PRAISE FOR *BETRAYED*

"Jeanette Windle authentically captures the sights, sounds, flora, fauna, and people of the cities, villages, and jungles of Central and South America. . . . She spins her tale as only one can who has herself lived and worked in this exciting and often contradictory subculture of the American Empire."

WILLIAM K. SMITH
Special Agent (Retired), U.S. Drug Enforcement Administration

"Jeanette's style of writing takes you to the place she is writing about. You see the smoldering fires of the municipal dump of Guatemala City and the beauty of the Guatemalan cloud forest. . . . Once again, Jeanette has taken you there and made you part of her adventure."

CW 3 LARRY TOMLINSON, SR.
(USA, Retired), Miami, FL

"Windle's amazing skill as a storyteller is equaled by her knowledge of the complexities of Latin America's darker side. *Betrayed* is a sure-footed journey into suspense and fear illuminated by hope."

PATRICIA SPRINKLE
Author of the best-selling Thoroughly Southern and Family Tree mystery series

"Just under the surface of the vibrant beauty of Guatemala's natural resources lies a seething cauldron of political turmoil. You can experience it all in *Betrayed.* Jeanette Windle is not only a great writer, she knows Latin America. I highly recommend this action-packed novel to any person who wants to better understand the Latin world or simply enjoys reading an intriguing mystery with a whisper of romance. This book is terrific!"

DR. RON BLUE
Coordinator, Spanish Doctor of Ministry, Dallas Theological Seminary

BETR

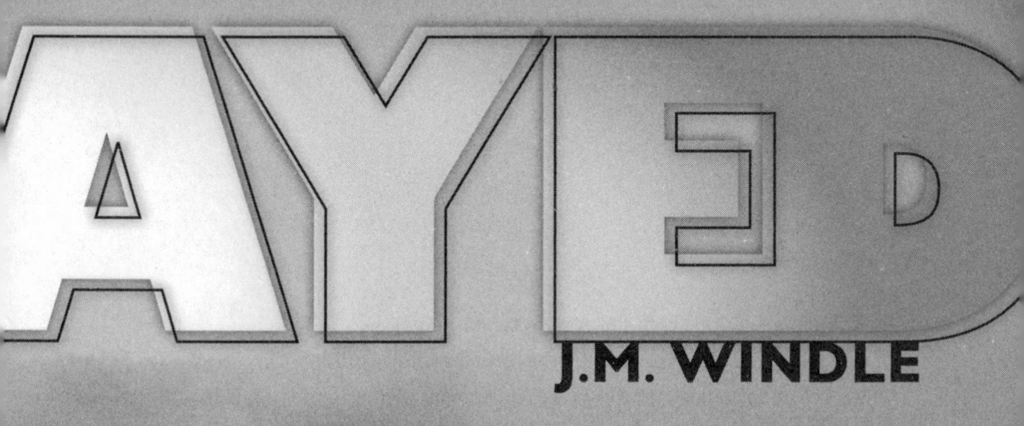

J.M. WINDLE

TYNDALE HOUSE PUBLISHERS, INC.
CAROL STREAM, ILLINOIS

Visit Tyndale's exciting Web site at www.tyndale.com

Visit Jeanette Windle's Web site at www.jeanettewindle.com

Betrayed

Designed by Mark Lane.

Edited by Lorie Popp.

Library of Congress Cataloging-in-Publication Data

Windle, Jeanette.
Betrayed / J.M. Windle.
p. cm.
ISBN-13: 978-1-4143-1474-7 (pbk. : alk. paper)
ISBN-10: 1-4143-1474-4 (pbk. : alk. paper)
1. Women anthropologists—Fiction. 2. Guatemala—Fiction. I. Title
PS3573.I5172B48 2008
813'.54—dc22 2007027444

Printed in the United States of America

14 13 12 11 10 09 08
7 6 5 4 3 2 1

DEDICATION

To the real Auntie Evelyns of my childhood, who could ride a mule up the Andes, face down a rioting mob, and assure a homeless child of a heavenly Father's love, and whose iron-spined commitment taught this small daughter of American missionaries what courage, love, and sacrifice are all about.

PROLOGUE

Sierra de las Minas, Guatemala

"'This is my Father's world. . . .'"

The crooning chimed with the screeching of macaws and the chitter of monkeys in the cloud forest canopy. Still, in the green hiding place made snug by wide, drooping fronds, curling ferns, and what had been a thick bed of moss, the singer checked herself, a raised finger hushing her companions. They'd never wandered this far or long without an adult hauling them back, and she was not ready to be dragged from this delightful new game.

There were three in all, two girls and a boy. The girls did not look like siblings. The singer was small with nut-brown hair and thin, sun-darkened features. Her younger sister, hardly more than a toddler, was flaxen blonde with skin pale enough to trace the blue of her veins. This oddity fascinated the boy, whose black hair and round, bronze features marked him as a native of these Central American highlands.

At the moment there was little distinction because all three were supremely dirty. Sharpened sticks had churned the firm springiness of the moss bed into a quagmire of loamy mud. The same mud caked woolen leggings and handwoven sweaters, plastering light heads and dark to an identical red-brown.

Their demolition was not without purpose. They were building a house, small hands industriously shoving bamboo canes into the mud, layering banana fronds and elephant ears across the top, patiently starting over again each time the structure overbalanced.

They were also extremely happy, as children will be with reasonable food and warmth, the security of adults in the background, and all of nature as their toy. At some point a crackling of thunder had presaged a storm, but when an exit from their hideaway confirmed blue sky between the thick branches of the forest canopy, they had returned to their labors.

They were blissfully unaware of the pit viper, green as the fern around which it coiled, just above their heads. Or the jaguar watching curiously from under a fern patch for a moment before it rose silently and wandered off.

Or the difference between rapid weapon fire and thunder.

The illusion of tranquility was so complete that the youngest ventured a low, contented humming as she patted and scooped. It was the same lullaby her sister had been singing.

Abandoning her caution, the older girl took up the words again. "'This is my Father's world. . . .'" Forgetting the rest of the line, she too dropped to a hum.

The Mayan boy had heard the tune often enough to add his own off-key whistle, while overhead the macaws set up a screeching counterpoint.

Yes, this was her father's world. And now he'd brought them along to this remote, secret paradise that was the most wonderful of any her short, varied life had yet known.

But even freedom palls in time.

After the corn tamales they'd provisioned for their adventure had been licked clean from their banana-leaf wrappings and the youngest child's hum subsided to a whimper, the older girl wondered why their escape had not yet been overtaken. Crawling out of their shelter, she was startled to see pink and orange through the breaks in the cloud forest canopy.

Back inside, she put her head close together with the Mayan boy, who was both playmate and guide. Even though they spoke no word of the same language, they understood each other well enough. Taking her little sister's hand, the older girl coaxed her to follow the Mayan boy's lead.

Out on the trail, the humidity that dripped from every leaf and frond soaked through mud-caked wool. For the first time the older girl questioned if they should have wandered so long and far. Papa and Mama were the loving bedrock of her small universe, but their displeasure could be as shattering as that earlier thunder.

But her young mind was not capable of guilt or worry for long. If the trail seemed much longer than their outward wandering, there was still much to delight. White wisps of a mountain mist curled through the trees, laying cool fingers against flushed cheeks. A flash of red overhead was the tail feathers of a quetzal bird. Orchids coiling down over the trail looked so much like tiny, peering faces that the youngest child giggled. With a handful of foraged bananas to quiet rumbling stomachs, the children let their tired legs lag while the sky paled to green and the first stars sprang out.

Only when they smelled smoke ahead and heard the raised voices did the older girl tug impatiently at her little sister. Smoke meant cook fires, and if a search party had to interrupt the evening meal, there would be more than just a scolding waiting for them.

It wasn't until they stepped into the clearing that she realized the smoke was all wrong, the flames leaping high against a backdrop that was no longer the quiet hamlet from which the children had slipped away. She did not understand this noisy invasion of strange men and vehicles. What were they doing? Why were they stacking human beings like sacks of potatoes?

And why was her family's home now a blazing torch? Why were their treasured possessions piled carelessly on the dusty ground for the invaders to ransack?

Above all, why were the most important people in her life not here to banish her terror and bewilderment? "Papa! Mama!"

Tall figures were striding toward the children, and the shifting patterns of shadow and firelight could not hide that they were strangers. Behind these men, the flames blazed higher, their ugly, red glare falling across the growing mound.

The girl caught sight of lighter strands among the black in the pile. Pale, familiar features that looked still and asleep. Tossed, sprawling shapes filthy with stains that were not mud. "Papa! Mama!"

She hardly heard her playmate's anguished screams as he hurled himself across the clearing. Her sister, still tight in her grip, was screaming too, but the older girl made no move or sound. Perhaps if she shut her eyes, this would all go away, like the bad dreams her father's strong arms and her mother's kisses so easily wiped away. *"This is my Father's world. . . ."*

Papa! Mama!

She did not immediately recognize the furious voices as a language she knew.

"No witnesses. Those are the orders."

"Are you out of your mind? They're children—babies! Haven't your goons butchered enough for one day?"

"You think this madness is our doing?"

"No, just our enabling."

Rough hands pushed aside the older girl's matted curls, wiping at the mud on her face. "Hey, take a look at this. These kids aren't locals."

"You're telling me they belong to—well, if this isn't . . . Hey, get away from those cameras! No records. Do I have to spell it out? *¿Qué hacen? ¡Muévense!*

Heavy footsteps moved away, the harsh shouts no longer intelligible. Then she was being carried to one of the strange vehicles, her sister's shivering small body settled into her arms.

"Don't cry, sweethearts," a deep voice whispered. "Everything's going to be all right. You're safe now."

Young though she was, the girl knew it to be a lie.

She would never feel safe again.

Twenty Years Later

So the rumors were true.

The stillness alerted the patrol even before their army Jeep jolted to a stop in the middle of the scuffed-dirt open space that was all this mountain hamlet boasted for a plaza.

There were no chickens or pigs rooting through the unpaved lanes. No women grinding maize or bent over the cooking pits. No shrill shouts of children's play. The patrol leader paused to dig at an ominously dark stain with his boot as his unit fanned out through the village, using automatic rifle butts to smash in rudely constructed bamboo doors.

"*¡Capitán!* Over here."

A box shape of cinder blocks roofed with galvanized tin across the village commons was the hamlet's only solid construction. The patrol leader strode over to where two of his squad had already battered in the door. A single blackboard and the wooden benches tumbled across the concrete floor identified the community schoolhouse/town hall/storm shelter.

And morgue.

The patrol leader snapped his fingers. "Tell the gringo we have found them."

His aide had no difficulty with the order. The army contingent was young, dark skinned, with the stunted growth and wiry leanness of the chronically underfed. Peasant conscripts too poor to buy their way out of military service.

The only exception stood under a nearby thatched cooking shelter, his height as conspicuous as the lightness of his hair and eyes. The recruit interpreted the thoughtful expression as the foreigner poked a stick into a pot of beans sitting on a burned-out cook fire. No villager would purposely abandon good food.

"Señor, *el capitán* requests your presence."

The gringo's long strides outpaced the recruit. As he reached the broken-down door, the patrol leader thrust out an arm. "It is not necessary to enter. There is nothing now to be done."

But the foreigner was already shouldering past. Crowding into the doorway behind him, the patrol leader and his recruits watched the gringo stop abruptly as his boots met the puddled stickiness that was everywhere across the concrete floor.

No one had been spared. The men of the village showed no signs of resistance, had perhaps not even known what was coming. Splayed half-sitting against the far wall or sprawled like tossed dolls on the concrete floor, they lay in an oddly tidy row where the rapid fire of machine guns had mowed them down. The women had not been allowed to die so quickly.

And the children . . .

Stooping, the foreigner ran a swift hand to close an empty stare of a boy not yet school-age. When he swung around to face the soldiers, the cold implacability of his expression was surpassed only by the ice chips of his gaze. "So . . . it begins again."

CHAPTER ONE

"Señoras y señores, AeroMéxico Flight 621 is now beginning its final descent into Aeropuerto Aurora, international airport of Guatemala City." The intercom announcement coincided with a flashing sign overhead: *Abroche Cinturón.*

Halfway down the crowded cabin of the 727, Vicki Andrews obediently fastened her seat belt, raised the shade of her window seat, and peered down. The landscape varied little from any one of a dozen developing nations into which she'd flown over the last few years. Admittedly spectacular scenery, followed inevitably by humanity's impact on that splendor. In this case Vicki couldn't tell if the white peaks of the hills and volcanic cones that ringed the highland basin in which Guatemala City squatted were snow or fog.

The plane banked to line up for approach to the airport. Beyond its control tower and terminals, Vicki could see the celebrated Zone 10 of Guatemala City. Sparkling glass towers that were luxury hotels and banks. The gracious, tree-lined Avenida de la Reforma with its nightclubs, American chain restaurants, high-priced boutiques, and foreign embassies. And terraced up hillsides, the mansions, bristling with security, where Guatemala's wealthy elite escaped the third world. An attractive scene and all that many international arrivals would ever see of the capital. Vicki was not one of them.

The plane tilted its wings as it dropped farther, offering beyond the glittering Zone 10 an excellent panorama of the other Guatemala City, where the overwhelming majority of its inhabitants lived and toiled. A warren of narrow streets. Crumbling adobe facades defaced by political graffiti. A sea of red tiles pockmarked with tin and Duralite roofing. Squeezed into every available opening and crawling up the steep sides of the mountain basin were the shanties of the poor, cobbled together from scrap lumber, tin, and even cardboard.

Far off to Vicki's right, one of Guatemala's less-advertised landmarks slashed through the shantytowns—a deep and wide ravine, originally a conduit for a major river tributary. Now a receptacle of a very different sort, its uneven and discolored surface reached within meters of the rim with what she knew to be thousands of tons of waste. Guatemala City's municipal dump. Vicki's destination.

If it was all depressingly familiar, it evoked no memories. So why had she been so reluctant to come here?

Giving up on the scenery, Vicki flipped back to the country info she'd printed out, picking up where she'd left off.

The heart of the Mayan empire, Guatemala fell to Spanish conquest in the 1500s. Centuries of colonial rule led to a highly stratified society with the indigenous Mayan majority relegated to a feudal-style peonage; a rising urban Ladino, or Spanish/Mayan, class; and a largely European ruling elite. . . . By the 1950s, US-owned United Fruit Company was Guatemala's largest landowner, giving rise to the term banana republic. With coffee and banana plantations dependent on Mayan forced labor, the election of reform candidate Colonel Jacobo Arbenz was greeted with dismay by both the local aristocracy and international business interests. A CIA-sponsored coup ushered in a half century of military regimes, punctuated by populist uprisings and army reprisals. . . .

By the time the 1996 Peace Accords marked a cease-fire of the civil war, more than two hundred thousand civilians had disappeared or been massacred. Though a UN Truth Commission found the Guatemalan army responsible for more than 90 percent of atrocities, the United States has maintained strong business and political ties, lauding Guatemala as one of their strongest allies in the war on socialism. . . .

Lush rain forests, sandy beaches, and a colorful blend of Mayan and Spanish cultures make Guatemala a tropical paradise. However, with social inequities remaining unaddressed and a spiraling crime rate, the US Embassy Watch advises caution for any of its citizens. . . .

Tropical paradise! Vicki began packing up her belongings as the plane landed and taxied to the terminal.

Vicki waited until the aisle was clear before sliding out of her seat and grabbing her purse and duffel bag—her only luggage. Experience had taught her the value of being able to sling all her belongings over her shoulder and walk away from a plane, a bus, a riot.

The immigration lines were still long by the time Vicki found the one marked *Extranjero*, "foreigner." A stamp in her passport, and she moved on to customs, a row of wooden tables set up beyond the baggage claim. Unsmiling guards with automatic rifles hovered near as Vicki's duffel bag was emptied out, the seams probed with the tip of a penknife. The same penknife dug into her deodorant, leaving white chunks like dandruff on her clothing.

Again, depressingly familiar.

It was also a routine part of her job, Vicki reminded herself sternly as she stuffed and zipped the duffel bag. So why was she being so sour?

I'm just tired. This last assignment had overrun her calculations by more than two weeks, and she'd barely had time to write up and fax the final report before boarding her plane for Guatemala City.

Shouldering her maltreated belongings, Vicki headed for the Plexiglas wall that separated the baggage claim and customs from a milling crowd waiting for arrivals outside.

A trick of lighting displayed her reflection, and Vicki took in the image she was about to accord her reception party. Rumpled jeans and a T-shirt. Shoulder-length dark brown hair pulled into a tight ponytail. The fine coating of perspiration and dust that was her only makeup. An amber glare blazing behind her lashes. No jewelry of any sort. Where Vicki spent her days, that was a red flag for a mugging.

Not a prepossessing first impression.

The image dissolved, and Vicki dismissed it with a shrug. Travel from one municipal dump to another hardly called for haute couture.

Vicki showed her passport along with her hard-earned customs clearance to a final armed guard and was out the door.

Outside, a metal railing held the crowd back from the Plexiglas, but with every emerging passenger, bodies surged against the barrier, calling out names, many holding up placards.

Vicki found herself instinctively searching the crowd for a familiar face before reeling herself in to read the placards. There would be no one she knew waiting in that welcoming throng.

She had traversed almost the entire gauntlet of reaching hands and pressing bodies when she spotted the one she wanted. A hand-lettered square of cardboard read *Casa de Esperanza,* "House of Hope."

Its bearer was as visibly expatriate as Vicki herself, an elderly woman not much shorter than Vicki but stooped and thinned with age to little more than a child's size. She looked so familiar that Vicki found herself stopping midstep until she realized the woman was a living embodiment of any number of black-and-white historical photos of American missionaries abroad that Vicki had come across in her research. The bun still showing a few threads of its original auburn in the white. The shapeless cotton smock reaching modestly to the tops of dark knee socks. Sturdy walking shoes.

Vicki swallowed a laugh. Was this already a total waste of her time?

Then she caught a shrewd, bright gaze, a smile that held so much understanding, warmth, and youth that Vicki decided to reserve her judgment. Walking forward, she set down her duffel bag, then held out her hand. "Hello, you must be Evelyn McKie, who founded Casa de Esperanza. I'm—"

But now it was the missionary whose aged features held startled recognition. "Victoria?"

CHAPTER TWO

"No, just Vicki—or so my birth certificate tells me. Vicki Andrews. From Children at Risk. My office did inform you I would be your contact, I hope."

"Yes, of course they did. And that was the name they gave." Evelyn McKie's confusion dissolved into a welcoming smile. "You just look so much like an old friend; it took me back a couple of decades. Though you're much too young to be that Victoria, if just as pretty. In any case—" she rejected Vicki's hand for a quick hug—"welcome to Guatemala. And thank you for taking the time to visit our project. This is *such* a blessing. I can't tell you."

"It's a pleasure, Ms. McKie."

"Oh, please, call me Evelyn. *Ms. McKie* makes me sound like such an old woman."

Vicki knew from her info packet that the founder of Casa de Esperanza was American by citizenship, but Evelyn's firm tones still held a trace burr of her Scottish roots as she swept on. "Now, dearie, you must be very tired from your trip. Why don't you let Alberto here—" she gestured to a slight, dark-skinned man Vicki hadn't realized was with her—"take that bag for you."

Alberto, at least five decades younger than his employer but already missing most of his upper front teeth, grinned at Vicki as he reached for her duffel bag.

"Alberto is one of our most valuable workers at Casa de Esperanza and is also my driver. Now if you'll stay close. The Jeep is just a short walk away."

Following them across the terminal and outside to the street, Vicki immediately understood her host's suggestion. While the arrivals hall had been crowded, the street was a seething mass of people and vehicles, the air noxious with exhaust fumes and a cacophony of honking and raised voices.

Evelyn simply walked into the crowd, Alberto right behind. And the sea of humanity seemed to part effortlessly for her.

Vicki was finding it more difficult to maneuver. A beggar thrust his remaining withered arm under her nose. A small boy with a wooden tray around his neck offered gum for an exorbitant price while an even smaller child reached to pull her purse from her shoulder. Whether would-be bellhop or pickpocket, Vicki had no idea, but she frowned and shook her head at him.

"Vicki, there you are. I was afraid I'd missed you. Wait up!"

The familiar impatient demand spun Vicki around. "Holly!"

The young woman pushing through the crowd was bigger than Vicki by several inches and at least thirty pounds, strawberry blonde hair tied back from round, freckled features, pale blue eyes blinking with irritation as she warded off vendors and beggars alike to reach Vicki's side.

"What a wonderful surprise." Vicki gave her a hug, then looked at her two companions, who were halted just a few feet ahead. "I wasn't expecting to see you. I thought you said you couldn't get into town to meet me."

"Actually, I just put a volunteer on a flight. In fact, I'm at the airport for the afternoon. We've got a work team coming in from London and a couple of more volunteers heading out. We're just getting their farewell party going here in the airport restaurant. I was hoping you could join us. I mean, I haven't seen you in *forever*."

"Well, it was only three months ago in Cancún on your way to Guatemala," Vicki reminded dryly. "And I don't know how many country-to-country phone calls, according to my cell phone bill."

"I really need to talk to you now. If you've got your luggage—"

"I can't do that," Vicki protested. If this wasn't just like Holly. "You told me you couldn't meet me, so I made my own arrangements. Not to mention, I'm hardly dressed for a party."

"No more than I am."

Yeah, right! Holly's safari outfit and hiking boots were top-of-the-line, while the gleam of gold around her neck would have drawn a mob in any of Central America's more marginal neighborhoods.

Vicki turned. "Holly, I'd like to introduce you to Evelyn McKie, my hostess and the founder of Casa de Esperanza, where I'll be spending the next few weeks. And Alberto, who is handling my transportation."

Vicki saw Holly's dismissive glance at the elderly missionary and her driver. "I'm sure they wouldn't mind sparing you for a few hours, would you, Ms. McKnee?" Holly smiled at Vicki's companions. "I haven't seen Vicki for *such* a long time. I promise she'll get to her lodgings in plenty of time for . . . well, whatever it is she's doing."

"Holly, I can't ask Ms. McKie to rearrange her—"

But arguing with Holly was something in the nature of blocking a tornado, and Vicki wasn't surprised when her hostess tapped her shoulder and said quietly, "If you'd like to stay, please don't hesitate on our account. Alberto can take your bag along, and we'll meet up at the project. You should have the directions we sent with the schedule, though any cabbie in the city knows Casa de Esperanza. In any case, here is our card."

Vicki tucked it into her purse.

"We have a team meeting this afternoon, and we try to finish before dark. So have yourself a nice visit until then."

"If you're sure—"

Holly was already pulling Vicki away.

Giving in, Vicki waved an apologetic farewell at Evelyn as she said to Holly, "I'm happy to see you, too, but what's the rush?"

"We don't have a lot of time. The others are waiting for us to order." Holly clutched a pendant at her throat as she eyed the same urchin who'd grabbed at Vicki's purse still dogging them. "Besides, it's dirty and hot out here, and I don't trust these street brats. Come on."

Reentering the airport rid them of their shadow as well as the noise and dust. As Holly dropped her hand, Vicki studied the pendant, an exquisitely formed gold jaguar with emerald chips for eyes. "Cute. Is that new?"

"Just picked it up when I got into town this morning to celebrate three months in Guatemala. At least that's the excuse. At the rate conservation efforts are going in this country, it'll soon be the only jaguar left. If that UN grant had just come through. We're hoping this team coming in from Hamburg, Germany, gets excited enough to go back and do some fund-raising. They're all pretty green over there, so we're keeping our fingers crossed."

All those calls that had run up her cell phone bill allowed Vicki to interpret the monologue. Still finishing up her veterinary studies, Holly had spent the last three months in Guatemala as resident staff at the Wildlife Rescue Center, or WRC, an endangered species rehabilitation program located in the mountains of a nature reserve.

At least Holly received room and board and a small living stipend for the privilege of overseas experience and an internship in her chosen field of animal medicine. The volunteer teams to which she referred, both American and European, actually paid for the privilege of spending a month or two feeding animals and cleaning out cages in a rustic rain forest environment.

"And now they're talking more budget cuts. Including personnel. Roger and Kathy's leaving is putting us in a real bind. And with this other thing . . . Let's just say I'm glad you're here."

As Holly led the way up an escalator and across a tiled landing, Vicki surveyed her. She was still rambling on, but she looked preoccupied as she glanced around in search of something—or someone. Her rapid blinking completed the illusion of a ruffled, blue-eyed owl.

A worried one.

"Hey, it can't be that bad." Vicki touched Holly's arm reassuringly as Holly pushed open an ornately carved mahogany door. "Let's just forget work for now and enjoy your party."

The door swung closed behind them, cutting off the noise and bustle of the airport. The restaurant with its rich wood paneling, sparkling chandeliers, and white-coated waiters was a world away from the dirty, congested street, and Vicki was conscious again of her disheveled appearance.

With reluctance, Vicki followed Holly through the crowded tables. Few here looked to be local, which was no surprise when the cheapest menu item would cost more than the average Guatemalan made in a week. A table of men wearing suits and ties stood out like overdressed crows at a lawn party of macaws. Embassy or big business, Vicki judged. One of the men had just pulled out a chair at the table when Vicki and Holly approached. He was younger than his companions, in the vicinity of thirty, with excellent height and build, brown hair several shades lighter than Vicki's, and a tan that hadn't been acquired behind a desk.

Vicki's glance had already moved on when Holly stopped. "That's him. I thought I saw him walking through the lobby when I went looking for you."

The words were barely above a murmur, but her subject had the hearing of one of Holly's endangered species, because the man turned leisurely, one hand still on the chair as a steel gray appraisal swept over Vicki and Holly. "Hello, Holly."

Holly was pale enough under her freckles for Vicki to see her blush. "H-hello, Michael. What a surprise to see you here. I-I didn't know you were back in town."

Holly was actually stammering. Not that it was difficult to understand why she was flustered. The man was attractive, more so because he showed no consciousness of his looks.

Embassy or business, I'll bet he's done military service—and not too long ago.

The man glanced at Vicki, and she dropped her gaze. His tone was grave as he turned to Holly. "I managed to thumb a flight heading this way. As you can see, I had guests to see off." He nodded toward the crowded table before he looked back at Vicki. "So, are you going to introduce me?"

"Oh, of course." Holly's flush deepened. "Michael, Vicki. Vicki, this is Michael Camden from the DAO."

So Vicki's assessment had been right. The Defense Attaché's Office staff was part of the embassy's military contingent.

Holly didn't add more in the pause that followed, breaking instead into hurried speech. "I was planning to call you, Michael, but I thought you were still out on some operation. If we could maybe get together to talk . . ."

"Sure; why don't you give the embassy a buzz and have my secretary pencil you in. My schedule's pretty crazy, but you are definitely a priority. Now, if you'll excuse me, I'd love to talk more, but I have guests to attend to." He slid into his seat, dismissing them.

Holly lingered so long that Vicki felt uncomfortable for her, so she urged her away from the table.

Was this Michael Camden the reason for Holly's preoccupation? At least he hadn't rebuffed her appeal, however tepid the assignation. Holly was as effervescent and friendly as a Saint Bernard puppy, Vicki considered with affectionate exasperation. And as easily hurt.

Like it's any of my business. She's a big girl now.

"Hey, Holly, over here."

"Where'd you get lost to? We were about to come looking."

The calls and waving came from two tables pushed together in a back corner.

Holly's face lit up, the troubled look evaporating, as they reached the group. "Sorry it took so long. But we're worth waiting for, aren't we, Vicki? Here, tuck yourself between these guys."

Vicki counted six others around the table as she sank into an empty chair opposite Holly.

Holly made the introductions. "Vick, this is Lynn Waters, Amazon Watch. Dieter, Greenpeace. And I've told you about Kathy and Roger, my colleagues at the center. Former colleagues, that is."

Lynn looked like an aging hippie with her flowing red hair streaked with gray and bright, flowered muumuu. A stocky German, Dieter's ample waistline was proof that his own consumption of the planet's resources was well beyond Greenpeace's stated principles. Roger and Kathy were youngish and blond.

"Roger and Kathy just finished their postdoctoral project," Holly explained with enthusiasm. "Sustainable logging and agriculture in a cloud forest habitat. A great project that fit rights in with WRC objectives. They're headed back to the UK tonight."

"Hence the celebration." Roger lifted a wineglass. "Tomorrow, London. Next week, a Cambridge fellowship. Maybe even a BBC documentary."

"And we hope a grant or two to keep sustaining our conservation projects. I really am happy for you, but I sure don't know what we're going to do without you." Holly let out an exaggerated sigh; then her face brightened. "At least we've still got Bill on the project."

She gestured at the oldest member of the group, though the man's lean, weather-beaten frame and buzz cut made it difficult to confidently guess his age, and a twinkle in his eyes held nothing of encroaching senility.

"Bill is WRC's most generous sponsor," Holly went on. "He's got property right outside the reserve near the center, and he's been helping us navigate local bureaucracy and security. You must be one of the longest-term American residents in this country; isn't that right, Bill?"

"Something like that," the older man agreed gravely.

"Señores, you are ready to order?"

"Oh yes, of course. Silly me!" Taking the menu a hovering waiter was discreetly pushing at her, Holly finished hastily, "And this is Vicki, everyone. She's a people hugger," she added as though that explained everything.

Why a foreigner was in a country like Guatemala defined largely—and quickly—who they were. The numerous aid organizations were popularly termed *people huggers*. Those groups represented here were dubbed *tree huggers*. Then there were the multinationals—country reps of the international corporations. The various diplomatic and consular personnel, military task forces, and other US government representatives were lumped together as the embassy.

So what category did that leave their final table companion? Did Holly realize she hadn't finished her introductions? Vicki took a menu and surreptitiously studied her neighbor. He didn't fall easily into any of the usual categories. *Give him an ax and one of those horned helmets, and he could stand at the prow of a Viking longship.* In fact, from his deep tan, long sun-bleached hair, sculpted muscles, and Hawaiian shirt, she'd have placed him as one of the many nomadic surfers or outdoor sportsmen who found Central America a low-cost playground for their hobbies.

And if that isn't stereotyping. So if you're the outdoor type and physically fit, dining in a suit and tie, you're military. In a Hawaiian shirt with sandals and bare legs, a beach bum.

"Joe." The Viking's drawl, at least, was pure American.

Startled, Vicki dropped the menu, meeting his comprehending green gaze. "Excuse me?"

His comprehension deepened to amusement as Vicki flushed, but he only said mildly, "My name." Lounging back, he stretched out his legs and crossed them at the ankle. "It's Joe. That's what you wanted to know, wasn't it?"

"Joe," Vicki repeated flatly. The incongruence forced a giggle to her lips, and she bent over her menu to hide a grin.

"Did I miss the joke?" Joe frowned and ran a large hand through his heavy mane, leaving it even more tousled.

A frowning Viking was an intimidating sight. *Off with my head.* This time Vicki let the giggle escape. "I'm sorry." Straightening, she made a helpless gesture. "It just caught my funny bone. Bill. Joe. It's so . . ."

"Tom, Dick, and Harry? Moe, Larry, and Curly?"

"Not exactly." Vicki smiled. "More like those macho types in a Western who are always sidling up to a bar—'Hi, my name's Joe.'" She dropped her voice in a caricature of his drawl. "Or Bill. And never any other alias other than that one-syllable name."

She must have imagined the brief narrowing of that catlike gaze, because the sardonic mouth was curving, Joe's strong features relaxed with amusement as he mimicked, "You got a point there, little lady." He gestured to Bill. "Let me disabuse you of that at least. I'm told that William Taylor's been kicking around Guatemala since shortly after Simón Bolívar. As for yours truly, would Joseph Ericsson—make that spelled with a *c* and two *s*es—have enough syllables to rank grade A?"

"Maybe." Vicki's eyebrows rose as she contemplated his name. "Ericsson. That's Scandinavian for 'son of Eric,' isn't it? Wasn't there a Viking ruler by that name?"

He laughed. "More like a common marauder. Why? Were you picturing me with a battle ax and horned helmet on some longship?"

Vicki was spared from answering as the waiter leaned in between them to take their orders. Joe requested a large steak, while Vicki settled for a chef salad. As the waiter collected their menus, Vicki asked neutrally, "So what brings you to Guatemala?"

Joe shrugged. "Great beaches. Warm climate. Cheap living. Nice people. But if you're asking what I'm doing here today with a tableful of tree huggers, it's nothing as mysterious as I can see going through your head. Okay, I'm guilty of inheriting those rover genes. Problem is, following the waves is a great life, but it doesn't exactly pay well. Your friends were looking for a handyman to help out at the center. Bill over there was kind enough to drop my name into the hat."

So she'd been right. Vicki felt a pang of disappointment. There was no denying a certain magnetic attraction about Joe, but the guy had to be pushing thirty, surely time to be thinking of the future and a steady job.

"Now, Joe, don't be selling yourself short," Holly chimed in. "Vicki, don't listen to him. Joe is one of the most multitalented people I've met. He can pilot anything from a boat to a small plane. Better yet, the local tradespeople *listen* to Joe, which is more than they do to me. *You* tell 'em, Bill; just who was being kind to whom when you steered Joe our way?"

"Don't kid yourself," Bill said. "When you've known me longer, Vicki, you'll learn I'm never kind. Joe here was simple self-preservation. He's bilingual, been kicking around the region long enough to cope with local politicians and red tape. Something you're not, Holly, and you might as well accept it, so don't shake your head at me."

Holly wrinkled her nose at him.

"Plus, I have it on good authority—his—that he can work as hard as he plays when he chooses. It was a logical recommendation."

"Well, I can tell you, we're glad to have him," Holly went on enthusiastically. "How many languages do you speak, Joe? He may not have come down here with an NGO, but Joe's not just a surfer. He can talk environmental issues and politics and—"

"Okay, Holly, enough already." Straightening up from his lounging position, Joe lifted both hands palm out in mock protest. "I don't think Vicki here's in the market for an entire biography. A misspent youth bumming around the planet may have been great for picking up languages and other useful skills, but don't make me out to be any kind of pro. I'm just happy to help out awhile. And pick up next season's living stake."

Under his admonition, Holly blushed and bit her lip.

Vicki frowned. Could Holly be interested in this nomad? She hoped not. And had she imagined Holly's interest in that embassy attaché?

Vicki glanced across the restaurant, caught Michael Camden turned in their direction, and looked hastily away. *Holly, what kind of heart tangle are you getting yourself into this time?*

CHAPTER THREE

CHAPTER THREE

"So, Vicki . . ." Lynn leaned forward. "Holly says you're a people hugger. What brings you to Guatemala?"

"I'm here with a children's project," Vicki answered. "Casa de Esperanza. They work mainly with the *basurero* population."

"You mean all those people living in the dump?" Lynn's thin eyebrows arched. "Sure, I know Casa de Esperanza. Who doesn't? So you're a missionary, then."

"Missionary!" Holly hooted, clearly restored to her usual ebullience. "Vicki a missionary? Though if you'd seen the specimen she was with when I caught up to her—" She stopped under Vicki's warning look, then said, "Vicki's an anthropologist. PhD from Duke. Fulbright scholar at that," she added with pride. "Though now she's more of a PI. She investigates projects and decides who gets all those millions her foundation has to hand out."

"Really!" Lynn's eyebrows shot higher. "So how does one go from anthropologist to private investigator?"

"It's not quite as glamorous as Holly likes to believe." Vicki threw Holly an exasperated glance, noting uncomfortably that the loud question had ended all other conversation. She caught Joe's sardonic smile before she faced Lynn. "I'm the project inspector for Children at Risk, an international foundation that funnels funds to children's projects around the world. Basically, it entails spending from a few days to a few months working directly with the project to see what's working and what isn't. Then I make a recommendation as to whether the project should be funded—at least by our foundation—and if so, how much. Or alternatively, what steps can be taken to salvage the project if its value merits the effort."

"It certainly sounds like an interesting line of work," Lynn said. "If you don't mind my asking, why you? Not that I'm questioning your competence, but I have to say you don't look much older than the children you work with."

"Yeah, and where can we sign up for one of those grants?" Dieter put in loudly. A pitcher of sangria stood at his elbow. "I'll take a million; two even."

"I'm twenty-five," Vicki said stiffly. She looked over at the German activist. "And I'm sorry, but we don't do environmental projects. The name is *Children* at Risk. As to why me—" Vicki shrugged as she turned back to Lynn—"I guess I just kind of grew into it. I did my doctoral thesis on the Colombian refugee camps. My original idea was to study childhood development in a refugee setting, but I ended up putting together a scathing—and accurate—analysis correlating international aid and corruption in the camp administration. It earned me a PhD and a commendation from USAID. That's where I first ran into Children at Risk, which had considerable money in that project. After they read my final report, they asked me to come on board to check out some of their other projects that were raising red flags."

Vicki hesitated, but seeing genuine interest around the table, she went on. "My last assignment in Mexico City is a good example. Children at Risk had been pouring considerable funds into a partnership with the local Department of Families to provide housing and medical care to children living in the municipal dump there. So they couldn't figure out why there never seemed to be any funds for food or medicine."

Vicki didn't even like remembering the horrific conditions she'd found in that so-called children's home. "After a few weeks I discovered that the department administrators had just paid cash for a brand-new mansion in the nicest neighborhood of the city."

"That's terrible." Kathy looked appalled. "You mean, they'd been siphoning off the kids' funds? And you're saying Casa de Esperanza . . . ? Why, that's one of the best-known children's projects in the city. I can't believe they'd be—"

"Oh no, not at all," Vicki cut in. "On the contrary, we've heard nothing but good about Casa de Esperanza. So much so that we're exploring the advantages of partnering with some of these faith-based NGOs instead of the usual local authorities."

"Personally, I think too much money is going into these groups already," Dieter interrupted again. "After all, it's Guatemala's environment that's at risk, not its juvenile population count."

Vicki didn't know what incensed her more—Dieter's attitude or the murmur of agreement around the table. She bit back a hot retort.

Lynn changed the subject. "Have any of you seen the news? what the army came across yesterday?"

"You mean that massacre up in the mountains?" Kathy shuddered. "I thought they'd put an end to all that."

"Oh, let's not talk about it," Holly pleaded.

Her plea effected silence just long enough for the waiters to refill glasses all around.

Then Dieter, recovering his aplomb in another glass of sangria, demanded, "So who do they think did it—the right or the left?"

"If they know, they're not saying," Roger said. "Of course, the army's denying any involvement."

"And the embassy?" Lynn lowered her voice as she glanced at the suit-and-tie table. "Do you think they had advance warning this time?"

"How can you say that?" Holly's eyes widened. "Do you really think anyone in our government would look the other way?"

A battery of derisive looks crisscrossed the table, but no one ventured to challenge her naiveté. How many embassy personnel had known of what Guatemala's military regime was doing with its American-supplied arms, training, and support during the last few decades of civil war was anyone's guess. That they'd been totally ignorant of the rampant human rights abuses was a fiction few were credulous enough to buy any longer, thanks to recently declassified CIA briefings.

"Speaking of your embassy—" Dieter injected derision into his mimicry of Lynn, sangria slopping onto the tablecloth as he used the glass to gesture—"did you see who's in town? Think it's connected?"

"Who are you talking about?" Holly turned her head. "Oh, you mean the big guy with the gray suit and beard next to the ambassador. He looks familiar. Where have I seen him?"

"Probably CNN," Lynn enlightened her dryly. "That's the administration's new drug czar. He was here for some big counternarcotics exercise our guys were running with the locals. They managed to snag half a dozen poppy fields and opium labs up in the mountains, and our drug czar has been patting the Guatemalans on the back, handing out medals left and right."

Roger shook his head. "How do you do it, Lynn? If that isn't classified, surely they don't go broadcasting it to the press."

She grinned at him. "I'm dating a guy in the air wing. He was out of commission all week while they were out playing with their toys up there."

"Yeah, well, they can pat themselves on the back all they want," Dieter snapped. "But for every lab they grab, there're a dozen others, and the growers just move on to a new patch of jungle. I don't know where we're losing more rain forest—the drug cartels or land-grabbing peasants."

"And going back to that, did you see where the massacre took place?" Lynn put in. "Right in your neck of the woods, Holly. Straight up past the center into the Sierra de las Minas."

Holly sat up straight. "The biosphere?"

Once again, it was due to all those country-to-country calls that Vicki knew what they were talking about. The Sierra de las Minas Biosphere was the highland nature reserve that opened up just beyond the Wildlife Rescue Center to preserve 150,000 acres of Guatemala's remaining cloud forest habitat.

"I thought the Ministry of Environment had cleared out that area." Holly spun around in her seat. "Bill, you know that area up there. There can't still be villages inside the biosphere, can there? I mean, we raised millions of dollars when we negotiated the reserve to pay for that land and recompense anyone already living inside the perimeter."

Bill hunched his shoulders. "From the coordinates they were giving, it looks as though it might have been within the perimeter. Bottom line: your environmental groups can pay off the government to sign over the land, but as long as people are hungry, they're going to keep finding soil to grow corn. And as long as they stay off the beaten track, it would take a better law enforcement than you've got to police a territory that size."

"Then maybe that makes one silver lining in all this, as you Americans would say." Dieter shot Vicki a malicious look. "After yesterday, the next bunch of *indios* looking to move in on the reserve will think twice."

"Isn't that a little harsh?" Lynn demanded. "After all, they're just trying to feed their families."

"Oh, come on," said Dieter. "Let's not be hypocrites. Aren't these Mayan peasants supposed to worship Mother Earth? Well, let them respect her before there are no cloud forests—or any other rain forest—left for the next generation. I'm certainly not applauding this massacre. It's a terrible tragedy, of course. But it may have never happened if these people hadn't been breaking the law out there to begin with."

"So what you're saying—" Lynn summed up with deceptive sweetness—"is that we're not talking leftist rebels or out-of-control military out there but maybe some kind of fanatic earth terrorists bent on saving their rain forest? Got any candidates in mind?"

Everyone started talking at once, but Roger's voice rose above the babble. "Okay, everyone, let's keep our eyes on the issues here. Yesterday's events have exposed a major systems failure in our conservation efforts. It's not going to do us any good to pour our funds and efforts into these projects if the locals are just going to come in behind us and erode everything we've done. What can be done to protect our perimeters from these kinds of incursions? Who can we get on board?"

The waiter was distributing their food now. Dieter inspected his double bacon cheeseburger before contributing. "For one, let's get more army patrols into the area."

Vicki picked at her chef salad as proposals and arguments ebbed and flowed across the table. For all Holly's insisting on Vicki's presence, Holly was as deep in the discussion as anyone. Worse, nowhere in all the talk of endangered species, biodiversity, tropical gene banks, and pristine habitats did there seem to be any consideration of the human link in the food chain.

Vicki checked her watch. If she didn't leave soon, she was going to have a hard time making that team meeting at Casa de Esperanza.

"In other words, Mayans aren't an endangered species; the cloud forests are."

The ironic drawl startled Vicki. Like her, Joe had remained silent during the debate, though his expression denoted no lack of interest. Was this all one more new "language" to the nomadic wanderer? And how did he keep reading her mind?

Vicki managed a rueful smile. "I'd forgotten you're not a tree hugger either. They're great people but a little single-minded. It just seems to me that *someone* might try asking the human inhabitants their opinion of what's being planned for them."

"So tell 'em."

"Oh no—"

Joe cut off Dieter, who was currently editorializing. "Hey, Greenpeace, put a sock in it and give Vicki a turn. After all, she's the only one here who actually works with these people."

Astonishingly, silence immediately reigned. As all heads turned to Vicki, Joe gestured to her. "So what do *you* think the answer is? How do you balance saving the environment and the complaints of the locals?"

The perennial people-hugger/tree-hugger debate. "What I think," Vicki said carefully, "is that while we're trying to save the rain forest, we need to figure out some way to feed the people as well. Or at least—" she glanced at the crumbs of Dieter's super-sized burger combo—"be willing to set an example. After all, gringos can hardly claim to be an endangered species either."

Her smile lightened the comment to a joke as she got to her feet. "Meanwhile, it's been a real pleasure meeting you all, but I need to get moving. Holly, I'll catch up with you later."

"Hey, you can't go already." Holly scrambled to her feet, rounding the table as Vicki dropped a bill on the table to cover her lunch. "I thought you came so we could talk. That's why I invited you, remember?"

And you didn't think of that earlier? Vicki maneuvered her purse to her shoulder. "I did."

"Look, my friends didn't mean—"

"I know. That's not it at all," Vicki reassured her as she started toward the exit. "I really am sorry. I had a good time; I promise. But I've got to get to Casa de Esperanza. Why don't you come over this evening, and we can talk as long as you like?"

"I can't. Once this German team is in, I've got to get them settled into the hostel, then on a bus to the center. At least let me walk you out. We can talk on the way." Holly was treading on Vicki's heels in her urgency, the worried owl look back.

Vicki stifled another sigh but slowed her steps. "Fine, talk."

"It's . . . well, I want you to come up to the center with me tomorrow. To do what you do in your projects—you know, an investigation."

"What?" Vicki stopped short to fix Holly with an incredulous stare before hurrying toward the escalator. "Are you crazy? Or are you forgetting that I came here to do a job? One I'm late for right now."

"They won't mind if you tell them you need to reschedule," Holly insisted. "I mean, you're not exactly talking emergency here, right? I'm just asking for a week or two, okay? After all, you've got to have some vacation time."

As they stepped off the escalator on the ground floor, Holly linked arms with Vicki, raising her voice above the noise of the arrivals hall. "I've been thinking about this since I found out you were coming to Guatemala, and now with this past week . . . Anyway, the interpreter who was supposed to work with the German team bailed out. They all speak English, so I figured you could take his place. Kind of undercover, you know?"

Vicki demanded, "Exactly how does that qualify as a vacation? Besides, you know I don't like mountains."

"Now *that's* crazy. I've never understood why you have such a thing about mountains."

"They're cold and wet and gloomy. Give me a warm beach if I'm going on vacation." Vicki couldn't keep the irritation from her tone. Trust Holly to turn this into something personal. *And* to expect Vicki to just drop her job and plans anytime she needed—no, *wanted*—Vicki to come running. "Holly, if this is one of your crusades, I just don't have time right now. I do need a vacation, but a real one."

"What do you mean, my crusades? When have I ever asked you to get involved before?"

"What about that spotted owl thing? You were so sure you'd seen one and that the loggers were covering it up. Except *that* one turned out to be actually quite common. But not before you'd used my name in a letter-writing campaign that had the EPA all over the local lumber industry."

"That was eleventh grade!"

"And the elephants in the circus? You discovered they were being used for heavy labor and called PETA. But these elephants were bred in India as work animals."

"I don't believe in exploiting performing animals. Besides, this is different. This is my job."

Holly's distress was so evident that Vicki stopped as they exited the glass doors onto the street. "Okay, what's so wrong with your environmental paradise that you need your own PI?" She looked at her watch. "And keep it to the condensed version."

"Well, the animals, for one." As though suddenly realizing some of this press of humanity might understand English, Holly lowered her voice. "I think the workers are stealing them."

"So what brought you to this conclusion?"

"I've been noticing that just about every time I get back from Guatemala City, there're animals gone. They're always the ones with value for the exotic animal trade. And when I ask, either suddenly no one understands my Spanish, or I get some song and dance. The short-term teams don't know the animals well enough to notice, and Roger and Kathy aren't out in the cages. But I'm the veterinarian. I'm the one who knows how badly they were hurt or whether they're ready for release. And there're too many to explain away."

"And . . . ?" Vicki prompted. So far she'd heard nothing to keep her from responding to the eager waves of the cabdrivers waiting for fares on the curb.

Holly chewed at the corner of her mouth. "Well, a couple of weeks ago we got our first jaguarundi. Female. A bad hind leg, so rehabilitation was out, but she was prime breeding age. I supervised her transfer to the zoo here for our breeding program. When I got into town this morning, I went to check on her, and she's gone. No one knows anything. I've talked to everyone from the zoo administrator right up to the minister of environment. I figured they'd jump on it, but they just brushed me off. I know I'm just a foreign intern, but WRC is footing the bills. Shouldn't we have *some* accountability?"

Vicki had to smother an impulse to laugh at Holly's outrage. *Welcome to Guatemala, Holly.* "Did it ever occur to you that you got the brush-off because it's not just your local workers doing the stealing?"

Holly bristled. "Are you suggesting that one of our Guatemalan conservationists would even think of such a thing? If that isn't a patronizing thing to say. You think they don't care about their own country a lot more than we do? If anyone, why not accuse one of the American volunteers—Roger, or Joe, or even me? Unless you're insinuating we're somehow morally superior?"

"That's not what I'm saying, and you know it. But you've got to look at the odds. Who's got the connections to pull it off? Not your short-term volunteers, American or otherwise. And let's not be so sanctimonious. You've been here long enough to know that kickbacks are practically a job perk. Or are you telling me your zoo administrator and minister of environment don't have houses in Zone 10? If so, they're sure not doing it on government salaries."

Holly looked appalled. "You're right. I . . . I never thought of it. But . . . environmentalists? It's inconceivable. Inexcusable. So what do you think I should do? Confront them? Maybe if I could make them see how important these animals are to their future, the future of their country."

"Confront them?" Vicki didn't know whether to laugh or cry. "You really think you're going to tell these people that you know they're lining their pockets? Or that you can just explain the environmental consequences of their actions? Now who's patronizing? You think because this is a third world country, they can't understand the implications of their actions? that if you beg them to be good, they're going to throw up their hands and promise never to do it again?"

"Should I call the police?"

"Even if they haven't been bought, you think they're going to take on the local aristocracy on your say-so?" Vicki glanced at her watch again. "Now, if you don't mind, I really do need to get out of here."

At that moment a hand tugged at her arm.

Instinctively tightening her grip on her purse, Vicki whirled around.

Sure enough, it was another beggar, this one a woman; her handwoven *huipil,* the brightly embroidered peasant blouse, and wraparound skirt of the indigenous Mayans were ragged and dirty, including the length of homespun binding a small child to her back. Pointing to the baby, she cupped a hand toward Vicki and Holly.

Vicki was about to ignore the woman when she felt the feverish heat of the fingers clutching her arm and noticed the baby's sunken eyes and mournful whimper. Closer scrutiny revealed that the Mayan woman was barely into her teens and little more than a child herself. Vicki dug into her purse.

"Vicki, what are you doing?" Now it was Holly clutching her arm. "Come away from there. Don't you know what kind of diseases these people could be carrying?"

"Probably better than you do," Vicki answered dryly. "Just hold on a minute. Can't you see they're sick?"

Digging in her purse for the card Evelyn McKie had given her, Vicki turned back to the Mayan beggar. Her Spanish was far from perfect, but it was fluent enough. "You and your baby need medical care. I'm not going to give you money, but I'm going to take you to the place on this card—Casa de Esperanza. They'll help you." She hoped she was telling the truth.

Vicki caught a flicker of recognition in the fevered eyes; then the Mayan girl nodded dully.

"You've got to be kidding me!" Holly grabbed at Vicki's arm again. "See what I mean? I ask you for help, and you brush me off. Someone else comes along, and you jump to be there for them. We're talking the future of our planet here, and you're worrying yourself over every beggar with their hand out. Where are your priorities?"

Vicki thought of several sharp retorts, but Holly looked so upset that she just said gently, "Right now my priorities are a couple of sick kids who need medicine and food and a bed." Switching back to Spanish, she said to the Mayan girl, "Wait here."

Vicki walked over to the nearest cabdriver and motioned to the waiting mother and child. “How much to take all of us to Casa de Esperanza in Zone 4?”

The driver’s nostrils flared into distaste. “One hundred quetzales.”

At least twice the normal fare, but Vicki was not in the mood for quibbling.

Wresting open a back door of the cab, Vicki half guided, half pushed her two passengers inside. Sliding in after them, she shut the door and looked at Holly. “I really am sorry. I don’t want to run off on you, but I need to go now. I hope you can understand. I promise I’ll call you as soon as I can, okay?”

“So that’s it?” Holly leaned on the door. “You’re turning me down without even talking about it? You’re telling me to just throw in the towel and let them get away with it?”

“I’m not *telling* you to do anything,” Vicki responded evenly. “You asked what I would do. Well, that’s easy. Exactly what I’m doing right now. Just walk away. Consider the occasional sidetracked animal the price for doing business in Guatemala and concentrate on all the other good you’re doing. If you’re really concerned, contact your superiors back stateside and ask them to require accountability for future funding.”

The driver had started the engine. Giving him a nod, Vicki added, “Holly, I promise we’ll talk more tonight. No matter how late you finish up, give me a call. Meanwhile, don’t do anything foolish.”

“Oh, don’t wait up for me.” Holly stepped back. “If that’s the best you can do for advice, I’ll handle the rest of it myself.”

“The rest of it? Holly, what are you talking about?”

“Oh, believe me, the animals are the least of it. But, hey, you’ve got your priorities.”

“Holly—”

She had already swung around on her heel, and the taxi was moving away from the curb.

Leaning back with a sigh, Vicki didn’t bother to watch her storm back through the glass doors.

In the years she’d been in this business, she’d seen countless volunteers like Holly come and go. Not just American. European, Australian—they were all the same. Young. Idealistic. Determined to save the world—or at least their third-world portion of it.

They arrived with backpacks over their shoulders, cameras around their necks—and a cause. Each sure his or her own cause was the most vital to the future of the planet.

And equally sure they had only to throw enough of their Western technology and money to solve the planet's problems. That the corruption and evils they encountered were never by any human choice but by unavoidable circumstance.

But most would be gone soon enough, anyway. Broken against the hard reality of this place and the enormity of the mess they'd found. Or because they'd accumulated enough picturesque facts and photos to put themselves on the map with a scholarly dissertation that established their own future in academia.

Or just because dirt and poverty and primitive living conditions and inept bureaucracy and never-ending insecurity lost their charm, and not even retreating to the air-conditioning and walled luxury of Zone 10 sustained an illusion of home.

It was better not to get involved. To let them come and go with their short-lived dreams and convictions and missions. To save the emotional energy for battles Vicki could win. A handful of garbage pickers. A Mayan baby. A mother.

Just walk away.

Except this time it wasn't so easy. Because this particular youthful and naive volunteer who had stomped with angry self-righteousness into the airport was Vicki's younger and only sister.

CHAPTER FOUR

Only for my sister would I put up with this.

Vicki pushed Redial on her cell phone. Eleven o'clock at night and Holly had neither called nor answered Vicki's repeated attempts.

"Hi, this is Holly. It's an awesome world. Help me save it."

Irritated, Vicki cut off the voice mail without leaving another message.

Walking across the smoothed concrete that was the infirmary ward floor, she looked down into a portable crib. *Maritza* was the hand-lettered name taped to the end. The sleeping baby girl was clean and freshly diapered, her thick black hair spiking with perspiration from a lingering fever, but the bronze features smoothed to peaceful lines, her rosebud mouth making contented sucking motions.

Sleeping beside Maritza in a narrow cot was her mother, her dusty homespun exchanged for a faded but serviceable nightgown. Even in sleep, her thin fingers clutched the bars of her child's crib. Casa de Esperanza's volunteer doctor had diagnosed her with malnutrition and a postpartum infection that had lasted for months.

In the end Vicki had been late to her meeting at Casa de Esperanza. It turned out to be a dilapidated colonial-era mansion in one of the oldest parts of the city, close enough to the ravine she'd seen from the air to smell the acrid fumes of burning garbage. Again familiar. *I could be back in Mexico City or even India.*

A small door set into the right-hand portal opened onto a courtyard that was scrupulously clean, even festive, with potted citrus trees and ornamental bushes. The house itself had been built two stories high around three sides of the courtyard, with all rooms up and down opening onto a wide veranda.

The verandas were made cheerful with potted plants, and though Vicki immediately spotted where gray Duralite slabs patched the original red tile roof, the interior walls were all freshly whitewashed, giving an overall effect of a peaceful, green oasis. Quiet it was not. In the courtyard, this was because of women and children, even some men, who waited their turn through a door identified by a square red cross as well as the words *Clínica Esperanza* hand-lettered above it.

But most of the noise came from over the wall to the right where a concrete building rose above the old colonial mansion to five stories. Vicki had recognized the sounds of playing children, presumably the subjects of her investigation.

Now Vicki smiled wryly at the recollection of the meeting. The short- and long-term missionaries were far different from what Vicki had expected. There were more than a dozen, some Guatemalan, others expatriates. Unlike Evelyn, they all wore jeans and yellow T-shirts with *Casa de Esperanza* and a child's rendering of a house printed on them.

Each team leader took Vicki through a neat printout of their particular responsibilities—including the clinic, the children's home next door, and a number of nonresident nutrition and educational programs—as well as their accompanying financial statements.

All of which Vicki would verify later. It was easy enough to write an impressive report. Though at first glance it looked almost too good for Vicki's inherent cynicism.

Once team members had been dismissed, Evelyn had given Vicki a tour, beginning with the clinic and offices housed in the original colonial mansion, then the concrete block next door.

This was no less crowded than that Mexican orphanage, but the children here looked well fed, their black hair shining with health, their chatter as cheerful as the yellow T-shirts they too wore as uniforms.

Though Vicki saw no toys or individual possessions, there was plenty of sports equipment. Surplus land between the building and property wall had been paved over for a playing field with basketball hoops and portable soccer goals on all four sides. All were in use as Vicki and Evelyn walked by.

Evelyn led Vicki upstairs to one of the dormitory wards. The girls who slept there had maneuvered the two rows of bunk beds together to make two opposing platforms, blankets forming walls around the sides and ends.

"We're *Cristóbal Colón* on the *Santa Maria,*" a pigtailed ringleader announced proudly from one set of bunks. "And they're the English pirates stealing our gold. The boys said girls couldn't fight to save their ships. But we can, can't we?"

"Of course you can," Evelyn assured her as she and Vicki moved between the battling quarterdecks.

Vicki found herself blinking back sudden moisture at the normality of the scene. "I remember playing just like that when I was a little girl."

"Yes, children really are the same the world over," Evelyn responded placidly. "It would be nice to give them an American standard of space and living conditions. But then, how many more would have nothing at all? As it is, we turn away dozens for every one we can squeeze in. Besides, this is the country they have to live in, and it's a poor one. Plenty of people outside these walls are crowding ten into a room or a thatched hut."

"Do you ever try to get them into foster homes?" Vicki asked.

Evelyn shook her head. "In Guatemala that would just mean becoming unpaid servants. Occasionally an expat will adopt, usually the babies, though the laws here make it a difficult process. Nor do we kick them out, like so many of the state homes do, as soon as they're old enough for manual labor. Our children stay until they're out of school and able to hold a job. And why shouldn't they? This is no holding station; it's their home. The other children and the staff here become their family over the years. A very big family but family nonetheless."

Family.

The word echoed now in Vicki's mind as she brushed gentle fingers over baby Maritza's soft, dark head. Was that the difference that set this place apart from any Vicki had surveyed to date?

Don't jump ahead. There's plenty I haven't checked out yet. How many other good impressions have turned out to be rotten underneath?

Satisfied her two charges were comfortable, Vicki gave the night attendant a smile as she left the ward. She dug into a pocket for her room key and headed to the taller building, where several smaller dormitories provided quarters for live-in nursing staff and visiting volunteer teams.

Vicki dropped the stack of reports she'd acquired on a nightstand and let her purse slide from her shoulder. Someone had already deposited her duffel bag on one of two single beds. The room was as austere as the rest of the building. High walls and ceiling painted a pale green. Mosquito nets hanging down over the beds. A single lightbulb dangling on a wire. A door leading to the room's one luxury, a private bathroom.

Tired though she was, Vicki was too keyed up to sleep. Crossing the room, she pushed the heavy wooden shutters open and wrapped her arms around herself as she leaned out. Her room was high enough to afford an excellent view of the city, and she saw the red, flickering glow of the fires that smoldered endlessly beneath the surface of Guatemala City's municipal dump.

Rather like the fires that must still be smoldering beneath the surface of Guatemala itself, Vicki thought reflectively, for all its theoretical peace. Fires of anger and greed. And revenge.

But not here at least. Not in this place.

Resting her arms on the windowsill, Vicki listened to the sounds wafting upward from other open shutters. A child sobbing in the dark. The soothing reply of an adult. Girlish whispers and giggles from a dormitory ward somewhere below the window.

Family.

If this noisy, restless, breathing building beneath her feet could be characterized so, then it was Evelyn McKie who was its matriarch. And a much-loved one. Vicki had stayed with the missionary during a supper of lentil stew and the madhouse of supervising each age group through bathrooms, story time, and lights-out.

Everywhere they had been besieged by excited cries of "*¡Tía Evelina!*" "Aunt Evelyn!" Small bodies hurled themselves against the fragile, straight figure for a hug. Teens paused to respond shyly to her interested queries about schoolwork or plans. And she'd called every one by name. How did she keep them all straight?

Family.

It had to be the smoke gusting from the ravine that burned Vicki's eyes. Impatiently blinking it away, she retrieved her phone and hit Redial, cutting it off with a stab as she heard Holly's voice mail. *Holly, come on, pick up. I know you're mad, but honestly . . .*

"Vicki, dearie, you're still awake after the long day you've had?"

Vicki hadn't yet closed the door, and as she turned, Evelyn stepped into the room.

"Forgive me for disturbing you this late, but I thought I'd leave these at your door." Evelyn handed Vicki two yellow T-shirts. "You'll want to wear them out on the project for ID and protection. Even *las maras*—the street gangs—will usually give Casa de Esperanza personnel a pass."

Her glance fell on the cell phone in Vicki's hand, and she added sympathetically, "Still haven't got through to your friend, eh? Is she with your children's foundation as well? I don't think I've ever met her in the expat community."

"Oh, definitely not. No, Holly's pure tree hugger." Seeing gentle interest in the bright gaze, Vicki explained briefly.

Evelyn nodded. "I've always worked with children myself, and for some people, that seems to put us in opposite camps. But to be honest, I've always felt a sneaking kinship with the tree huggers. You couldn't even imagine what this country was like when I arrived fifty years ago. Green and wild and beautiful—and no garbage. Back then we'd never have imagined anything like this would ever be possible." She gestured at the fiery glow of the dump through the window.

"The children's needs come first, of course," Evelyn continued, "but it really would be a shame for them to grow up with nothing left of the incredible beauty God put into their country, and for that I applaud people like your friend. It always reminds me of an old hymn no one sings much anymore." Her voice was surprisingly strong and steady as she started singing, "'This is my Father's world: I rest me in the thought of rocks and trees, of skies and seas—His hand—'"

"Don't sing that!" Vicki's sharp rejoinder cut through the melody.

As Evelyn stopped and stared, Vicki caught herself. "I'm so sorry. You caught me off guard. I . . . I've always hated that song."

It was hardly an adequate explanation for rudeness, so she added quickly, "When I was a kid, I always thought the song was talking about my biological father. And since he never figured in my life, it always rubbed me the wrong way."

"And now?" There was something uncomfortably *seeing* in Evelyn's shrewd gaze, the gentle question.

Vicki shrugged. "You mean, the Father being God the Creator, Father of the world and all that? Sure, I managed to figure out my error as I got older. I'm certainly no atheist, if that's what you mean. I went to Sunday school. I believe the Bible. It's just . . ."

Under Evelyn's steady, encouraging gaze, the words twisted out of Vicki as she whirled back to the window. "Just take a look at that. The starving kids. The dirt. The wars. The . . . the pain. My Father's world—it . . . it's like a bad joke. What kind of sick parent creates a world like that and calls it beautiful?"

Evelyn shook her head slowly. "Do you think it's really fair to blame God for that mess? It's we humans who've played havoc with His creation, after all."

"Oh, sure," Vicki said impatiently. "We humans made the mess, and we probably do deserve anything we get. But if God bothered enough to create all this in the first place, it seems He should care enough to do *something* to clean it up. Then maybe people like you wouldn't have to give up your whole life—" She stopped, astonished at herself. What on earth was independent, hardheaded Vicki Andrews doing spilling her guts like this to a total stranger? There was something about this old woman.

She managed a rueful smile. "I'm sorry. This all started as an apology for cutting you off. I must seem pretty silly to you. It's just . . . well, I hadn't heard that old song in years, not since I finally broke my sister of singing it over and over."

"Of course you don't seem silly," Evelyn answered firmly, "and you really don't need to apologize. You mentioned your sister. Would that be Holly?"

Vicki's eyebrows shot up. "Yes. How did you know? Not many people guess; we don't look anything alike."

Evelyn smiled faintly. "For one, you act like sisters."

"Yes, well, you're right. Holly is about two and a half years younger. She used to drive me crazy singing that song. There were times I wanted to strangle the person who taught it to her."

"Actually—" Evelyn coughed before she finished apologetically—"that would be me."

CHAPTER FIVE

Vicki was so dumbfounded she could do no more than stare.

"You *are* Vicki and Holly Craig? Or were, since I see you now go by the name Andrews. Your parents were Jeff and Victoria Craig?" Evelyn looked at Vicki with bright eyes. "I thought I was mistaken when you told me your name. But when you introduced your friend—sister, that is . . . after all, Vicki and Holly are not a particularly common combination, and you do look very much like your mother. Add to that a favorite hymn two little girls I once knew loved to sing over and over again. That's when I was sure."

Vicki's head was whirling so much that she could hardly breathe, and she found herself groping for the support of the windowsill. "You're saying you met my parents and knew Holly and me when we were children? Then that's why you—this place—seemed so familiar. I thought I was imagining it. But I don't understand how you could know us. And who were my parents? Where did you meet them—and us?"

"Why, right here. Your parents were living in our guest quarters when you were born. " Evelyn leaned forward to study Vicki's face. "You really have no idea what I'm talking about, do you?"

Vicki shook her head. "I never even knew I'd been in Guatemala until my birth certificate was turned over when I went off to college. Not the original either, since Holly and I are adopted. But it lists Guatemala as my birth country. Are you sure you have the right people? that this isn't some kind of weird coincidence?"

"Well, that's easy enough to establish. Come with me." Evelyn took Vicki by the arm.

Vicki was too stunned to talk as she accompanied Evelyn out of the room, into the freight elevator, through the connecting gate into the Casa de Esperanza courtyard, and up a veranda stairway into an upstairs apartment.

It was small with an open kitchen and living area. The furniture was sparse and well-worn. One wall held floor-to-ceiling bookshelves, a scattering of bright, newer book spines amid the ancient mildewed bindings. Like everything else Vicki had seen, the place was ruthlessly clean, and its very simplicity held a certain attraction.

"My retreat when things get too noisy around here," Evelyn said with quiet humor as she ushered Vicki in and began rummaging through a bookshelf. "Though back when you were born, it was our guest quarters. Such a sweet baby you were. And Holly, though of course she was already a toddler before I saw her. Sit! Sit!"

As Vicki sank obediently into the armchair, Evelyn came back with a photo album, old enough that its binding was cracking. Carefully she spread it out on a coffee table.

"There you are—the whole family. That was the last time you were here, just before . . ."

Vicki stared in astonishment at the photo. The background was easily identifiable as the courtyard below, the broad staircase behind the group the same she'd just climbed.

There were four people in all. And, yes, the blonde toddler being held up for the camera was definitely Holly, while the small, brown girl in front looked much like Vicki's early school photos. Though none of those had carried such a joyous grin. Vicki studied the two adults. Could these really be her birth parents? The woman holding Holly looked startlingly like the image that confronted Vicki in the mirror. Her hair was long and parted down the middle. The man was tall and blond, one hand resting protectively on Vicki's shoulder.

"It *is* us," Vicki said blankly. "But how did you—?" Then she saw the picture on the opposite page, identical except that in this one a younger Evelyn replaced the man.

"I took that one." Evelyn tapped the first photo. "The only picture I've got with your father in it, since he was always behind the camera, of course."

She caught Vicki's puzzled look. "Jeff was a photojournalist; didn't you know? He was hitchhiking through Central America, right out of journalism school and determined to find a story that would win him a Pulitzer. He was fascinated with the *basureros*, a phenomenon that was new back then as peasants displaced by the civil war flooded into Guatemala City. I'd just raised the funds to buy this place for a children's home. Your mother was one of our volunteers. Your father arrived and fell in love with the children, the country—and your mother. He went home with some news stories that roused enough interest and funds to get this place outfitted for the first fifty kids."

Evelyn's smile was reminiscent. "Then he came right back and proposed to your mother. They got married and stayed here, your mother working as our nurse, your father taking pictures and writing. They traveled together until you came along, though it was none too safe with all the warfare going on, but Jeff never worried. He had this *fearlessness*, almost recklessly so, as though nothing could touch him. He was outraged about injustice, especially the civil war. He wanted the world to know what was going on down here."

She's describing Holly, Vicki realized.

"And he *was* getting noticed. Associated Press and Reuters were beginning to pick up some of his photos and news coverage." Evelyn turned the album pages as she spoke.

There were group pictures of Evelyn and Victoria with Guatemalan children. Close-ups of haunting faces and sad eyes. Photos of *basureros* and Casa de Esperanza, clearly before its renovation.

Vicki stared at a photo of Victoria with a baby in her arms, then bent forward to read the tiny lettering on the bottom right-hand corner. The date was followed by *Jeff Craig Productions*.

Evelyn nodded. "Yes, Jeff always stamped his pictures with name and date to protect his copyright. That one would be you at . . . three months. Which sounds right because that's when he was offered a graduate fellowship back at Columbia. I didn't see Jeff and Victoria for several years after they left, but they always kept in touch. I knew Jeff was doing well because I'd see his name on a news photo from Sri Lanka or a magazine spread on Kenya. He *did* have itchy feet."

Like his daughters. Vicki bent forward again to look at a *National Geographic* layout of an African refugee camp that might easily have been one she herself had surveyed. For the first time she was beginning to feel that these unfamiliar people in the photos really might be connected to her and Holly. Her parents.

Then why was it all such a blank, as though she were listening to a story about total strangers? She strained to remember something—*anything*—but the effort brought a familiar queasiness to her stomach. She asked hastily, "So how did they end up back here? By the photos they must have come back. *We,* I mean."

"Jeff had been given a grant to do a book on the modern-day Mayans. He believed the beauty of this country needed to be preserved on film before it was gone forever, and he wanted to include the *basureros* in the book, since they're Mayan too. I invited him to bring the whole family here. So you came. Victoria settled right back into helping with the children while Jeff traveled around the country, taking pictures, doing interviews. You girls loved it. Playing with the children. Having tea with me in this apartment. Singing."

Evelyn gestured to the ancient pump organ in a corner, a worn hymnbook lying open on its rack. "That's where you learned 'This Is My Father's World.' That's even the same book. I sang it for you one day because it seemed to fit what your father was trying to do. You and Holly latched onto it and begged me to sing it, though you never managed to get past the first line. Funny to think that stuck even when you forgot everything else."

"I can't believe it." Vicki shook her head. "I always assumed we'd learned that song at Sunday school. I can't imagine *choosing* to sing it."

"Well, you did, over and over." Evelyn gave a ghost of a smile before she went on. "I'd have been happy to have kept you here forever. But Jeff persuaded the leaders of a Mayan village to allow him to live there and photograph their daily lives for his book. He convinced them that this would be an opportunity to communicate their plight to the outside world. It was the height of the civil war, and the Mayan peasants were getting the worst of it. Jeff was sure this would be Pulitzer material. The only drawback was leaving his family for such an extended time.

"Victoria dug in her heels and said you'd all go. It would be safe since you'd be under the auspices of the Mayan tribal leaders, and there was a strong army presence in the area as protection against any guerrilla activity. Besides, as a nurse, she could handle medical emergencies, even make herself useful in the village while Jeff was working. I'll never forget you and Holly climbing into the Jeep to take off, still singing 'This Is My Father's World' at the top of your sweet little voices. That was the last time I saw you."

"Because Jeff and Victoria were killed?" Vicki was touched to see tears in Evelyn's eyes. It seemed odd that to this woman these people were friends—even family—while to Vicki, their daughter, they were strangers.

"Yes. There was no easy communication in those days, certainly not in the mountains, so it was no surprise for a month to go by without hearing from Jeff and Victoria. In fact, the first I knew of any trouble was when the embassy announced that two Americans had been killed in the Mayan highlands east of here. The bodies had been recovered and turned over to a local military unit who'd brought them into Guatemala City—" Evelyn broke off. "I'm sorry, Vicki. I forget how difficult this must be for you. Does it bother you to talk about it?"

"Not at all," Vicki said truthfully. "I never knew them, after all. But if this is hard for you . . ."

"It's been twenty years," Evelyn said gently. "It's time they were remembered, especially by their daughters."

"Then I'd like to hear the rest," Vicki said. "How were they killed? Was it a car accident?"

"Oh, it was no accident. That was in the news coverage, though not much more. I guess it was assumed to be one more carjacking or robbery. When they were identified, my first concern was you and Holly, so I went to the embassy. All they would tell me was that you two girls had already been evacuated to the States. I was sorry I couldn't say good-bye or keep in touch. You both were so precious to me."

Evelyn stopped again to scrutinize Vicki. "You really don't remember any of this? I mean, you were five. Surely you must have some memory."

Vicki lifted her shoulders. "I don't remember anything that far back. My first memories are the orphanage where Holly and I used to live."

Evelyn looked at Vicki in dismay. "I . . . I had no idea. I'd always assumed you went home to family. At least . . . Well, I knew Victoria was raised in foster care—one of the reasons she was so interested in my work—but I thought Jeff had family. I am so sorry." Her hands shook with distress as she closed the photo album.

Vicki gently touched Evelyn's arm. "Really, it's okay. We weren't always in an orphanage. We were in and out of foster homes until we finally settled down with Mom and Dad Andrews."

Vicki had always known that it was her fault. Many families were anxious to take in an adorable blonde toddler, but a stubborn first grader who refused to speak was a different story.

"Andrews. The people who adopted you?"

"Yes. They were retired schoolteachers. They'd never had children of their own, and they missed them when they stopped teaching, so they volunteered as foster parents. We were their first—and last—assignment. After a couple of years, they adopted us."

"Were you happy there?" Evelyn asked. "Were they good to you?"

"They were very kind to us. More than I deserved, I'm sure. Holly doesn't remember anything earlier. They were just Mom and Dad to her, and she loved the farm and the animals. I'd always thought that was where she'd picked up that song. Holly just wouldn't *stop* singing it. To her it was about God making a beautiful world. To me it was about a father who wasn't there. I mean, I loved the farm and Mom and Dad too, but I could remember the other foster homes and the orphanage, and I guess I was always waiting for the ax to fall and us to end up alone again."

With an embarrassed laugh, Vicki added, "I guess a psychologist would say that's why I drifted into working with abandoned children while Holly ended up in the tree-hugger camp. She was always more of an idealist and thought she could save the world, but I always knew better. In fact, Jeff sounds a lot like her."

"And you never tried to find out more about your birth family when you grew up? Your adoptive family never told you about them?"

Vicki shrugged. How could she explain the unease that gripped her every time she tried to push back the dark veil of her early childhood? "They told us what the foster system had on record, namely that our parents hadn't abandoned us, which mattered most. But family records are sealed with adoption, so all they knew was that our parents had been killed when we were very young. Guatemala hardly seemed relevant, especially since Holly's birth certificate stated she was American born, and it wasn't as though we were immigrants from here. We were both registered as American citizens by birth, so Mom and Dad Andrews figured our birth parents must have been traveling down here when I was born.

"I'm not sure why I never told Holly about it, except that . . . well, she was happy and settled there. The past was the past."

Again that feeling of queasy unease.

"And Mom and Dad Andrews weren't young. They died just a few months apart when Holly was a freshman in college, so if there was anything else they knew, it went with them. Holly and I were grieving enough over losing the only parents we'd ever known. What good would it do to stir up more past hurt or loss? After all, if we'd had any family, we wouldn't have ended up in the foster care system, so what was the point? I never expected that either of us would be in Guatemala, much less that I'd run into you. Who would have believed such a coincidence?"

"I don't believe in coincidences," Evelyn said soberly. "Not in God's economy." Then, fixing Vicki with a steady gaze, she asked, as she'd asked earlier, "And now?"

"Now?" Vicki ran a tired hand over her face. "It doesn't sound like we'll ever be able to find out how our birth parents were killed, but I'll definitely have to tell Holly about them. That is, if I can ever get her to pick up her phone."

A sigh escaped Vicki as she fiddled with the Redial on her cell phone. Catching Evelyn's questioning glance, she added a rueful explanation. "Holly's not too happy with me. I'm afraid I didn't take her latest crusade as seriously as I should have."

"She'll call when she's had time to cool down," Evelyn said quietly.

"That's what sisters do. As to just how your parents were killed . . ." She hesitated. "There is at least one person who knows what happened that day, however locked away that knowledge might be."

"Really?" Vicki sat up straight. "Who would that be?"

"You."

CHAPTER SIX

Vicki glanced at the dark heads bent studiously over open notebooks before completing the final spelling word she was writing on a portable blackboard. Wiping her sleeve across the dust and sweat of her face, she signaled to Consuelo, her assistant, and ducked out of the thatched shelter to cross a dirt courtyard to the cook shack at the back.

The large A-frame shelter, the narrow wooden benches with their wriggling occupants, and the open courtyard with its low, adobe wall was another of Casa de Esperanza's neighborhood outreach projects. This one offered elementary schooling to children whose *basureros* parents were willing to spare their labor for a few hours a day. Vicki had little illusion that her patient reading and math tutelage were as big a draw as their daily reward of a nutritious noon meal, which was not far off according to the sun gleaming palely through the haze of smoke almost directly overhead.

Vicki filled an enamel cup from an enormous pottery jar that held boiled water; she drank deeply, then splashed the remaining drops across her hot face before murmuring thanks to a plump, black-braided woman in indigenous dress patting out tortillas in front of the cook shack.

This was the third day Vicki had taken over the teaching responsibilities here, replacing a volunteer currently battling a bout of dengue fever. It was also exactly one week since she'd arrived at Casa de Esperanza. In that time she'd seen every one of its neighborhood projects, pored over financial statements, visited extensively with volunteers, and taken every opportunity she could to spend time with the children themselves. An excited *Tía Vee-kee* now greeted her every time she stepped through the gate of the children's home.

Far from modifying her original perceptions, Vicki remained thus far reluctantly impressed. The work was not easy, as Vicki was experiencing firsthand, but the volunteers seemed genuinely committed to their cause and, more importantly, to the children. Certainly they were not profiting personally. As to wasteful spending, Vicki was instead astounded at just how much these people were accomplishing with the very limited funds they had.

Maybe not all faith-based NGOs were as exemplary as this one. But unless some red flag was raised in the next few days it would take to write her report, Vicki saw little reason to postpone her seal of approval for a partnership between Children at Risk and Casa de Esperanza. And since Evelyn had informed Vicki at breakfast that she'd found a volunteer to fill in, there was nothing to keep Vicki from booking her flight to that long-earned vacation.

But not without seeing Holly.

Annoyed, Vicki strode back across the courtyard. An entire week and not so much as a message from Holly on her voice mail. The second day Vicki had even called the Wildlife Rescue Center's Guatemala City headquarters. There were no landlines as far up into the mountains as the biosphere, but the local office maintained a radio-phone network. Yes, Holly was back up at WRC, an Australian soprano had informed Vicki. No, she didn't know when Holly would be in town again. Yes, she'd pass a message on for Holly to contact Vicki.

And there Vicki had left it. She might have worried if she didn't know her sister so well. Holly was going to show Vicki by doing on her own whatever it was she'd wanted Vicki to do. Vicki likely wouldn't hear from Holly until she'd succeeded—or thrown in the towel.

One thing Vicki had taken time for was a visit to the American embassy in Zone 10. A Google search had brought up nothing on the deaths of Jeff and Victoria Craig—no real surprise since local news archives from twenty years past were not likely to have made it to the Internet.

So the previous afternoon after finishing with the children, Vicki had taken a cab down to the fortress she'd seen from the air.

The consular office open to the public was staffed in its totality with local hires rather than actual Americans, right down to the guards at the gates. But for a fee, a Guatemalan clerk had unhesitatingly looked up the appropriate Death Abroad file and printed Vicki a copy. To her disappointment, the report added little to what Evelyn had told her except that there had been multiple gunshot wounds involved, so it was definitely no accident. Assailants: unknown. Presumed motive: robbery. An addendum gave the only mention of Vicki and Holly. A note that since no family members had come forward, the Assistance to Distressed Citizens Abroad Fund had paid for a cremation and the return of two surviving minors to their point of origin.

Later that evening she'd shown the report to Evelyn. "I was just wondering . . . I guess this means Jeff—I mean, my birth father—never finished his Mayan book. So what happened to all the pictures he'd already taken when this happened?"

"I have no idea. I have only the prints he gave me of his Casa de Esperanza pictures; he always developed his own." Evelyn shook her head. "He was paranoid about his copyrights and losing his pictures. He didn't want anyone getting hold of them before the book was finished. He couldn't just send photos off to his publisher by computer like you can now, and he certainly wouldn't have been foolish enough to drop them in the Guatemalan mail system. It's gotten better, but back then if you wanted to send something stateside, you found someone traveling north and asked him to deliver it for you. If Jeff did that, I have no idea who or where. He didn't leave anything here."

All in all, another closed door.

A side note was that Vicki had run into both of Holly's male interests, as Vicki had cataloged them. The first had been the embassy staffer Holly had introduced as Michael Camden.

As the clerk was running off Vicki's photocopy, Michael had walked past, then swung around immediately and walked back to Vicki. "You're Holly's friend from the airport the other day. Vicki, right?"

"Yes. And you're . . . Michael? The defense attaché from the DAO."

"Michael Camden. The defense attaché would be my boss. I'm simply a lowly attaché attached to the defense attaché's office, if that isn't too redundant." For a lowly attaché, he certainly managed to project a persona of cool authority. He glanced from Vicki to the clerk behind the counter. "Is there any way I can be of assistance?"

"No, I'm just doing some research." Vicki was not going to discuss her birth parents with a stranger before she'd even shared that information with her sister. "But thank you for asking," she added with belated politeness.

Michael knit his dark eyebrows together. "Holly was going to set an appointment with my secretary to get together. I still haven't heard from her. Do you know how I can get in touch with her?"

"I'd like to get ahold of her myself," Vicki answered. "But she's not in town right now anyway. As far as I know she's up at the wildlife preserve where she works."

"If you hear from her, let her know I'd still like to sit down with her." With a courteous nod, he walked away.

Vicki's second encounter was Joe, the WRC handyman and pilot. He'd been walking rapidly toward the high guarded gate of the embassy just as Vicki was flagging down a taxi to return to Casa de Esperanza. At first she didn't recognize him. In his tucked-in, buttoned-up shirt and pants, his blond mane slicked back and tamed, he looked more like a businessman than the surfer she'd met.

Vicki would have liked to ask him for news of Holly, but she was already in the taxi when she realized who he was. He'd glanced up just as the cab was pulling away. He raised a hand in greeting, the corner of his mouth sloping down in that derisive smile of his, before striding into the embassy.

Which brought Vicki back with annoyance to her sister. *Holly, I love you, but honestly!* If Holly was going to keep sulking much longer, it would serve her right if Vicki just booked that ticket home.

I'll call the office and have them radio a message that I'm winding down here. Then it'll be her call if she wants to see me before I leave.

Vicki checked her watch. Just enough time before lunch for her students' favorite part of the morning studies—the Bible lesson that was an integral part of any Casa de Esperanza project. At the moment, they were working their way through the Creation story, and as Vicki had placed the colorful images of animals and plants and flowers on a flannel board, she wondered if these children had any concept that such a world even existed beyond the surreal landscape they woke up to each morning.

"This is my Father's world."

Vicki's mouth twisted wryly. Not for these kids at least. Still, what would be the possibilities of some field trips? Maybe even a campout? That would be something to bring up with Evelyn before she left.

It was the vultures that detoured Vicki's steps before she reached the thatched schoolroom. She paused to check that her students were still bent over their assignment, then quickly crossed the scuffed earth of the courtyard.

This project compound had been built right on the edge of the dump, offering an unrestricted vista of the landscape that greeted Vicki's students every day—a wasteland of refuse as far as the eye could see.

Ignoring the streaks mud brick left on her T-shirt, Vicki leaned over the low adobe wall. Tears burned her eyes as a sudden updraft caught her nostrils.

That stench was a combination of rotting garbage and fumes from the fires, some set purposely to diminish the trash hills, others the spontaneous combustion of methane gas generated by tons of decomposing compost. There'd been a time when Vicki had found it inconceivable that human beings spent their days toiling in that reeking inferno, much less lived there.

Vicki could see cardboard and scrap wood shacks climbing the slopes of the ravine. Permanent paths wound through unsalvageable garbage and rusted car frames to the dirt tracks where rusting yellow trucks dumped fifteen hundred tons of trash each day. Riches to be fought over with the vultures and scrawny mongrels—and each other. Rakes hammered from foraged metal pulled apart fresh loads as fast as they could be shoveled. Deft fingers shook off vegetable peelings to pick out glass, plastic, cardboard, cans, rags—anything that could be sold to the recycling merchants keeping a prudent distance beyond the top of the ravine.

Children were there too, those not fortunate enough to be squirming on the benches behind Vicki. Babies tied to their mothers' bent backs or tucked for safety into an old tire or box. Older children picked through their parents' rakings. Just down the slope from where Vicki stood, two boys struggled to roll an old tire up a muddy path. Farther down, a toddler screamed as a stray dog snatched away the half-eaten melon she'd unearthed.

Filthy, their scavenged garments tattered, rags binding hands and feet against the constant cuts and scrapes, hair matted and strawlike from malnutrition, these waifs were distinguished from the debris through which they foraged only by their movements.

But it was the vultures that drew Vicki's intent gaze. They were always out there by the thousands, wheeling lazily above the mountains of garbage or perched hunch-shouldered on the smoking heaps.

These vultures were different. Their tight pattern circled above a single, distant mound, dropping lower and lower. Spooked by some movement, they scattered upward, only to begin their slow circling again.

Vicki had seen that patient waiting game before. There was fresh meat out there.

And it was still alive.

Brushing back a wisp of hair the breeze had tugged from her ponytail, Vicki leaned precariously farther, blinking away the burning in her eyes. Had that blur of black beneath the circling carrion birds just moved?

Then, in one of those glimpses of clarity where tears themselves act as a magnifying lens, the blur coalesced into focus. Black plastic. One of the industrial trash bags in which wealthier Guatemalans disposed of their waste.

And, yes, a definite movement had just sent the vultures fluttering upward again. Had one of the mongrels infesting the dump crawled inside and been stuck? Maybe even a child?

Vicki rushed to an opening in the adobe wall, where two boys sprawled against the mud brick. She'd tried earlier to coax them into the schooling program but to no avail.

"*Hola,* Pepe, Luchito." In local custom, her chin pointed the direction rather than her hand. "I think there's something hurt out there. Would you go see what it is? *Se los pagaré.*" "I'll pay you." The five-quetzal note dangling invitingly from her fingers should have had the boys scrambling to their feet.

Apathetic stares were explained as they dropped filthy faces back to sniff at disposable plastic cups filled with a pungent, golden molasses. They'd already earned the few cents needed for their ration of industrial glue and would spend the rest of the day lost in the illusion of warmth and food and comfort. The street kid's best friend.

Exasperated, Vicki stepped from the opening into a rutted alley that petered a few meters away into the path leading down into the ravine. Threading single file up that path, a procession of *basureros* emerged over the rim of the ravine, backs stooped under their gleanings.

"Señores!" Vicki called. The title was a courtesy few would give these laborers. This time she forgot her training and used a finger to point. "There's something out there moving. I think it's hurt. *Si me podría ayudar.*" "If you would help me."

Heads swiveled to follow the foreigner's rude gesture, then swiveled back. Vicki recognized astonishment behind the impassive blankness of dark faces.

"A dog, perhaps," one man called from under his pack. "Or rats."

"But it might be a person. Maybe a child." Vicki displayed the five-quetzal bill. "Look, I can pay if you'll just go take a look."

The column didn't even break its slow, measured pace as it came abreast of Vicki. *Crazy, rich gringa,* she read in the flicker of black eyes.

Only the laborer who'd spoken paused to shake his head. "No one goes out that far, señorita. It is too dangerous, and there is nothing left of value. *Los gringos preocupan demasiado.*" "You foreigners worry too much." Like most people here, the man was Mayan, stunted by life and diet to little more than five feet tall. He added, "If it is a person, it is dead. The destitute leave them there. Cemeteries cost money. Do not worry. The vultures will take care of it."

As though he considered it payment for his advice, the man snatched the bill from Vicki's hand and fell back in with the procession.

"Hey!" Vicki exclaimed, then subsided. *Count it as a contribution to the local economy.* The man was probably right. The movement she'd seen was far out on that wasteland of smoldering fires and rotting debris, well beyond where trucks and bulldozers or the *basureros* themselves dared venture.

Stepping to the edge of the slope, Vicki squinted against the fumes. Yes, there it was, swimming into watery focus. A black trash bag. If the movement had been a small animal trapped inside, it was no longer moving, the vultures now beginning to settle. Her stomach roiled as beaks ripped into the plastic. Time to retreat to a more savory meal, if she could stand to eat with this stench lingering in her nostrils.

But just as she was blinking the tears from her eyes, she saw a human hand thrust upward imploringly from that black bundle. This time it was no illusion that it moved.

"*¡Esperen!* Wait. It *is* a person! And it's still alive!"

The *basureros* did not even look back.

Anger propelled Vicki across that wasteland. Not at the garbage pickers toiling up out of the ravine nor at the sprawled teens drowning one more day's misery in a chemical haze. At a world where a human being tossed on a garbage heap for the vultures was too commonplace for even a moment's concern.

The trail downward was as slippery with rotting foodstuff as mud. Vicki's shoes and clothes were saturated with muck, her lungs burning by the time she reached the landfill and ventured out onto its precarious surface. A nearby bulldozer shoveled trash deeper into the gorge without regard for the workers still picking through it. Following the operator's example, Vicki shook filth from a bandanna tied around her ponytail and retied it to cover her mouth. How did the *basureros* breathe this all day?

When Vicki had covered fifty meters, she understood the Mayan's warnings. The landfill was dangerous, glass and metal shards too small for salvage cutting into her rubber soles. Decomposition and the fires smoldering continuously underground created sinkholes that could swallow the unwary without a trace. After a near miss, Vicki slowed her pace, the heat underfoot burning through her soles to a painful level no matter how carefully she chose her path.

Vicki was close enough now to see she'd been right. The black of the trash bag covered a human shape, and where the plastic was torn, she could glimpse cloth. More horribly she could see bloodied flesh, the upthrust hand torn by sharp beaks. Vicki snatched up a rusted length of tailpipe that burnt her fingers before she threw it. It had the effect of fluttering some of the scavengers skyward.

The last meters were a difficult scramble over a metal jungle of stripped car frames, the rusted edges dangerously sharp. Vicki was bleeding from half a dozen nicks before she reached the mound that was her destination.

Which brought forcefully to mind the *basurero*'s insistence. The industrial-size trash bags that held wealthier Guatemalans' garbage served as housing and bedcovers for street kids. Or burial shrouds for the poorest of poor. But neither had cause to be out this far.

More oddly, sprawled like a tossed potato sack on top of the mound, this trash bag was still largely intact where the vultures had not ripped at it, untouched by *basurero* rake or bulldozer. And it was clean, the black plastic still shiny. It might have dropped from the sky for its unlikelihood here.

There was no time to be wasted on questions. The heap was ominously still. Had Vicki imagined that earlier movement? Grabbing a broken-off car door to shield against angry beaks, she shooed away the remaining vultures and dropped to her knees for a closer look.

The rips in the plastic—whether from the birds or the victim's own efforts—were largely at the upper end, exposing head and shoulders and one arm. Vicki's stomach rose into her throat as she saw the ruin the sharp beaks had made of the exposed half of the face.

Tearing at the plastic, she pushed aside matted hair for a clearer view. Her heart grew hot and tight in her chest. The victim was female. And she was neither a strayed *basurero* nor pauper burial.

Nor Guatemalan at all. Where not darkened by dried blood, the hair was blonde, newly exposed skin freckled and pale. Both only too familiar.

Please, no! Sick and trembling, her fingers fumbling, Vicki felt the slow pulse at the girl's neck. Incredibly, even horribly, she was still alive. Vicki began to rip further at the plastic, then stopped. Her medical knowledge covered only basic first aid, but she could see enough to recognize what had happened. The girl had been shot point-blank in the chest after being forced into the trash bag, the powder burns and bullet hole still distinguishable against the plastic.

And that alone was why the victim was still alive. The bullet must have missed any major organs, and the plastic sack itself had acted as a pressure bandage, the blood flow that had drawn the vultures coagulating beneath the victim to seal the exit wound. But for how long?

Rocking back on her heels, Vicki glanced around wildly, her mind dizzy with helplessness. Even if she could attract the attention of the *basureros*, it would take far too long to track down a medical team and get them here across that dangerous surface.

She's going to die! What do I do? Hurry, hurry! A rapid beat was pounding at her temple, her breath coming so quickly that she felt herself beginning to black out. Clenching her fists, she dug fingernails into her palms, welcoming the sharp jolt of pain. *Take a deep breath. Hold it. Let it out. Take a deep breath. Hold it. Let it out.*

Vicki's fingers brushed against the cell phone in her pocket as her head began to clear. She tugged the phone free and slapped it open. There was no 911 service here, but 125 was the emergency code for the International Red Cross. *Please let them have a chopper in town!*

But the phone was overly hot to the touch, and even as Vicki began inputting the number, she could see there was no service, whether from heat or some interference from the twisted metal and mounds of rubble all around.

Her next action was not even a conscious decision. Jumping to her feet, she began screaming and waving her arms to attract attention. It might have been hours, minutes, or maybe seconds before Vicki caught the attention of a single file of *basureros*, perhaps even those she'd begged earlier for help, starting down the path into the ravine.

Vicki let her arms fall in exhaustion when she felt a featherlike touch against an ankle. Glancing down, she sucked in a sharp breath. The one exposed arm was moving, the hand groping pleadingly. As Vicki dropped again to her knees, a moan confirmed an unwelcome return to consciousness. Vicki reached to catch the bloodied fingers, and as they moved against hers, the mutilated mouth moved, the sounds so garbled Vicki had to strain to interpret.

"I'm . . . so sorry. . . . You were right. . . . No, I was right. . . ." The last word came out with a whistle of exhaled breath. The head sagged back, and the fingers clutching at Vicki's went limp.

Vicki fumbled frantically for a pulse, forced her own breath into the girl's lungs. *Oh, please!* What began as an exclamation became a cry of despair. *Oh, please, no!*

Admitting failure at last, she bent her head. Tears that were no longer from smoke and fumes spilled down her face onto the bloodied material of the girl's T-shirt, washing a bright trail across a gold chain Vicki's administrations had dislodged around the slack neck. The original green of that material was no longer discernable, and only a sharp eye could have made out the single word of its logo presently exposed. But Vicki did not need to rip the plastic further to complete the Save the Rain Forest slogan hidden beneath or to identify the flawlessly shaped gold jaguar with brilliant emerald eyes that dangled at the end of the chain.

"Holly! Oh, Holly, no!" Only as Vicki struggled to regain some control did she realize that other words were intermingled with that despairing cry. "Mama! Papa!"

CHAPTER SEVEN

CHAPTER SEVEN

Anger and disbelief sustained Vicki through the next hours.

The tears had time to dry, her face to set into stone by the time the *basureros* made their way up the mound, tongues clicking astonishment and sympathy in their own Mayan dialect.

She waved them back as they crowded around. "No, don't touch her. We have to wait for *la policía*."

"They will not come out this far." The Mayan laborer who muscled forward was the same who'd snatched Vicki's five-quetzal bill, his labored Spanish patient but adamant. "And it is too dangerous to stay here longer. Look."

Vicki took in the explosive pop of a methane leak igniting just a few meters away, recognized dully the painful heat burning through the knees of her jeans. She made no further protest as the *basureros* unslung the lengths of Mayan homespun used to bind packs to their backs, maneuvering them under the black plastic to form a sling. Prompted by a lifetime of cop shows, she tried to explain the concept of fingerprints. But she'd neither authority nor language to contradict their rapid discussion as they lifted Holly, three men to a side. Those not occupied as bearers spread out in front to warn of obstructions.

By the time they'd all stumbled and jostled and clawed their way back up the side of the gorge, she had to concede the near impossibility of separating the *basureros'* grimy, if well-meaning, handling from any marks previously on the black plastic.

Reaching the school compound brought no relief to her nightmare. Vicki's students had been served their noon meal, but when they spotted the strange procession, enamel plates clattered down. A shrill, excited babble pierced at Vicki's temples as the children swarmed around the bearers.

Then came the hurdle of finding a resting place off the dirt floor. The only table was piled high with cooking preparations, the rickety benches only inches wide. The *basureros* stood patiently with their burden while Vicki scurried around the compound. Finally in desperation, she ripped the portable blackboard from its frame to balance across three of the benches.

In all of this, the heat and noise and confusion didn't abate. Vicki's assistant, Consuelo, had shooed out most of the students, but they'd been replaced by a sizable portion of the dump residents. Curious gawkers swarmed the mud-brick enclosure, crowded into the patio, and perched on the walls like so many vultures.

It isn't fair, some back corner of Vicki's mind wailed. This still shape on a propped-up slab of wood, covered only by a *basurero*'s carrying cloth, hemmed in by strident, unruly strangers of another nation and tongue, was her young sister. Surely she'd every right to give way to her grief, dissolve into hysterics, and allow some authority somewhere to step in and take charge.

Instead the very absurdity of her circumstances kept Vicki dry-eyed and numb as she dealt with each obstacle. She thanked the *basureros*, digging up a few more quetzales to press into their leader's hand. Enlisting Consuelo's furious vitriol when her own protests proved futile, she drove the gawkers back outside the walls. Vicki's phone was still not working, and the school compound didn't have one. Corralling a lingering student, Vicki thrust another five-quetzal note into his hands and sent him at a run to Casa de Esperanza.

"What is happening here?" The four khaki-uniformed police marching through the opening in the mud bricks had arrived too promptly to be in response to Vicki's messenger. This was neighborhood muscle, hard-faced and hard-eyed.

The local precinct's arrival scattered the crowd, shutters and doors slamming shut up and down the street. Vicki's *basurero* bearers and the students still lingering outside the walls melted into the landfill.

The police listened with patent disbelief, only briefly pulling back the woven cloth to glance at the victim and not bothering with so much as a cursory survey of the dump site. Eyebrows rose at Vicki's inability to produce witnesses to verify her story, unfriendly eyes zeroing in on the dried rusty blotches and muck staining Vicki's clothing.

"Who was the shooter?"

"Was there a fight?"

"Where's the gun?"

"Was this a domestic dispute? A boyfriend involved?"

The questions pounded at Vicki with the hammer force of the blood throbbing at her temples.

The testimony of Consuelo was waved aside as the corroboration any hireling would be expected to offer her employer.

"Isn't it obvious she wasn't killed here?" Vicki cried out with frustration. "There isn't even any blood." Where was the assistance she'd sent for? Had her errand boy absconded with those five quetzales?

"Then produce your accomplices who brought the body here."

In all this, the patrolmen remained standing, thereby keeping Vicki on her feet, her hands balled up at her sides, her body taut with holding in her anger. *I'm not in America,* she reminded herself. *I have no rights to demand.*

"Vicki!"

"Evelyn!" Vicki spun around, her relief coming out suspiciously like a sob as she caught sight of the thin, straight figure marching into the compound. "Then Jaimito did get through to you."

"Yes, I was at Casa de Esperanza when Jaime arrived. But I had to walk over because Alberto has the Jeep. I am so sorry. This is a terrible tragedy." Evelyn looked even smaller and more fragile next to the four patrolmen, her white bun barely reaching their lapels. But there was nothing frail in the cool survey behind thick-framed glasses as she summed up the uniforms, the emptied courtyard, the still shape on the benches, and Vicki's filthy clothing.

"Let me deal with this." Evelyn patted Vicki's shoulder before singling out one of the patrolmen. "Robertito, how tall you've grown. I haven't seen you since you left Casa de Esperanza, *sí*? I'm glad you joined the police force. This country needs good and honest police officers. Your grandmother must be very proud of you."

The patrolman was the unit leader and the most brutal in his interrogation tactics. Now he was actually shuffling his feet. "*Sargento* Roberto Torres now." He proudly indicated his insignia. "I received my promotion just last month. Not so bad for a child with no parents nor home but the streets."

"And Casa de Esperanza."

Under Evelyn's stern look, the sergeant had the grace to look abashed. He glanced at Vicki. "You know this woman, *doña Evelina*? You can vouch for her?"

"Yes, of course, I can vouch for her. And you know very well that she is one of my volunteers." A sharp gesture indicated Vicki's stained yellow Casa de Esperanza T-shirt. "Now where are your manners that you have kept the poor child on her feet all this time?"

From his surly expression, Vicki wasn't going to get an apology, but he allowed Evelyn to urge Vicki to a bench. Whipping out her cell phone, Evelyn went on briskly, "Now, Robertito, I can see you've become a capable police officer, but this is the homicide of a foreign woman. Their American embassy will be involved. You know your barrio station has neither the resources nor the experience for this kind of investigation. I am going to call the chief of police right now to send a special investigation unit. And *los americanos. La profesora* will need representation from her embassy."

Under the calm authority of the older woman's voice, Vicki felt the tension begin to leave her shoulders. Tugging the bench over to one of the beams holding up the thatched roof, she let her body sag against the hard wood and closed her eyes.

Vicki was not surprised when a half hour later a marked police van and ambulance jolted up outside the compound.

Then a dark green Land Rover with the double-paned tinted windows that meant bulletproof glass pulled up.

Embassy. She felt too numb for surprise when she saw Holly's State Department acquaintance, Michael Camden, get out. She pushed herself to her feet.

The embassy attaché walked to the thatched shelter and stopped short when he saw Vicki. He took in her disheveled appearance, and his mouth tightened to a grim line as he demanded, "Is it true about Holly?"

Vicki could only make a hopeless gesture.

Spinning around on his heel, Michael stalked over to the make-shift bier and looked down. Then he swung back. "We're going to need to notify the next of kin. Would you know where we can contact her family?"

Vicki swallowed. "That would be me."

"You!" The muscles of his jaw bunched.

"Yes, this is Holly's sister, Vicki Andrews." Evelyn tucked her palm into the crook of Vicki's elbow, her calm voice at her ear. "And you?"

Now it was Evelyn who bore the brunt of his scrutiny. "Michael Camden. DAO. American embassy."

"DAO?" Evelyn's question conveyed her surprise. "I'd expected at the most a consulate staffer. To what do we owe this honor? I wasn't aware our embassy had begun affording this level of service." Her comments held dry irony.

"Yes, well, I've been running some training courses for local police officers. The commander of the special homicide unit was one of them." Michael indicated the police lieutenant who was organizing the new arrivals. "He called me as soon as they were told an American was involved."

Evelyn didn't look particularly impressed. "Then maybe you can make yourself useful by clarifying to your . . . local colleagues that Vicki is a victim and very distressed family member, not their prime suspect."

"The embassy is not authorized to interfere with the local judicial system. Only to monitor any legal proceedings and ensure that they abide by international treaties." Michael's glance went from Evelyn to Vicki, and the grim line of his mouth relaxed a fraction. "But as a private citizen, I will do anything I can to help. Excuse me."

He joined the special unit lieutenant, and soon all the uniforms Vicki could hope for were swarming around dusting for prints, exploring the canyon rim, even making their way out over the landfill to the mound Vicki showed them.

Vicki had to tell her story again, but at least this time the questions were courteous. Michael lingered, leaning against a pillar within earshot, not speaking or interfering in any way. But his solid, observant presence was impossible to ignore.

During the interrogations, Alberto arrived from Casa de Esperanza with Evelyn's Jeep and a change of clothing for Vicki. Gratefully changing in the cook shack at the back of the compound, she emerged to find a crime lab technician waiting to bag the clothes she'd stripped off.

Later Vicki borrowed Evelyn's cell phone to call the local WRC office.

"Vicki! I've been trying to reach you all morning. Where's Holly?" Vicki recognized the exasperated voice of Alison, the Australian volunteer she had talked to before. "I thought she'd at least call. Is she there with you?"

"That—" Vicki had to clear her throat before she could answer. "That's why I'm calling. Holly . . . she's dead."

The shocked silence allowed Vicki to explain quickly. Then she got in her own questions. "When did you last see Holly? The police need to know." *And so do I.* "I didn't even know she was back in town."

"She flew in with Joe and Bill yesterday. The second half of our German volunteers arrived on the afternoon flight. Holly came in to take them to the Wildlife Rescue Center on the bus."

"Yes, I saw Joe at the embassy," Vicki said automatically as Alison paused. "Then Holly was with them?"

"Oh no, the Cessna had to be back on the ground at the center by dark. Joe and Bill flew back out even before Holly had the team settled into the hostel. That's when I talked to her last. She said she had a visit to make, and she'd see us at the bus in the morning. I gave her your message. Are you saying you never saw her at all? Then where was she? Where did she spend the night?"

"I don't know. That's what I'm trying to find out."

"What are you going to do? Do you have someone there with you?"

"I'll be fine. Can you ask around to see if anyone knows where Holly went or why?" Vicki noticed that the crime scene technicians were back from the landfill. "Please excuse me. I'd better go." She hung up.

Whatever evidence they'd collected, they didn't say. But after a huddle with the special unit patrol, they announced they were finished.

A new dispute arose when ambulance personnel began moving Holly from her makeshift bier. Vicki insisted on accompanying her sister's body. The lieutenant in charge of the unit asserted that no civilians could ride in a police vehicle. Vicki would have appealed to Michael, but he had disappeared into his own vehicle, and Vicki could see through the windshield that he was conversing on a hand radio.

The standoff ended when Evelyn handed the lieutenant her cell phone, his supervisor on the line. Under other circumstances Vicki would have smiled. Was there anyone the missionary didn't know?

A police guard climbed in after Vicki, inexplicably feeling the need to rest his automatic rifle across his thighs as he settled down across from her.

Ignoring him, Vicki reached for Holly's hand that had slipped out from the sheet now replacing the *basurero* homespun. But the fingers were cold, the vital life force that was Holly no longer in any way connected to that unyielding grasp. Folding her hands instead in her lap, Vicki stared at the white wall of the ambulance, avoiding the curious gaze of the guard and the city streets flickering by outside. *Don't feel. Don't think.*

The ambulance pulled up at the gates of a sprawling installation whose crenellated ramparts, arches, and statuary looked more like a medieval castle or palace than a police headquarters. Vicki was reassured to see Evelyn's battered Jeep park behind the ambulance. But this time her fierce persuasion was not enough to get Vicki through the gates.

"You will be informed when the medical examiner is finished," the lieutenant told Vicki. Until then, she was not to leave the capital, though he stopped short of demanding her passport.

Then the gates slammed shut on the police unit and the gurney. The ambulance sped away, leaving Vicki standing in the gravel, for the first time bereft of a clear next step.

"Come on, honey. There's nothing more you can do here."

Numbly, Vicki allowed Evelyn to steer her toward the Jeep.

Before they could climb in, the embassy Land Rover pulled up beside them with a spurt of gravel. Climbing out, Michael handed Vicki his business card. He studied Vicki's face before he said with more gentleness than she'd heard from him so far, "I never did express how sorry

I am about your sister. I wish I could stay to be of assistance, but I've already delayed too long the departure of a field op that's been on the books for some time. In fact, that's why I was trying to catch Holly. I wanted to see her before I left. I'll be gone a few days, and if there is anything you need in the meantime, please don't hesitate to contact my assistant. The number is on the card. And I will definitely be in touch as soon as I get back."

Then he was gone, and Evelyn ushered Vicki into the Jeep. The soothing murmur of her small talk flowed over Vicki as Alberto drove them back to Casa de Esperanza, but she heard none of it. Staring out the window, she watched the sky pale and lights blink on along the narrow streets. What was she forgetting? What needed doing next?

Vicki roused herself when they bumped through the huge portals of the children's home, parking in the cobblestoned courtyard.

"I'd better start a list of people to call," she told Evelyn as they crossed through the gate to the children's home and up the freight elevator. "Here and stateside. The WRC headquarters. Her friends. Oh, and Roger and Kathy. I don't even have their number." She paused outside her door to rub a hand over her face.

Evelyn lifted the key from her hand. Pushing the door open, she shepherded Vicki inside.

The apartment was as bare and orderly as when Vicki had arrived a week ago, her few belongings tucked out of sight under the beds, the covers and mosquito nets tidily pulled up. But a card table and pair of folding chairs had been added as a work area for Vicki's computer and piles of paperwork.

Evelyn took out one of the chairs. "Honey, just sit down."

Vicki resisted Evelyn's hand on her shoulder. "I can't. There's too much to do. The funeral arrangements. I'm not even sure who to call. And how am I supposed to make them if the police are holding the . . . the . . . If I could just think straight."

"Sit down."

At the authoritative command, Vicki sank slowly into the chair, trembling, suddenly as exhausted as though she'd been physically instead of mentally beaten.

Settling into the other chair, Evelyn leaned forward to fold Vicki's cold fists in her small, warm hands. "There, dear; let it go. You've been brave and strong and capable all day. But you don't have to be strong any longer. Just let it go."

Vicki looked at her blankly. The shrewd kindness behind the thick-framed glasses dissolved something tight and hot in her chest. She blinked slowly. *Holly is dead. My sister is dead. My family is gone. It's happened again. It isn't a dream. I won't wake up.*

Then in a burning flood that was at once painful and yet somehow the beginning of healing, the tears began, and they did not stop for a long time.

"Señor, please come this way."

The thin gray-white beams of the fluorescent lanterns were enough to illuminate the camouflage nets and the scattering of inflatable shelters beneath them but not to pierce more than a few meters through the thick foliage and underbrush of tropical rain forest. Leaving the four-wheel drive under a patch of giant elephant ears and ferns, he followed the sentry to the nearest shelter.

The personage supervising activity from the ease of a canvas lounge chair in front looked up at him impassively. "So, the gringa—she has been found."

"Yes."

"Dead?"

"Of course dead! That was the objective; was it not?"

"What took so long? I expected your communication hours ago."

"A miscalculation." His Spanish was idiomatic, if accented. "The locals are less inquisitive than one might expect. You're safe—*we're* safe."

"This time."

His eyes narrowed at the flat statement. "What do you mean?"

"You are not the first to give me news." The occupant of the canvas recliner waved a hand toward the radio set perched on a packing box beside him. "I am told there is another gringa, maybe more, now making noises. If more questions are raised, they too will have to be dealt with."

"I told you that equipment should be used only for emergencies." His teeth gritted with the effort to keep his voice even. "As for these others, of course there are noises. Did you think the woman's friends would ask no questions? Give them the right answers, and they will go away soon enough. It's over; do you hear me? Over!"

"Just ensure that it is. Or we will begin making our own choices . . . and allies."

He chose to leave before the speaker's gesture made it an order. Ducking under an anchoring rope, he hurried beyond the feeble reach of the fluorescent beams. He felt out a rock outcropping he knew to be there. Clambering up the brief incline, he braced himself against the sudden cold draft, letting the night winds sweep over him with the rich, damp growing scent of the rain forest and the chitter and caws and chirps of its restless animal life.

Without the contaminating haze of city lights or any other human habitation, there was presently only deep darkness. The horizon itself across the void was the far-flung black shadow of another mountain range so that only directly overhead twinkled the cold, hard-edged sparks of the constellations.

His kingdom, he occasionally let himself reflect before iron pragmatism forced such dangerous contemplation under control.

It really was too bad about the girl. He paused to feel the twinge any decent human felt for the loss of a life. He'd felt similar regret for the majestic tapirs the men occasionally butchered to supplement their MREs.

Leaving the outcrop, he strolled back to the circle of fluorescent beams. The workers were unloading the supplies he'd delivered. As he checked manifests and snapped out orders, it was not regret that occupied his thoughts. Nor guilt. Nor worry. Nor even satisfaction.

The predominant feeling was righteousness.

So he'd guessed right.

No, this had been a studied calculation. After all these years, the equipment was still out there—and still in use.

It was carelessness not to consider that others might be listening. But then, how could they? That frequency and scrambling technology had been phased out a decade ago.

Or so the records showed.

When the crackle of voices didn't return, he reached out and flicked off his own communications system. From that transmission, they were not likely to be back tonight, and the kerosene for the generator was too scarce in these parts to waste.

Walking out onto a veranda, he leaned against one of the concrete pillars that held up the tile roofing. The night was empty of music and voices, the locals long since having blown out candles and lanterns to retire to their hammocks. The only illumination came from a single generator-powered bulb dangling from a rafter through the open door behind him and the pale twinkle of starlight stretching to the jagged black of the mountains.

His eyes narrowed against the darkness. That transmission had originated somewhere out there. His preliminary assessment would seem to be right on every point. This was no new threat. They had returned. Nor had the intervening years curbed their tactics.

Still, the years had brought other changes. Maybe this time an end could be made. With equipment he didn't presently have, it might be possible to triangulate both those transmitters. And there were other options, even with limited resources.

He felt neither anger nor righteousness, only cool, focused concentration.

CHAPTER EIGHT

"I don't want assistance shipping remains home."

Heads turned all around the lobby of the Guatemala City police headquarters. Behind the clerk's desk, a guard cradling an M16 took a step forward.

Vicki lowered her voice, if not her frustration level. "I'm not here about the Certificate of Death Abroad, as I've already explained. I'm here to find out the status of my sister's murder investigation. It's been four days."

Four interminable days since the horror of finding Holly on that trash heap in the middle of Guatemala City's municipal dump. Four days of unanswered questions compounded upon unanswered questions. Four days of pounding her fists against bureaucratic concrete walls. "In all this time, I haven't received so much as a police report or *anything* about where the investigation is going. Now, all of a sudden, I'm told the body has been released, and I'm free to leave the country and take my sister with me. Well, I don't *want* to leave the country. What I *want* is to know just what is being done to find my sister's murderer.

"As for this—" Vicki slapped a photocopy on the desk—"how can this be the final investigation report? 'Holly was the victim of assault, by person or persons unknown, for probable ends of robbery.' That doesn't say anything. Where are the interviews? the evidence reports? the suspects? Have they even tried to find out who did it?"

"*Lo siento.* I am sorry. This is all I was authorized to release to you." The police clerk did not shift a muscle of his stony expression as he shoved the report back toward Vicki. "Perhaps things are done differently in your country, but this is not America."

Vicki gritted back a response. Levelly, she said, "Fine, then. If you can't release anything further to me, I'd like to speak to someone who can. Who is the officer in charge of my sister's investigation?"

The clerk tilted back in his chair. "*El teniente* is already occupied with another *homicidio.* He does not make appointments with civilians."

Vicki forced her hands to unclench. "Then I want to speak to your chief of police."

"*El comandante* does not make appointments with civilians."

Bloodred fingernails plucked at Vicki's sleeve. Marion Whitfield, the consular aide assigned to Vicki in due course, was a breathless young woman in a power suit and precariously high heels. "Ms. Andrews, I don't think you appreciate how cooperative the locals have been to secure your release as well as your sister's in just four days. At least you're now free to leave the country and make arrangements for your sister. Meanwhile, let's allow the authorities to do their job."

From blank expressions across the desk, neither the police clerk nor the guard understood English.

Marion lowered her voice to a conspiratorial murmur. "Ms. Andrews, if it's a matter of finances, the embassy does have at its discretion a program of aid for distressed citizens abroad. We can at least cover your passage home."

"I don't *need* aid. Haven't you heard me? What I need is answers!" Vicki heard her voice rising again and seized on the shift to English to vent her frustration. "Look, Marion, I know you're trying to help. But you're basically telling me that I should be grateful *not* to be arrested for a crime I didn't commit and forget all about who actually murdered my sister. You say we should let them do their job. Well, I don't see that they *are* doing their job. I mean, how can a murder case be wrapped up in four days? This should be the beginning of an investigation, not the end."

"I'm sure the police do their best, but with their limited resources, there is only so much we can expect. Unfortunately, they do have full jurisdiction. We can ask for cooperation, but we cannot demand it."

Yeah, right! As though Vicki didn't know just how much political clout the United States carried around here. "Holly was an American citizen. Shouldn't the embassy be interested in finding out who murdered one of its citizens?"

Marion's lips pressed together in a stiff line. "We care about all our citizens, of course. But you must understand the justice procedures you take for granted as a citizen back home do not for the most part exist around here. The embassy's primary responsibility is to ensure our citizens get a just representation under local law. Which is why our first concern has been that you no longer be listed as a suspect or prohibited to leave the country, if you so choose."

"I appreciate that—," Vicki began.

Marion went on unsmilingly. "If you've been in Guatemala any time at all, you must be aware of the situation. Hardly a day goes by that the embassy doesn't get a distress call from some American tourist who's been robbed at gunpoint, hijacked, or worse."

"I'm sorry, but I can't accept that." Vicki looked at the police clerk as she shifted back to Spanish. "I don't want to be difficult, but I'm not leaving this country—or these premises—until I speak with someone who knows what's going on. If not the chief of police, then at least the officer in charge of the special homicide unit."

"I don't know if I can arrange that."

Vicki looked from the police clerk to Marion. "Fine; then I'll camp out on the front steps until someone can."

Any response was interrupted by the tap of footsteps across the tiled floor behind Vicki.

Marion smiled. "Michael!"

The police clerk, who had not budged from his lounging position since their arrival, sprang to his feet.

Vicki turned. So the DAO attaché was back in town. She hadn't heard from him in the last four days. Nor had she bothered calling his secretary.

Michael reached them and waved the police clerk back to his seat. "Hello, Marion. I didn't realize you had an appointment here."

"Just handling our latest death abroad, Holly Andrews. Michael, I'm so glad you're here. I don't know if you've met the victim's next of kin, Ms. Vicki Andrews. We're having a bit of a communication difficulty you might be able to help us with."

The melting look Marion bestowed on Michael held both relief and adoration. So much unadulterated approval couldn't be good for a man, Vicki concluded ungraciously, reminded of Holly's own agitated reaction.

Vicki kept her voice carefully neutral as she stepped forward. "Actually, we have met, and I do have some questions I hope you can answer for me, Mr. Camden."

"Why, yes, of course. I'm sorry I didn't . . . Please call me Michael."

Vicki suppressed a wry grimace at the immediate warming of his gaze. She could construe the lack of recognition as an insult or a backhanded compliment, so she'd choose to presume the latter. A glimpse of herself in a gilt-rimmed mirror on the wall behind the police clerk was explanation enough. The usual efficiency of her ponytail had been released to a shining, shoulder-length wave, a suit replacing her work uniform of T-shirt and jeans while her makeup brought out the green flecks in her amber eyes and lengthened already long lashes. High-heeled sandals and a gleam of gold at her earlobes and throat completed an image unfamiliar even to herself. But Vicki hadn't chosen today's ensemble for the surprised appreciation in Michael's eyes. In this place where power suits and high heels determined social status, she'd dressed to do battle.

"Thank you, Michael. You mentioned you work with that homicide unit who's supposed to be handling my sister's case."

"I teach a few classes for their training program," Michael corrected.

"And that's where you're headed now, if I remember," Marion broke in brightly, "so we wouldn't want to delay you. But if you could take a minute to help Ms. Andrews understand that the embassy has no jurisdiction in individual police investigations. I've been trying to explain that her best option is to take advantage of her release to travel and let the investigation take its course."

Lifting her chin, Vicki said evenly, "All I'm asking for is a reasonable explanation of what is being done about my sister's murder investigation. This is as ridiculous as the runaround I've been getting for the last four days."

Vicki handed Michael the police report, then looked over at Marion. "Again, I really appreciate the assistance and time you've given me. But I too am at the end of my options. If I have to, I'm perfectly willing to sit here until I can speak to someone—anyone—who can give me some straight answers."

"And I've already told you," Marion cut in sharply, "that we can't make those types of arrangements. This is a sovereign country."

Michael's expression was unreadable as he studied the police report. Then he smiled. A singularly charming smile that relaxed the stern planes of his face. Suddenly Vicki could empathize with Marion's adoration.

"Vicki's right." Michael rattled the report. "This says absolutely nothing. And if speaking to someone else in authority can bring her some closure, make it possible for her get on that plane with a clear heart and mind, then by all means let's make it happen." He talked with the police clerk in low, fluent Spanish.

Beaming, the clerk picked up a phone, spoke briefly, then held out the receiver to Michael.

He took it. "*Sí, ¿cómo le va,* Gualberto? How are your children? your wife? . . . I have a friend here who would like to speak with you. Señorita Vicki Andrews. . . . Yes, the same señorita who has been making *representación* about her sister. . . . We'll be right there." After replacing the receiver, he said, "All set. Vicki, you've got a conference with the chief of police as soon as we can get you to his office. Marion, I'll take over from here. "

"But your class."

"There's still plenty of time, and if they have to wait—" Michael shrugged—"then they wait. Vicki, if you'll come with me." He was already striding across the lobby, his glance back over his shoulder an impatient order.

Ignoring Marion's unhappy expression, Vicki murmured a quick thank you, then stretched her legs to catch up. The teetering of her high heels was a reminder of why she usually wore jeans and sneakers. As she reached Michael's side, she smiled and said fervently, "Thank you! I can't tell you how much this means to me."

"You're welcome." Michael guided her out of the lobby and down a wide corridor.

The vast courtyard onto which the corridor opened was barren of green things, the original cobblestones paved over with concrete. An ornamental fountain in the center was dry, its basin cracked. Gracious colonnades were crowded with marching uniforms and stoically waiting lines, while the high-ceilinged salons where Guatemala's aristocracy had once dined and danced held only filing cabinets and desks and endless rows of tables, where clerks typed on the most antiquated computers Vicki had ever seen.

Everything was painted a depressing army beige. A curious decorative pattern reaching partway up the walls proved on closer look to be thousands upon thousands of fingerprints and scuff marks.

And the smell. Did every police headquarters smell like ammonia and dusty files and the pungent, acrid musk of human fear and despair?

Once Michael steered Vicki up a flight of stairs to the second-floor colonnade and down a corridor, crowds and smells evaporated abruptly. A guard sprang to open a door into another narrow corridor, this one empty except for a handful of striding uniforms.

Only then did Michael slow his steps to look down at Vicki, his firm mouth crooking into a smile. "I'm still trying to process that you're Holly's sister. You really are nothing like her. I would never have guessed the relationship. In fact, I didn't even realize she had family in this country. She didn't mention it when she introduced us."

"No, she didn't." That fact hadn't struck Vicki till now, and she found it vaguely troubling. There'd been times in high school, especially after a certain romantic interest had transferred his sights to Vicki, when Holly had deliberately frozen Vicki out of her male relationships. But surely the sisters had moved well beyond that. "She was a little preoccupied. And I haven't been living here. I arrived only a week before—" Her throat closed so she couldn't finish.

Michael's glance held sympathy as he prompted, "So you came down for a visit and walked into this. No, wait, you were out at that children's project when this went down. So was this a work trip or vacation?"

"I'd hoped both." Vicki felt tears prick at her eyes and raised a hand to brush them away before they spoiled her careful makeup. *Oh, Holly, I didn't even get to tell you about our birth parents.*

She was relieved when they reached an ornate hardwood door at the end of the corridor, putting an end to their conversation. Two guards, both with automatic rifles, stood at attention outside. At Michael's terse "*Con el comandante,*" one stepped back to open the door while the other moved aside.

Despite her urgency, Vicki paused as they stepped inside. If the rest of the headquarters had been strictly utilitarian, this room was a throwback to palace days. The carpet was handwoven, the furnishings polished hardwood and leather. A wall of glass-fronted bookshelves held tall leather-bound tomes that looked as though they'd never been opened. Behind a massive mahogany desk hung a huge portrait of a military commander in Napoleonic dress right down to the sword. Only when Vicki's fascinated gaze dropped to the customized armchair behind the desk did she realize it held the same man, though notably older and heavier than when his image had been painted.

The portrait subject surged to his feet as Vicki and Michael advanced into the room. "May-kole." He rounded the desk for the hearty hugs and back pats of an *abrazo*, the Latin American greeting.

"Gualberto, thank you for seeing us at such short notice," Michael answered as he detached himself. "I know how busy you are."

"Not at all. It is my pleasure." Waving away Michael's appreciation, the chief of police turned to Vicki. "And this is your friend of whom you spoke."

"Yes, this is Señorita Vicki Andrews. Vicki, this is Commander Gualberto Alvarez, chief of the Policía Nacional Civil."

"Truly precious." Alvarez leaned forward to kiss Vicki noisily on each cheek. Then he waved his guests toward a pair of armchairs. "Sit! Sit!" He returned to his seat on the other side of the desk. "So, May-kole, what do you think of my men? Much improvement, no?"

"Well, they have certainly come a fair way."

As the two men talked, Vicki settled into the chair and looked around the room. Between tall French windows was a cluster of framed photos: a studio portrait of a well-groomed woman with the European ancestry of Guatemala's ruling class, two pretty teenage girls in party dresses, and a young man in military cadet uniform. The wife and children to which Michael had referred?

Below these, a dozen men in camouflage fatigues posed against a background of army vehicles—transport trucks, Jeeps, a tank, and to one side, the squat green-gray of a Vietnam-era Huey helicopter. Vicki leaned forward to study the photo. Yes, there—third from the left—was a younger, leaner version of the man behind the desk.

Noting Vicki's interest, Alvarez leaned over to say proudly, "As you can see, when I was in *los militares*, I was one of those chosen to receive training from the Americans."

Now that Vicki looked closer, she could see that the two men at either end of the group carried the red, white, and blue of a small American flag on the lapels of their fatigues. A patch visible on one shoulder read *SOUTHCOM*. A third American, in civilian khakis and shirt, stood slightly back from the group. Or at least Vicki assumed he was American by the light hair and paler skin, though his turned head and tilted floppy hat made it impossible to see his features clearly.

Alvarez beamed. "And now the Americans are helping me to train my police. Perhaps May-kole here has told you that he has been helping to instruct our new special homicide unit. In fact, your sister's case is their first investigation."

Alvarez opened a file in front of him and folded his hands on top of it as he looked at Vicki. His florid features radiated solicitude. "First, may I express our condolences to you in the loss of your sister. That she should come to this beautiful country to help our people and then be killed in such a way—it is truly a disgrace, and I must apologize on behalf of my countrymen. But you must have seen how things are these days. The crime that goes up and up since the peace accords, with *la guerrilla* turning to theft and violence instead of the peace they promised. And these *maras*—the street gangs they have spawned. They are truly vicious, and they do not respect the police as they did *los militares*. It is not safe any longer for women to walk our streets alone, especially foreigners like your sister."

Vicki fought a grimace. It was the official mantra of the Guatemalan authorities, the excuse for any authorized human rights abuse. Guatemala had one of the highest crime rates in the world, and it was increasing rapidly. Part could be blamed on the lack of jobs and education and opportunities, which had also been promised in the peace accords. On the other hand, two generations of armed conflict had bred on both sides a lawlessness that was as quick to pick up a gun or machete as mediate any other solution.

The thousands of *maras*—tattooed, swaggering members of youth gangs, without hope of a future or any societal restraints—were admittedly as vicious as the chief of police claimed, however much one might sympathize with their circumstances. It was no wonder that a sizable segment of law-abiding Guatemalans secretly applauded whatever strong-arm tactics their authorities chose to employ.

"Discipline. Respect. Order. That's what this country needs to turn it around. Is that not so, May-kole? But, please, you did not come to speak of philosophy." Alvarez's solicitous expression turned into a smile. "What is it that you wish to ask of me? It will be my pleasure to be of service to such a beautiful señorita."

Vicki hesitated, unsure of herself now that she'd actually attained her objective. "The investigation, for one. Why has it been closed after only four days when nothing has been found out about who killed my sister? And what about the fingerprints? the police interviews? the autopsy report? I know the special unit did all of that. I'd at least like to know what the evidence reports turned up."

Alvarez shook his head. "Yes, of course the special homicide unit employed the techniques May-kole here has taught them. But no evidence was found to indicate which *maleante* was responsible for your sister's tragedy. After all, there are thousands of such criminals in Guatemala City. And we are a poor country without the resources you have in your cities. I am deeply distressed for the loss of your sister. But can it truly matter to you which of these *maleantes* pulled the trigger? It will not change what is done. They will receive their punishment soon enough—of a gun or a knife or sickness or drugs. Life expectancy is short on these streets. You will only make yourself sick if you continue to fret over this. If you are sensible, you will go home to your own country to lay your sister to rest and then put this terrible thing behind you and move on with your life."

This would be easier if the police chief wasn't making some reasonable points. Doggedly, Vicki persisted. "I appreciate all your work and your men's. But I just can't accept . . . I mean, I don't think my sister was killed by a *mara* or any other stranger to her. Surely that possibility should at least be investigated."

Alvarez's smile evaporated suddenly. "You cannot accept. You are saying you do not trust our investigation? that my men are incompetent?"

"No, of course not. It's just . . . well, there are so many unanswered questions."

"Unanswered questions. Such as?"

"Why my sister was where I found her. She couldn't have been carried out there. The plastic bag was too clean. And why would *maras* bother to go so far? It looked to me like she must have dropped there from the air."

Alvarez turned a page in the file. "I see nothing of that in here. The plastic was torn and dirty."

"That was only after we carried her out. I told the police. It should be there in my statement. And the necklace she was wearing—it was pure gold. Any *mara* would have stolen it."

"What necklace?" Now any remnant of friendliness was gone. "The victim was wearing no jewelry when my officers examined her."

"But there had to be. It was there when I found her. A chain with a gold pendant—a jaguar—with inset emeralds. The police took everything. It has to be in the inventory."

"Are you accusing my men of theft? Or perhaps one of your *basurero* clients took it. If you did not imagine it in the stress of the moment."

"I didn't imagine it." Vicki was trying not to get heated. "There's more. She'd been really upset lately. She was sure something was wrong at her job. And what was she doing out there in that part of town anyway?"

"That is simple," Alvarez said coldly. "She was there to meet you."

CHAPTER NINE

"But—," Vicki began.

Michael stood. "Thank you, *comandante*. You have been most gracious in sparing this time for us. Now, if Señorita Andrews and I are not to be late for another appointment . . ."

Strong fingers were biting into Vicki's shoulder, and she found herself on her feet, steered toward the door. She got out something she hoped was a thank you before she was outside the door.

"What was that for?" Vicki twisted from Michael's grip as the two guards sprang to close the door behind them. "I was just starting—"

"You don't tell the chief of police in a country like this that he's incompetent. Not unless you're on your way to the airport with a ticket out."

"I wasn't—"

"Not here," he said, cutting her off.

Vicki was propelled in silence down the corridor and stairs. "What about your class?" she got out as she half trotted across the courtyard.

"It's been canceled." Michael paused in the lobby to exchange a few short phrases with the police clerk. Then they were outside.

When Vicki opened her mouth, he shook his head warningly and led her across the busy street. A sidewalk café on the corner catered to supplicants waiting to be attended at the police headquarters. The music blaring over the cacophony of traffic was an atrocious Latino techno-pop.

Michael glanced around with unsmiling satisfaction as he guided Vicki to a small round table. "We can talk here."

Vicki reluctantly sank into the chair he pulled out. As soon as he'd dropped into a chair opposite her, she leaned forward to demand again, "So what was that about? I hadn't even started getting the answers I was looking for."

She didn't get an immediate answer from Michael either. He snapped his fingers for an attendant. "Two *cafés con leche* and two *empanadas*," he said to the teenage Mayan girl who hurried over. He glanced at Vicki. "Will that do for you? They don't do tea."

When Vicki nodded, he waved the waitress away before adding tersely, "The way you were going about it, you weren't going to get any answers. And since I've got to work with the guy, I'd just as soon you didn't mess up every bit of capital I've built in that relationship."

"So what am I supposed to do?" Vicki demanded. "I already tried to get answers elsewhere, as you well know. What was the point of talking to the chief of police if I wasn't supposed to get any answers from him either? Why did you even bother?"

"I bothered because I expected you to accept his quite reasonable explanation and head home with your heart and mind set at ease." Propping his forearms on the table, Michael leaned forward and lowered his voice. "I understand what you're going through; believe me. It's perfectly natural to want to know just who did this terrible thing and to bring them to justice. But Alvarez is right. Few crimes in this country are ever prosecuted and not just because police are incompetent or corrupt, though there's plenty of that. They simply don't have the resources. You do understand that for any continuing investigation, someone—usually the family—has to foot the bill. Maybe you can afford it, but most victims here just cut their losses and move on."

The waitress delivered the milk-laced espresso, a sugar bowl, and the *empanadas*, crescent-shaped corn flour shells stuffed with spiced meat and deep-fried.

Vicki was reaching for the sugar when angry and loud voices exploded above the normal background noises.

Michael was on his feet in one fluid motion, and Vicki's own instinctive tension was echoed along the street, heads shooting up, hands stilled on their eating utensils. But even as a human mass turned the corner and became visible, Vicki saw Michael relax, and a moment later, he slid back into his chair, though his gaze did not leave the street.

Vicki eyed the parade with curiosity. They were mostly women, the majority of them in the Mayan wraparound skirt and embroidered blouse, their dark faces unsmiling and purposeful. Vicki saw placards that read *GAM* and *Justicia* and a banner that read *Solidaridad* in bright red letters. Then she noticed the photographs. Some were hanging on cardboard backing around necks. Others had been blown up and pasted to placards carried high above the crowd. One of a young girl in a school uniform read across the bottom, "Where is Anna?"

"Who are they?" Vicki asked. "What are they doing?" Where they were going, she didn't add. Their target was clearly the police headquarters, and as they filled the plaza outside, the chants grew louder and separate.

"Justice!"

"Solidarity!"

"Never again!"

Michael glanced at Vicki as he answered, "GAM. Grupo de Apoyo Mútuo, or Group of Mutual Support. They are the widows and mothers and other family members of *los desaparecidos*, or 'disappeared ones,' of the civil war. Periodically, they still march, insisting the government has records somewhere of what happened to their family members."

"And do they?"

Michael turned back to the march. "Who knows? Maybe those involving some local authority might have some moldering files somewhere. The military was almost pathological about maintaining a paper trail of nearly everything."

Catching Vicki's grimace, Michael said, "I can see what you're thinking. But keep in mind that this was a war with casualties happening on both sides. The army grabbed leftist subversives and those they figured were funding or supplying them. The guerrillas did their own grabbing of those they considered to be traitors helping the army."

"But I thought the UN Truth Commission found that almost all the atrocities were committed by the Guatemalan army and leadership. And what about all the reports of entire villages being massacred and all that?"

"So it's been said—and I'm not questioning the accuracy of the reports—though it's hard to know who was telling the truth and who was maybe exaggerating atrocities for their own political bandwagon. There's no doubt civilian deaths happened, especially on the battlefield, but as far as the 'disappeared,' the majority were listed as enemy combatants and socialist subversives by the Guatemalan authorities. It certainly is not the way we would deal with enemy subversives. But like I said, this was a war—the Cold War—and just like the present war on terror, unfortunately, there are always collateral damages."

The sincere regret of his tone made Vicki wonder if Michael was speaking from some personal experience. Vicki wondered whether he had been in Iraq or Afghanistan at some point. And like the police chief, he had some logic on his side.

But as Vicki watched the photograph of the girl in a school uniform move toward the police headquarters, she had to wonder. Just what kind of subversive had the authorities considered that underage student to be?

She turned to find Michael's eyes on her, meditative under lowered lashes, his firm mouth pressed into a sober line. As their gazes collided, he said abruptly, "Please believe that I don't mean to be indelicate. But you're at least fortunate enough to have found your sister when you did. Even one more day in that environment, and you may never have known what happened. She'd just be another *desaparecida* on the books down here. At least you have the closure; these women don't."

"Closure!" Vicki cried. "You call this closure?"

"Okay, maybe that's the wrong term. What I'm trying to say is that Alvarez has a point. I have seen too many Americans pouring out years of their lives and energy down here in some fruitless quest for vengeance and closure. And in the end, they're no further along than you are right now. I just don't want to see that happen to you. I cannot urge you enough to get on that plane. Put Guatemala and this nightmare behind you. Get on with your life before this eats you up inside." Sincerity was again unmistakable in his eyes, the somberness of his expression.

Vicki bit at her lip before she answered. "You think I don't know all that? I'm not a tourist either. If it were just some *mara*, I'd be out of here on the next flight. You think I'd take some desperate, starving, drugged-up teenager personally? In fact, I wish I could believe it was *las maras* because it would be so much easier."

Michael ran a hand over his face, then picked up the coffee cup with a shrug. "Okay, I'm listening. Explain to me just why you're so certain it isn't *las maras*."

Vicki chewed again on her lip as she marshaled her thoughts. If she could just get this well-connected embassy staffer on her side. "Well, I already mentioned the clean plastic of the bag and the necklace—which I *didn't* imagine. As for Holly coming to meet me—that's lazy, if that's really what the police want to think. Holly would never have come looking for me at that hour. And if she had, she'd have come to Casa de Esperanza. She didn't even know I was helping at that *basurero* project because I hadn't talked to her since I got here."

"That's right; you mentioned that when I ran into you at the embassy. Though she could have called someone and asked."

"Maybe. Though in that case, why wouldn't she just call my cell? Besides, what she said just before she . . . before she died . . . I *know* it was connected to whatever it was she was so worried about. If I hadn't . . . if I'd just taken her seriously!" Vicki had to tighten her mouth to keep it from trembling.

"Are you saying she was alive when you found her?" Michael's coffee cup settled back into its saucer as quietly as the question, but as she caught the intentness of his gaze, the rigidity of his jawline, Vicki realized with a sudden skip of a heartbeat that she now had his full attention.

"Yes, I . . . I guess I forgot to mention that. It was so fast. And then . . ." *And then the nightmare!* "It was only afterward I really started thinking about what she meant—that she was trying to tell me something."

"Tell me everything from the minute you set foot in this country."

It took some time, and more than once Vicki had to stop and grope back in her thoughts to remember. She did not talk about Casa de Esperanza or Evelyn, nor did he show any interest in them, hurrying her on impatiently through her airport conversation with Holly, her attempts to make contact, and in further grim detail, that terrible last hour in the dump. Vicki's coffee and *empanada* were stone-cold before she was done, and when the waitress stopped by, Vicki pushed them with distaste away from her.

"Well?" Vicki prompted Michael when the serving girl had carried the dishes away. "Holly said I was right. That can only mean what I'd said about someone in her project, someone local, being the one who was ripping the center off. And she was trying to tell me that was who'd attacked her. So you see why I can't just let this go. At the least, I want to see the full transcripts of the investigation. Who she talked to last. What her final days and hours were. What exactly was in the autopsy report. What kind of weapon was used. Surely they did that much."

Michael didn't answer immediately. When he did, the grimness of his mouth relaxed into a sardonic half smile. "I was wrong. You really are Holly's sister, aren't you? You've got the same bulldog streak when you want to find something out."

Vicki felt her face burning. "For that matter, what was it she wanted to meet with you about? That is . . . I mean, if it wasn't something personal. I . . . I just thought maybe it had something to do with all this."

The line of his mouth curved to a full smile. "Not at all. I knew your sister only casually. We'd crossed paths at a few expat functions."

"Then why did she want to talk to you so urgently?"

"That we may never know," Michael said soberly. "I ran into her briefly on a field op in the Sierra de las Minas Biosphere, just days before that airport run-in. That was the first time she mentioned wanting to speak to me. I told her to give me a call when she came into town. As to her reasons, I assume it was something related to my official capacity at the embassy, since I did not know her personally, nor am I so conceited to think a woman would be making excuses just to talk to me."

Yeah, right. Did this guy really not know just how attractive his smile was? "Exactly what would that official capacity be? You keep mentioning field ops. Why would a homicide unit be doing field ops in the biosphere? For that matter, isn't the DAO connected with the military, not the police?"

"No, not the homicide unit." Michael shook his head. "My principal mission is actually right down your line—or rather your sister's. I've been helping in the development of the newest branch of the PNC—Policía

Nacional Civil. The Unidad de Protección de la Naturaleza or UPN. 'Environmental Protection Unit' in English. The military base from which the unit has conducted its last several training missions is right on the perimeter of the biosphere. And quite close as well to WRC's rescue facility up there, which is how I happened to run across your sister.

"As to why DAO, naturally the embassy has civilian police advisers in this as well. But there's a lot narrower dividing line between military and police down here than back home. In fact, until recently, the police force here *was* under the military. UPN will be responsible for policing all the national reserves as well as enforcing the environmental protection laws, and that mission includes a lot of elements that are more military than law enforcement. Border enforcement and smuggling interdiction. Patrol and surveillance of large territories."

"Then this new unit is more military than police?" Vicki remembered the photo on the police chief's wall. "I mean, what difference does it make what you call it if they're all the same people anyway?"

"There are a lot of former military," Michael admitted. "And that's not all bad. The peace accords slashed the army by a third. If we want that to stick, those people are going to need civilian employment. Of course that is part of the mission—teaching them to apply civilian parameters of law and human rights to their procedures.

"On the flip side, trained soldiers already have a lot of the very skills UPN's mission will entail. Not to mention narcotics interdiction. My unit has already been responsible for shutting down a number of illegal cultivations and drug ops in protected areas. In fact, they were recently decorated for their efforts."

The pieces suddenly clicked. "You were at the airport that day with the US drug czar. Lynn, one of Holly's friends, mentioned the awards ceremony. Dieter's going to love you."

At Michael's raised eyebrow, Vicki amplified. "Another of Holly's tree-hugger friends. Greenpeace. He was complaining that they needed some serious environmental enforcement presence in the biosphere." She studied him. "So, did Holly know what kind of field ops you were involved in up there?"

"Probably. News travels, and like I said, the fact that Holly chose me to approach would indicate she knew of my connection."

"In all this discussion and investigation, it never occurred to you to bring this up till now?" Vicki demanded with some heat.

Michael spread his hands, palms up, but there was no apology in his expression. "It was the briefest of contacts and of no particular relevance to an expat mugging here in the capital. I made every effort to follow up with her, but reports of poaching in the biosphere and local corruption are hardly big news. Nor do they fall within any scope of embassy involvement. Now, though, if I get you those transcripts, can I count on you to get on tonight's flight out and leave this to the professionals?"

"Professionals," Vicki scoffed. "Your police buddies?"

"No, me. I *will* follow up on this. If there're any merits to your theory, I'll find them. And you can rest assured I'll communicate with you anything that emerges. Is it a deal?"

"Well, I certainly can't fly out tonight. Tomorrow is Holly's memorial service. Or funeral actually, now that the . . ." Vicki couldn't put it into words. No wonder people used euphemisms for death. "Now that the paperwork has come through. That's the only good that's come out of this."

"Funeral?"

"Yes, at the Union Church. The embassy circulated an invitation to the expat community."

"I just got back from that op this afternoon, remember?" Michael said. "So you're having the burial here? I assumed you'd be flying home to your family."

"We don't really have family stateside," Vicki answered simply. "Besides, Holly is—was—a strong proponent of cremation. It's the only plan she ever made for a funeral."

Vicki could remember that conversation only too well, as much because it was so typically Holly as for the occasion. They'd just endured the second funeral in a year—Mom Andrews—at the city cemetery where generations of Andrewses were buried. "Dirt to dirt is right," an eighteen-year-old Holly had defiantly informed Vicki. "So why do we waste so much of the planet's resources and its land trying to slow down the process instead of contributing to the circle of life we're created to be part of? When the day comes that I don't need this body anymore, I want to be cremated and spread out as fertilizer for the prettiest spot on the planet I can find. You remember that, Vicki, if I happen to go first, which I've no intention of doing for a good long time."

Vicki's thoughts were interrupted when Michael put in tersely, "Fine, then as soon as it's over, you'll be on that flight."

"Why? If you really believe maybe I'm not so crazy, that it wasn't just some *mara* who shot Holly, why in the world would I want to pick up and leave now?"

Michael's tone was bleak. "I'm not saying you're right. In fact, like you said earlier, I really do hope Holly was a victim of some random *mara* assault."

As Vicki stared at him, his voice grew harsher. "Don't you get it? If this wasn't a *mara*, if it was someone Holly actually knew, then you're talking someone a lot more influential—and dangerous—than some street thug. Which is why I want you on that plane, because personally, I don't want to see you end up just like your sister."

CHAPTER TEN

"'This is my Father's world: He shines in all that's fair. . . .'"

Vicki kept her eyes, wide and unblinking, on the stained glass window at the front of the sanctuary as the harmonious chords, contributed by volunteers from Guatemala City's Union Church, rose to the vaulted ceiling. The small, round glass mosaic was of Jesus kneeling in prayer in the garden of Gethsemane. Something in the patient sorrow the artist had somehow captured in that two-dimensional image conflicted with the jubilation of the song and shook Vicki's control, blurred her focus.

Just don't think. Don't feel. I can get through this.

"'This is my Father's world, O let me ne'er forget that though the wrong seems oft so strong, God is the Ruler yet.'"

As the last triumphant chord faded, Vicki smoothed her skirt down over her knees with damp palms. She was wearing the black dress she'd tucked in her luggage for those inevitable occasions when it became necessary to mingle with local dignitaries. This was not where she'd expected to wear it.

Vicki walked to a lectern at the front of the church. Next to it was an easel surrounded by flower displays, which held an enlarged photo of Holly cradling a baby jaguarundi. Vicki didn't look toward it. It was just a focal point for the stares of this assembly of strangers.

There were far more of these than she'd expected, given the shortness of notice and limited acquaintances either Holly or Vicki had in this country. Almost all the seats in the sanctuary were full.

Vicki recognized faces from that airport party—Lynn, Dieter, Bill, and Joe. Evelyn had come as well and a surprising number of Casa de Esperanza volunteers, considering none had ever met Holly. Marion Whitfield was here, red power suit toned down to gray, with half a dozen others doing their duty as embassy representatives. Michael Camden was not among them.

Vicki had no idea who the rest were. Expatriates, for the most part. Maybe members of the English-speaking church. Vicki knew Holly had attended here on occasion when she was in the capital. However at odds the various aid and environmental and multinational organizations might be, in times like this, business and politics were tacitly laid aside, leaving simply compatriots banding together in a strange land. One of their own had died. They were here to lend their support. That was all that mattered.

Vicki's gaze fell on a row of local police and military dignitaries in khaki uniforms at the back of the sanctuary. Was this to pay honor to a high-profile death in their country or some kind of apology for incompetence? Among them, Vicki recognized the chief of police. He was in full dress uniform with medals and ribbons, and under his dark unflinching gaze, she felt chilled.

I can't do this. Vicki forced herself to focus on her typed notes. Catching Evelyn's encouraging nod from the first row, she took a deep breath, her fingers turning white where they gripped the sides of the lectern. "I'm Vicki Andrews, Holly's sister. If you knew Holly, then you understand why I asked the choir to sing this particular song."

The words in front of Vicki were beginning to clear, and she managed to relax her grip. "It's not a song I would have chosen. While Holly and I are sisters, we are as different as tree huggers and people huggers. To be honest, I never really understood Holly's fascination with plants and animals above people. We spent a number of years as children on a farm, and it was there that Holly's interest in environmental issues was born and she started down the path that led her to the Wildlife Rescue Center. It was there, too, where she used to drive me crazy singing the song the choir just finished. It was her theme song as she became a veterinarian and got involved in environmental issues.

"But the truth is, for all her talk about saving the planet, that was never really what she was about for one very simple reason: she believed that song. She believed with all her heart that this was her heavenly Father's world. A world created by an almighty God who really cared about His creation. And she was always optimistic that no matter how much wrong was out there, the world itself was quite safe already in the hands of the Father who created and ruled it.

"I was never so hopeful about that, but I appreciated it in her even when her enthusiasms about trees or animals drove me up a wall. If Holly never bought that we humans were big enough to destroy a world God created, she felt strongly that it was our responsibility to tend that world and keep it beautiful. That's why she came to this country. She thought this was one of the most beautiful spots on the planet, and she wanted to make a difference by keeping people from trashing it. In the end, her fight to do that lasted only three months before she herself became a casualty."

The page was swimming before Vicki's eyes again, and she tightened her grip on the edges of the lectern. "I'm not a tree hugger. But Holly's life made sense to me. Her death makes none!"

Vicki lifted her eyes. Most faces were somber, even expressionless, leaving no hint as to how her words were being received. But her gaze clashed with stony stares from the back row.

Her voice faltered, then hardened. "But I intend to make sense of it. I won't leave this country until I find out what happened to my sister. So if any of you has any information about what Holly was doing during that last night or week, please contact me. Thank you." Abruptly picking up her notes, she walked to her seat.

Behind her, with some confusion, the choir broke back into "This Is My Father's World."

Vicki was sinking down next to Evelyn when she saw the commotion in the back. The police chief and at least half the khaki uniforms were marching out the back door.

Others came forward to pay tribute to Holly, including a young blonde woman whose Australian drawl Vicki recognized as the Alison she'd spoken with on the phone.

A government official with the Ministry of Environment called Vicki forward to receive an award bestowed on *la americana* who'd given her life to serve Guatemala's environment. Only as he held up the shiny medal did Vicki take in the flash of cameras. *Great, so my sister's funeral has turned into a government PR event.*

Don't think, Vicki reminded herself fiercely. *Don't feel. Don't cry.*

Then the service was over. Under the Union Church pastor's discreet direction, Vicki stood beside Holly's photo, numbly receiving condolences from more strangers. At some point the government official pressed her hand, whispering something solicitous, and Vicki caught again the flash of a camera before he swept down the aisle toward the sanctuary exit, news crews at his heels.

As the crowd dissipated, Lynn, the Amazon Watch ecologist, approached Vicki. Dieter was behind her. He offered Vicki only a curt nod. So he hadn't forgiven her for her contradictory opinions.

Lynn squeezed both of Vicki's hands. "You pegged Holly just right. She had me humming that song myself. She was always so enthusiastic. It was part of what made her so sweet." She released Vicki's hands to pat her shoulder. "Please know your sister isn't gone. I've never been sure whether I believe in reincarnation or a higher existence, but I'm sure she's happy, wherever she is."

Vicki murmured a polite reply. Her head was beginning to pound unmercifully, and she was grateful to find her hand folded suddenly in a very large grasp and a tall, broad frame inserting itself between her and the lingering mourners to give her breathing space.

That gratitude lasted only long enough for a grim voice to drawl above her head, "Quite a challenge you threw down there, Ms. Andrews. You sure that was wise?"

Vicki's gaze traveled up a purple-splotched tie until her head tilted far back. She'd forgotten how tall Joe was. The height and the broad-shouldered power of his frame at the moment seemed ready to burst the constraints of that surprisingly conservative dark gray suit. Maybe it was the restless energy of his body language, the long fingers tugging at the tie knot, already ruffling the slicked-back neatness of his hair that made the space around them seem cramped.

Withdrawing her fingers, Vicki asked coldly, "And why wouldn't it be? Is there something wrong with wanting to find out what happened to my sister?"

"The top brass back there sure didn't seem too happy with your assessment."

"I wasn't challenging them. I was—"

"Hey, I'm with you." Joe raised a hand. "I'm not too fond of the local authorities in any country. I'm just saying announcing on public television that you're going to do the job they're not—that might not be the best way to get some cooperation."

Joe's tone softened. "Hey, I didn't mean to be abrupt. I'm not good at these things, but I'm really sorry about Holly. From what I was able to get to know of her, she was a very special person. She didn't deserve this."

He glanced toward the funeral display, and Vicki could sense anger simmering in the tautness of muscle under the sober suit, the blaze of his eyes. The anger warmed Vicki toward him. "Joe, do you know—?"

"Vicki, dearie."

Vicki turned at the light touch on her arm.

Evelyn gave her a quick hug. "I don't know what your plans are, but Alberto needs to get our bunch back. If you'd like me to stay with you, he can come back for the two of us."

"No, please," Vicki said swiftly, "you go on with Alberto. I don't know how much longer I'll be. I still have to deal with the mortuary."

"Well, if you're sure, there is one teeny emergency that's come up at the home. But I could go and come back. Or at least send Alberto back with the Jeep."

"No, please, I couldn't ask that. The easiest would really be to grab a cab and meet you back at CE."

"I just don't like leaving you to deal with this alone."

"She won't be," Joe said. "Ma'am, if you're willing to entrust Vicki to us, we'll make sure she's delivered to your door."

"And who might 'we' be?" Evelyn demanded, her head tilting birdlike as she rested her small, capable palm in Joe's offered grip.

"Joe Ericsson and my employer, William Taylor." He gestured to the tall, white-haired older man in conversation with the WRC delegation a few meters away. "We're Holly's colleagues from Wildlife Rescue Center.

We've got a project vehicle with us, and we'll be happy to run Vicki home when she's ready."

Evelyn's nod stamped her approval. "Thank you, young man. That would be of real service." She gave Vicki a final hug. "I'll see you later then."

"Quite a lady," Joe commented as Evelyn bustled away. He looked at Vicki. "I guess I should have asked you first."

"I'd appreciate the ride," Vicki answered. "In fact, I'm glad you offered. I want to talk to you about Holly. No, not the 'challenge,'" she added hastily as his eyes flared. Couldn't she have one conversation with this man without sparks flying? "Though at some point I would like to interview everyone who worked with Holly. This is about . . . Well, she wanted to be cremated."

This had been in the program handed out at the church door, the reason no burial service had followed the funeral, and was certainly no news to any of Holly's colleagues at WRC.

"Holly told me once that if . . . if anything ever happened, she wanted to be taken to the prettiest place I could find, to be part of the flowers and grass and living things there. And there's only one place I can think of. She'd been telling me for months that the Sierra de las Minas Biosphere is the most beautiful place she'd ever seen. And I—I just kept putting off ever visiting there. Now I was wondering—"

"If I could fly you out there?" Joe supplied.

"Yes, if it's convenient, of course." Catching his sudden frown, Vicki added hastily, "I can pay to charter the plane."

"I think we can work out something equitable," Joe said, waving to Bill. "It isn't that."

Bill strolled up beside her and expressed his condolences quietly. "Holly was a special person to all of us. We appreciate your letting us know about today in time to change our flight."

"As I was saying," Joe cut back in, "we came into town to trade in our ride for a new plane. Well, new for the center. A 1966 de Havilland DHC-2. Bottom line: we won't be heading back out to the center until we've taken possession and finished the paperwork to get the plane in the air. It'll be a few days, maybe even a week. But you're welcome to hop a ride then, right, Bill?"

"By all means." Considering the subordinate relationship, Bill seemed surprisingly tolerant of Joe's assumption of authority. "It would be our pleasure."

"That is, if you're still planning to be in town. I'm assuming that challenge of yours wasn't as open-ended as it sounded. You do have employment stateside to get back to?"

Vicki stiffened at the dryness of Joe's tone but refused to be pulled into further debate. "I can wait a few days. I have matters to attend to here in town anyway. Can you let me know when you'll be flying out?" She addressed the question to Bill instead of Joe.

"Just leave me your cell phone number. And now that we've broached the subject—"

"*Con permiso, señorita.*" the mortuary director interrupted. He looked from Joe to Bill as though under the impression that they were Vicki's escort. "Please, señores, if you will leave us now to handle this, it is less distressful for the family in these arrangements that they are not here. Señorita Aan-droos, we will call when all is in readiness."

Though he'd been able to rush the funeral services, the cremation arrangements would take a few days, which worked out with Bill and Joe's scheduling neatly.

Vicki stifled a sigh as the mortician ushered them down the aisle, his crew moving in behind him. The sanctuary had emptied out, the last lingering knots of mourners drifting toward the doors.

She'd probably done this all wrong. Certainly her adoptive parents' funerals had been very different. But she'd done her best, and at least in this alien country that was also inexplicably Vicki's birthplace, Holly had been honored and remembered.

The pastor of Union Church met them at the door. He could not have been more helpful to Vicki in the overwhelming confusion of these last days. "You know you have only to call," he assured her as she expressed her fervent thanks.

Then they were outside, though not on the street, since the Union Church, like any edifice of size in Guatemala, had spacious outdoor courtyards and walkways. As they cut across the grass of one of the courtyards, Vicki caught Bill's eye and was reminded of their conversation when they'd been interrupted. "You said there was something else you needed to discuss?"

Bill looked uncomfortable. "I don't know if anyone's contacted you from WRC. Maybe this isn't the right place, but I wanted to let you know we brought Holly's personal effects in with us from the center. We've got them in the Montero. If we're going to be driving you home, maybe we could drop them off as well."

Bill raised none of the antagonism his younger employee did. Vicki smiled at him gratefully. "Thank you. I'd really appreciate that."

"And speaking of Holly's things, there is just one other matter." When Vicki reluctantly turned her attention back to Joe, he frowned. "Naturally, what we brought down isn't all of Holly's things, just what she had at the center. When I flew her in last week, she had a backpack and her computer, not to mention her cell phone and other personal items. Do you know how much of that has been recovered?"

"Holly's personal stuff was at the WRC hostel where she was supposed to be spending the night. That's one place the police investigated; they confiscated everything. They released it to me when they released Holly. I . . . I haven't even looked at it."

That was because it had been returned to her bundled up in Guatemala's ubiquitous black plastic sacking, so evocative of Holly's death that Vicki hadn't been able to bring herself to do more than shove the stuff under her bed.

"If you're really so determined to launch your own investigation," Joe went on coolly, "that might be a good place to start. Holly spent a lot of time on that computer. There may be something in there that would give an idea of what was on her mind. And there's her PDA. I know I've seen her with one."

So now he decides to be helpful. "Yes, I got Holly a PDA for Christmas a couple of years ago. She kept everything that really mattered backed up on it. That's a great idea. Thank you."

"Yeah, well," Joe said, "I probably shouldn't be encouraging you. But about that computer—"

The two men exchanged glances.

Then Bill spoke up. "You've made a good point, Joe. In fact, Vicki, if it would be at all helpful, Joe and I can certainly spare the time to take a look at it ourselves. Maybe when we drive you over? At the least, we could help you sort through which of the files are center business. Likewise with that PDA."

"Computer. PDA. You wouldn't be talking about Holly Andrews?"

Vicki spun around as she recognized the new voice. "Michael."

He closed the distance across the grass quickly. "Vicki, I am so sorry I didn't make the service. I came as soon as I was free." He didn't wait for Vicki's introduction but thrust out a hand to Bill. "Michael Camden. Defense Attaché's Office. And you are William Taylor, if I'm not mistaken."

"Yes, we've met. The embassy Fourth of July bash last year."

"Of course. You have that coffee plantation up in the Sierra de las Minas near the biosphere. Beautiful country. And didn't I see you at the airport with the WRC party? I'm told you donated the land for the wildlife rescue facility where Holly Andrews was working."

"It's been my privilege to be a part of that effort," Bill responded. "So you know the area."

"I've been in the area a few times, though I haven't yet made it out to your facility yet. Sierra de las Minas will be a strategic mission for the unit I'm working with."

"Really." Bill didn't look particularly impressed. "So you're part of that bunch that's been buzzing around the biosphere lately, scaring the wildlife. Well, you're welcome to stop by the center. We can at least give your people some tips in sensitivity and environmental impact on the fauna. And speaking of WRC, may I introduce you to—"

"Joe," Bill's companion finished laconically, stepping forward with outthrust hand. "Center handyman."

And pilot, Vicki amended mentally, then stopped. She was *not* going to follow Holly in jumping to the defense of a perfectly capable grown man.

"An interesting choice of profession." Michael seemed tall next to Vicki, but beside Joe, he would have looked slight except for the flex of muscle as his grip tightened, then released Joe's hand. "Unusual for an expatriate, isn't it? I thought that kind of thing was usually hired out locally."

"It pays the bills." Joe's tone was as impersonally courteous as

Michael's, but as Vicki looked from one man to the other, she noticed a similar unreadable expression on their very different features, an equally measuring appraisal in the clash of gazes.

"Well, to each his own." The turn of Michael's body was dismissive as he faced Vicki. "You were mentioning a computer and PDA when I walked up. If that's Holly's you were talking about, we'd appreciate taking a look at anything you've got."

"We?" Joe asked, making no effort to remain dismissed. "Is that a royal 'we' or split personality you're talking, Camden? Or are you speaking on the authority of a particular department of the United States government? And if so, would you care to specify?" His expression held only detached interest, his tone bland.

Vicki intervened hastily. "It's fine, Joe. I'm happy to cooperate with Michael or anyone else in the embassy. They are certainly welcome to any information I've got."

To Michael, she added, "Holly's computer should be back at Casa de Esperanza if it's in the luggage the police released yesterday. And the PDA. We're heading over that way right now. In fact, Joe and Bill brought the rest of Holly's things."

"Good. I'll give you a ride over there, and we'll go through them."

"Actually, Ms. Andrews already has transportation," Joe reminded mildly. "With us."

Michael appeared controlled, his expression neutral, but Vicki had learned his body language enough to know he was displeased. He swung around to Joe. "I'm sure Vicki appreciates the offer. But that won't be needed now. As I said, I have business to discuss with her. Embassy business."

"Maybe we should let Ms. Andrews make that decision. Vicki?"

Again the exchange held nothing but courtesy. But Vicki, glancing from one man to the other, had a sudden hysterical fancy of a pair of jungle creatures facing off over a bone. *Except I'm the bone.* Vicki fought an exasperated impulse to laugh.

"Joe, Bill, I'll meet you two over there," she decided quickly. "I'm so sorry to have kept you waiting for nothing, but Michael really does have some data I've been waiting for."

"Your choice." Turning on his heel, Joe headed across the grass. Bill followed.

As Michael led Vicki to his Land Rover, he demanded, "So what do those two have to do with your sister's investigation?"

"They're friends of Holly's from the center. They thought it might be a good idea to take a look at her computer files—maybe see if they offer any clue of what she'd been up to."

Michael's dark eyebrows rose. "Well, they're right enough about that. Though I really don't think it's a good idea to have a couple of extraneous civilians getting involved."

"They're just trying to be helpful. After all, who better to explain anything that might have to do with the center?"

"Maybe. Okay, then, let's see what's on the computer, and we can go from there. Now, if you can read on these roads—" Michael handed Vicki a folder before starting the engine—"there're your police reports."

"Wow, that was quick! Thank you. Uh . . . do you know where Casa de Esperanza is?"

"Doesn't everyone?" Michael shot Vicki a charming smile as he pulled out into traffic.

Vicki smiled back, suddenly glad it was Michael who was driving her home—and not only for the gift he'd brought. At least one person was not only on her side but competent—and willing—to do something about it.

The file itself was far more complete than anything Vicki had seen to date but still less than an inch thick. Michael wove expertly in and out of the congested traffic while she skimmed through it in silence. It was distasteful reading, and only by detaching herself from it as though this were just another investigation on which she'd embarked could Vicki bear to read it.

They were turning into the narrower side streets of the old part of the city when Vicki looked up. "So the weapon used was a .38 service revolver. Isn't that what the police carry?"

"Sure. And every lowlife who's ever stolen or purchased one off law enforcement," Michael said.

Vicki shuffled a few pages. "Except for our statements at the scene, the only person they've interviewed was Alison at the WRC hostel."

"That's because Alison told them Holly had left to meet you. Since Holly had just come into town, the assumption is that she was jumped on her way to see you, so the homicide unit felt there was no reason to waste further manpower." Competently dodging a donkey cart, Michael glanced at Vicki. "Okay, so you don't agree with that, but read incompetence into it if you like, not conspiracy."

The most useful item Vicki found was a catalog of Holly's belongings the police had taken possession of, presumably the contents of that black bag under her bed. The gold and emerald jaguar pendant was not in it. *Some police officer's salary will be augmented this month,* Vicki thought sourly.

"They have the computer listed here with her things but not the PDA. Nor Holly's cell."

"Which could mean they simply didn't recognize the PDA unit as separate from the computer. Or there's the very likely possibility Holly's assailants grabbed her purse with the cell and PDA and just didn't even notice the jewelry."

At least he didn't suggest Vicki had imagined the pendant. "Right. The world's greatest pickpockets, and they don't check for jewelry. Okay, we can agree to disagree since neither of us really knows. Holly might be foolhardy enough to wear jewelry in the streets. I've seen her myself. But that you can replace. Holly was paranoid about her PDA ever since she had one stolen back in college. I can't see her carrying it in the streets at night any more than she would her passport. It's probably in with the computer."

Vicki slapped the file shut. Looking over at Michael, she studied his handsome, tanned profile before saying hesitantly, "Would you mind if I asked one more question?"

Michael threw her a look. "By all means. You've hardly been shy about it so far."

"Joe and Bill back there at the church—did you know them before?"

Michael turned a corner, revealing the concrete box of the children's home before answering casually. "Bill Taylor, sure. At least I know *of* him. He's the biggest landowner—expat or otherwise—up around the biosphere. The other guy—the handyman, Joe." He shook his head. "Just by sight from that tree-hugger party of Holly's. He's kind of hard to miss. Why?"

"I don't know." Vicki was embarrassed to put it into words. "There just seemed to be some kind of—"

"Animosity?" Michael supplied quickly. "So you caught that too?" He grinned. "Of course, it could just be a tug-of-war to chauffeur the prettiest woman around." Before Vicki's cheeks could turn red, he turned his attention back to the street. "Still, he's an unusual type to be content burying himself out there in the middle of nowhere. Maybe it would pay to do some homework there."

His statement invited comment, and Vicki saw no reason not to oblige. "All I know is he's a surfer, and he's trying to earn money to get back to the beach. He does fly planes as well as doing handiwork."

"Well, that explains why the center hired him on instead of someone local. There aren't a lot of pilots for hire down here. He'll likely move on as soon as he gets a stake. That kind of expat drifter usually does."

They were at the gates of Casa de Esperanza now. They stood open, and a jungle green Mitsubishi Montero with the logo of a jaguar was in the courtyard. Joe and Bill had made it before them. A doorman closed the gates after the Land Rover, the inevitable throng waiting for clinic services scattering as Michael pulled up behind the Montero. Vicki spotted Evelyn on the veranda in animated conversation with the two WRC men, a large duffel bag slung over Joe's shoulder.

Joe lowered the duffel bag to the ground as Vicki reached them. "Here you go."

"Thank you." Vicki gestured toward the children's home next door. "The computer is in my quarters. That would probably be the easiest place to hook it up."

"Can I offer you all some tea first?" Evelyn studied Vicki. "You're looking all in."

"No, thank you." She suppressed a shudder. The last thing she wanted was to drag this out into a social event with these not particularly compatible virtual strangers. "I . . . I'd just like to get this over with."

"Here, I'll get it." Joe took the duffel bag just as Michael reached for it.

Evelyn turned away as a clinic volunteer in a white coat approached.

Vicki led the way through the connecting gate and up the freight elevator, feeling claustrophobic and somewhat ridiculous with three tall men looming over her. Even before she reached her door, she saw that it was standing slightly ajar.

A cry of dismay burst from her as she stepped inside. Nothing in the room remained untouched. Vicki's duffel bag had been pulled out from under the bed, her clothing ripped to shreds. Shampoo was spilled, toothpaste sliced open. Mosquito netting was pulled down, the bedsheets torn. The black plastic sack Vicki had shoved out of sight was ripped too. She recognized pieces of beige canvas as the backpack Holly used for travel.

Worse were the shards of computer components all over the floor. Even the files that had been with Vicki's computer on the card table, now overturned, had been methodically ripped to unsalvageable scraps.

Directly across from the door, between the two shuttered windows, words had been spray-painted in red. The meaning was unmistakable even with its Spanish misspelling:

Yanqui go jom

CHAPTER ELEVEN

The maliciousness of the vandalism got at Vicki more than the loss of possessions.

"Don't go telling me this was just a robbery," she cried as her companions joined her in picking through the debris. "I told you someone doesn't want me digging into Holly's death. I told you it was no mugging."

"Maybe," Joe said, shaking fragments of the motherboard from the largest remaining piece of Vicki's laptop. "Or it may just be some local police types—like the ones who walked out of your service this afternoon—who figured there'd been an aspersion cast on their competence and decided to teach you a lesson. Your pal Michael here would probably know better than I, but from what I've seen of law enforcement here, it wouldn't be hugely out of character."

"He's right." Michael sounded rather surprised at his own statement. "I did warn you, Vicki, that challenging the locals isn't the best way to make allies around here. May I suggest again that you continue your inquiries from the safety of your home stateside? I hope you'll believe me that the embassy will continue to pursue this case with every resource at our disposal."

"You're not going to try to tell me that if I pick up and go home, the embassy is really going to find out what happened to my sister."

"Not at all. I wish I could guarantee that. But I can guarantee that anything you think you can do here, the embassy can do better—and certainly with a lot more discretion."

"He's right, Vicki." This time it was Bill's quiet tones, the sharpness of his blue eyes softening to concern as he walked over to her. "I've been here a long time, and I can promise you that staying and banging your head against the wall of local bureaucracy is a one-way ticket to a nervous breakdown. I knew Holly too well to think she'd want an obsession with her death to keep you from going on with your life."

"Why do people keep saying that?" Vicki asked. "Why is everyone in such a hurry to put me on a plane and send me home?"

"Maybe because they have your best interests at heart," Joe said. "And because they know this country better than you."

They were all being so reasonable. But Vicki didn't have to respond because by now passersby had spotted the destruction through the open door, and the room was filling up with sunshine yellow T-shirts and exclamations.

It took Michael's authority to keep the scene from being totally trampled while Joe and Bill continued picking up the debris. It was immediately clear they wouldn't be recovering any data from either Vicki's computer or Holly's.

"Please, it's just a machine," Vicki reassured when a horrified Evelyn showed up. Digging into her purse, Vicki pulled out a flash drive. In her opinion it was the greatest invention of the computer age for a frequent traveler like herself. "I have everything backed up here. And I've already e-mailed all the reports to headquarters."

"Unfortunately, we can't say the same for Holly's computer." Bill shook his head over the smashed fragments. "If we could just find that PDA."

There were not even fragments to suggest Holly's PDA had been among the destroyed items.

While Vicki changed into a Casa de Esperanza T-shirt and the one pair of jeans that remained intact, Michael accompanied Evelyn to make inquiries as to who had seen what. Vicki knew their questioning was pointless. With any number of staff quartered on this hallway and dozens of local volunteers rotating through, she doubted that anyone could pinpoint a stranger or two who might have slipped up here.

"I guess we need to review our security protocol," Evelyn said mournfully when she and Michael returned to Vicki's room. "There're always so many people going in and out. We do keep medicines, supplies, and personnel quarters under lock. But you said yours was locked, Vicki."

An examination showed the door had been expertly picked.

Vicki looked at the broken and ripped debris now neatly gathered in two large trash bags. An enterprising volunteer had managed to scrub the graffiti into a pink smear, and one of the nursery personnel was wielding a broom.

Michael's mouth tightened before he said mildly, "That could have been construed as evidence. Vicki, did you want to call the police?"

"Is there any point?" she asked wearily.

"Not a whole lot," Michael admitted. "But if there's insurance involved, you'll need a police report to put in a claim."

Bill was examining the pink smear left between the windows. "I must be slipping. We should have taken some photos of all this before cleanup."

"I did." Joe pulled a cell phone from his pocket. "I'll JPEG them if you need them for insurance, Vicki."

"No, I don't carry insurance." Vicki shook her head, then wished she hadn't. The headache that had abated since the funeral service was back in full force.

"If that's settled, then I'd say we should call Alison at the office." Bill had taken Joe's cell phone from him and was sifting through the pictures. "If Vicki's right and Holly wouldn't have been carrying that PDA on the streets, Alison might have some idea where she'd stash it."

"Good idea," Michael said. "On behalf of the embassy, I'd like to be there if it turns up. Vicki, can you think of any place Holly might have stored it for safekeeping?"

"Not tonight!" Vicki didn't realize how high her voice had risen until all three men turned to look at her. Wiping a suddenly trembling hand over her face, she used it to wave to the door. "You've all been very kind. But can't we leave everything else until tomorrow? I . . . I just want to be alone. Please go away, all of you."

"Yes, can't you see the poor girl is worn out? And no wonder after such a day. Come, all of you out of here!"

If Vicki's head wasn't pounding so, the sight of Evelyn shooing away three large men like so many chicks would have brought a smile.

As the room emptied and the door clicked shut, Vicki sank onto the edge of her bed, still stripped of bedclothes and mosquito netting. After a few seconds she rose and walked over to the nearest window. The shutters were open, and through the protective bars, the evening sky had darkened enough to see the smoldering glimmer of the dump. An explosive spatter of sound in the distance could have been firecrackers or gunfire from some *mara*, a reminder of the violence that gripped the city.

A commotion below drew her attention across the dividing wall to the courtyard. The yellow glow of its outdoor lighting illuminated a horse cart clattering across the cobblestones. Vicki watched a man with the wool poncho of a Mayan peasant walk around the back to lift a child from the bed of the cart. A nurse came out of the clinic, and the two carried the child through the bright yellow rectangle that was the open clinic door. Tonight in the drama being played out on that dimly lit stage, the child would live or die. Either way the child was only one; thousands more would never make it to these gates. Millions across this continent and the globe. If one less died tonight, what difference had they really made?

"This is my Father's world."

Is it really, God? Was Holly right?

Vicki rested her forehead against the iron bars. Anger and disbelief and then sheer stubbornness had carried her this far, permitting her the dignity of remaining dry-eyed in front of all those strangers. But now beyond her exhaustion, she felt more helpless than she ever had in her life, as though she were pounding futile fists against a cosmic brass wall, accomplishing nothing but the bruising of her own flesh. The demolition around her had been the last straw, though not for the loss of possessions. She never traveled without the possibility of such loss, and she could—and would—walk into a Zone 10 electronics boutique tomorrow and replace everything on Visa. She had little enough on which she spent her salary.

No, it was the reminder of how vulnerable she was in this country, how easy it had been for an adversary to invade her private space. Despite her declaration of defiance at the memorial service, she hadn't the slightest idea what she could do or where to go next.

The worst was that all these well-wishers in such a hurry to get her on a plane were right. The measured, logical course was to follow their advice. And Vicki had always been a prudent person. Holly had been the fearless one, charging in where angels feared to tread. Like her birth father, it would seem now.

So why not just take that commemorative flight with Joe, then head stateside to pick up the carefully frantic life track that for so long had kept Vicki too busy to feel and think? After all, did it really change anything whether it had been some *mara* or some corrupt local colleague or government official who was responsible for her sister's death? It was still just part and parcel of what this country was—and so many other countries she'd visited around the globe. A jungle where human predators were far more dangerous than the remaining jaguars in Guatemala's rain forests.

And like every war zone into which Vicki had ventured, you watched your back, took your best precautions for survival, and occasionally counted your casualties and called a retreat.

Oddly, if it were just Holly, that retreat would be easier to accept. But though she'd no memory of it, though it was only a story told of strangers, Vicki could not forget that this had happened before. Her family had died in Guatemala. And she'd turned her back on it and run away. Not by choice, of course. But the truth was that no one had stood up for her parents, fought to find out what happened. Not the embassy. Not family. And as a result her birth parents had been forgotten, their memory buried so deep that their own children had not known of them, leaving the Craigs as *desaparecidos* as the thousands whose cause they had championed.

On the other hand, what had been the alternative?

The images of yesterday's marching women rose in Vicki's mind, those pitiful black-and-white enlargements, the determined but somber dark faces. Those people had been searching for years for the truth of their disappeared loved ones. Was she being naive—or even arrogant—to think she would be the exception? *Here comes the gringa. Just because she's an American, she thinks she should get the answers no one else has.*

Still, they were marching.

Hopeless or not, certainly at the risk of their own lives, in defiance of the brutal powers responsible for their loss, they were doing *something.*

"Vicki."

Vicki hadn't heard the door open. Startled, she spun around.

Balancing a well-laden tray, Evelyn walked into the room. Behind her one of the volunteers carried a stack of fresh bedding and towels. After placing it on the nearest bed, she retreated, shutting the door behind her.

Evelyn set the tray on the card table. "I've brought you some supper. I know you're tired but you'll feel better with some nourishment inside you."

The tray held a small hot water pot, and the fragrance from a covered plate was a reminder of how long it had been since Vicki had eaten. But she didn't immediately move.

Pouring hot water into a mug and adding a tea bag, Evelyn asked quietly, "What is it? What's eating you up inside?"

"It's just . . ." Vicki made a helpless motion with her hand. "I don't know what to do. No matter what I do, it could turn out wrong."

Taking a step from the window, Vicki studied Evelyn as she set the mug in front of a chair and added the covered plate and cutlery to make a neat place setting.

"Evelyn, what would you do if you were in my place?" she asked suddenly. "You were here through all of it—the dictators, the massacres, the disappearances. What did you do? How did you decide when it was best to keep quiet or give in or make a stand? How could you be sure you weren't making the wrong choice?"

Evelyn waited until Vicki had slid into her seat before she answered. "I did exactly what I'd been called here to do. Feeding children. Teaching them to read and their parents how to make a decent living. And sharing God's Word and His love."

"But that was dangerous too, wasn't it? How many teachers or social workers who tried to help the peasants 'disappeared' over the years? Weren't you ever afraid? Didn't you ever wonder—agonize, like I'm doing—over what was the right thing to do?"

"Of course I've been afraid." Evelyn slid into the other plastic chair opposite Vicki and stretched out her legs with a sigh. "And I used to worry about what to do. Then I learned to remind myself that I am Sarah's daughter, and it became easy. The decisions at least. Not necessarily carrying them out."

"Sarah's daughter?" Vicki echoed, puzzled. "You mean, like from the Bible?"

"That's right. Abraham's wife. Mother of Isaac. And through him, of the nation of Israel. Genesis tells us the story of Sarah and Abraham. But interestingly, the most revealing biography we're given of Sarah isn't in the Old Testament but the New Testament." Evelyn dug into a pocket of her ample skirt and emerged with a Bible. Flipping through the well-worn pages, she handed it to Vicki. "Read me what it says here in 1 Peter 3; start with the third verse."

The Bible was the smallest complete volume Vicki had ever seen, the print so fine that she couldn't believe the elderly missionary could decipher it. *She's probably got the whole thing memorized.*

With some reluctance, Vicki read aloud, stumbling over the unfamiliar words. "'Your beauty should not come from outward adornment, such as braided hair and the wearing of gold jewelry and fine clothes. Instead, it should be that of your inner self, the unfading beauty of a gentle and quiet spirit, which is of great worth in God's sight. For this is the way the holy women of the past who put their hope in God used to make themselves beautiful. They were submissive to their own husbands, like Sarah, who obeyed Abraham and called him her master.'"

Vicki stopped, uncomfortable and confused. "I don't get it. Isn't this the kind of thing preachers read to tell women not to pierce their ears or wear makeup? You know: Keep yourselves ugly so the men don't notice you. You're going to hell if you wear pants, and all that. We're a long ways past that in the twenty-first century—" Suddenly she took in Evelyn's old-fashioned dress and scrubbed-clean face, and she turned her last words into an embarrassed cough.

There was a twinkle behind Evelyn's thick lenses. "You're not understanding what I'm trying to say. Or what Peter was saying. He wasn't telling women to disregard their physical appearance, though there have been those who've misused it that way. After all, if you know the story, you know the Bible tells us Sarah was the most beautiful woman of the land. So beautiful that twice she was carried off to a king's harem. And where was her husband, that great hero of the faith and founder of a nation, when it happened? Not mustering his forces to storm the harem. No, he just stood by and let it happen. No, not just stood by. He actually planned it to save his own skin—and made a hefty profit off it."

Taking a second mug from the tray, Evelyn poured hot water and added a tea bag. "Abraham really didn't deserve Sarah—like a lot of husbands, from what I've observed. Finish reading the passage."

Obediently, Vicki finished the verses. "'You are her daughters if you do what is right and do not give way to fear.'" She looked at Evelyn and repeated slowly, "Sarah's daughter?"

"That's right. Here, let me take that so you can eat your supper before it gets cold." After lifting the Bible from Vicki's hand, she removed the tea bag from Vicki's mug and uncovered the plate, revealing pan-fried steak, rice, and fried plantains. Then she bowed her head. "For this bounty You have given us, our Father, may we be truly thankful." The grace was clichéd, but in Evelyn's Scottish burr, it breathed absolute conviction.

As Vicki picked up her fork, Evelyn went on placidly, "You're a beautiful young woman like Sarah was. But the point Peter was making is that Sarah's beauty was not a matter of fancy clothes or jewelry but a beauty that was from within. I see that in you, too—a caring spirit and a strength that some lucky young man is going to appreciate far more than your pretty face. And like Sarah, you've found yourself in a serious predicament, not because of any choices you've made but through the wrongdoing of other people. Maybe very powerful other people. As powerful as that rich king and Sarah's own husband. You asked me what I would do, how to know what you should do. It's really simple—so simple people miss it at every level. And you've already given it to me."

Her pause demanded an answer, and Vicki supplied it, with amazement in her tone. "'You are her daughters if you do what is right and do not give way to fear.'" Then more slowly she said, "'Do what is right. Do not give way to fear.'"

"That's right. Just those two simple steps. Let's not forget that in the harem, Sarah had no way of knowing how her predicament was going to turn out. Yet look at the biography Peter leaves us of her. A gentle and quiet spirit. An inner beauty. A woman whose hope was in God. Which was just as well because in the end it wasn't anything Sarah engineered and certainly not her loving husband galloping in to save her that got her out. God had His own plan.

"You see, we keep thinking that if we can just figure out how to manipulate the situation, if we can read the future and make the right decisions, we can make things turn out the way we want them. The problem is, we don't know all the facts, and we can't read the future. Nor are we called to. All you and I are called to do in any situation is to be Sarah's daughters. Do what is right. Do not give way to fear. If you just do that, believe me, our heavenly Father your sister loved to sing about will take care of the outcome, just as He did for Sarah. It might not be the outcome we planned, but it'll be the right one.

"After fifty years in this country, I can bear witness to that a hundred times over. It's when we forget—or figure the end justifies the means to get what we want—that we really mess things up. Again, Sarah is a good example. Just once, she got tired of doing right and gave way to fear, and we're still paying the price thousands of years later."

"She did?" Vicki was realizing despite all those years in Sunday school how little she knew of that worn volume Evelyn handled and quoted with such familiarity. "What happened?"

Evelyn laid the Bible back on the card table. "Go back to Genesis and read it for yourself. Meanwhile, eat, and then let's get your bed made up. A full stomach and a good night's sleep are as much an aid to good decisions as knowing the right thing to do."

CHAPTER TWELVE

"Do what is right. Do not give way to fear."

Vicki stared up at the fluttering shadow that was the mosquito netting above her bed. Despite her exhaustion, she had not been able to sleep after Evelyn had collected the supper tray and left her alone.

Vicki had finally turned the light back on and reached for the Bible Evelyn had left behind. What a story that had turned out to be. She remembered bits and pieces from Sunday school: Abraham receiving a call from God to leave his city and people and step out in faith to an unknown land where God would make Abraham's descendants His chosen nation. And Sarah, his wife and half sister, had gone with him. What had it been like for Sarah to leave the security and wealth of Ur for that nomadic existence in a dry and dusty land where water was the greatest treasure, obediently following her husband, never knowing where she was going? Vicki had lived in tents in more than one refugee camp and knew the relief of returning to a clean living space and hot water.

How beautiful Sarah must have been for rumors of her to reach the local king's ear. And here was her celebrated husband, the man who talked with God, who had trusted Him enough to pick up all he had and head into the unknown at His call, begging Sarah to say she was his sister so he wouldn't be killed to possess his beautiful wife. How frightened and alone and betrayed had Sarah felt in that harem while her husband was accepting a bride price of valuable livestock?

"Do what is right. Do not give way to fear."

Vicki had reread the biography given of Sarah. And she'd been fascinated at how God had reached down—not once but twice—into a harem to secure Sarah's release. Abraham had walked away richer on both occasions. Had Sarah ever been able to trust her husband again with the same obedient faith that had followed him into a wilderness? Maybe that was why she'd forgotten just once the creed that had been her enduring memorial.

That part of the story at least was familiar to Vicki. How Sarah had despaired of God fulfilling His promise to build a nation—at least through her infertile womb—and talked Abraham into sleeping with her maidservant, Hagar. So Ishmael was born, and when the son of God's promise was finally born, Isaac already had a rival whose descendants, the Arabs, would hate Isaac's descendants, the Jews, to the present day.

Yet Sarah's final biography had not been of that scheming doubter who'd messed up international politics for thousands of years ahead. That second harem experience had been long after Ishmael's birth and not long before Isaac's. And like Abraham, the friend of God, she must have learned her lesson because the Bible's final appellation of Sarah was as Evelyn had made Vicki read. A gentle and quiet spirit. A woman of hope and faith. An inner beauty far greater than the exquisite outer form that had captivated the hearts of kings.

"You are her daughters if you do what is right and do not give way to fear."

Sarah's daughter.

Vicki's wide-open eyes were suddenly wet. Holly had been a daughter of Sarah. She'd rushed fearlessly—if not always wisely, in Vicki's sober opinion—toward what she believed was right. Vicki had been the prudent one, whatever Michael and Joe and others seemed to think, always considering the consequences, thinking of the future.

It was an irony that Holly had asked Vicki the same question Vicki had demanded of Evelyn. What should I do? What would you do? And what had been Vicki's response? Walk away. Don't get involved. Watch your own back, or you might get hurt.

And now?

The tears became hotter, spilling out of the corners of her eyes as she gazed up at the ghostly flutter of the mosquito netting. She hadn't shed so many tears since . . . Had she ever? Had she wept for her birth parents in those forgotten days behind the dark curtain of her past? If only she could remember! Certainly not in the orphanage or foster homes or even when Mom and Dad Andrews had died. She'd been the tight-lipped child that all her own early photos revealed, so different from the joyous little girl in Evelyn's album, allowing no one and nothing to touch her. Or Holly. Another reason she'd been unpopular with those multiple foster parents. She'd been as forcefully protective of her younger sister as a hen with one remaining chick.

But Holly was gone. In the end, Vicki had not been able to protect her, to keep her safe. As she had not been able to save her parents.

Now why had that thought sprung to mind? Though Vicki was lying flat, she felt a sudden vertigo, a familiar nausea gripping her stomach. *That's ridiculous. Whatever happened back then, I was only a child.*

But that was no longer true. Was pursuing her sister's killer futile, an attempt perhaps to assuage her own feelings of guilt? If she'd gone after Holly, left her own assignment to track her down, however unnecessary and even irresponsible it had seemed at the time . . . But, no! While she might always carry that regret, Vicki hoped she was too levelheaded to be making present decisions based on guilt.

No. Vicki cataloged the facts: Holly's dying words, the bizarre setting of her death, the pendant, the demolition of her own room.

I can't let it go because I know there's more that could be done, and I'm the only one who seems interested in doing it.

There was Michael. But would he really follow through? Besides, he didn't know the way Holly thought or what to look for.

Vicki could talk to that zoo administrator and Department of Environment minister Holly had mentioned and try to find out if anyone saw her that night. *Even if her cell phone's gone, our account should have a record of her last calls. The police didn't even ask for it.*

And the center. Vicki could question the locals Holly worked with, however distasteful the cold, wet mountain cloud forest might be.

If Vicki couldn't guarantee any better results than that incompetent—or indifferent—homicide unit, at least she'd have the consolation that she'd tried. The path seemed very clear. So why was she shivering despite the warmth of the heavy, handwoven Indian blanket that had replaced her ripped bedding?

"I'm afraid."

There, she'd said it aloud. For all the public defiance Joe had derided, Vicki hadn't missed the stony glares of those uniforms in the back of the sanctuary. Nor did she share Holly's optimism—or naiveté—that a few signatures on a peace accord had changed the impunity with which power and evil operated in this country. The warning of today's vandalism was only too real.

With longing, Vicki thought of the quiet apartment in a secure, upscale DC suburb that was her refuge and sanctuary between assignments. No one would fault her if she took everyone's advice, bought that ticket, and retreated from the fear and horror this place had come to mean to her.

But then, when hadn't she been afraid? While others might raise a skeptical eyebrow at her career, it seemed to Vicki that she'd always walked a line of caution, watched her back, carefully judged circumstances. Even in the comparative safety of the Andrews family farm, even when she was enjoying a place or a person, there'd always been that tight knot of fear in the pit of her stomach. Fear that the bubble would burst, the ax would fall, and disaster would strike again.

I've been so afraid of what life might hand me, Vicki admitted with sudden stark realization, *I haven't let myself experience life.*

Maybe that was the reason she'd never let any of the relationships men had tried to pursue with her develop beyond lukewarm, not the excuse she'd always made that her career kept her too busy. While Holly—for all the rashness that had so often driven Vicki crazy—had rushed toward life, thinking not of what might happen to her but of what needed to be done.

If I were the one lying on that trash heap, Holly'd go after this without thinking twice. And it sounds as though Jeff, our father, would have done the same.

And look what it got them—killed.

Still, there were worse things than death. At least if you had the faith Holly'd had that this life was only a prelude to something far greater.

Vicki threw back the Indian blanket and lowered her feet to the floor, an action that left her shivering in earnest as her flesh came in contact with the cold concrete. Ignoring the chill, she walked over to the window, stepping into a gray and black pattern the paleness of moonlight and protective iron bars cast on the floor. A full moon gave strength to that pale light, but Vicki could not see it or the stars as she looked out. The *basurero* children didn't even know such splendor existed behind the pall of smoke from the dump that left the night permanently overcast.

Staring up at that sky, Vicki searched futilely for a glimmer of the silver globe responsible for the gray radiance in which she stood. As invisible behind those clouds was the God in whom Holly had put so much trust.

As Sarah had in that harem.

"This is my Father's world."

Father God, is that really who You are? what You are?

There was no answer any more than a glimpse of that full moon. That there was a Creator of the universe, Vicki didn't doubt for a moment, as she'd told Evelyn. That was too evident in the very complexity of the world. And she'd never doubted any more than Holly that He had a plan for the universe and the power to accomplish that plan.

But if the billions of crawling little beings caught up in the accomplishment of that plan really mattered, then would that desperate father she'd spotted earlier be hauling his sick child in the back of a donkey cart in a frantic search for aid? Would a Mayan teenager be cradling her dehydrated and malnourished baby on a street corner? Would precious children be crawling through the planet's waste for survival?

Father God, if that's really what You are, I don't understand what You're doing or why You're doing it.

"Do what is right. Do not give way to fear."

Was that really the answer?

Vicki felt suddenly paralyzed with the weight of her decision. Beyond a shadow of doubt, she knew this was the pivotal point of her life. She could walk away and go on through life governed by fear. Or she could follow a path whose end was no clearer than that pattern of gray and black on the floor and trust the outcome, as Evelyn had told her, to that distant, invisible God somewhere beyond the cover of smoke and cloud.

"This is my Father's world."

"Do what is right. Do not give way to fear."

Vicki's thoughts went to Holly. To Jeff, her birth father, so like his younger daughter in his pursuit of justice and abandonment to life. To Victoria, in that old photo so strikingly like Vicki herself, but who had followed her husband beyond civilization's safety net. To the GAM marchers, who after all these years were still keeping faith with their lost loved ones. Would the remaining member of the Andrews—no, Craig—family be the only one unwilling to risk the challenge?

"I'm going to do it. At least as long as there's one more step ahead of me to take."

Just as the spoken words echoed against the cinder-block walls, a cloud or maybe a gust of smoke from the dump abruptly winked out the pattern beneath Vicki's feet.

Suppressing a sudden shudder, Vicki crawled hastily back into bed.

The first angling ray of dawn through the glass allowed him to make out the concealed edging. Prying open the compartment, he felt around inside. Yes, buried under other contents, his fingers encountered a smooth rectangle, the synthetic material cool to the touch. He'd known where it was the instant they'd confirmed it was missing. Tugging the device free, he powered it up. There was still battery. Now for a log of recent activity.

A photo came onto the screen, then the text. After he read through it with chilled incredulity, he pulled up the next file, then another.

He slid the unit into his pocket. Had its owner even guessed how explosive this material was? It was no wonder the girl had needed to die.

"So . . . the sister is still here. And as I forecast, she promises to be more trouble than the other. Perhaps it is now necessary—"

"No, don't touch her!" The loud *throp-throp* of the rotors was as exasperating as the static of outdated communications equipment. "Don't you understand? *Los americanos* are not like your peasants. Prodding them with a stick will not make them run away. They will simply dig their heels in and choose to do the opposite. What your people did today—that was foolishness. To this point, no matter what questions the woman asks, the official tale is one more tourist in the wrong place. *La embajada* is as anxious as you that this go away. But a mishap to her, too, and you cannot know how many eyes and ears will be drawn here, how many questions raised. No, let the sister ask her questions. She will find nothing, and it will not be for much longer in any case."

"Then she is your responsibility. Keep a close eye on her."

A low chuckle. "That will be a pleasure."

The radio went dead. The brief amusement vanished from his face. Replacing the handheld communicator, he lifted the glittering decoration that hung from a knob. As it dangled from his fingers, the light glinted green in the eyes of the tiny jungle cat. It had proved easy enough to repossess, and while it was a shame to waste either its value or beauty, he was not about to repeat the stupidity or greed that had already caused so much inconvenience.

Below the runners of the hovering aircraft stretched the vast wasteland with its scattered plumes of smoke, its crawling specks that at this altitude could hardly be differentiated between human and avian scavengers.

Opening a small access pane, he dangled his fingers outside, feeling the wind snatch away what they held even before he let go. A fluttering upward of black wings told him where his toss had landed.

Satisfied, he nodded. The aircraft rose, then banked away. The fury of that subterranean furnace would swiftly erase the mistake his associates had been careless enough to leave behind.

CHAPTER THIRTEEN

Resolve is easier by daylight.

In the morning, Vicki approached the task to which she'd set herself with the same cool, analytical logic with which she approached each project investigation. She deliberately set Holly to the back of her mind as though her sister were only away from her for one of the long assignments that so frequently—and temporarily—separated them.

And that's all this is, Vicki cried silently with sudden passion. *I believe it; I do. It's just a little longer than it's ever been before.*

Vicki's first action was to call Alison at the Wildlife Rescue Center's Guatemala City office. "Are you still looking for a translator up at the center?"

"Are we! And just about everything else until Roger and Kathy's replacements arrive next month up there. Why? Do you have a candidate in mind?"

"Myself," Vicki said. "I have a few weeks' vacation accumulated, and I'd like to spend some of it seeing why Holly was so in love with that area and the center."

All perfectly true, as far as it went. Vicki would fly up with Joe and Bill as already planned and stay on. What the two men would think of her decision, Vicki preferred not to speculate.

Walking over to Casa de Esperanza, she found Evelyn in her living quarters.

"I've got to be honest," Vicki told her. "I'm basically done here except for hearing back from the foundation on my recommendations. But if you still have the room—"

"Oh, of course you can stay as long as you need to," Evelyn cut in.

An answer to be expected considering the lucrative funding these people hoped Vicki could facilitate for them. But the warmth of Evelyn's response held no iota of self-interest, only genuine and fervent welcome.

The rest of the morning Vicki spent replacing her ruined possessions, including a sturdy and relatively inexpensive Korean-brand laptop, to which she began the tedious process of transferring her files from the flash drive. This wasn't the first time she'd gone through the process. Vicki had learned to keep operational as well as work files backed up. But it was still late evening before she had the Internet up and was able to download her most recent cell phone log. The next day Vicki was on the phone as early as local office hours began. Her immediate goals were to talk personally with the zoo administrator and minister of environment Holly had mentioned visiting. Vicki learned that the zoo administrator was out of town, treating his children to a Disney World vacation. *So what's his local salary?* But she was able to make an appointment with the minister for the next day.

Then Vicki began calling Holly's section of the phone log, ignoring anything further back than two weeks ago or any number outside Guatemala. The list wasn't long. Holly's phone hadn't been used since the evening before her death—another stroke against the theory of street thieves, as those typically ran the bill up as high as possible, selling minutes to whoever wanted them until service was cut off.

Vicki worked backward from the last day. One frequent repeat was now familiar as the local WRC office. Another proved to be the WRC hostel, where Holly had checked in. The very last number Holly had called was a radio taxi service.

"Do you keep a record of pickups?" Vicki asked the dispatcher. "I'm looking for a request to pick up a gringa at the WRC hostel in Zone 4 called in six nights ago at 7:58 p.m."

"Yes, we often supply service to that locale," the dispatcher answered indifferently. "But we do not keep such detailed logs."

That had been no more than Vicki expected. Keeping meticulous logs only invited a government probe into sales tax and other regulations inconvenient to taxi drivers, who worked largely under the radar of the official economy.

Vicki tried a tactic more likely to succeed. "Please ask your drivers if any remember such a pickup. For information, there will be a generous remuneration for both your office and the driver."

There was not one call, Vicki noted somberly, to her own number. The only other calls that last afternoon had been to the airport—by its timing presumably confirming her volunteer team's arrival—and another number repeated twice earlier in the time frame. It wasn't familiar, so she entered the number with cautious hope.

A terse baritone answered, "Michael Camden."

Vicki was too stupefied to respond.

The DAO attaché's voice sharpened to impatience. "Who is this? *¿Habla español?*"

"Michael, I'm sorry. I didn't realize I was calling your number." Vicki scrabbled through her handbag as she spoke, coming up finally with the card Michael had given her the day of Holly's death. Yes, the number printed there matched the one she'd just keyed in.

"Is this Vicki Andrews?" His voice warmed immediately. "Don't apologize. It's a pleasure to hear from you. What's new?"

"I was just . . . Actually, I don't understand it. I was calling through Holly's cell phone log to see if anything might turn up. She called this number several times, and it was the last one she called except for a radio taxi the evening she died. I . . . I thought you'd never been able to get ahold of Holly, or did I misunderstand what you said?"

"Holly's cell phone log," Michael's calm voice held none of Vicki's surprise or discomfort. "Brilliant. That's data I couldn't easily access from here. If you can print me off a copy and drop it by the embassy, it would save me some time in my own investigation. As to Holly's calls—no, you didn't misunderstand. Holly did leave several messages here at my office after I'd asked her to get in touch. But I managed to be out in the field every time she called, so all she got was my voice mail.

There was a message from her logged that last day after I ran into you at the embassy. But I was out on a training op that night, and I'm afraid I didn't even get around to my voice mail until shortly before the police called. It was the same as the others—wanting to set a time to consult with me."

His voice turned grave. "If I didn't bring it up, it wasn't just because there was nothing relevant in that voice mail. Truth is, I just . . . well, I can't help feeling if I'd been around to get that call, if I'd been able to meet her request, even if I'd checked my messages right away when I got in the next morning—"

"No, you can't go there. What's done is done. And even if you'd listened earlier to the messages, it couldn't have made any difference since Holly was already—" Vicki's throat closed up, and she forced the images her mind insisted on conjuring up back to the cold discipline of her investigation. "But would you mind if I listened to the message myself? Just to get a sense of her tone, how she was feeling. I know Holly. I might pick up something someone else would miss."

"That I can't do," Michael said regretfully. "I get such a backlog of calls that I don't save messages unless there's data I need to file. I'd have certainly saved it if I'd known then . . . But in any case, I don't remember any urgency in what she said."

As Vicki swallowed her disappointment, Michael added, "Actually I'm glad you called. I've been successful in tracking down the perps responsible for that little escapade with your room the other day."

Vicki's disappointment vanished immediately. "You're kidding! Who did it?"

"Well, under conditions that no charges were being filed and totally off the record, I was able to squeeze out an admission that some local uniforms who'd been at the scene decided to take exception to the TV coverage. I'm afraid they figured your commentary made them look bad, and much as your handyman friend suggested—" Michael's tone grew drier—"decided to do something to recover their honor."

"But how did they get in and out so easily without anyone even seeing them?"

"It would appear one of the neighborhood patrol knows your project well enough to play tour guide."

"Roberto Torres, the sergeant who used to attend one of the Casa de Esperanza school projects. What a lowlife!"

"There's no way you could prove it," Michael cautioned. "But I thought you'd like to know it wasn't connected to your sister's death. Or at least only indirectly."

Making it one more dead end. At least it showed Michael was keeping his word not to let the investigation drop.

"Thank you for telling me," Vicki said warmly, then filled Michael in on her travel plans.

He responded slowly. "Well, it's probably safer than Guatemala City. I'm assuming it would do no good to try to talk you out of it."

"No, it wouldn't. I don't know how long I'll be up there. There's no cell phone access, but in an emergency, I can be contacted through the center radio phone. I would be grateful if you could let me know when anything else comes up on Holly."

"That you can count on. The UPN is still running its ops out of the army base up there, so you might see me. Assuming the welcome mat is still out for extraneous humanoids over at the center."

Vicki could hear the smile in his voice, see in her mind's eye the curve of his mouth and the softening of his handsome features. She felt warmth rise to her face before catching herself sharply. *He's just thinking of his investigation and trying to be nice about it.* "I don't know about the center, but you're certainly welcome anytime as far as I'm concerned. I'll definitely keep you informed if anything turns up on my end."

A prospect that was attractive only because of what it signified to her investigation, Vicki assured herself.

She chose not to tell Evelyn about Sergeant Roberto's duplicity. The attack had been on Vicki, not Evelyn, and as Michael had said, nothing could be proven now. It would only distress Evelyn that one of her former protégés had stooped to such juvenile spite.

The rest of the call log was unfruitful. Most numbers were related to Holly's work, including suppliers and a veterinary clinic under which Holly was officially interning.

There were also a few personal calls, all within the tree-hugger camp. Lynn was one of them but not Dieter. None had anything to add. Whatever Holly was up to, she hadn't confided in them.

Because she was waiting to confide in me. I'm wasting my time.

Not unexpectedly, another of the numbers proved to be Joe's cell.

He showed no surprise at Vicki's call. "We just confirmed delivery of the plane," he informed her. "We take possession tomorrow and leave first thing the next day. Can you make it?"

Vicki hadn't heard back yet from the mortuary, but with her change in plans, she'd be on that plane regardless of how it fit in with her original arrangement with Joe and Bill. "Give me a time, and I'll be there."

Only one number roused even a modicum of interest. "Archivo General de Centro America," a female voice answered.

Vicki could think of no possible work-related reason Holly would have contacted the national archives. She decided to stop by after her appointment with the minister of environment tomorrow.

There was little else Vicki could do that day except hassle the mortuary. "No, next week is not acceptable," she countered the mortician's smooth excuses. "You said forty-eight hours." She reminded him that she'd paid with Visa and could reverse the charges.

The mortician scrambled to be helpful, promising that a delivery messenger would drop by her lodgings by the close of business hours tomorrow.

The next morning a secretary ushered Vicki into the minister of environment's office and murmured that the Honorable Doctor Francisco Soliz would be right back. "He can spare you fifteen minutes, no more," she warned as she returned to the reception area.

The office had Vicki wondering if all government appointees lived and worked in the sumptuousness of the colonial Spanish aristocracy. She sank into the red leather couch and looked around. If not as big as the police chief's, the office was furnished with the same rich wood and polished leather, deep-piled carpets, and well-filled, glassed-in library shelves. And the same photo display.

No, not quite. The group of framed pictures on the wall between two windows held a different woman and three much smaller children in various poses. But the largest photo . . .

Vicki rose and walked over for a closer look. Yes, it was the same group shot of men in uniforms she'd seen at the police headquarters, the same American colors on the lapels of those on either end, the same third American with his head turned away, hat tilted over his face. Like its counterpart, the photo was black and white. Vicki guessed it had been shot for press purposes because even then surely color was the norm for photography.

"You find it of interest?"

Vicki turned around and realized Soliz was the same man who'd presented Holly a posthumous medal at the funeral. A short, pudgy man, he rocked forward on his feet in a way intended to make him look taller, but which only made him seem self-important. If he was one of the men in that photo, he'd left behind any military discipline long ago.

Returning hastily to her seat, Vicki said cautiously, "Yes, very interesting. Wasn't that the American training program carried out here? *El comandante de policía* has the same picture in his office."

"You know Gualberto?" The minister of environment looked pleased. "Yes, we were brothers then, specially selected from the best officers of our army to receive the *americano* training. Ah, those were good times with *los americanos*. This year is the twentieth anniversary of our brotherhood. See—there I am." He pointed out a slim, wiry young man Vicki would never have recognized, adding as he took his seat behind his desk, "It was good training, too. Your country is most expert at such things. It proved very useful in pursuing the vicious war *la guerrilla* had unleashed on our country at that time."

"But you didn't continue in the military. The Ministry of Environment is a very different career." It was a question.

"No." The minister's face clouded over. "The peace accords stripped our military of strength and international support. So, one looks for other opportunities."

And other international funding. Vicki's distaste must have shown because Soliz added with an ingratiating smile, "Of course the preservation of our beautiful land is also a vital war. Which is why I would again express my appreciation for your sister's service to my country."

Vicki jumped at the opportunity to steer the conversation to her purpose for this appointment. "Yes, it is of my sister I wish to speak. You know I am looking further into her death. I understand she visited you to share some concerns a couple of weeks ago."

The minister's geniality faded instantly. "Yes, she did come here. You must realize your sister was young and inexperienced. She did not understand how things work in this country."

You mean, like bribery and corruption? Vicki let go of that thought and said evenly, "She was worried that animals—endangered species the center was rehabilitating—were disappearing. I know she had some concerns about the zoo. She talked to the administrator there the same time she talked to you. Unfortunately, he appears to be out of the country right now. Is it possible he might know of these missing animals that distressed my sister so?"

Soliz looked even more wary. "What I assured your sister was that she was mistaken. I have known Samuel Justiniano at *el zoológico* for many years. He comes from the most respected strata of Guatemalan society. Like mine, his family has served this country in maintaining law and discipline for generations. In fact, it was I who recommended him for the position."

None of which addressed a single concern Vicki had raised.

"No, if there has been a difficulty, it is possible that there has not been sufficient discipline among certain employees. The people do not respect the strong hand of the law as they once did. I assured your sister the matter would be addressed, and I can assure you that it has been done. We are not children to need foreigners to instruct us in how to preserve our patrimony. Now if you will excuse me." He stood.

His secretary appeared at Vicki's elbow to steer her out. For all her caution, she'd fared no better than she'd once warned Holly, Vicki admitted resentfully. As to the absent zoo administrator, it was clear class and family counted for more than whatever the truth might be. But unlike Holly, Vicki hadn't come for the truth. Especially since she cared only academically whether this man or his associate had been using their positions to feather a replacement nest for those lost with the loosening of the military's stranglehold on this country.

No, Vicki was here only for Holly. And though she might have her doubts as to whether this particular minister was more committed to his cause or the fat funding of the international NGOs, Vicki couldn't see him killing an American volunteer to silence her complaints. Not when he had only to ignore her or pass the blame back down the chain of command. And since according to his secretary, who'd had no reason to fudge the dates, the zoo administrator had been out of the country since before Holly's death, he too was cleared of murder, if not fraud.

Not a dead end; just elimination.

CHAPTER FOURTEEN

The national archive was a tired-looking building, its atmosphere as heavy with dust inside as the exhaust and smog and dirt of the street outside.

Vicki handed the clerk a photo of Holly.

The young Ladino woman took one glance and shook her head. "I'm sorry. I may have seen her or I may not. There are many foreigner scholars who come, and you must forgive me if I say that they all look much alike."

The apologetic expression drew Vicki's first real smile in a week. "I'm afraid a lot of gringos say the same about Guatemalans," she said candidly. "I was just hoping you might have a record of what she was looking for."

"No, if materials are removed, they must be signed out with the proper identification. But just to look, it is not required."

"Well, let me leave you my phone number in case you remember something." Vicki was scribbling on a business card when she had another thought. "Would it be possible to look at any of the major newspapers you have from twenty years ago? Specifically any coverage of an *americano* military exchange program that was training Guatemalan army officers. I'm looking for a picture with some of the Guatemalan officers and their American trainers."

"That's it!" The clerk's pretty olive features lit up. "That was her. That was what she asked about too. Come."

The archives were little more than tied-up bundles of every newspaper or magazine that had ever sprung up and died in Guatemala. Despite a card catalog whose contents were as dusty and dog-eared as the bundles, Vicki could not see how any effective research could be done. Fortunately, several of the larger and more enduring periodicals had been transferred to microfiche. In minutes the clerk had pulled up a front-page spread dated twenty years earlier. There was the photo, a much smaller version, and above the accompanying columns of print was the headline: "*Estados Unidos y Guatemala: Aliados Contra el Comunismo.*" "America and Guatemala: Allies Against Communism."

The article gave details. The dozen Guatemalans in the picture were a unit of D-2, the elite Guatemalan military intelligence branch handpicked to participate in a counterinsurgency course sponsored by a US MAP—Military Assistance Program—training team on loan from the American military base in Panama. Such training programs were common enough throughout Latin America: counternarcotics and military police courses such as Michael was teaching, weapons training, war games.

Of more interest to Vicki was the caption below the pictures listing the names of the officers who'd graduated from the program. She picked out Colonel Gualberto Alvarez and Colonel Francisco Soliz. But when the name *Samuel Justiniano* looked familiar, she dug into her handbag for the notes she'd made for her last appointment. Then the zoo administrator was part of that same brotherhood Soliz had mentioned.

Vicki frowned. Even she, a newcomer to Guatemala, had read of the infamous D-2, responsible by all accounts for thousands of *los desaparecidos* and political assassinations of the 1980s and 1990s. Under international pressure, the D-2 had been disbanded after the 1996 peace accords. But far from paying any reparations for their actions, it would seem this unit at least had simply shifted to other powerful and lucrative positions. *And after all these years they're clearly still scratching each other's backs,* Vicki thought bitterly. *No wonder their wall of silence is so powerful.*

The American advisers were not named. An oversight or an intervention by the embassy or Pentagon?

"Do you know what else this woman was looking at while she was here?"

The clerk shook her head. "She was here a long time, but this is the only one I am sure of because I helped her with the finding of it."

"Would it be possible to print this picture out?"

The printout was a full 8½ by 11 page, and a chill raised hairs on the back of Vicki's neck when she saw the words *Jeff Craig Productions* at the bottom right-hand corner.

Her birth father. What bizarre coincidence was this? Was this what Holly had been after?

As Vicki studied the picture, logic restored her equilibrium. Evelyn had said Jeff Craig had been earning a name as a photojournalist when this picture was dated. The picture involved a US embassy–sponsored event right here in Guatemala City. That her birth father would have provided the photo to a local Guatemalan newspaper wasn't a coincidence.

Besides, to Holly, the photographer's name would have meant nothing.

Vicki understood exactly what Holly had been doing. She must have seen those photos and figured there was a conspiracy—or at least a cooperation—among the men, so she was digging out anything she could find on their background.

No doubt Holly had thought it would be enough to force some action. Except she didn't realize the whole country—or at least the ruling class—was one big network. *Hermandad*, or "brotherhood," got things done around here.

Still, Vicki folded the photocopy carefully. This was one small link she now possessed with her birth father.

Vicki's cell phone rang as she was walking down the cracked marble steps.

"Señorita, you are the one offering a reward for certain information?" a man asked.

Vicki questioned him, but he refused to talk over the phone. *Afraid I won't pay his reward once he's coughed up the data.* So she gave her present location.

Less than ten minutes later, a yellow cab drew up at the archive steps.

Climbing in, Vicki counted out the one hundred quetzales so the driver could see them and added directions to Casa de Esperanza.

When she showed the driver Holly's picture, he only waved it away. "I never saw the woman. But the request I received from the dispatcher was to pick her up outside the hostel. That girl in the photo—I have picked her up there on other occasions. I cannot say it was her because I did not speak to her directly. But if the request was made at the time you say, it was her. There was none other from that location."

"But where did you take her?" Vicki asked impatiently.

"That is what I am trying to tell you, señorita! When I arrived, she was not there. I honked. I waited. Then I knocked. The doorkeeper told me the fare had already emerged. I assumed she had grown impatient and taken a taxi that passed by. A dangerous practice for a young woman," he added severely, "for one never knows what such a driver might be."

A reality of which Holly had been well aware.

Vicki handed over the one hundred quetzales and redirected the driver to the WRC hostel instead.

This was siesta hour, when few people visited, so the doorkeeper was dozing in the watch shack that was also his home just inside the walled compound. He was as helpful as the taxi driver. Yes, he'd let Holly out that night, as he'd informed *la policía*. No, he had no idea where she was going. No, he hadn't seen who'd picked her up. His responsibility was to keep watch on the interior of the compound, not what was happening on the street.

"Vicki!"

Vicki swung around into an enthusiastic hug. "Lynn, it's good to see you. Hey, are you staying here?"

"Just for a day or two. My apartment's being fumigated." The Amazon Watch environmentalist grimaced. "Cockroaches."

Then she hadn't been here during Holly's stay. A sudden thought had Vicki digging out the photograph she'd copied. "Lynn, you've been here awhile. Do you recognize any of these people? Think twenty years back."

Lynn glanced over the printout. "Why, of course, there's Soliz, our beloved local minister of environment. Who'd have thought he ever had that much hair! And that's Justiniano over at the zoo. I hadn't realized they were ex-military. The others . . ." She studied the photo again. "Can't say I recognize any of them. The embassy could probably ID the Americans, though I doubt they'd just hand out that kind of info. Especially Mr. CIA there."

"CIA?" Vicki eyed the turned figure in a floppy hat under Lynn's tapping fingernail. "Why do you say that?"

"Come on—an American civilian in there with our military advisers? Trying to hide his face from the camera? If that guy's not CIA, I'll give up my time-share in Cancún."

"You think? But what would he be doing down here in Guatemala?"

"Oh, my dear, where have you been?" Lynn's exclamation sounded pitying. "You're in Guatemala, and you've never bothered to learn the story of the United Fruit Company and their nice, little CIA-sponsored coup? President Arbenz and Guatemala's famed 'ten years of spring'?"

"Well, I read something—"

Lynn interrupted Vicki inexorably. "Back then in the fifties, the American-owned United Fruit Company was the largest landowner in the Caribbean. So large the locals called them *El Pulpo* or 'The Octopus.' Banana and coffee plantations. Railways. Roads. Postal system. Then comes reform candidate Jacobo Arbenz. He had wild ideas like a minimum wage law, freedom of speech, education, health care, redistribution of unused land back to the Mayan communities from which it had been originally misappropriated. Worst of all, taxes to redistribute some of the country's wealth from the 1 percent enjoying it back to the other 99. All the things American workers had fought for and won.

"The Guatemalan aristocracy was screaming. But nothing like the United Fruit Company. Fortunately for them, Eisenhower was in the White House, and two of their major stockholders just happened to be Allen Dulles, Eisenhower's CIA director, and his brother, Secretary of State John Dulles. They yelled "Communist plot," and Eisenhower signed on the dotted line to send in the CIA. Arbenz was replaced with a US-backed military regime that immediately rescinded all those nasty tax reforms. That was the end of Guatemala's experiment in democracy. And the beginning of a long and close relationship between the Guatemalan military and the CIA."

Vicki felt as though she'd been caught inadvertently in a flash flood. "But that's all ancient history. I mean, that was more than fifty years ago!"

"Yeah, well, tell that to the Guatemalans."

CHAPTER FIFTEEN

Well, she'd certainly chalked up a civics lesson, if nothing useful. Vicki spent the next hour working her way down the street, showing Holly's picture to store clerks, dropping coins in beggars' cups, knocking on doors before giving up and returning to the taxi, whose driver had been happy enough for another fifty quetzales to settle down to his own siesta. No wonder the local police had thrown in the towel, Vicki thought despondently as the taxi dropped her off at the children's home. Nobody sees anything, hears anything, or knows anything.

A messenger from the mortuary was waiting for her at Casa de Esperanza. Vicki didn't bother opening the carefully wrapped box before signing for it. If its contents were randomly scooped from someone's fireplace, she'd never know anyway.

She blocked her mind to the lightness of weight as she carried the box up to her quarters and set it carefully with the belongings she was readying to bring with Joe and Bill in the morning. How was it possible that this small cardboard receptacle held all that was left of what had been a living, breathing human being?

Forcing her thoughts back to the task at hand, Vicki dialed up the local Internet connection. As it downloaded her e-mail, she browsed through some Google searches. Checking data was second nature to Vicki, and Lynn had thrown some new curves at her. *It can't be true! We're the good guys!*

But Lynn had her facts correct enough. UFCO, Arbenz, the CIA's 1954 coup—it was all public record. As were the decades of brutal military repression that followed. So brutal that those ten brief years of reform were referenced in everything Vicki read as though the so-called "ten years of spring" were the only positive note in Guatemalan history. *So what were we doing arming and training these guys?*

And not just in Guatemala. Vicki was astonished to read that the same Dulles brothers had engineered a similar coup just a year earlier in Iran, where a democratically elected president had threatened to redirect oil revenues to modernize his own medieval state. While the oil companies recovered their monopoly, the Iranians got Shah Reza Pahlavi. Then there was El Salvador, the Philippines, Chile, Argentina, Iraq, the pattern depressingly similar. In Iran, of course, that intervention had backfired badly, with the oppressiveness of the shah and his American-trained SAVAK secret police giving rise to the Ayatollah Khomeini's Islamic revolution and its legacy of hatred for which the US and the entire Western world were still paying.

We were fighting Communism, and they were our allies. Maybe they weren't always the best. But by making a stand, we did create the freest and richest society on earth.

At least for ourselves.

Vicki propped up the group photo she'd recovered from the archives. Had her birth father known the American advisers shown here? Or had he simply been making an extra commission for the news service? Vicki studied the turned figure in civilian clothing and a floppy hat. Had he really been deliberately trying to keep his face out of the picture? *Are you really CIA?*

The only good news was waiting on her e-mail. Vicki immediately set off to find Evelyn.

The elderly missionary was in the CE thrift store, a former salon set up Goodwill-style with clothing and other items donated by the expat community. With her was Adriana, the local volunteer who'd replaced Vicki at the dump school. Adriana was sorting through racks of children's clothing, while Evelyn was picking through the infant supplies with a young Mayan woman carrying a baby.

Evelyn looked up as Vicki approached, and as she saw Vicki's face, she straightened. "You've heard."

Vicki ended the suspense quickly. "The proposal was approved. You got the grant." She threw an arm around Evelyn's shoulders, touched and astonished to see tears pouring down the woman's cheeks. "What's wrong? Aren't you happy about it?"

"Oh no, no! Nothing's wrong. It is all *so* right!" She hugged Vicki fiercely. "Here it was your father and my dear Victoria who helped out here. And now it is so fitting that their daughter, my sweet little Vicki grown up, is making it possible for this to go on no matter what should become of me. Thank You, heavenly Father above. Thank You for bringing my little Vicki back to be such a blessing to me."

"Hey, don't be thanking some heavenly Father above—or me," Vicki said lightly, pulling away, uncomfortable at the accolades. "Thank the foundation. They're the ones with the cash."

Vicki regretted her levity as she caught sorrow in Evelyn's eyes and corrected herself. "It's just . . . you're the one who's been trying to save all these kids on your own, and it's about time you caught a break. I'm glad for anything I could do to help."

"Oh, Vicki." Evelyn sighed.

As though adding her own protest, the baby Evelyn had been outfitting when Vicki burst in set up a wail. The teenage mother loosed the carrying blanket from her back so she could comfort the child in her arms. The baby was adorable with silky, dark hair and plump cheeks, its rounded, brown limbs flailing vigorously.

"You do remember Carmen and little Maritza?" Evelyn prompted.

"Of course," Vicki said. "I just wouldn't have recognized them."

Maritza and her mother had been released from the clinic forty-eight hours after Vicki had brought them in. Vicki knew Evelyn had made arrangements for their convalescence, but she hadn't seen the pair in the last two and a half weeks.

"One of the mission organizations has a home for street girls and their babies. A lot of them don't stay long—especially since they allow no drugs. But Carmen here has settled in well and is volunteering with the nursery."

"*Hola*, Carmen." Vicki shifted to Spanish with a smile. "It's good to see you again. Maritza is looking very beautiful."

Now that eyes were on her, Carmen drifted close enough to snatch Vicki's hand, the black eyes that had been so dull with despair now passionate with gratitude. "*Que Dios te bendiga.* 'May God bless you,'" she answered fervently before bursting into a flood of her own language.

"She is thanking you for saving Maritza's life and her own," Evelyn translated, then added with gentle implacability, "Don't downplay how our heavenly Father uses His own human children to work in His world, Vicki. After all, you too are a part of the beauty of God's creation. You questioned how a loving Creator can see what's happening in His world and do nothing about it. But if you asked Carmen, she'd say He did do something. He sent you to her and her child. You see, He never asked you or me to fix the whole world, just to—"

"I know. I've got it now," Vicki interrupted. "'Do what is right. Do not give way to fear.'"

"Don't you laugh at it. Because when enough ordinary people choose to do just that, then you'll see change in this world and not before. And when more people don't do it than do, that's what gets you the kind of world we're looking at. I'm happy doing what God's called me to do and leaving the rest to Him."

The kindness in Evelyn's keen hazel gaze leavened the reproof, and Vicki impulsively threw her arms around her again. "And you just keep on saving the world, Evelyn. I'm happy to help, even if it isn't really much—" She stopped as a glint of light across the room caught her eye. Slowly, she lowered her arms and straightened.

As Adriana reached for a girls' rack, Vicki spotted a dainty gold chain around her neck with a beautifully crafted jaguar hanging from it, the eyes a green gleam of emerald chips. For a long heartbeat, then another, Vicki couldn't breathe. Then she crossed the floor in two long strides. "Where did you get that?"

At the harsh Spanish, the volunteer took a step back. Vicki reminded herself that Adriana hadn't even been at the school compound when

Holly's broken body was brought there. Yet the pendant had to be Holly's, its handcrafted design too unique for coincidence.

"I'm sorry. My sister, Holly, was wearing that necklace when she died. At least it looks like the same one. Could you tell me how it came to you?"

Like all the volunteers, Adriana knew of Holly's death. She unfastened the chain from her neck. "Oh, please, then you must take it. I purchased the chain today from one of the *basurero* children. For only a fraction, I am sure, of its value, though of course it cannot be real gold. Not if he found it, as he says, in the *basura*."

"Thank you. If you don't mind, I will take it because it is a precious memory for me of my sister. But you must let me reimburse you for what you gave the child."

After Adriana reluctantly admitted what she'd spent, Vicki went on to her most urgent query. "Would you be able to take me to the child who had the pendant? I'd like to talk to him about where he found it."

"You should know him. Pepito, just down the path from the school. His mother would not let him come to classes, if you remember."

Pepito didn't look happy to see Adriana and Vicki when they made their way down the muddy path to where his scrap-wood shack clung to the side of the ravine. No, he wasn't in trouble, they had to reassure him and his mother before he would talk about the pendant.

"I found it out there." He indicated a direction far afield from where Holly had been found.

"That isn't possible," Vicki probed gently but firmly. "My sister was wearing it when we carried her up to the school."

Pepito wouldn't back down. "It was there. I am not lying. It was a miracle from God."

Vicki knelt to look the boy straight in the eyes. "What do you mean? What was a miracle?"

"You will not believe me," Pepito answered.

"Try me." Vicki produced a twenty-quetzal note.

Pepito's face lit up. Snatching the money, he said eagerly, "It dropped from the sky when I prayed. I swear, it was not there, and then it was. As though it came from the very hand of God."

The sky!

Vicki's thoughts leaped to Holly's broken form on the garbage mound. The shiny black plastic in which she'd been encased. As clean and untouched, Vicki had puzzled over, as though it had dropped from the sky.

"You see! You do not believe me." The sullen look was back on Pepito's face.

Vicki straightened, her voice ringing with conviction as she gave him a pat on the head. "Oh no, I believe you. I believe you absolutely."

CHAPTER SIXTEEN

"You're late."

Vicki skidded to a halt on the tarmac as a long body separated itself from the fuselage of the single-engine plane.

Joe had reverted to his surfer look. He wore Bermuda shorts, despite the coolness of the highland morning, and a dizzyingly bright Hawaiian shirt. His hair tumbled to his broad shoulders. Nor was there any hint of the sympathy that had warmed Vicki toward him at the funeral. His eyes swept over Vicki's face. "And what is this I hear you're not making the return trip?"

So that was why the sympathy had vanished. Joe hated having his advice ignored, even if it was none of his business.

Vicki gritted her teeth. What had started out as a good morning was already turning into an ordeal. She'd made her good-byes to the Casa de Esperanza staff, the affection of their hugs chasing away some of the heart chill of Holly's death. An e-mail from Children at Risk's home office offering condolences and congratulations had also extended her available leave by two weeks. Adriana's announcement that Pepito's mother was going to let the boy attend classes was an added gratification.

Then the late arrival of her radio taxi dropped Vicki into rush hour. A traffic jam involving a mule cart and garbage truck had been compounded by a lineup at airport security. Her duffel bag was heavier than usual, thanks to the coroner's box, reinforced now with duct tape and padded with clothing, so that by the time Vicki had found the parking berth matching Joe's directions, she was breathless and damp with perspiration. A definite disadvantage as she tipped back her head to glower at Joe.

"I have some vacation time coming, and the center needs a translator," Vicki answered coolly. "You've got a problem with that?"

"Hey, it's your funeral." The WRC handyman had the grace to catch himself. "Sorry! Poor choice of words. You do what you have to. If HQ says you're welcome, it's none of my business."

"Precisely. As to schedule, I'm sorry I'm late. There was a traffic jam and a mule—" Vicki broke off. Why was she defending herself to this man? She let some of his sarcasm creep into her tone as she glanced around. "I hadn't realized a one-passenger charter flight was on such a tight schedule. I mean, what's the penalty? Dumping the passenger or firing the pilot for taking off a whole ten minutes late?"

"More like a fine." Joe lifted Vicki's duffel bag from her grasp. Ducking his head under the strut, he swung it effortlessly through an open side door.

From a distance the plane had looked tiny, its body boxlike with square-tipped wings, rather like a bumblebee compared to the sleek aerodynamics of the 727 loading passengers over at the terminal. But in this parking field among other private aircraft, the wings clearing Joe's height by several feet. Through the open door Vicki could see a two-person bench just behind the pilot and copilot seats. The rest of the cabin had been stripped for cargo, currently a stack of boxes and crates and one empty cage.

"We may not be on a tight schedule ourselves, but air traffic control still has to coordinate our takeoff with other flights."

The liftoff just then of a two-engine Fairchild commuter jet bore out his rebuke. Vicki opened her mouth for a real apology when he said, "However, since I always play it safe, I factored in a woman's tendency to run late. You've actually got fifteen minutes if you'd like to make use of the facilities. May I remind you, there are no restrooms aboard a DHC-2."

The snapping shut of Vicki's jaw cut off any conciliatory words.

"I've flown on small planes before. And for your information, I am more punctual than any man I've worked with. It wasn't my fault—"

At his low chuckle, Vicki spun around. Though she'd have liked to defy his advice, she had too much experience with small plane flight to pass up using the facilities before finding herself in a confined cabin a few thousand meters above the ground.

And though annoying Joe would be a pleasure, she also hurried to get back before the fifteen minutes were up. It wouldn't do to repay Bill Taylor's kindness by jeopardizing their takeoff window. *It's just a few hours. I can visit with Mr. Taylor and ignore surfer boy.*

When she returned to the DHC-2, the cargo door was shut and Joe was looking pointedly at his watch. His elderly employer was still nowhere in sight. "So where's Bill Taylor? It looks like I'm not the only one running late."

He raised his eyebrows. "Bill? I thought you knew. He headed home overland the day after the memorial service. No sense two people sitting around in this smog waiting for delivery."

The glint in Joe's eyes told Vicki he'd read her dismay. Perversely, he was courteous as he helped her into the copilot's seat. Handing her a pack of mint chewing gum and an airsickness sack, he reached to start the engine.

"Planes this size don't have pressurized cabins," he informed Vicki as she fished for her seat belt. "The gum will help equalize the pressure in your ears. I'm sure you can guess what the bag is for. We don't fly above weather in this thing. We fly through it. I've got some Dramamine, too, if you need it."

Vicki forbore reminding him this wasn't her first small plane flight. Accepting his offerings, she swallowed a Dramamine, popping in a stick of chewing gum to wash it down.

His presence beside her was more of a problem. The pilot's seat was too small for his bulk, so his long limbs brushed against hers as he adjusted controls, a faint but unambiguously masculine musk warm in her nostrils. Vicki wanted to scream with the claustrophobic closeness of the cabin. She dug through her carry-on for the paperback she'd tucked in for the flight. *Why couldn't it be Michael I'm cramped with in here?*

"You're perfectly safe, you know," an ironic drawl murmured above her ear. As Vicki's head shot up, Joe patted the closest portion of the control panel. "She may be old, but the Beaver here is the best bush plane that was ever invented. This gal's seen plenty of tough country, and she'll get us through plenty more."

"I'm not worried about—," Vicki began.

Joe reached for the hand mike and in reasonable Spanish read off his flight information to the air control tower. Then the half circle of the throttle came back, and the plane taxied down the runway.

For all her boasted experience, Vicki held her breath as the wheels left the ground, chewing furiously at the gum while her eardrums popped and her stomach plunged in inverse proportion to the rising of the plane.

Since he'd delivered his directives, Joe had fallen silent to concentrate on his flying, which he seemed to be doing expertly enough in Vicki's amateur judgment, so she was able to ignore his closeness, turning her attention to the landscape falling away below.

This was the same picturesque panorama that had greeted Vicki just two weeks earlier, but as the single engine of the DHC-2 beat its way upward to bank above a ridge, disappointment snatched away Vicki's exhalation of pleasure.

She'd known what would be there. It was in her briefings. It had been there, though obscured by the altitude, when she'd arrived.

As the small plane droned low enough that Vicki could make out the individual thatched houses and cobbled streets of villages clustered in the valleys, the rising folds of mountain ridges passing so close under the wheels of the plane it seemed they should collide, Vicki saw what her first appreciative survey had missed.

Landslides wiping away entire mountainsides where deforestation was too great to anchor the topsoil. Rivers visibly polluted from the waste of mining operations and sugar cane mills on their banks. Green ridges that became sparse patches of remaining forest interspersed with cornfields and coffee plantations. Clearings where the infertile soil had been surrendered back to weeds.

It was like a hideous canker eating everywhere at what had looked from a distance like endless green waves of a forest-cloaked mountain range.

"We'll be about three hours in the air." It was the first time Joe had glanced Vicki's way since the wheels had left the ground. "That isn't as the crow flies. Bill wants me to pass over the biosphere—check out some reports we've been getting of unauthorized clearings. Will you be okay that long?"

"Just don't offer me any water." Vicki summoned up a smile as her hand went to the window. "I didn't realize it was so bad. I guess I understand Holly—and even fanatics like Dieter—a little better. I mean, people need to eat, but I didn't see this much devastation even in India."

"Yes, unfortunately, best estimates are that the last cloud forests may be gone within the decade unless something is done. That includes the natural reserves if they don't crack down on illegal invasion and poaching. Sad thing is, this kind of destruction doesn't really help the peasants either, because the deforestation and landslides are destroying so much topsoil they have to keep moving on and clearing more."

Joe banked to aim the plane between two peaks. "Of course it's not just the peasants. Mining and lumber are destroying as much as slash-and-burn. And then there's that."

Vicki spotted a flash of red tucked into a valley between the two peaks. "What is it?"

"Poppies. Heroin. The 'cocaine' of Guatemala."

Vicki knew more than she cared to about the heroin trade after a project in Myanmar, formerly Burma, hub of the famed Asian opium triangle. Too many of the children in that particular relief effort were already addicted to a cheap version of opium gum. She craned her neck for a better look. "Michael's new Environmental Protection Unit has been involved in that."

Joe's eyebrows shot up. "Really? I've seen that unit in action up around the center. They're kinda hard to miss. I just hadn't realized that was Camden's show."

Vicki thought she caught a derisive note under the neutral statement and bristled. "It isn't. The Guatemalan forces are independent of any outside interference. Michael's just been helping with some training exercises as . . . as an adviser."

"And you got that from Camden, I'm sure." Joe raised a hand in surrender. "Hey, I've got no beef with Camden. I'm all for what he's doing.

This country needs some serious environmental law enforcement—as long as it doesn't trample all over people and their lives. Especially since poppy fields and land grabs are far from the worst problems out here."

Joe pointed out a valley below where they'd glimpsed the poppies. A stream winding through it looked clear enough, but the vegetation along the banks was bleached yellow and patchy.

"The processing into heroin and cocaine is what's killing these mountains—literally. The chemical runoff into these streams is a hundred times worse than the industrial pollution."

Mollified, Vicki eyed Joe curiously as the valley dropped behind a ridge. "You sound like a tree hugger after all."

A flowered sleeve brushed Vicki's arm as Joe shrugged. "Hey, you can't be around them—or this—for long without facts and figures rubbing off. Besides, I hate waste. There's a lot of good country being ruined here. Remember me—surf, sand, and the great outdoors? You can't enjoy nature on a bunch of polluted beaches or mountain trails."

He looked over at Vicki. "And you? Holly never made a convert out of you? No, wait. You're firmly on the people-hugger side. So tell me—how did the two of you end up so different? You'd never guess you grew up in the same house."

"Holly didn't tell you about us?"

"Sure. She's hardly the reserved type, as you know. She mentioned that you two were adopted, grew up out in the country. But I'm interested in your point of view." He appeared relaxed, his hand so light on the control yoke that the plane seemed to be flying itself. His eyes met her scrutiny with wide-open guilelessness.

For someone so critical and opinionated, Joe was being uncharacteristically affable. On the other hand, maybe he too considered three hours a long time to sit in silence.

Vicki gave him a colorless version of the story she'd told Evelyn. Briefly, she considered adding what she'd learned from the missionary about her birth parents. But Holly's death had made her the target of enough sympathetic interest. She didn't need the added curiosity and probing her prior connections to Guatemala were bound to arouse.

So she let her story trail off, turning her attention back to the landscape below. They were now well into those green folds she'd seen from

Guatemala City, the thatched hamlets and fields farther apart, the few unpaved roads snaking down mountainsides.

The DHC-2 tilted in a long, lazy curve to the left before Joe broke the silence. "Sounds like you two had a rough start in life. At least you landed on your feet okay."

Vicki looked at him in surprise, then said slowly, "Yes, I guess we did. I never really thought of it that way. Maybe never even appreciated it as much as I should have. The Andrewses were very good to us."

Uncomfortable with the subject, she changed it abruptly. "And what about you? Where did you learn to fly? It sure wasn't offered with driver's ed in my school."

"My father was a pilot. My grandfather was a pilot. I probably teethed on the controls of a bush plane like this one."

"Commercial? Or peace corps?"

Joe didn't answer immediately, and from the withdrawal of his expression, Vicki had the impression he wished he'd never spoken. But turnabout was fair play.

"Well? You said you'd grown up overseas. At least that's what I assume you meant by a misspent youth. Unless you were a *really* underage surfer, you had to be tree hugger, people hugger, embassy, or multinational yourself. Which was it?"

A feather touch on the controls tilted the wings. It wasn't until the plane leveled out that Joe responded. "None of the above. My father was military."

It was the last thing Vicki would have guessed. "So that's why you were in all those countries, because you kept moving to a new base?"

"Every year. My father never could sit still." Joe grinned. "Before you say it—okay, just like his son, I suppose. Hey, I'm not complaining. I saw a lot of countries and found out I had an aptitude for languages. And extreme sports."

"You never wanted to be a soldier like your father?" Vicki asked cautiously.

Joe gave her an unreadable look. "Let's just say I learned early on that a life of rules wasn't for me."

"So you became a surfer instead." Vicki tried to keep disappointment from her tone. "Didn't your father mind?"

"Possibly. I never asked."

"And your mother? Any brothers and sisters?"

"No siblings. And I haven't seen my mother since I was a kid. One thing I guess we've got in common. She left my dad and me when I was about eight or nine. Make that nine, because we were heading overseas to Germany that time. For a while, I was sure she'd come back. But . . . she never did."

"And you never saw your mother again? That's awful. That . . . that's worse than her dying." For an instant the tough, self-reliant giant sprawled next to Vicki wavered into a vision of a small blond boy waiting at a window for his mother. "I'm so sorry."

"Don't be. I came to terms with it years ago. At the time I was sure that if I'd been a cute, well-behaved child like I bet you were—" he turned to Vicki—"instead of an exceptionally naughty little boy, she might have stayed. But I came to understand she had issues of her own. Besides, my father was a good enough parent. Don't count my lack of spit and polish against him. It wasn't a bad life for a kid. Since my father found it easier to hire a nanny in some third world country than to find a relative to put up with a rowdy and not particularly well-disciplined little boy, I ended up seeing a lot more of the world than I would have otherwise. I've got no regrets."

"Is that where you learned Spanish, then? Were you in Panama before the US pulled out?"

Again a long pause. Why was he so reluctant to talk about himself, especially after the way he'd pumped her for information? Then Joe nodded. "Sure, we did a couple of tours down there when I was a kid."

Vicki sighed. "It's funny to think you were born stateside yet grew up in countries all over the world. While I was born in Guatemala, and all I really remember is the Andrews farm."

"Born in Guatemala?"

Vicki wished she could bite back her slip. "Yes, at least that's what my adoption papers said. Don't ask me for more, because that's all I was ever told. Mom and Dad Andrews figured my birth parents must have been tourists or something since Holly was born stateside, and we were both American citizens."

All perfectly true, and thankfully, Joe didn't pursue it. Now it was

Vicki who was anxious to avoid further questions, so she focused on the new terrain flitting past under the rectangular shadow of the DHC-2's stubby wings.

The plane had been gradually rising as they talked, and there was no longer any sign of mankind's devastation. Or human habitation at all. Just fold after fold of the mountain range that made up the most remote region of the Guatemalan highlands, the steep slopes cloaked in unbroken and virgin cloud forest. It was the wildest landscape Vicki had ever seen. *And the most beautiful,* she thought.

Lush, vibrant greens held every conceivable shade from the palest yellow-green of palm fronds in the valleys to the emeralds of the hardwoods so prized by illegal loggers to the evergreen of wind-twisted pines on the higher elevations. Those infinite shadings, along with the constant movement, created the illusion of a restless sea, the ridges and valleys forming the crests and troughs of colossal green waves. Peach and lavender and orange of flowering trees added bright notes of color.

Threading through it all were glittering ribbons of water, leaping out into the white froth of waterfalls where the mountainside fell steeply, winding as lazy, brown ribbons between ridges.

And floating as wisps through the canopy, settling in thick, white pools that filled a valley, were the mists that gave the cloud forests their name.

"This is my Father's world."

The world as its Creator had designed it to be. Before His final and greatest creation had worked its devastation.

"The Sierra de las Minas Biosphere. Pretty, isn't it?" Joe commented unnecessarily. "You said you wanted to choose a location." He glanced over his shoulder to where Vicki's duffel bag had been dumped on the bench seat behind them.

The question raised a sudden panic in Vicki. How had she actually put out of her mind her original purpose for this charter? Now that it was time, she had no idea what to do. Should there be some ceremony involved? Did she just pry open one of these windows?

I can't do this! Not here. Not now. And not in this company.

"Unless you'd rather look now and come back later by land or air," Joe added quietly. "It would be no problem to take you up again. Or there's a lot of beautiful country around the center where Holly worked."

Vicki grabbed at the reprieve with relief. "Yes, yes, thank you. That would be best." She waved a hand at the windshield. "It looks so pure and untouched—like the Garden of Eden."

"The largest remaining cloud forest habitat left on the planet."

"Yeah, well, I don't suppose it'll last much longer," Vicki said lightly, but her mouth twisted as she turned her gaze back toward the beauty outside the cockpit. "Like the Garden of Eden, human beings will destroy it soon enough, and you can bet neither God nor man will lift a finger to stop it."

"You sound angry. If you feel that way, then why are you coming up here?"

Vicki met his eyes. "You know why. It certainly isn't for the hopeless—and thankless—task of saving some other country's environment."

"Holly didn't feel it was such a hopeless task," Joe said mildly, but Vicki was sure she read censure in his measured words.

She drew in an angry breath. "Holly was an optimist."

"No, Holly had faith."

Joe's response was so unexpected that Vicki stared at him.

"You look shocked. Let me guess: a beach bum can't have a strong work ethic or morals or faith."

"I'm sorry. I didn't mean to be sarcastic." Vicki gave an unconvincing laugh. "I mean, come on. You've been around the world as much as I have. Enough to knock off any illusions. I wouldn't put either you or myself in the same head-in-the-clouds, rose-tinted-glasses category as Holly."

"Is that where you put faith? Hey, don't count me in with you. If I didn't have faith that Someone far greater and better than I was in charge of this universe *and* its outcome, if I believed it was up to my puny efforts to make things come out right, I'd swim out into the ocean. Or just give up on life."

Again his tone was neutral with no suggestion of criticism, but something in his expression stung Vicki. "I haven't given up on life. I'm just . . . I believe in being a realist."

"A realist!" Now he did sound angry. "Is all that down there or a perfect sunrise over the ocean any less real than war and dirt and suffering? Oh no, it's more than that, Vicki Andrews."

The penetrating intentness of his gaze was so uncomfortable that Vicki wanted to scream at him to watch the road. Or the sky. Anywhere but her flushed face.

"No, I heard you loud and clear at the funeral. Oh, sure, you and Holly may have started off life rocky. But it sounds like you grew up in a home with plenty of faith and love. What happened to make you so different from Holly? to sour you on faith?"

Vicki was silent, her lashes dropping to shut out Joe's look. She'd given him the bare outline of her biography. How did she add in the fear and darkness? the helplessness of feeling out of control in a world so torn and hurting that any momentary resting place or pleasure was only an illusion? the dread of greeting the brightest day with the certainty disaster could be a tightrope step away?

They were flying now between two ridges that rose higher than the plane. On her side was a cliff face dappled with browns and reds and grays so close that it seemed Vicki could open a window and touch it. A waterfall shooting over the cliff had caught the sun to form a rainbow, both cascade and arch losing themselves in the mists that filled the valley below. Above the falls, a pair of condors wheeled on outspread wings. The beauty and peace made Vicki's throat ache.

"Holly doesn't—didn't—remember the before. And I always made it my business to protect her. Not that I did a very good job, evidently." Vicki's teeth closed on her lip to keep it from trembling. "It's not that I don't see the good and the beauty. I do. It's just that I see so much more ugliness and suffering and pain and killing. And that's what's winning, not the good. Whatever little bit I can do—or *anyone* can do—is only holding back the inevitable. Including all this. I just . . . I can't understand a God who could create something so unbelievably beautiful and let the bad guys win. Watch it all be destroyed."

"Yet you keep trying. You really believe you can't make a difference, but you don't head home and settle down to a comfortable life of shopping malls and cable TV. Why? I saw what you were doing with those kids. You are a total contradiction."

Again Vicki thought she detected censure. "At least I'm trying. Isn't that better than burying your head in the sand—or surf, or pretty mountains?"

"If that was meant for me," Joe answered, "you're wrong. Of course I see the pain and the ugliness. But maybe I just look at it the other way around. If the Creator of this world *is* who He says He is, if He made all this—"

They were flying past the waterfall now, the spray leaping out to grab at the wings. For a moment the rainbow enclosed the plane in its jeweled prism before falling behind them.

"—and He allows human beings to spoil it all with their own bad choices, then what value does He see in that freedom of choice? After all, God could turn us into robots with a snap of His fingers, assuming He has fingers. So what value does He see in *us* that's worth all the pain and ugliness to which we have submitted His creation? Hey, I'm just a simple guy—"

Yeah, right!

"—and I'm certainly no theologian. But I choose to believe God *is* who those military base chaplains always told me He was when I was growing up. Otherwise this world really wouldn't be worth living in. Okay, I'm not saying it isn't everything you say it is. But . . . maybe it's like a butterfly coming out of its cocoon. Maybe there's something of value in what we learn from the suffering. Something of more value than making this world easy and pretty for us, which if you believe God's real, you've got to admit He could do easily enough. Something we can't get a glimpse of because we can't see far enough ahead to understand it. But it's got to be beyond imagining to be worth all this."

With a crook of his mouth, he added dismissively, "There's a lot of time to think on a surfboard."

But Vicki wasn't fooled by his lightness. Maybe not a theologian but a philosopher certainly. It was this man, not Vicki, who was turning out to be a maze of contradictions. *I could like this guy.*

Yet an instinct she'd learned to trust, honed by too many years of sifting through lies and deception, made her wary. *Anyone can spout off nice-sounding philosophy. I know he's hiding something.*

Joe was clearly not expecting a reply from Vicki, so she made none.

He'd fallen silent again, not with his earlier caustic reticence but because he was occupied.

The plane had dropped farther between the two ridges, and the mist was actually boiling up over the windshield. Through it Vicki could see the cloud forest canopy only meters below. Not the pines that cloaked the higher slopes but broad leaves and rounded crowns, punctuated by odd, pencil-straight trees topped with a single tuff like upside-down brooms. Looping it all together were the liana vines that offered the monkeys and other canopy dwellers a transportation system the length and breadth of the cloud forest.

Vicki knew what he was looking for—the unauthorized clearings of which he'd spoken. But if there was any break in that green sea, she couldn't spot it. They rose over a ridge and into another valley, this one with only wisps of mist. Joe slowed over a hillside opening, looping a lazy circle. It was clearly an old one, already grown back over with elephant ears and saplings.

But another ridge and valley later, Joe slowed to trace another circle. This time she could see the signs of recent clearing. There were no accompanying indications of human presence, and if a crop had been planted, it was already being overtaken by weeds and wildflowers.

Joe nodded past Vicki to where a cliff face directly ahead made the valley a dead-end canyon. Above the cliff face, the mountain slope rose to a steep crest. "We're almost to the end of the biosphere here. The center is maybe ten minutes over that mountain. The village that was massacred a couple of months back was just up the ridge between here and the center. I'd say that was probably one of their clearings."

Dropping lower, he looped a wider circle that revealed half a dozen more of the abandoned clearings. The removal of the original undergrowth had allowed the clearings to be invaded by a virtual carpet of flowers. The petals were dropping, but there were enough remaining on the stalks—white, pink, lilac, red—to visualize the swathe of beauty it must have been in full bloom.

"Well, Greenpeace was probably right about one thing. It would seem the massacre has scared the local peasants from crossing the line. Okay, let's head home." Joe vigorously added power and pulled back hard on the yoke, the plane rising so steeply it felt as though they were flying up the side of the ridge in front of them.

Vicki, who hadn't yet felt the need of that airsickness bag, grabbed at her shoulder strap, her stomach flying into her throat as Joe banked right to head down the valley toward the cliff face. The only sound was the roar of the propeller. When the plane jolted, Vicki thought they'd hit an air pocket or even a bird. Then she saw the stitching of light through the material of the wing just outside the window. "Joe, there're holes in the wing!"

"Bullet holes," Joe gritted between his teeth, fighting grimly with the controls. "We've been shot! Hang on!"

This time Vicki saw the light burst of tracers shooting up from the green tangle of the hillside. The plane fell sideways so sharply that she was thrown against Joe's shoulder.

It was an eternity before the wings finally straightened out. The DHC-2 raced up the valley toward the cliff face beyond which Joe had promised sanctuary. Vicki could see no other damage to the plane as she fell back into her seat. They had reached the cliff face now and were rising steeply to clear the ridge above. But even as she let out the breath she was holding, she heard the *throp-throp* of another helicopter.

The propellers rose first above the ridge, then the long, sleek gray-green shape of the military helicopter. A Vietnam-era Huey, Vicki recognized from a thousand news shows and movies. Donated as war surplus by the US to allies around the world. The side was open, and there was no blinking away the machine gun staring at them through the doorway.

CHAPTER SEVENTEEN

This time Vicki could hear the *rat-tat-tat* of rapid gunfire as well as see the flicker fire of tracers streaking across their flight path. Was she screaming, or was Joe? Or maybe both.

Now Vicki was able to judge the fluency of Joe's Spanish as he grabbed the mike. "*¡Socorro! ¡Socorro!* Don't shoot. We're unarmed. We're civilians. Call numbers N62513. Don't shoot!"

For an endless moment Vicki was sure they hadn't heard or had chosen to ignore Joe's call. Banking, the Huey took up a flanking position beyond Joe's window. Looking past him, Vicki could make out at least half a dozen men in khaki uniforms inside with that huge, bolted-down machine gun.

Vicki closed her eyes as the gun barrel swiveled toward the DHC-2's cockpit. When she thrust away cowardice to force them open again, it wasn't to machine-gun fire but the arm gestures of a uniform crouched in the open door of the Huey. The gist crackled over the radio in Spanish. If some of the terminology was unfamiliar to Vicki, she had no problem translating their general meaning: "Follow us and land where we tell you, or we'll blow you to bits."

Then they were over the ridge. All she saw was the asphalt runway rushing up to meet them. Beyond the airfield and sweeping up into the mountains was uncleared cloud forest that marked the beginning of the biosphere. Bordering one side of the runway was a high chain-link fence, topped with barbed wire and broken by guard towers and a wide gate. A collection of army trucks, Jeeps, and other vehicles lined the edge of a packed-earth parade ground.

Marking the far end of the runway was an open-sided hangar and a small air control tower. Outside the hangar a second Huey sat alongside a DC-3 military cargo plane.

As the DHC-2's wheels touched the ground, running figures in army fatigues boiled out of the control tower and hangar. Through the fence, Vicki could see an army Jeep and a pickup speeding from the parade ground, guards hurrying to open the gate.

The most bizarre sight to Vicki was a huge pair of army boots, as broad as the gate and taller than the base wall, topped with an equally oversize army helmet, both painted in camouflage greens and olives. It was the most blatant advertisement of the central status of the military she had yet seen in Guatemala.

"We're landing at the military base?" Vicki demanded. "Where's the airport?"

"This *is* the airport." Joe's expert hand on the throttle slowed the plane to a taxiing speed. As he pulled in next to the DC-3, their helicopter escort settled to rest on the opposite side, the wind of the propellers rocking the lighter DHC-2.

Men in khaki uniforms spilled out of the Huey, the automatic rifles unslung in their hands considerably smaller than the Huey's machine gun but no less intimidating.

"The center pays a ridiculous rent to park their plane here. What kind of hornet's nest we've stumbled into, I can't imagine. But just sit tight and let me do the talking. A simple explanation should clear this up." Joe's tone was even and cool, but the clenching of his fist as he reached to unbuckle his seat belt gave away his anger.

At the sharp tap of a rifle butt on the fuselage, he opened the cockpit door and climbed out, hands outspread.

A moment later Vicki's door was yanked open. A hand grabbed at her forearm as she clambered out. She miscalculated the short jump, landing hard on her knees.

By the time she'd scrambled up, brushing off her jeans, Joe was being driven around to her side of the plane. He didn't look at all cowed by the rifle barrels directed at him. Maybe it helped to be head and shoulders above your captors. Vicki's guard was not only double her body mass but standing close enough to overpower her with the rankness of sweat and body odor.

"Don't touch that!" Joe barked at two men in army fatigues who had opened the plane's cabin door and were wrestling out a cargo crate. "Those are medications belonging to the wildlife center. If any are broken, you will be held personally responsible."

Hastily, but carefully, the pair lowered the crate.

Joe turned to the nearest khaki uniform, whom Vicki recognized as the one whose gestures had directed them to land. He was tall for a Guatemalan, with a strong European infusion into his gene pool, curly hair more brown than black and a beard that bore a striking resemblance to a younger Castro.

"What is the meaning of this unprovoked attack?" Joe demanded in Spanish, motioning toward the bullet holes stitched across the wing overhead. "This is a private aircraft belonging to the Wildlife Rescue Center and authorized to land at this airstrip. We informed your radio control of our arrival."

"You lie!" the man who looked like Castro returned. "I know the center aircraft and its pilot. Where is Ro-hed?" It took a moment for Vicki to realize he was referring to Roger, Holly's British WRC colleague, whom Joe had replaced. "As to an attack, do not think you can escape blame for this. Our radar caught your evasive maneuvers. We saw you trying to flee. What are you transporting? Narcotics?"

"We weren't trying to flee. We were trying to keep from being shot down."

At their leader's gesture, the two men who'd lifted down the crate used rifle butts to smash in the lid.

"Hey!" Joe took a step forward, then as rifle barrels came up, relaxed, his hands spreading wide. "Please, there is clearly a misunderstanding. Yes, you are right; this is not the same aircraft we had stationed here before. We just purchased a new one. The papers have been filed with your *comandante*. And I am the pilot now. Roger returned to his own country. Again, you have only to check with your headquarters. I have flown in and out of here several times over the last weeks."

"I was not present then," the man said arrogantly, as though that negated anything Joe had said.

"Coronel." A man in army fatigues held up a vial he'd lifted from the crate. "It is true this contains medicines. The label says this is an *antibiótico*."

"It could be a trick to disguise *narcóticos*," the colonel snapped back. "Anything can be printed on a label."

"Why would anyone smuggle drugs into here?" Vicki had been silent till now, the adrenaline jolt of their forced landing leaving her shaking and nauseated.

Though the sun was high overhead, a brisk wind blew across the mountain plateau, so heavy with moisture that Vicki could taste it. It was an unpleasant reminder of how much she disliked mountains. And soldiers. The running uniforms, dozens of them converging. The harsh shouts and hard dark faces. The black boots pounding on the asphalt. The smell of burning.

Wait a minute; there was no burning.

Vicki took deep breaths to blink the dizziness away. It had to be the altitude that was making her heart pound so hard. "I thought people tried to smuggle drugs *out* of these mountains, not in," she got out between chattering teeth. "You're not making any sense. Just let us go!"

Vicki caught Joe's warning glance, saw it shift to concern.

The colonel's expression bristled with anger. "That remains to be decided. What makes sense is that you are both under arrest." He snapped his fingers at a knot of soldiers who had just arrived from the direction of the hangar. "You—secure the plane. And you—escort the prisoners to headquarters."

A roaring filled Vicki's head as fingers tightened on her upper arm. The dark faces crowding in above her seemed oddly distant and hazy, her breath coming fast and shallow. She was going to faint or throw up on the colonel's polished black boots.

The blare of a horn scattered the soldiers. As the grip on Vicki's arm dropped away, the army Jeep she'd seen from the air slammed to a stop, the pickup pulling up behind it.

A dozen uniformed men were crowded into the Jeep, squeezed into seats, squatting on the floor, perched on the tailgate. Vicki spotted the lighter head and taller frame of the man seated beside the driver. She could have wept with relief as he jumped to the ground and strode in their direction.

"Michael, what are you doing here?"

"Hello, Vicki." He reached her and smiled. "I told you I'd be shuffling my training schedule around, though I hadn't expected the pleasure of seeing you this soon." He stopped to exchange a brief handclasp with their captor. "Coronel Alpiro. So you made it back. And I see you've brought a couple of my countrymen with you."

Michael turned back to Vicki. "May I introduce Ramon Alpiro, commander of the new UPN and my local liaison for this training program."

"UPN . . . ? But . . . I thought they were soldiers." Even as her head whirled, Vicki realized there were indeed two distinct uniforms facing her: the camouflage fatigues that had raced toward them from the hangar and the solid khaki of the helicopter contingent. Only now did Vicki take in the *UPN* across upper sleeve and lapel, the khaki beret replacing army caps. Michael's Jeep companions wore the same uniform.

"Yes, well, you're partly right. The local military command is working closely with UPN. Pooling resources is the only real way to accomplish this mission." Michael's hand shot out to steady Vicki as she swayed. "Are you okay?"

"Okay? Of course she's not okay." Shaking off restraining hands, Joe took a step forward that put him face-to-face with Michael. "Can't you see you've scared the poor kid half to death? Your goons could have killed us. Tell me, is shooting down civilian aircraft always part of your training exercises?"

"Shooting?" Michael glanced at the wing damage above his head, and the smile abruptly left his face and eyes. "What are you talking about?"

"I'm talking about the fact that we could have been killed," Joe said icily. "In fact, it's a miracle nothing vital was hit."

The two men had spoken in English, and Vicki shifted to the same as she spoke up. "He's right, Michael. Someone fired on us from the jungle.

And then these . . . these police, soldiers, whatever—" her voice shook as she indicated the helicopter crew—"arrested us."

"I can assure you it wasn't *my* 'goons' who did the shooting. To start with, these people aren't my men. As Americans, we are here only in an advisory capacity." When Joe's expression didn't lose one degree of skepticism, Michael went on shortly. "In any case, all ground personnel involved in the training exercise were back over an hour ago, as half the base can attest. Colonel Alpiro and the helo unit just happened to be making a final surveillance sweep of the biosphere when they radioed that a suspicious aircraft was buzzing in a restricted zone and trying to evade pursuit."

"Buzzing! Evading! What I was trying to evade was being shot out of the air and not just by ground fire. Your colonel friend there is as trigger-happy as whoever was on the ground."

"And for that I really have to apologize, Joe."

Vicki spun around at the interruption. Only when she saw Bill did she realize that the pickup behind the Jeep wasn't the army green of the Jeep but a lighter shade, and the WRC sponsor was the driver.

He hurried over. "I am so sorry! I'd expected to be on the airstrip to meet you, but my meeting with the base commander ran late. When word came there was trouble with an aircraft, I was afraid it was you. I filed the appropriate paperwork, but you'd think I've been here long enough not to count on the changes getting down to people on the ground. Or in this case, air traffic control. Ms. Andrews, please accept my apology for this unfortunate welcome to our little community. I hope you won't consider it indicative of what you're going to encounter here. It isn't."

"Please don't blame yourself, Mr. Taylor." Michael turned and smiled at Bill. "It was just an unfortunate mix-up. No one was hurt, so all's well that ends well."

"That's fine and grand, but have we forgotten the little matter of who shot at us? And that we're currently under arrest?" Joe reminded in a hard voice. A dozen weapons were still leveled at him, the dark eyes above them as intent on the big American as so many mice watching a cat. "Camden, you want to tell your goons to at least point their toys elsewhere?"

Michael narrowed his eyes but said calmly, "You can be assured the situation will be thoroughly investigated. Your shooter was probably some poacher worried you'd caught sight of them." Turning to the UPN commander, he switched back to Spanish. "Coronel, let me congratulate you and your men for an excellent job. You executed the operation precisely as we rehearsed. This has been a profitable additional training exercise for your unit. But as you can see, there has been a misunderstanding in detaining these two."

Colonel Alpiro looked from Michael to his captives. "Then it is done." Snapping his fingers, he shouted an order Vicki didn't catch but which had the effect of lowering every weapon.

And with that it was over. Within moments men who'd been pointing lethal weapons at them were cheerfully transferring crates from the DHC-2 to the back of Bill's pickup, the rest drifting back to their interrupted duties. The three American men and the colonel, joined now by the helicopter pilot, were in a huddle under the plane's wing, inspecting the damage.

Only Vicki seemed to be still shaken by the incident. Was violence so much a part of these guys' lives that it could just be shrugged off? She wandered away. This at least brought heads up, but when Vicki pointed toward the air control tower and mouthed *baño*, they turned instantly back to their discussion.

A guard inside the control tower directed Vicki to a restroom that was far from clean but at least functional.

When she emerged, she turned into an alley running between the hangar and tower. The alley dead-ended in a narrow strip of trimmed vegetation that separated the runway from the uncleared rain forest beyond.

An armed sentry watched Vicki as she stepped out into the open, but he made no move to interfere.

In front of her reared a tangle of trees and vines and undergrowth, dark and alien and chill. The brisk wind had thickened to a mist that was not quite fog or rain but humid enough to bead on Vicki's face and bare arms. She wrapped her arms tightly around herself to control her shivering.

I shouldn't have come. Vicki knew she was behaving badly. Yes, it had been a frightening few minutes. But she'd been in tight corners before, and it was over now. So why was her heart still racing, her stomach roiling with nausea?

She'd had a similar reaction once in Sri Lanka when their aid convoy was stopped on a mountain pass by government troops. The altitude, the cold, wet, *green* rain forest smell, and the shouting soldiers had precipitated a panic that startled and shamed Vicki, since for all their sternness, the government troops had shown the aid workers nothing but courtesy.

But this was worse—the pounding boots so terrifying, the smell of smoke so real, the tangle of vegetation so dark and cold, it was as though Vicki were fighting her way out of some forgotten nightmare instead of what actually lay around her.

Maybe I am.

Vicki let her hands slide slowly from the cold flesh of her upper arms. Maybe that was exactly what she was experiencing. Hadn't Evelyn said her birth parents had taken Vicki and Holly to live in a highland Mayan village? Probably in surroundings much like these. Maybe even in these same mountains.

And somewhere in this mountain range her birth parents had died. According to that death report, a local army unit had brought the bodies in to the embassy. Had they brought two surviving children as well? Was it possible Vicki's unreasoning distaste for mountains and forest that so annoyed Holly, the panicky racing of her heart every time she saw an army uniform, the images of running boots and leaping flames that matched no conscious remembrance were no imagination but real happenings? Happenings traumatic enough to impact Vicki, even while remaining buried in the fog of her past, but not a much younger Holly?

If only I could remember. Why can't I remember?

Well, Vicki couldn't change a past she couldn't even remember. But she could do something about the present.

A worn footpath leading across the perimeter strip into the rain forest indicated Vicki wasn't the first to take this shortcut between the hangar and the tower.

Crossing the open ground quickly, Vicki allowed the underbrush to close around her. Here she could no longer see the runway or army base, and ahead the path curved to disappear into the vegetation, leaving her alone in a world of green. Standing still, Vicki quieted the panic welling up in her. *Let go of the past. Let go of the prejudices. Just look at it objectively, the way it really is.*

Vicki turned a slow circle. Next to the path arched the perfect curve of a giant fern, the droplets of moisture that beaded its feathery lace catching the light to refract the jeweled spectrum of a rainbow. A wisp of fog coiled through pines and broad-leaved hardwoods, and above her the mist had now become the lightest of rain. *Chipi-chipi.* The word came to Vicki from nowhere. The constant drizzle that kept the cloud forest so green.

How did I know that?

Just ahead a stream bubbled across the path to spill down an embankment. The stepping stones across the stream looked slippery with moss, so Vicki went no farther. She listened instead to a noisy scolding above her. Tilting her head back, she glimpsed a wrinkled furry face among the tangle of vines and leaves. It was joined briefly by another larger one before both disappeared. A baby howler monkey and its mother. Among the trees Vicki caught a flash of bright feathers. The fabled quetzal bird? And here beyond reach of the airport's diesel fumes, the moist scent of the vegetation was fragrant and suddenly—astonishingly—familiar.

I've been here before. At least in these mountains. And it isn't ugly and dark. It's so beautiful. No wonder Holly loved it. No wonder my father wanted to come here.

Vicki brushed back the lilac and cream and orange velvet of a cascade of orchids curling down from a tree branch. *This really was my father's world. I remember now. I remember singing that song. I was playing. I was . . . I was happy. And then . . . ?*

The sudden pang of joy evaporated as Vicki strained to remember, the beauty of her surroundings dimming. Her heart began to race again.

Then what happened?

CHAPTER EIGHTEEN

"Vicki?"

Vicki whirled around, her hand going to her throat. She'd been so lost in another world it was as though the voice—masculine, sharp, and American—were calling to her from across the years.

Then Vicki reoriented herself to the present. She'd been gone longer than she'd planned, and someone had come looking for her. She realized that her face was wet, though she didn't remember crying. Hastily, she mopped at her face as she heard footsteps approaching. What kind of a wreck must she look? *Get a grip.*

"There you are." Bill stepped around a tree trunk into the opening on the path. "I was concerned you were lost. We're ready to move out." His eyes darkened as he took in Vicki's damp face. "Are you all right? You weren't hurt back there?"

"No, I'm fine, really. Maybe a little shaken up." Bill still looked worried, so Vicki went on hurriedly, indicating her surroundings. "It's just . . . it's all so beautiful, it . . . it got to me. The sounds. The smells. It brought back memories I didn't even know I had."

"Memories?" Bill said. "Then you've been here before?"

"Apparently." Vicki hastily downplayed her slip. "Not necessarily here. But somewhere in these mountains. Close enough this seems very familiar. Though I would have been so young at the time, I'm not sure what's real and what's imagination."

At his expression, Vicki knew she'd have to explain fully. "I was born here in Guatemala. My birth father was an American photojournalist working here, and my parents were killed somewhere in these mountains. Or so I've been told. But—" her gaze drifted back around the tangle of trees, ferns, and vines, the orchids and the rush of water across the path—"something in all this sure strikes a chord."

"Your parents were Jeff and Victoria Craig?" Bill's expression went as blank as his tone but not before she glimpsed shock. "The American couple killed up here twenty years back?"

"You knew them?"

"I knew of them, certainly. Any expat with contacts in Guatemala at the time knew the case. Is that why you're here? And is that why you're pursuing Holly's death so hard? Because you think there's a connection?"

It was a thought that had never even occurred to Vicki. "No, not at all. Holly didn't even know about it. I . . . I just found out myself when I came down here."

She explained briefly and reluctantly. "It really is just a coincidence. Strange though, isn't it? Do you think it's possible I was up in these very mountains?"

"Anything's possible," Bill said flatly. "Though one of these valleys is much like another. Now, are you done here? We do need to move out."

Vicki caught his glance at his watch. "I'm sorry for holding you up."

She'd been lost in the past for longer than she'd thought. Except for a handful of sentries, the airstrip was deserted when they emerged into the open, the cargo loaded neatly into the pickup and tied down under a tarp. Vicki looked around for Joe and Michael. She should thank Joe, who for all the cool censure that seemed to accompany every exchange between them, had at least delivered her—and the plane—here in one piece.

As for Michael, that he'd so quickly rearranged his own schedule proved again that he really was pursuing Holly's death. She would like to express her appreciation—and find out if there was any news.

"Joe asked me to make his apologies for the rough landing," Bill said.

"Alpiro took him and Camden back up in the helo to see if Joe could pinpoint the exact ground area from which you were shot. He said to let you know your things are in the backseat. Camden asked me to make his excuses as well. He expects to catch up with you over at the center today if this investigation into the shooting moves quickly. If not, tomorrow."

So she hadn't just been forgotten. The warmth of that chased away the last chill and unease so that Vicki could take in the last leg of her trip with interest. This was over a dirt road so rutted and uneven it clearly carried more pedestrian and cart traffic than motor vehicles. At first the track followed the airstrip, where Vicki spotted a group of Mayan women sweeping for debris with hand-bound straw brooms. Their male counterparts chopped brush along the runway and base perimeter. Armed guards—army, not UPN, by their fatigues—stood watch over their labor.

Then the tarmac gave way to small plots of corn and beans and larger plantings that were coffee bushes. Here, too, Mayan highlanders labored with wooden hoes and machetes. The pickup passed a woman carrying firewood on her back, a boy prodding a donkey piled high with bundles.

"This plateau is actually within the Sierra de las Minas Biosphere." Bill eased his cargo over hillocks of dried mud so carefully that Vicki could have walked faster. "As you can see, it's suffered its share of human impact. But this at least is the last human settlement before what we call the nuclear reserve, one reason WRC chose to locate here."

Bill indicated the steep, green folds over which the DHC-2 had dropped. Below on the plateau, the human impact was more visible as the road became the main street of a village. Under the shade of citrus trees and banana palms, Mayan women pounded corn into flour, tended cook fires, scrubbed clothing in metal basins. Toddlers scampered around the beaten-earth yards while older children looked up with solemn, dark eyes as the pickup jolted by.

It was all a familiar scene to Vicki. The life of a rural village in any number of the developing world cultures.

What was not familiar was the impression of an armed camp. There had been soldiers overseeing work crews among the coffee plantings. The pickup had already passed through two military checkpoints, and even in the center of the village there were men patrolling and doing sentry duty on the steps of a squat cathedral with a single bell tower.

"The lake down there is Izabal, the largest freshwater body in Guatemala. This town is called Verapaz." Bill braked to avoid a speeding army Jeep. "Named and built by the army, as you may have guessed, as part of their model village program."

He expanded. "The model village, or 'strategic hamlet' as it was also called, was part of the army's rural pacification program during the civil war. A highly effective one too. Build a town center outside an army base. Then bring the survivors in from all the farms and destroyed villages around and give them a home."

"That seems kind," Vicki said doubtfully. "I guess you hear so much about army abuse, but you never really hear of anything good they might have done."

"The reconstruction money came from international aid organizations. From the army's point of view, it's just plain smart. Move a hostile population to where you can keep an eye on them and have a convenient workforce as well. Beans and bullets, the program was called. The concept was if you cooperated, you got food and shelter. If not, that was the bullet part."

Vicki took another look at the cathedral. Only now did she take in a crack that ran down the bell tower, then in a jagged diagonal across the front of the building. Closer scrutiny revealed other cracks and patches of missing facade that had been painted over. There was no bell.

Bill's glance took in her interest. "The church foundation shifted somewhat after construction. The army blames an earthquake. The locals mutter about the hired architect, who retired to the capital's Zone 10 after his involvement in the reconstruction efforts."

A third roadblock marked the end of the village, a soldier running forward to raise the bar as he recognized Bill's pickup.

Vicki looked back to see the bar drop back into place. "It doesn't look like that big of a town."

"Yeah, well," Bill said dryly, "there weren't a lot of survivors."

It was the opening Vicki had been looking for. "Yes, I've been meaning to ask about that. Why is everything so militarized here? Not just back then but now? You'd think they were preparing for an invasion, except they're up here in the middle of nowhere. And that new Environmental Protection Unit—I don't really see much difference between them and the army."

As though to punctuate her statement, a Huey roared overhead, flying in low toward the army base. Joe and Michael heading back? It conjured up an unpleasant image of that deadly machine gun facing her from the open Huey door.

"I mean, isn't this a lot of overkill for patrolling a national forest? Whatever happened to some nice park rangers with a guide book?"

"You're still thinking like an American," Bill said. "In Guatemala the army's main purpose has always been maintaining internal law and security, functions that belong to the police back home. In fact, the police have traditionally been the eyes and ears and hands of the military. As to why here, the Guatemalan army has considered itself at war within its own borders for at least the last fifty years. These mountains were a hotbed of guerrilla fighting."

Michael had said as much. With some hesitation Vicki asked, "Is it true that the Americans put the military into power here and armed and trained them all these years? I just don't get why."

When no response came, Vicki turned her head.

Bill looked troubled, his gnarled hands tight on the steering wheel, his eyes fixed straight ahead as though staring into some distant past. The road made a turn that dropped the roadblock out of sight before he let out a sigh. "You've got to understand it's easy to look back and point fingers. At the time it wasn't quite so black and white. Not even with Arbenz."

"You were here with Arbenz?" Vicki studied him curiously. Had the elderly expatriate maybe been in the military? "But that was more than fifty years ago."

"I was new and young, to be sure. The point is, back then all we saw was a beautiful country, full of opportunities—and available land.

"Even the United Fruit Company—it's popular now to make them the scapegoat. But from their point of view, they were helping build a modern nation. Oh yes, they were making huge profits for themselves. But they also built schools and clinics and roads and at least offered better treatment and wages than the local aristocracy."

"That may be, but what about human rights and working conditions? And the Mayans—all those massacres and *desaparecidos* I keep hearing about? Was that all an exaggeration?"

"No. That was . . . regrettable. But you can't grow an economy without stability. And there was a lot of instability. Let me tell you, there were plenty of ordinary, decent-minded people—including expats—who considered army control, iron-fisted though it might be, an acceptable exchange for anarchy."

Bill slowed to ease through a pothole before he admitted, "Maybe there was a certain amount of fear involved too. At least half the population here is Mayan, much of the rest Ladino and plenty of them as destitute as the Mayans. Then you have a small, largely European upper class that actually owns most of the wealth. And the expats. I think there's always been a fear here that the Mayans would rise up someday and demand their share. Which is what happened with the guerrilla insurgency. Unfortunately, when people are afraid of losing their way of life, they tend to overreact and lash out. The army had a saying: 'Drain the sea, and the fish will die.' The sea was the Mayans. The idea was that by destroying the Mayan way of life, the guerrillas would have no support to keep them going.

"Believe me, we—the Americans, that is—didn't sanction excesses on either side down here. And we *did* encourage democratic reform. But the ruling classes just weren't ready for those kinds of changes. And they happened to be our staunchest allies in the Cold War, not just in Guatemala but across the region. The US reasoning was that whatever our disagreements with their government policies, the war on socialism took priority. Once that was won, we could go back and touch on some of the other issues. Which of course is what we're doing now. Programs like Camden's are a good example."

"The Environmental Protection Unit, you mean."

The conversation had come full circle to Vicki's original question. The dirt track too had curved back toward the steep slopes of the ridge that backed the plateau. On either side stretched neat rows of coffee bushes, and up a knoll to the left was a solitary one-story house with a veranda running around it. Against the red tiles of the roof, Vicki spotted the metallic gleam of a satellite dish.

Straight ahead the road ran right into the tall trunks and tangled green crowns of the cloud forest rising unbroken from the plateau up the mountainside to disappear into a mist that had settled thick now over the mountain crest.

Bill nodded in that direction. "Exactly. One thing the war did was clear out the villages from those mountains, making it a whole lot easier to turn it into a nature reserve. But that still leaves a few million land-hungry peasants, and whether it's Camden's UPN or the local army battalion or both working together, it's going to take an iron hand to keep them out of the remaining rain forest. It may seem harsh to outsiders, but there is no other way if any of this is going to be left in another ten years."

Maybe Bill was right. There was no black and white here, just so many complex shades of gray that Vicki certainly couldn't sort them out. Then a thought struck her. "The massacre up here . . . You don't think—?"

"Whoa!" Bill lifted a cautionary hand from the steering wheel. "Whatever you think of our local authorities, I can assure you they are long past murdering an entire village just because they'd squatted on restricted land. There *are* easier ways to run them out."

"Then who?"

"Who knows? It could be anyone. Raiding bandits. A drug deal gone bad. A land dispute. Even a faction of the villagers themselves. That's just the point. Too many of the combatants on both sides have never given up their arms—or the vigilante mentality." He shook his head sadly. "No, I'm afraid it's going to take a lot more than a few signed pieces of paper before the first reaction to a problem in Guatemala isn't to pick up a weapon."

"So does protecting the rain forest include pointing guns at coffee pickers? Or is it usual to have soldiers patrolling fields here?"

Bill chuckled. "With the security situation as it is, I've got the occasional armed guard on my land too. But the fields you're talking about belong to the army base. Part of their appropriation when they built up here. Planting the extra land in coffee helps subsidize the base—and the officers' salaries."

"Your land. That's right. Holly said you had a coffee plantation here."

Only now did Vicki take in that the coffee plantings on either side of the road were no longer open fields but neatly enclosed behind barbed wire. She saw the gate to her left before the pickup drew up to it. Just inside the gate stood a guard shack, and from it a gravel driveway ran up to the red-tiled house on the knoll.

A tall Ladino with tight curls denoting some African ancestry and a shotgun over his shoulder stepped out to open the gate, but Bill rolled down his window to shake his head. "I have a delivery for *el centro*. I'll be back shortly."

"Then that's your house up there?" Vicki asked as Bill pulled back out onto the dirt track. Ahead on the opposite side of the track, she spied another shotgun. Unlike the army patrols, this security guard faced his weapon outward to watch the road and fence line.

"That's right; and the center is just ahead through there." Bill motioned to the wall of uncleared forest only a few hundred meters ahead. "An easy walking distance, if you get tired of nature and all those German volunteers. We can offer quiet and solitude, something you'll find is at a high premium over there. Or to borrow some reading material. You won't find much at the center."

Vicki looked back at the small, whitewashed house sitting alone on its knoll and wondered again about its landlord. "It looks . . . isolated. It must have been lonely living here all those years before the center and modern communications. And dangerous too with the guerrillas and everything. You sure have a lot more courage than I'll ever have."

Bill's eyes crinkled into a smile as he glanced over at Vicki. "I can see I've given you the wrong impression. I didn't move here until after the peace accords, when the army started selling off some of the land it had acquired during the war. Dirt cheap too. It was a good investment, not courage."

"Then you weren't actually up in these mountains when my—when Jeff Craig was killed?" It wasn't a question Vicki had intended asking.

"I've done business in and out of Guatemala since then," Bill said. "This place gets under your skin, especially these mountains. I was recently retired when the land sale came along—and bored. The road and airstrip had made the area accessible to market. The army base guaranteed security. So I grabbed at the opportunity. Bought myself a

Cessna, built that house, and hired the villagers to clear the land for coffee. In fact, you can blame me for most of the deforestation in this zone, I'm afraid. It was my success that prompted the base commanders to turn their remaining landholdings to profit. Of course, the area wasn't part of a reserve at the time. Truth is, there was so much wilderness, we never thought it might one day run out."

Vicki caught the regret in Bill's tone as he looked out across the neat rows of coffee bushes. "But you donated the center. You pushed for the biosphere."

"Yes, I did that much. I guess I figured it was one way to make atonement."

He hadn't specified what business had brought him to Guatemala so often. Did he have a family here? Had he ever encountered Vicki's birth parents in person? The investigator in Vicki had a dozen more questions. But the dirt track was now leaving the open fields and entering a tunnel of green that was the uncleared cloud forest Bill had indicated. Around a curve and through a tangle of leaves, Vicki glimpsed stained-wood construction that must be the center.

Bill stopped the pickup and cut the engine. He turned to look at Vicki, and his deeply etched features were now grave. "Just one thing before we get to camp. May I suggest you consider keeping your relationship to Jeff Craig to yourself? At least as long as you're at the center."

CHAPTER NINETEEN

Vicki stared at Bill. "Why?"

She had the impression Bill discarded his first thought before he said carefully, "Memories run long, and there are a lot of scabbed-over wounds you're not aware of. Embers of hate and revenge simmering under the surface of these so-called peace accords that wouldn't take much to blaze into a forest fire. I know these people—how they think. The assumption will be that you're here to open those wounds and dig up those embers. If that isn't your intention, I can promise you'll get a lot further in your present mission if you let the past stay buried."

He had a point. Vicki had endured enough explosions already in her pursuit of truth in Holly's death. Sidetracking twenty years into the past would only complicate her mission. She nodded. "I can do that. It isn't as though it's relevant to why I'm here."

"Why you're here—yes." Bill leaned over to turn the key in the ignition. "You're a nice person, Vicki, as Holly was. And you deserve better than maybe you've experienced in your life so far. If you don't find the answers you're looking for, I hope you will find some measure of peace and solace in these mountains—as I have."

The remaining meters of track dead-ended in a gravel cul-de-sac. A rude wooden sign announced *Centro de Rescate.*

Bill pulled up at the door of a two-story building with large screen windows. Straight ahead was a large, open-sided thatched shelter, where a number of volunteers could be seen chatting around plastic tables, typing on computers, writing in journals. Vicki's throat tightened as she looked around. So this had been her sister's last home.

Vicki welcomed the distraction when a group of volunteers erupted into the open, laughing and chattering in German. As they clustered around the pickup, tugging knots loose and lifting the tarp free, Vicki spotted the Australian team leader, Alison.

She rushed toward the pickup. "I'm so glad you're here, Vicki. Now I can get back to town. Here, let me make some introductions."

The German team was a boisterous university-age group of men and women whose English ranged from excellent to barely intelligible.

A Ladino couple appeared briefly before disappearing inside with Bill.

"Rosario and Beatriz are the center administrators. The two of them and Cesar, our veterinary resident—" Alison indicated a slight young man with solemn, dark features—"speak only Spanish. And of course the Germans don't. So you'll need to translate to English. Good news: they'll be here only another week. Bad news: we've got no other teams on the horizon, so that'll leave a lot more chores for you once they're gone. *If* you decide to stick around."

Alison waved to the resident. "Cesar, would you please show Vicki around? I'd better get these stores checked into the dispensary before any of your medical supplies get smashed."

Cesar wore Western-style shirt and pants but looked more Mayan than Ladino. He obediently gestured for Vicki to follow him and introduced her to the last on-site staff member. A middle-aged Mayan woman was patting out tortillas in a smaller open-sided structure behind the communal shelter.

Here the roof overhead was tin instead of thatch, for food hygiene, Vicki guessed. Waist-high brick walls kept out chickens and a rooting pig, but Cesar shooed a spider monkey off a worktable as he exchanged a few phrases in the local Mayan dialect. The woman snatched browned tortillas from a hot plate and added fresh ones before offering Vicki a dignified nod. Behind her two huge metal pots steamed on a low gas grill.

"Maria is a very good cook," Cesar assured Vicki. "She understands Spanish well enough, though she prefers not to speak it."

Neat gravel paths edged with white-painted rocks connected buildings and the animal enclosures. Scattered in small clearings among the trees, these were mostly cages built up on concrete slabs. The strong musk of animal fur and urine explained why they'd been placed out of sight—and scent—of the main living quarters. Signs on the cages identified howler and spider monkeys, a raccoonlike coatimundi, ocelots, and pumas. Two fenced enclosures held animals that could be trusted not to climb out. Mountain deer no larger than a fawn stateside. Pig-size animals identified as peccaries. A juvenile tapir with the thick, black thread of sutures across one brown flank.

The animals themselves were as boisterous as the volunteers, the raucous screeching of monkeys and macaws and toucans so unrelenting that Vicki understood Bill's offer of quiet.

"They are not always this noisy," Cesar told Vicki solemnly. Did the young resident ever smile? "They are excited by the arrival of the truck."

Most of the animals had been brought into the rescue center by concerned citizens, the young veterinarian explained, though some were seized by authorities from illegal traffickers. An assortment of splints and bandages explained why each was here. But they looked content enough, their cages clean despite the strong odors, water and food in ample supply. All in all, a testimonial to the hard work of the volunteer team and Cesar himself.

And Holly, of course. This quiet young man must have been Holly's closest working colleague. Definitely someone on Vicki's interrogation list.

The gravel path continued past a row of storage sheds, and from somewhere not too far away, a rush of running water began to drown out the noise of animals. Following close on Cesar's heels, Vicki almost ran into him when he stopped abruptly. Stepping back, Vicki caught her breath in a sharp inhale of delight. They had emerged onto a rock outcropping, and for the first time she could see more than a tangle of vegetation because the mountainside dropped steeply away. The swaying carpet below their feet was actually the tops of oaks and pines and firs.

Around them, the *chipi-chipi* still dripped from every leaf and frond, the mountain heights still gray with mist. But straight ahead over the vast, blue expanse of Lake Izabal, sunlight sparkled off dancing waves, reflected white from spread sails. To Vicki's left, the rush of water they'd been hearing had become a stream tumbling merrily over a rock face to splash with a churning of foam into a pool some twenty meters below them.

"El Pozo Azul." At Cesar's gesture Vicki saw the white stones edging the path wind their way down the side of the outcropping to the pool. "You may bathe here if you wish."

Vicki scrambled down the incline. The pool was no more than ten meters across. At the far end, the water bubbled through a pileup of boulders to spill down the mountainside toward Lake Izabal. Flat stones had been pressed into the soft earth where the path ended to make a shelf from which bathers could step into the water. Down here the view of the lake was again hidden by vegetation. But the pool nestled like an aquamarine in its setting of ferns and flowering bushes and orchids, and despite the milky froth of the cascade, the water was clear enough to make out rocks on the bottom.

Dipping her fingers into the pool, Vicki was surprised to find the water warm, the mist rising from it not just the waterfall's churning but steam. The volcanic activity that had forged this mountain chain still simmered somewhere deep under the surface. The height of the rock face shut off any glimpse of the center, so she might have been alone in an unspoiled paradise.

Not quite alone. Nor a paradise.

Vicki straightened to see Cesar making his way down the path. She waited until his feet touched the stone shelf before asking abruptly, "You worked with Señorita Holly Andrews, didn't you?"

"Yes, we worked together." Cesar's gaze slid sideways toward Vicki as he added hesitantly, "They say you are her sister. Is this true?"

"Yes."

"And that she is dead?"

"Yes."

"I am very sorry. I hoped . . . I could not believe it was true." Vicki was startled to see moisture in his black eyes. "She was a good person and a good veterinarian—very passionate about the animals. I learned more from her than in all my classes at the university."

So here was someone else who had been touched by Holly's death. And maybe an ally among all these strangers.

"Cesar, you must have known my sister well if you worked together with the animals. Did she ever talk to you about something—or someone— troubling her? Or do you know if she left any of her belongings behind? Maybe left them with someone to take care of? Computer disks or . . . or maybe electronics?"

She'd gone too far too fast, Vicki saw immediately. Cesar stiffened, his expression turning hostile and wary. "I do not know of what you might be speaking. Señor Taylor gathered Señorita Ho-lee's belongings personally. If you believe one of the staff has taken some of her possessions, it is not so. We are not thieves."

"I didn't mean—," Vicki began hastily.

"Vicki, there you are!" Alison's flushed face appeared at the top of the cliff. "So you found our hot tub. I'm leaving with Bill pretty quick, so if you can tear yourself away, I need to get you registered."

"I'll be right up." Vicki swung back around. "Please, Cesar, I wasn't accusing anyone of taking anything that was my sister's. I'm just . . . I'm trying to make sense of how and why she was killed."

"We all are," he responded simply.

No, you aren't, Vicki cried passionately to herself as she scrambled back up to Alison. In fact, just about everyone had already made what they thought was perfect sense of Holly's death. She glanced back over the cliff. Cesar had made no move to follow her but was staring into the churning pool. Vicki stopped short at his expression. Was that sorrow she'd caught on his face? Or fear?

One way or another, Cesar was definitely someone she'd be interviewing again. Vicki hurried after Alison.

"Isn't it cool down there?" Alison called over her shoulder. "Our own little spa. Wait till you try it after a hard day's work. For that alone, I'd consider transferring to the center. If the social life wasn't so limited. One thing this year in Guatemala has taught me: however much I may respect the environment, I'm made for the bright lights. I'm back to the city—and next month to Sydney."

"Uh, Alison?" Did she realize the WRC plane was out of commission? "Just how are you getting there? You did hear what happened to the plane."

"Oh yes, Bill told me," Alison said airily, leading Vicki in a shortcut across the wood flooring of the thatched shelter. "I'd have had to take the bus anyway, since Joe isn't scheduled to go back in for a week. But Alpiro and his unit don't know that, so I'm thumbing a ride on one of their choppers. They're always dropping into the city. It's all the apology we'll get out of them; you can be sure."

In front of the main building, Bill's pickup was empty, the volunteers scattered.

As Vicki and Alison arrived, Bill broke off conversation with a tall, bearded German to raise five fingers.

"Okay, okay! Make it ten, and I'll be there," Alison called, steering Vicki into the building.

Vicki found her duffel bag deposited just inside the door. Through a door to the right was an office where she could see the two center administrators working.

"They did tell you it's a hundred dollars a week?" Alison demanded anxiously as they entered. "I know it doesn't seem fair to pay for the privilege of working like a dog, but it's what keeps this place going."

"I know. . . . It's fine, really." Counting out the first week's payment, Vicki handed it to Rosario.

The man accepted the cash without a word, while his wife unsmilingly wrote down the deposit in a well-worn ledger.

"Don't mind them," Alison said when they emerged into the hall. "Rosario and Beatriz believe in the mission, but I don't think they really like all these gringos coming and going—or being here at all. It's a bit isolated for a couple of university graduates, especially if you can't just take off the way we can. They'd like to go back to the university and teach, but they were assigned here by the minister of environment, and it isn't like there are a lot of paying jobs in this field."

Grabbing her duffel bag, Vicki glimpsed a dispensary and rudimentary vet clinic before Alison hurried her up a staircase.

"Cesar seems happy enough. Not that he's been here long. He just finished his class studies, and this is his residency. He's smart and hardworking, but . . ." Alison sighed. "We're sure going to miss Holly."

The second floor was living quarters. On opposite sides of the hall were bunk-lined barracks for male and female volunteers. Not even the open screens could blow away a certain locker room smell.

Alison wrinkled her nose. "Some of our back-to-nature types seem to feel that natural body odor makes them more appealing to the animal life. Count your lucky stars you don't have to bunk in here. Come on."

Vicki followed her through an open door between two bunks. A concrete floor divided rows of stalls, and Vicki was thankful to see showers and actual flush toilets. Living wouldn't be as rough as she'd prepared for.

"We pipe water from the hot springs, so the showers are reasonably warm. For laundry you'll have to settle for a scrubbing slab out back. Electricity is available three hours every night when the generator is booted up. Enough for everyone to charge their laptop batteries. What we need is solar panels, though with the rain we get, that's probably not practical."

Alison opened another door at the far end of the bathroom area. On the other side was a tiny room, the reason they'd entered through the bathroom immediately apparent since the only other door was set in the outside wall.

She pushed it open to show a staircase leading down. "The royal suite for resident WRC staff. It's a little awkward. Rosario and Beatriz's quarters are right through that wall, hence no proper door. But at least it's private. Just be sure to put the bar across at night."

Vicki looked around. Resident staff? Then this must have been Holly's room.

"I think that should be it. And now, I'd better go. My ten minutes are *so* up." She took the back stairs two at a time.

Leaving her duffel bag, Vicki followed at a less dangerous pace and thanked Bill. As soon as he left, she was back up the stairs. If Holly had left a clue anywhere, her living quarters would be the most likely place.

The room was the size of a closet and had perhaps originally been designed as such since there were no windows except a screened slit over the outer door. Besides the bunk bed, there was a shelf with a bar underneath for hanging clothes, a wooden chair, and a packing crate, painted white and fitted inside with shelving that did double duty for storage as well as a stand for a Coleman lantern. The walls were empty.

Leaving both doors open improved the lighting. Vicki pulled the crate away from the wall and stood on the chair to check that the shelf and crate were empty before turning her attention to the bunk. She climbed up, shaking out the sheets and blanket and removing the pillowcase, then turned the mattress on its edge. Nothing.

Tossing the bedding down, Vicki scrambled after it. The bottom bunk was already stripped, clean sheets, blankets, and pillow stacked neatly at the foot for its next occupant.

Vicki was bracing herself for another disappointment when she saw what poor lighting and shadows had hidden. The inside walls of the bunk were not empty like the rest of the room. There were tacked-up paper items, a calendar, a daily schedule, and a list of center regulations. But there were photos and other papers taped there as well.

Pulling the mattress free, Vicki checked underneath with new hope. Maybe something had fallen underneath—even the missing PDA. But the camp's cleanliness extended to here, and there wasn't more than a thin coating of dust under the bunk.

Replacing the mattress, Vicki turned her attention back to the walls. The photos were all computer printouts from a digital camera. Mostly of the center itself—perhaps why they'd been left up. Shots of volunteers washing dishes in the kitchen shelter. Splashing in *Pozo Azul*. Cesar and Holly splinting the front leg of a jaguarundi. The one Holly had sent to the zoo?

More photos were taped to the bottom of the upper bunk. As Vicki stretched out to look at them, her throat tightened again so that she had to swallow. Just above where Holly's head would have lain was a photo she recognized—a close-up of the two sisters, wind-tousled and sunburned, arms around each other's shoulders. Another tourist had snapped it for them in Cancún.

Vicki's gaze traveled to a second picture tacked right beside the smiling faces, and she stiffened. It was the same printout Vicki carried in her new laptop case, the photo she had seen framed on two government office walls. Then this was the copy that clerk at the national archives had made for Holly. And her sister had thought it important enough to tack up where she'd be staring at it every time she lay down to sleep.

A sheet of computer paper surrounded with snapshots of Lake Izabal and the Sierra de las Minas and close-ups of the center animals was titled "This Is My Father's World."

Leaning close, Vicki read the lyrics, slowly, curiously. If she'd ever seen the entire song that had played such a role in her life, she had certainly never taken notice.

This is my Father's world,
And to my listening ears
All nature sings, and round me rings
The music of the spheres.
This is my Father's world:
I rest me in the thought
Of rocks and trees, of skies and seas—
His hand the wonders wrought.

This is my Father's world,
The birds their carols raise,
The morning light, the lily white,
Declare their Maker's praise.
This is my Father's world:
He shines in all that's fair;
In the rustling grass I hear Him pass,
He speaks to me everywhere.

This is my Father's world,
O let me ne'er forget
That though the wrong seems oft so strong,
God is the Ruler yet.
This is my Father's world:
The battle is not done;
Jesus who died shall be satisfied,
And earth and heav'n be one.

"Ms. Andrews?"

Vicki sat up so quickly she banged her head against the wooden planking that supported the bunk above her.

Standing in the bathroom door was Johanna, one of the German volunteers she'd met. "If you would please speak to Beatriz about the kitchen assignment. I cannot pluck chickens. I am a vegan. I do not touch animal products."

The rest of the daylight hours were too busy for Vicki to even think. No sooner had Beatriz sourly exchanged Johanna's chicken duty for swabbing out cages than Vicki was called to translate Cesar's instructions to a German veterinary student helping suture a barbed wire tear on a howler monkey. Tripping over the medical terms, Vicki made a mental note to spend a few hours with an English/Spanish dictionary.

Above the leaves and vines of the cloud forest canopy, the sky faded from overcast gray to black with equatorial suddenness so that by the time a cowbell signaled supper, served on the plastic tables of the open thatched shelter, the generator was lit. Fluorescent tubing suspended from the rafters illuminated beans, rice, and tortillas but also drew legions of insects. Brushing yet another moth from her plate, Vicki wasn't sure she wouldn't prefer eating in the dark.

After supper, laptops and playing cards came out, the former plugged into a selection of power strips. The Germans formed a tight group, laughing and talking loudly, and the Guatemalan staff disappeared. Vicki took her turn uploading e-mail to the camp laptop to be transmitted by radio phone in the morning, then headed back to her room.

There a single twenty-five–watt bulb dangling overhead was now operational. By its dim light Vicki made the bed and unpacked her few belongings. Last of all she picked up the box cradled at the bottom, still swathed in the sweatshirt with which she'd safeguarded it.

As Vicki unwrapped it, she found herself shaking. *No, I can't do it yet. I'm not ready.*

With violence she pushed the box under the bunk as far as it would go. Grabbing the sweatshirt, she tugged it over her head and flung herself out the door and down the stairs. Even with the sweatshirt, the mountain night had grown chilly. Vicki walked quickly, her feet seeking out the gravel paths, not even sure where she was heading, only spurred to get away from the raucous laughter of the volunteers, the fluorescent lighting, the generator's rumble. The animals were quiet as she slipped past the cages, presumably asleep, so that Vicki heard only an occasional stirring or rustle of feathers.

I should have brought a flashlight, Vicki thought, for once she was out of sight of the generator lights, it was as dark as a cave. Now she understood those white-painted rocks edging the paths, their pale glimmer on either side of her feet guiding her cautiously forward. Only as a rush of water grew to thunder did Vicki realize where she'd been instinctively heading. Stepping out onto the solid footing of the rock outcropping, she went no farther though she could see phosphorescent blotches winding down the cliff. Instead she stood looking out on the night as she had . . . Was it just three weeks ago when she'd first looked through the barred windows of Casa de Esperanza onto a Guatemalan night?

But this was a vastly different panorama. Replacing the acrid smell of burning garbage was a fresh, moist fragrance that spoke of growing things and life. With nightfall the mist had crept down the mountain to pool gray and thick at Vicki's feet so she could make out no suggestion of the pool and treetops she knew to be below her. But the roar of water and spray reaching her face pinpointed where the falls crashed down to her left. Far above Lake Izabal, with neither mist nor smoke to cloak them, stars splashed luminous patterns across the night while other twinkling constellations marked villages along the lake.

It was all undeniably beautiful, and though for a moment—an eternity—familiar panic welled up to choke Vicki, racing through her heart, pounding at her temples, this time she thrust it away. Breathing deeply of the night's sweetness, she listened to the rushing music of the falls. An orchestra of tree frogs offered counterpoint, and somewhere nearby a wakeful bird added a flutelike soprano.

The smells, the sounds, the mist drifting damp across her face were all so *right* that a tight, hard knot that seemed to have been there all her life loosened in Vicki's chest. Sliding to a sitting position, she hugged her knees.

This really *was* her father's world.

"This is my Father's world."

Which was it? Or could it be both?

Vicki raised her eyes to the stars jeweled across the night's black velvet. *God, are You really out there? No, I know You're out there. But are You listening to me? Do I matter enough for You to look through all this and see me? I know it's been a long time since I've talked to You. I remember I used to. At Sunday school and bedtime prayers. Even when I was afraid, I prayed. I still believed You were out there, and if I prayed hard enough, You'd hear me and change things.*

Yes, she had prayed. When had she stopped? She couldn't even remember.

I guess it was when I grew up and realized the world wasn't going to get better no matter how hard I prayed. It was all so out of control and so ugly. I forgot how beautiful You'd made it. I forgot all this that I must have loved once upon a time.

I still don't get it. All this up here—this is Your world. This is You. The beauty, the peace. But down there where those lights are—no, not even that far—people are hurting and dying. Other people are doing the hurting and getting away with it. And I feel so helpless to do anything about it. I couldn't save my sister or my parents. I can't save the world. I know that's supposed to be Your job, but I don't see it happening.

This time it wasn't cold or panic shaking Vicki until she wrapped her arms tight around her body but a grief that tore at her heart so that she didn't think she could bear it. Not just for her own loss nor for Holly but for an entire world that seemed to be crying out with her in pain.

"That though the wrong seems oft so strong, God is the Ruler yet."

"Do what is right. Do not give way to fear."

Is Joe right, God? Is Evelyn right? Is there something You're doing that I'm missing? Something that's worth all this?

No audible answer came. But the stars twinkled down. The mist laid soft, comforting fingers across Vicki's hot face. The sweetness of the air seeped deep into her lungs, bringing with it a calm she didn't even recognize as the beginnings of peace.

Vicki had no idea how long she'd sat there when she heard raised voices, then saw the bobbing of lights approaching on the path behind her. She climbed stiffly to her feet and jumped behind an oak trunk as a dozen laughing shapes crowded out onto the rock outcropping. The volunteer team coming down for a night swim in the hot spring.

Vicki waited unmoving until they had disappeared down the rock face into the mist. Then she hurried back up the path.

With tight self-control, he restrained from slapping the fat, satisfied face in front of him. "Your men are undisciplined *idiotas*. Do you realize what they could have done? The orders were to not fire without express authorization."

The man in uniform lounging in front of the command tent slammed a bottle of golden Palo Viejo rum down on the crate beside him. "We had no knowledge who was on board. Only that the plane was unidentified and circling low. It seemed we would be seen. Are my men not to defend themselves?"

"Defend—?" He cut himself off with gritted teeth, forcing himself to explain patiently. "You cannot be seen from above. That was the purpose of our exercise. I myself have tested it. As for the plane, I personally delivered the description and call numbers. If your men follow my instructions, there should be no need for further bloodshed. Is it understood?"

He stood up to go. "I cannot protect you forever. One more month, and then it is over."

The fat face showed neither concern nor apology as a hand reached again for the rum bottle. "This time."

CHAPTER TWENTY

Joy comes in the morning.

Standing on the rock outcropping, Vicki wasn't sure from where those words had come. But they seemed fitting to a sunrise over Lake Izabal, the gray of waves and sky lightening through pale green to pink and orange, stray tendrils of dawn tinting the pooled mist below to rose.

The warmth of the thermal pool was as delicious as Alison had promised. With lightness of step, Vicki headed up the path, rubbing her hair dry, as a clanging bell signaled the beginning of the day's schedule.

In this place animal needs took precedence over human. Vicki pitched in filling bowls with diced fruit or meat scraps. Buckets of water from *Pozo Azul* sluiced the concrete cage flooring, the water system having chosen this morning to go on the blink. The center cook Maria didn't arrive this early from the village so other volunteers set out fruit, bread, and coffee for the team's breakfast.

Cesar, on the other hand, was already hard at work. Popping into the clinic to pick up some forms, Vicki found the young veterinarian measuring medications into plastic cups. Behind him, an open door revealed a crumpled cot and tossed clothing in a space that made Vicki's room seem palatial. Though she too would have chosen a storage closet to the locker-room atmosphere of the barracks.

Animal and human breakfast over, Vicki found her translation skills in demand as the volunteers huddled together with the camp administrators, Rosario and Beatriz, over a cage improvement project. They were marking off a less constricted enclosure for the wild cats when Bill's pickup pulled into the cul-de-sac.

"Now we will have water again." Rosario hurried over to the pickup as Bill and Joe got out. The three men were disappearing around the main building when it occurred to Vicki that Joe had never turned up at the center after yesterday's adventure.

As the planning session broke up, she drifted back to the concrete water tower. Rosario and Joe were bent over a bundle of plastic piping that ran up the mountainside to the stream. Bill stood watching.

Vicki joined him. "Hey, did that army thing take all night? Or doesn't Joe stay here with the rest of the center staff?" A recollection jumped to her mind. "Wait a minute. You said 'we' yesterday when you invited me to drop by your house."

"That's right. Joe's bunking with me." Bill looked at Vicki. "And to clarify a certain misapprehension, Joe likes to refer to himself as the center handyman, but he's actually employed by me. I've got a number of odd jobs he's working on at my place. However, since the center is my principal project at the moment, I'm happy to make his services available here anytime they're needed. Just as I've made my plane available." He nodded toward Joe, climbing a metal ladder up the side of the water tower. "He can fix—and fly—just about anything."

"Yeah, well, maybe working for the center sounds more professional on his résumé."

Not that Joe seemed the type to care what anyone called him.

"Vicki! Beatriz is looking for you."

Heading indoors to the office, Vicki wrote out the chore assignments in English, then wandered over to the animal enclosures. The rising sun had burned away the mist. A half-grown tapir thrust its long snout through the mesh to sniff at Vicki. Wandering farther to chatter with a spider monkey, she untangled her hair from the grasp of an adorable baby coatimundi. Down the path volunteers were hammering in stakes for the new cat run.

I could get used to this. That tranquil thought was shattered by a roar of engines. Screeching and cawing and howling erupted around her. Chittering its terror, the baby coatimundi scuttled into its sleeping shelter. Then human yells joined the animal uproar.

Sprinting up the path, Vicki pressed her lips together with annoyance to see the cloud of dust hanging over an army transport truck and Jeep parked in the cul-de-sac. A dozen troops—UPN, by the khaki uniforms and berets—spilled out of the truck. As they fanned out through the center and into the main building, their thudding boots and shouts sent the animals into an even noisier frenzy.

Vicki marched over to the Jeep. "Michael, what's going on? You said you'd be dropping by this morning. You didn't say anything about bringing half the army with you."

He swung down from the Jeep. Beside him, Vicki recognized her captor from yesterday, Colonel Alpiro. The Guatemalan commander's glance was appraising and cold before he turned his back to issue orders to his men.

Michael's smile was warm enough to make up for it. "Hi, Vicki. I trust you slept well after yesterday." He winced as the sounds of excited animals rose to a new pitch. "This is quite a place. Is it always this noisy?"

"Only when your soldiers are scaring the animals out of their wits. Can you make them stop before they drive one of the poor things into a heart attack? What's going on anyway? What is it with the escort?" Vicki repeated with exasperation.

Michael murmured something in Alpiro's ear. He in turn snapped out a loud order and walked away.

Michael faced Vicki. "What's going on, my dear, is that I've been busy since our encounter yesterday. You'll be happy to hear that after the run-in, the powers that be have agreed not only to reopen your sister's investigation but assign it high priority."

Vicki ignored the warm glow of that *my dear*. "But you don't think yesterday had anything to do with Holly? I thought they said it was just some poacher."

Michael looked amused. "We have no idea. That's the point of an investigation—to eliminate those possibilities. That doesn't mean Chief of Police Alvarez is admitting you were right. Only that they're willing to explore the possibility. Or rather let UPN explore it since the options are pretty basic. Either your sister was a victim of street crime or her death was somehow involved with her work with WRC and the nature reserve. Which puts it under the jurisdiction of the Environmental Protection Unit."

"And all of this?"

Whatever order the UPN commander had given, the truck and Jeep engines abruptly died, the running boots and shouts gradually quieting. As the dust cloud settled, so did the panicked noise of the animals. But there were still men everywhere, and now from upstairs in the living barracks, Vicki could hear angry German.

"Well, again, you've been granted what you asked for. After reviewing the case files, Colonel Alpiro is in agreement. If there's more to be uncovered about Holly's death, the key lies in that missing PDA. Since the Guatemala City police didn't consider it relevant, no serious search was ever made for it. Alpiro has ordered it to be done now."

At Vicki's involuntary sound of dismay, Michael asked, "What is it? I thought you'd be ecstatic."

"No, you're right. I'm the one who asked for this. It's just . . ." Vicki grimaced. "The volunteers aren't going to be too happy with your people rummaging through their stuff. Or me if they find out I'm responsible. I don't get why Alpiro's searching here either. Isn't it more likely Holly took that PDA with her? For that matter, how do we know those police who smashed up my room didn't steal it?"

"Which is precisely why the center hostel is being searched at this same minute. Believe me, this isn't the first time Alpiro—or I—have organized a search. As for your neighborhood patrol, they've been picked up for questioning too. Though if they were going to steal instead of smash, they'd have taken the computer gear with them. Alpiro has given strict orders to deliver all electronics down here. You can go through them yourself and see if you recognize anything. He will organize your interviews as well."

Michael added, "You've forgotten you asked to have anyone acquainted with Holly questioned as to what she might have been doing or confided?" He gestured to a unit of soldiers—no, police—herding the camp administrators into the thatched shelter, where Colonel Alpiro was already at a table.

"Of course. I've been trying to do all that myself, but I'm sure your police will be able to get more than I can. Oh, Michael, I can't believe you've managed all this. And after all that stonewalling. I can't thank you enough."

"It's the right thing to do. I'm just glad I was in a position to help make it happen. Now, come on. I'm sure you're going to want to get in on these interviews."

Vicki followed Michael over to one of the plastic tables where troops were laying out electronic devices, presumably seized from the barracks upstairs. Vicki noted a PDA lying on the next table.

Michael nodded toward it. "Mine. Their sample. They've got orders to leave anything else alone."

Behind them, the kitchen shelter was still minus its cook. UPN troops were crowded inside, lifting every item, emptying containers of rice and corn flour into pots, then back again. They were showing commendable care, even putting things back as they'd been on the shelves.

The volunteers were being herded into the community shelter too. Vicki didn't need to know German to see how angry they were. *I'm just glad they don't know this is my doing.* Vicki spotted Bill talking quietly to one of the team leaders. Her intervention wouldn't be necessary. Joe was there too, sprawled out at a table as unperturbed as though waiting for meal service.

Then Michael steered Vicki to the table where Colonel Alpiro was interviewing Rosario and Beatriz. His many questions were repeated in any number of variations, but they boiled down to two: "Have you seen the electronic device in question? Did the deceased confide any concern that was troubling her?"

However little Vicki had taken to the pair, she could empathize with the anger and nervousness they were visibly holding in check under Alpiro's implacable scrutiny. Their answers were consistent. Yes, they knew the electronic device in question. No, they hadn't seen it since Holly left for Guatemala City. Nor had it been in the personal effects they'd packed up for Señor Taylor. Yes, Holly had made some complaints of animals being improperly released or dying in custody, but they'd been able to reassure her from the records that her concerns were misplaced. Rosario looked away at that last statement. But if the camp administrators were being less than truthful about Holly's concerns, they seemed sincere enough in their protest over the PDA.

The German team had arrived in Guatemala only hours before Holly's disappearance and had all been strangers to Holly, but that didn't prevent the UPN commander from interrogating each in turn. Michael handled the translation, his calm English defusing Alpiro's stern questions. A team leader did any necessary translating to German. Halfway through the lineup, even Alpiro seemed to recognize the futility of his questions, confining himself to gathering contact data.

Bill and Joe were next, giving their answers directly in Spanish, Bill with bland, unconcerned courtesy, Joe looking openly bored.

Yes, everyone who knew Holly had seen her PDA.

No, it had not been left with them when Holly traveled or among the belongings Rosario and Beatriz turned over for Holly's next of kin.

No, Holly had not confided in them more than a normal frustration with the deteriorating ecological situation.

Alpiro treated Bill with a polite deference he showed no one else. Just what influence did the American wield up here? Michael, his translation services no longer necessary, watched both Americans instead, his features impassive. What was he thinking?

Cesar was last. Vicki, as bored by now as Joe looked, straightened up as two uniforms pushed the veterinary resident to a seat. This time there was no mistaking his expression. He was absolutely rigid with terror. Yes, he had carried out Holly's instructions. No, why would she confide in him? He was only a lowly resident. If she had complaints, she would raise them with his superiors, Rosario and Beatriz.

No, he had never diverted any of their wildlife charges to the black market. This last accusation stung him to a forceful denial. He leaned forward earnestly, indignation for the first time overcoming fear.

Michael gave Colonel Alpiro a slight gesture. Then the UPN commander waved for Cesar to go. Vicki swallowed her distaste at the complacent approval with which Alpiro followed Cesar's unsteady progress across the thatched shelter to where volunteers and staff alike were still corralled under the intimidation of three automatic rifles.

Alpiro likes people to be afraid of him. No, he takes it for granted.

The search had petered out by the time the interviews finished. Vicki counted seven PDA units of various brands. None matched Holly's, but under Alpiro's scrutiny, Vicki went through the motions of turning each on. Colonel Alpiro and Michael verified the language involved to be German.

As Alpiro's frown deepened, Vicki caught the urgent murmur of a squad leader. "There is equipment that could hide such a device. The clinic. The office. The animal quarters. Perhaps if your orders were modified—"

Vicki was about to voice her protests, but Michael intervened. "Coronel, if *la americana* left behind such a device, it would be for safekeeping and to be easily retrieved, not inside equipment that is in use or under an animal cage. The minister of environment would not appreciate having to replace—"

To Vicki's relief, Alpiro nodded. She felt let down and not just because of angry glares from volunteers repossessing their electronics. The Germans hadn't missed Vicki's silent participation in the interviews. She didn't expect it to be so easy, but she'd hoped for something!

Only now did Vicki realize how late it was. The sun was high above the forest canopy, past time for the midday meal. The kitchen shelter had been restored to reasonable order. But the gas burners were still off with no signs of meal preparation. Or Maria.

Vicki heard a child sobbing only because the turmoil of soldiers, angry volunteers, and excited animals had largely abated. And because she'd heard it so many times in so many places. She turned to see Maria stepping noiselessly from behind a tree toward the kitchen shelter. She wasn't alone. Clinging to her were two smaller versions of the black braids, hand-embroidered shirts, and red wraparound skirts. The girls were maybe five and seven years old.

Vicki noticed a flash of emotion as Maria took in the uniforms and weapons before her round, dark features settled into stoical lines. Slipping into the kitchen shelter, she turned on the burners.

The UPN troops were starting back toward the transport vehicle, allowing their recent captives to scatter. The volunteers headed immediately toward their quarters.

Catching sight of her tardy cook, Beatriz started toward the kitchen with a frown. Vicki didn't need to overhear to know she was giving Maria a tongue-lashing. The cook showed no reaction. Was it five hundred years of subjugation that had given the Mayans the ability to withdraw behind lowered eyes and blank impassivity?

If so, Maria's companions had not yet learned to school their emotions. The frightened wail of the younger child drew Vicki over.

Beatriz pushed by as Vicki entered the kitchen shelter, pausing only to snap at Vicki, "Let the volunteers know dinner will be an hour delayed."

But Vicki wasn't the only one who'd responded to the children's distress.

"*Tío* Cesar!" The two girls threw their arms around him. Still looking shaken by his ordeal, he stooped to shush the girls in mixed Spanish and Mayan.

"Uncle Cesar?" Vicki stared at him with surprise. "Then you're from the village here? These are your nieces?"

"Not my nieces, but family."

Vicki knew the custom of calling any close adult acquaintance aunt or uncle, as the Casa de Esperanza children had called her *Tía* Vee-kee.

Cesar straightened, the girls still clinging tightly to him, to address Maria.

Joe must have fixed the water problem before things had broken loose, because Maria had a pot filling up and was dumping onions, garlic heads, and tomatoes on the wooden table. A sharp knife sliced briskly through the vegetables as she answered Cesar in her Mayan dialect.

Cesar turned to Vicki. "She is late because the army came to the village this morning. They took everyone to the plaza and searched every house before anyone was allowed to depart. She apologizes that the food will be tardy. And for bringing her cousin's children to work."

"The food doesn't matter. Please tell her that. But I am so sorry about this morning." Vicki looked down at the girls pressed close into his sides. "Why are they so upset? Did they hurt them?"

"No, no. No one was hurt. Nor did the soldiers steal anything this time. They said they were searching for valuables stolen from the center." Cesar studied Vicki. Did he realize this was all her doing? "Alicia and Gabriela are just very frightened. They are . . . their families were killed—shot—not long ago. They're afraid the soldiers are here to destroy this village too."

"Oh no!" The realization was a sickness in Vicki's stomach. "You mean the massacre up here a couple of months ago? They were there? But I thought there were no survivors."

"No, their father—my cousin—had brought them here to Maria to go to school until a teacher should arrive at the schoolhouse there. They know only that their parents and younger brother are dead. When they saw the soldiers and the army, they believed . . ."

Vicki could imagine only too well what these girls had believed. The images were real enough in her mind to be her own. Their distress was tearing at Vicki's heart. She tugged at their embroidered *huipiles* until two tear-filled pairs of eyes looked at her. Vicki had no idea how well they understood Spanish, but she put all the authority she could into her voice. "You are safe now. The soldiers won't hurt you. I won't let the soldiers hurt you."

Then Vicki stormed back through the thatched shelter. Michael was talking with Colonel Alpiro beside the command Jeep when she caught up to him. He smiled at Vicki.

Vicki burst out in English, "Did you know your soldiers invaded the village this morning? They dragged everyone out of their houses searching for Holly's PDA. Scared those two little girls *sick*! I thought the days of army brutality were over!"

Bill and Joe, lifting some tools into the back of Bill's pickup, stopped to listen with undisguised interest.

Michael was no longer smiling. "You're upset, and you don't know what you're saying." As Vicki gritted her teeth at his sharp rebuke, he dropped his voice to calm reasonableness. "Look, you complained that the Guatemala City police hadn't done a proper investigation. Well, this *is* the investigation you asked for. This is the way it's done here. Quick and efficient and over. Have you heard that anyone was hurt? Anything stolen? Any property destroyed?"

Vicki shook her head.

He hammered in his point. "Then you've no idea what army brutality down here entails."

Vicki was feeling hugely deflated. If Michael had wanted to convince her to quit this quest altogether, he couldn't have gone about it better. What had she put in motion? That he was right didn't make it more palatable. Bill and Joe turned away as she glanced at them. She swallowed, searching for an apology that wouldn't further her humiliation.

But static from a radio at Bill's belt interrupted them. It was followed almost instantly by a crackle in Colonel Alpiro's hand.

Bill looked across at Michael to announce coolly, "It seems your men—or Alpiro's here—also feel the need to invade my home."

Alpiro said in Spanish, "Señor Taylor, my men inform me that your guards have prevented them from completing their orders. They have taken up defensive positions on the perimeter of your property." He drummed his fingers against the radio. "Your residence alone remains of our search. Perhaps it is not necessary. The army lieutenant accompanying my men tells me his commander has given special orders concerning you."

"No!"

Alpiro looked at Bill with as much surprise as Vicki.

Bill held up a hand. "No, I wouldn't want anyone to question later why my home alone remains unsearched. I'll give my guards instructions to cooperate. As I'd have been happy to do, had I known in advance of your intentions. I would appreciate, though, if they could hold off until I can be present. Then I can reassure *el comandante* that your men didn't damage my property."

Colonel Alpiro nodded.

As he spoke tersely into his radio, Vicki spun around to Michael. "I want to go too." If she'd loosed this on Bill, the least she could do was be there for support.

She tensed herself for an argument, but Michael just jerked his head toward the front seat. "Then climb in."

Bill's house was less than five minutes away at the speed with which the army Jeep took the dirt track. Another Jeep was pulled up outside the gate, its contingent hunkered down behind its cover, weapons trained on the knoll where Bill's house sat. The workers were nowhere in sight, but as Colonel Alpiro had indicated, the plantation guards were very much in evidence, at least three shotgun barrels visible above the planters that lined the veranda.

The pickup pulled up behind the army vehicles. As he got out to open the gate, the guards on the veranda stood up and lowered their shotguns. Bill took the lead to the driveway, the three army vehicles parking behind him. Only the command vehicle unloaded. Colonel Alpiro waved for the other troops to stay where they were.

Bill led the way inside. Despite the unpleasantness of the visit, Vicki looked around with interest. The interior was largely open, the walls whitewashed plaster, the flooring a red-earth tile. Beyond a huge stone fireplace was a surprisingly modern kitchen and doors opening into two bedrooms and a bathroom.

Couches and chairs upholstered in tanned cowhide were grouped around the fireplace. The walls held bookshelves and native tapestries as well as beautiful specimens of *típica*, the handwoven Mayan clothing, hats, and bags. Bill had his own generator because there were floor lamps. An entertainment center held a stereo, VCR, DVD player, and flat-screen TV. Through the office door Vicki could see a computer and radio equipment.

No wonder Joe prefers to bunk here.

The search was carried out as carefully and professionally as Vicki could hope, books and dishes lifted from shelves, furniture patted down. She wandered over to the office, keeping a vigilant eye on the handling of delicate computer and radio equipment. The latter was set up on a long table shoved under a window whose shutters the guards had flung open to offer a view of the veranda and coffee fields beyond. The back and left walls held bookshelves. But only the one straight ahead was full, the left one holding a scattering of Mayan pottery, perhaps because heat from the fireplace would be right behind that wall.

Sensing the warmth of another person behind her, Vicki glanced over her shoulder. Joe too was watching.

But any concern proved unnecessary. For this base commander's friend, it was hardly a search at all, quick and almost perfunctory. Then Colonel Alpiro excused himself.

Michael lingered. "I apologize, Taylor, for the inconvenience. I trust you understand."

"Of course. If there's anything we can do to find Holly's killer, you have only to ask."

"Well, I'm not sure how much more we can do here. At most, we've eliminated possibilities. What we will do is increase patrols on the biosphere. At the least we can make sure there're no more incidents like yesterday's."

Joe transferred himself to his usual lounging sprawl in one of the cowhide chairs. It wouldn't hurt him to make a gracious response to Michael's apologetic smile, but he only lifted an eyebrow.

Vicki compensated for his boorishness with a warmer smile than she'd planned.

She was rewarded by the appreciative glint in Michael's eyes. "May I run you home, Vicki?"

She shook her head. "That won't be necessary. It's a short walk. I know Colonel Alpiro is in a hurry to get back to base."

"Then I'll catch you later. I have to fly back to the city this afternoon. Tom Casey—you saw him at the airport—is in town again, and I've got a report to make. I'll be popping back this way in a couple of days. By then I should be able to fill you in on the search and interviews we're running down there. Unless you'll already be in town. Then maybe dinner?"

Vicki dropped long lashes over her amber eyes, cheeks burning at the warmth of Michael's smile, the sudden derisive twist of Joe's mouth. Michael was definitely the kind of guy consular aides or expat volunteers might find attractive. Not just the good looks and lean, muscular frame but the cool confidence, discipline, and self-control. He was a leader who knew his own mind and was committed to making a difference in his society. Vicki liked that.

But at the moment she had more compelling interests occupying her mind. "I won't be back in town," Vicki said quietly, "but I'd appreciate an update when you're back this way."

Silence reigned for two heartbeats after the door closed behind Michael.

"Tom Casey. That's our new American drug czar," Joe repeated ironically. "And Michael boy has to run to make his report. Just who did you say this Camden fellow is?"

His question was directed at Bill, but it was Vicki who answered shortly, "He's an attaché with the embassy. The DAO's office."

"Yeah, right, that's what they all say," Joe snorted.

Vicki looked from one man to the other. "What do you mean?"

Joe just shrugged.

Vicki was not in the mood for any more of Joe's cryptic insinuations. She glanced at Bill, but he was looking at his employee, white eyebrows raised. "Come on, Joe," Vicki challenged. "What do you mean? I know there was a nasty dig in there somewhere. What do you have against Michael, anyway?"

Bill said resignedly, "You might as well spit it out, Ericsson. She's not going to let it go."

Joe's gaze shifted from Vicki to a spot behind her. "I'm not slamming your pal. But growing up around all those embassies taught me some things. Extraneous attachés—especially hotshot ones running around with the locals and holding meetings with VIPs—are usually code for CIA."

"What?"

"Ignore him—and his conspiracy theories," Bill advised Vicki. "Ericsson's unfortunate upbringing hardly qualifies him as expert testimony. In my opinion, Camden seems like a decent young fellow. Hardworking. Steady job. Safe. You could sure do worse. It's not like there's a lot of pickings up here, and Camden seems eager to make you welcome. If I were you, I'd take him up on that dinner offer before some embassy secretary grabs him."

"Oh, really. If that's another hint to give up this investigation, it won't work." Vicki met Joe's sardonic look with a caustic one of her own before adding sweetly, "And what about Joe here? Isn't he a decent young fellow? Hardworking? Steady job? Safe?"

Bill stared at her. "Ericsson is hardly a safe person for anyone to know. And if I had a daughter, I couldn't give her better advice than I'm giving you now. As I should have given Holly. Stay as far away from this man as possible."

Joe was on his feet with an abruptness that belied his indolent slouch. A moment later the back door slammed.

CHAPTER TWENTY-ONE

CHAPTER TWENTY-ONE

"Bill, I can't believe you said that," Vicki said. "I think you hurt his feelings. He thinks you meant it."

"I always mean what I say."

There was little to be said to that. Vicki started for the front door. She turned back in the doorway. "Bill, there's one other thing I don't understand. You told Colonel Alpiro that Holly had said nothing to you about what was bothering her. But Holly thought the world of you. You worked with her. If she talked to anyone, I'd have thought it would be you."

Bill sagged as though she'd struck him, and he looked his true age. "Yes, I thought so too. That she didn't has troubled me more than anything else."

Vicki headed back to the center. Incredibly, when she emerged from the coffee fields into the center cul-de-sac, the scene was as peaceful as though the morning's invasion had never happened. Volunteers gathered for lunch in the communal thatched shelter. The tame spider monkey perched on Johanna's shoulders. A tranquil twittering and chatter carried from the cages. Even the two little girls were industriously eating plates of pasta at the farthest table.

Which didn't mean Vicki's part in the morning was forgiven. An angry rumble rose as she stepped into the shelter. *How am I going to work with them a whole week?* Vicki did the only thing she could think of. She threw herself on their mercy. By the time she finished explaining, angry mutters had shifted to sympathy.

"The young woman who met us at the airport was your sister?"

"Yes, we heard she'd been murdered."

"But of course you're trying to find out what happened!"

Bemused, Vicki watched as they scattered to their chores. *Why didn't I just tell them from the beginning? Because I've always got to stand alone. And I can't stand pity.*

By evening, when the German volunteers coaxed Vicki to join them in *Pozo Azul,* she was part of the team. Though that proved the only benefit of the UPN investigation.

Michael dropped by two days later. "The UPN helo flew me straight here from seeing Tom Casey off again." He looked around. "Wow, this really is beautiful. A little quieter than last time."

"Yeah, well, it does make a difference when it's not swarming with soldiers. How about a tour?" Vicki excused herself from Cesar and the German vet student for whom she'd been translating. Cesar didn't lift his gaze from the clipboard as he nodded. Vicki sighed. The Guatemalan veterinarian had withdrawn completely since the UPN invasion. So much for gaining his cooperation in her quest.

"So how did your report go?" Vicki asked as she led Michael toward the animal enclosure.

"Well enough. Casey seems to be impressed with our program. UPN was able to search and destroy two opium plantings within protected habitat while he was here. In fact, he rode along on the last one. Now to see if he's impressed enough to talk Congress into shelling out a bigger appropriation." Michael's face went rigid. "Just a minute. Isn't that . . . ?"

Vicki's hand rose to the object of his gaze. She'd started wearing Holly's pendant since her arrival, if only because it was too valuable to leave lying around unlocked. But it was usually tucked under her shirt. The spider monkey she'd been cuddling earlier must have tugged it loose. "Yes, it is. I guess I never mentioned it turned up."

After she explained, Michael shook his head. "If that isn't the mother of all coincidences. Unless it really did just slide loose while they were carrying her out of the dump." He lifted the pendant for closer scrutiny.

"Is there anything else you're forgetting to tell me? It really is important that I stay informed, no matter how small a detail you may consider it. If anything like this comes up again, contact me immediately. Now, about the searches in Guatemala City . . ."

Michael updated Vicki as they walked. "They've searched everywhere. Interviewed every person who's ever talked to Holly. It's been a great training exercise for the unit, the only reason Alpiro's been willing to take it this far. But we're exactly where we were before UPN got involved. Whatever happened to that PDA—stolen, destroyed, or just fell out like that necklace and burned up in the dump—I think we've at least established it's not going to show at this date."

His gaze roved constantly, taking in every detail.

When they stopped under the water tower, Vicki laughed. "Is this a tour we're doing here? Or another police search?"

Michael's grin was sheepish. "Sorry. I was just hoping I might see something we missed." Running a hand through his hair, he sighed. "I wish I didn't have to say I've no idea where to go next. Even by stateside standards, we've turned over every rock we can find. Unless a new rock turns up, I can't ask too much more of Alpiro."

"Well, at least you tried." Vicki's sigh matched his own. "That's all I ever asked."

However disappointing, it was hard to remain depressed when Vicki stepped outside every morning to the sweet, moist fragrance of the cloud forest, a dawn orchestra of caws and squeaks and the bass thunder of water, a luxuriant tangle of ferns and leaves and vines color accented with orchids and flowering trees. Whether or not she'd indeed been in these mountains as a child, her surroundings had very quickly become familiar and pleasant. And, oh, so peaceful.

With the cloud forest spreading its green canopy overhead, the center might have been in a bubble or alternate universe from the world of problems Vicki had left outside.The animals too were becoming individual. Vicki could now tell the monkeys apart by more than size. The half-grown tapir followed her around its enclosure like a puppy. The baby coatimundi rode around the center on Vicki's shoulder, prehensile tail wrapped around her arm.

It wasn't that Vicki had forgotten why she was here. But she'd done all she could do for now. The animals were cute and needy, but they didn't rend the heart as the *basurero* children had. As days slipped by with no greater decisions than chore distribution, Vicki felt herself unwinding and simply relishing the present. Splashing in *Pozo Azul*. Playing with the animals. Laughing with one of her new friends.

Maybe I'll just stay here forever.

Though in time the tranquil confinement seemed cramped. Especially with the map on the hall bulletin board showing the center as just a dot on the edge of the steep, majestic sweep of the Sierra de las Minas Biosphere.

I want to see the country Joe and I flew over. At least some of it.

Vicki hadn't forgotten the box under her bed. She'd thought it would be a simple matter to trace on the ground some of the wilderness she'd flown over. She hadn't figured on lack of transportation. Or restrictions on exploring the biosphere itself.

An opportunity came as the Germans completed their volunteer stint. The cat run was finished, a long mesh enclosure that allowed pumas, ocelots, and other felines to stretch their legs to a lope. To celebrate, an outing was scheduled to follow the biosphere's only nature trail. It veered off the main road at the last military checkpoint on the village outskirts, winding up into the mountain range that rose behind the plateau. A main track when villages had still dotted the biosphere, it was overgrown now, threading the cloud forest like a cool, green tunnel, but it offered some spectacular panoramas where it emerged to overlook mountain valleys.

It would have been a pleasurable experience if two Jeeps of UPN troops hadn't tagged along, neatly sandwiching the group's pickup between them. For protection, the patrol leader had assured them. The Germans seemed pleased enough.

But back at the center as the volunteers packed up to catch a tour bus into Guatemala City, Vicki protested to Cesar. "Isn't there any way to get up into the biosphere ourselves? I understand UPN needs to patrol the place and keep poachers and developers out. But we *are* the Ministry of Environment here. I mean, I'm not officially. But you are. Shouldn't the center be in there studying the biosphere?"

A rare smile lit Cesar's face as he slid a bowl of fruit and lettuce into a cage. "You sound like your sister. She always wanted to go into the mountains on her own. To see the animals in their own homes. To walk where no one else had been."

"She did?" Vicki's hand went out so suddenly she knocked the next bowl from Cesar's tray. Retrieving chunks of orange and banana, she demanded eagerly, "Do you know where she walked? Could you take me there? Please. I have a reason."

Cesar's expression shuttered. "That is not advisable. It is not safe."

"But if Holly did it . . ."

"And Señorita Ho-lee is dead."

But she didn't die here. It was no use. You couldn't argue with someone who just slid away into their own thoughts and refused to talk. In any event, in the following days, there was little extra time between feeding animals and cleaning cages. These tasks being beneath the two camp administrators, Vicki deduced sourly.

Cesar and Vicki weren't left with all the work, though. Bill made an appearance every day, and Joe was over for longer periods. His powerful build hadn't come from lounging around, Vicki had to admit. He worked hard and steadily, building a fresh fence when the tapir flattened one, digging up the water piping and replacing it with new, and tinkering the generator back to health when it refused to start.

Bill always paused to chat with Vicki after checking in with the center office. But Joe didn't approach her.

One day, having exhausted the center library's meager English selections, Vicki trekked through the woods to Bill's property. The curly-haired guard was at the gate, another walking the fence line. She didn't bother alerting them to her presence but slipped through the coffee rows. Reaching the back veranda, she tapped on the door to the kitchen. When she heard no response, she opened the door.

Back stateside, she'd have walked away. But expat hospitality went by different rules, and she'd been given an open invitation. She'd go in, borrow a few books, and leave a note for Bill.

Stepping inside, she called, "Hello!"

Silence.

No longer hesitating, Vicki entered the living area. The remnants of a small fire smoldered in the fireplace. She walked over to the nearest bookshelf. She was perusing a mildewed Reader's Digest Condensed Books collection when she heard a sound. At first she thought it was the snapping of kindling in the fireplace. Then she heard a soft scraping coming from the office.

So the house wasn't empty.

With two volumes in her hand, Vicki hurried over to the office door, calling, "Hi, Bill. I'm out here borrowing some books. Sorry—I didn't hear anyone when I knocked." She stopped as the door swung open under her touch.

It wasn't Bill who hadn't responded to her knock. Joe had been making some repairs, because the pottery shelf to her left was slightly out from the wall. Vicki heard again the scraping sound as he finished pushing it back. He dusted his hands off on a rag as he turned around, a frown giving him such a dangerous look that Vicki moved backward.

"What are you doing here?" he demanded.

"I'm sorry. I knocked," Vicki said defensively. "Didn't you hear me?"

"Actually, I was working and not paying attention." A step forward left Joe looming uncomfortably above her. "Hey, I didn't mean to startle you. I'm just wondering how you got past the guards. They do have a job they're supposed to be doing."

"I . . . I walked around the back through the coffee bushes." Vicki backed into the living room. "I'm sorry. I'm leaving. Where . . . where's Bill?"

Joe relaxed at her action, the dangerous look giving way to amusement. Following her into the bigger room, he said mildly, "No need to hurry. Bill ran into the village, but he should be back shortly. " He nodded toward the volumes in Vicki's hands. "By all means help yourself. Bill would be disappointed if you don't take what you want."

When Vicki didn't move, the books clutched against her like a shield, he added dryly, "I won't bite. I promise. It's just—if you could slip by security so easily, so could someone else. And they might not be as *safe* as you."

From the sudden twist of his mouth, Vicki knew he was thinking of Bill's warning. Her tension dissolved to sympathy. "I'm sure Bill didn't mean all that the other day. He was just kidding around. As I was."

Joe shook his shaggy head. "Bill Taylor never kids." His eyes lingered on her face. Then he took a long step backward. "And he's right. You should stay away from me. If you'll excuse me." The office door clicked shut behind him.

Vicki didn't even look over the titles in her hands. She just grabbed a couple more off the shelf and fled out the back door.

When she returned the books some days later, a Ladino with a shotgun was patrolling the veranda. He'd had orders, though, because while neither American was home, he led Vicki inside to choose fresh reading material.

Vicki didn't speak to Joe again until a few days later. Restless, she'd taken advantage of the siesta hour after lunch to explore the mountainside above the falls. She'd gone longer and higher than she'd planned, following an animal trail through thinning ground cover toward the top of the ridge. Joe stepped directly into her path.

Vicki hadn't recognized him at first. In fact, she'd thought he was one of the army troops. Then she realized his camouflage fatigues and cap were the type civilian hunters wore, the weapon in his hand a sporting rifle, a pair of binoculars around his neck.

"You don't want to go any farther," he said. "It's easy to get lost out here without a guide."

"And you?" Vicki demanded indignantly.

"I know my way." He didn't move from her path but waited for her to turn around.

Though she'd been planning to return to the center, it was with a furious flounce that Vicki started back down the trail. Joe followed so close on her heels that she could feel his warmth behind her. She reached the rock face above the falls when he left her, striding off through the trees.

The laborers were hard at work now under the bored surveillance of the guards, stooping and slashing in a thousand repeated gestures as they moved along. The leader had abandoned his usual canvas lounge chair to wander into the fading twilight. So much planning. So much sweat, if not his own. So much investment.

And now the payoff. Wealth beyond any of his original calculations.

He turned to beckon to the visitor, still standing in the concealment of camouflage netting and forest canopy. An irritant he might be, especially with his constant warnings and caution, but he was useful.

"Did I not tell you all this would be worth it? Come! Why are you so apprehensive? Have you not ensured there will be no more prying eyes?" An expansive arm took in landscape, workers, guards. "You worry too much. A week from now, perhaps two, this will all be finished, and it will no longer matter how many questions are asked."

"Until next time," his visitor said.

"Next time we will commit no errors."

"Next time I won't bail you out."

Neither believed the other. Tilting his hat low over his face, the visitor strolled out to survey the scene with satisfaction of his own. It was not wealth this place represented to him.

It was power.

His keen gaze searched the fading twilight. They were out there. He was sure of that now, even had a good idea where. But though he'd searched with every instrument available to him, the evidence they needed was still eluding him.

Should he make the call now?

But that would put a stop only to this time, this place. A way must be found to end this forever. Only then would the sins of the father finally be atoned.

So he would patiently wait and watch, as hard experience had schooled him so well to do.

If only the urgency wasn't so strong on him that time was running out.

CHAPTER TWENTY-TWO

"Why is Joe exploring the biosphere?" Vicki asked. "And if he can be out there, why shouldn't I?"

Cesar handed Vicki the blood sample he'd just drawn from a peccary. "He's been working on our water source. Perhaps he was following the stream. Besides, he is a man, not a woman. It is not so dangerous for him to travel alone."

There were infinite responses to this but none that would carry the day in this macho culture. "And the gun? Maybe he's poaching."

Cesar looked puzzled at the accusation. "Carrying a weapon in this region is wise. There are *bandidos,* if not animals. As to poaching, was he carrying anything?"

"No."

"In any case, Señor Taylor would know if *el americano* was doing such a thing. Be assured he was simply carrying out a task for Señor Taylor."

Vicki spoke to Michael more frequently. His responsibilities ranged across Guatemala, even to Washington DC, but every few days the unwelcome intrusion of helicopter rotors low over the canopy signaled some army and UPN exercise. Within the next hours, Vicki would hear the rumble of an army Jeep and Michael's quick stride on the gravel.

By his third visit Vicki couldn't even pretend he'd come only because of the investigation since there was never any news to add. As they sat over coffee in the shelter or strolled out to *Pozo Azul,* Michael drew from Vicki the tranquil happenings of the center and told of his own more exciting activities.

"Thanks to UPN success, Congress has doubled counternarcotics appropriations for Guatemala. DEA, State Department, local government—they're all smiling big right now. Enough that UPN is taking over a second army base up in the Petén to patrol the rain forest reserves and Mayan ruins."

The Petén was the tropical counterpart of Sierra de las Minas in northern Guatemala and home to some of the more spectacular Mayan archeological discoveries.

"This base is a lot closer to Guatemala City, so Alpiro will maintain it as his primary operating base. He's been in and out of here for months. But as of this week, Alpiro's taking full command of this base for UPN."

"And the soldiers?"

"Oh, the army contingent will stay. They're mainly area recruits doing their required military service, and UPN doesn't have a large manpower reserve of its own. But they'll be under UPN command—here and in the Petén. It's a step to reining the military back under civilian control."

If UPN could be called civilian. But Vicki didn't say that aloud.

Michael went on. "Meanwhile, Guatemala is small enough that with Alpiro's second-in-command up in the Petén, the helo wing alone should be able to patrol every nature reserve in the country."

Michael was charming, his smile alone attractive enough to keep Vicki's ears pricked for a helicopter rotor or a Jeep engine, and flatteringly attentive. So why after more than two weeks did Vicki feel she could no more read what lay behind his eyes than when Holly had first introduced him at the airport?

He says what he does but not what he thinks. I know more of Joe's opinions, even his past, than I do of Michael's.

Nor was Michael ever able to stay long or give any indication when he might be back. Vicki should have been lonely since Rosario and Beatriz ignored her now that her translation services were no longer needed, and Cesar was as silent as ever. But she found the solitude refreshing after the crowds and frantic pace of the last years. The animals were all the companionship she needed. And once the Germans had left, any lingering restlessness found its own outlet.

"So where have these been hiding?" Vicki demanded when Cesar wheeled a mountain bike from one of the locked sheds.

"A New Zealand foundation donated them for environmentally friendly transportation," Beatriz informed brusquely. She emerged from her office to take inventory of the supply sheds. "We lock them away when the teams are here. There are not enough for all, and it would only create more work to search for the gringos when they get lost. Cesar, if you are riding to market for Maria, I have a few items for you to bring back as well."

Vicki registered the empty backpack Cesar was wearing. "May I come along, please? There're a few things I'd like to look for at the market as well."

"It is not for me to say yes or no. The bicycles belong to the center. They are free for the use of any of their personnel." Cesar had mounted his bike but hadn't moved off.

Choosing to interpret his lingering as an invitation, Vicki grabbed one of three remaining bikes in the shed. She'd ridden only a regular bike around the Andrews farm but quickly discovered the versatility and sheer pleasure of the sturdy, lightweight mountain bike. It made easy work of the bumpy track into Verapaz.

In the days that followed, the bike gave Vicki a new freedom she relished to its fullest.

At first she rode into the village, but the poverty and soldiers were an unpleasant reminder of the world she'd left behind. So she rode instead along trails worn by animal and human feet across the plateau and lower slopes behind the center. Vicki chose the siesta hour when the Guatemalan staff disappeared into their quarters. Since she was always careful to be back by afternoon feedings, no one questioned her activities.

Vicki even made an attempt to follow the biosphere nature trail, but she'd hardly started up the dirt track when one of the army Jeeps that had accompanied their earlier outing came down the trail. Politely but firmly, they'd insisted on giving Vicki and the bike a ride back down to the plateau.

What I need is to find some trails that go over that ridge into the biosphere. But such a trek would take far longer than her free periods, and Vicki wasn't unmindful of the dangers of wandering these steep mountains alone. *All I need is for Beatriz to have to call out a search for me.*

Vicki hadn't given up either on breaking through Cesar's reserve. With no one else to help, the Guatemalan veterinarian grew easier with her presence as days passed, even occasionally speaking more than absolutely necessary.

Vicki had finished the feeding and watering one morning when she spotted Cesar mounting his bike. Wandering over, she asked, "Are you heading into market? Do you mind if I ride along?"

"Not to market. To church."

Days were so much alike up here, Vicki had lost track of the calendar. Yes, this would be her second Sunday since the Germans had left, her third up here in the mountains. It had been five days since Michael's last appearance. At least two since she'd seen Bill and Joe even at a distance. Feeling restless for human contact, Vicki asked impulsively, "Would you mind if I went with you? That is, if these are okay." She gestured to the jeans and sweatshirt she was wearing against another drizzly morning. "I didn't bring much else."

Cesar wore the same cheap cotton pants and shirt he always wore, but he'd changed into fresh ones since the morning rounds. "You are welcome to come. And they will not care what you wear." A smile flickered on the thin features. "They do not expect gringos to dress as they do. But it is perhaps very different from the churches you know. It will not all be in español."

"All the better. I'd like to see what a highland church is like." Vicki was suddenly eager to escape the center. She hadn't been to church since she'd accompanied other Casa de Esperanza volunteers to the expat Union Church on one of her Sundays in Guatemala City. And this might even be the opportunity to break through Cesar's reserve.

Vicki had expected to head into the central plaza, but Cesar turned his bike at one of the thatched homes on the outskirts of the village. A dirt yard held fruit trees and a banana patch. A large pot balanced over an outdoor cook fire, and a hammock hung under an orange tree. She spotted two pairs of solemn black eyes watching from the hammock.

"This is Maria's home. We'll leave the bikes here. They will be safer where no one will see them." Opening a bamboo door, Cesar lifted Vicki's bike along with his own inside, throwing a burlap sack over them before pulling the door shut. Then he hurried over to the hammock. "Alicia. Gabriela. Why are you not in church?"

The tearful murmur and Cesar's coaxing answers were in the local Mayan dialect.

"What's wrong?" Vicki asked.

"They do not wish to leave the house." Cesar sighed. "They're afraid they will see the soldiers. They say they want to go home to their own village."

"Are they okay here by themselves?"

By stateside standards the two were still young enough for a babysitter, but Cesar shrugged. "Maria knows they are here. And the church is only a short distance away."

Vicki seized the opportunity to introduce her own interest. "You said Maria was your cousin. Is this where you were born then? In this village? No, I guess you couldn't be since the army built this after . . ." Vicki trailed off.

Cesar finished simply, "Yes, I was brought here from one of the villages that was destroyed. My cousin Maria's village was destroyed too. She took me in like Alicia and Gabriela many years ago. Not here, because this place was not yet built, but the refugee camp where I found *Tía* Maria and where we lived while we built this place." He waved a hand in the general direction of the army base.

"And your own family? Are they here too?"

His expression went instantly somber. "I was the only survivor of my village."

"Oh." Vicki had hoped to ease the conversation somehow to Holly. She *knew* this young highlander had more to say than he was letting out. He *had* to know something useful, because if not, there was nowhere left for Vicki to go in this quest. But his statement was so matter-of-fact, so unbelievable on this quiet, dusty village street with the sun shining, the cook pot simmering deliciously on the fire, a macaw offering glowing color and raucous commentary from an orange branch overhead that Vicki stared at Cesar. "You mean, your village and Maria's and the girls'—all of them were destroyed? By whom? The army? And why?"

Cesar's shoulders hunched. "I do not know of the others. I wasn't there. But in my village, yes, it was the army. They destroyed many villages in these mountains. As to why, they said we were helping *la guerrilla,* that we were all *comunistas.*"

"And was it true? I mean, your village? You had to have been a small child at the time. Is it possible that there was provocation? Maybe not for everything that happened. But why the army thought they had to go in and fight . . . If there really was a war going on—"

"I was not so small!" Cesar cut her off. "I don't how old I was. They do not give birth certificates in the villages. But seven or eight was decided in the army camp when I started school. Old enough to remember clearly what I saw. Was the village—my family—*comunista*? The army called them so, to be sure. I do not know politics. But was it *comunista* to want freedom for our people? the right to work for ourselves and to feed our families, not to slave and starve and die on the plantations of the wealthy so that they could live in luxury at the cost of our sweat and labor and blood? Is it *comunista* to want an education? to organize the cooperatives, so that together we could bargain for better equipment and prices than we can achieve on our own? to sell together our goods at the market? Tell me, did your own labor class never fight for such rights? Or did the landowners and factory bosses surrender them willingly?"

"Well, no, of course not."

"The guerrillas would come into the town, yes. We did not ask them to come or want them because we knew they would cause trouble. But they too had guns, so what could we do? They didn't hurt us. Why should they? Many had relatives in the village. They were fighting for our people, our future. Then the army came and told us that because we had allowed the guerrillas in, we were sympathizers. And for that they destroyed our village."

"It just seems so unbelievable. I understand war. I've seen it in other countries. But that government forces would target civilians—women and children—right here in the Americas under the eyes of the international media and never be held accountable—"

"Yes, that is what all the gringos say," Cesar said flatly. "Either they do not believe it could be so bad, the people must be exaggerating, or they throw money at us as though rebuilding houses or schools will wipe away all that has happened."

Vicki was dismayed. She hadn't meant to provoke such an outpouring of emotion. And after all her effort, she was losing him, the dark features shuttering into that stoical Mayan reserve.

"And Holly?" she asked with some anger of her own. "Which was she?"

Unexpectedly, it proved the right question this time. Cesar relaxed visibly, even smiling briefly. "She did not ask such questions. She spoke only of the animals, the trees, the water. Those who come to the center are like that. They are interested only in the land, not its people. In the future, not the past. It is why I chose to work there. Because there it is possible to forget."

Vicki saw horror lingering in Cesar's fixed gaze, felt the tenuous peace she'd found in this remote place draining away.

"I . . . I don't think I should have come. I shouldn't be intruding on your people, your church. Maybe I'll just ride back."

"No, no!" Cesar looked dismayed. "No, please, you must not leave. I am sorry if I should make you feel so. You must be thinking it will be sad. But it isn't. If the past is not so easily forgotten, nor is the future. Our church meeting is a time of rejoicing and hope, not sadness. You will see. Come! Come!" He grinned. "Your sister loved to come to our services."

That did it. Cesar wasn't quite as passive as he'd schooled himself to be in front of his Ladino and expatriate colleagues. Meekly, Vicki followed him on foot down an alley. They'd turned a corner when she heard music. A minor atonal singing that wound through an intricate beat sharp enough for Vicki to feel it in her molars. As they headed toward it, she glanced around at the thatched-roof homes.

"What I find really unbelievable is that you came from here to become a veterinarian. How in the world did you make it to the university? That is really impressive."

He looked pleased even as he waved away the praise. "It is true there haven't always been many opportunities to study. But there were teachers at the army camp where I was brought. They took an interest in me. A scholarship was found to permit me to go to the city to study. Later when I worked hard, the scholarship became enough for the university."

"From the army, you mean? To compensate for destroying your village?"

"No, not the army, never the army." Emotion flashed in his eyes. "To compensate would be to admit they had done wrong. No, I truly do not know where the scholarship came from. I was very young, and there have been many programs of *extranjeros* and *misioneros* to benefit the poor in Guatemala. But I have always believed it was the gringo."

"The gringo?" Vicki found herself actually holding her breath, willing her companion to keep talking. But just then they crossed an alley into a large corner lot worn bare of grass. The singing became abruptly louder.

Vicki had assumed they were heading toward the town cathedral. But this was a much simpler affair similar to the communal shelter at the center. Stripped tree trunks held up a thatched A-frame, the dried palm fronds hanging low enough to keep out all but the worst weather. Behind a platform at the far end, adobe bricks had been built up to about ten feet high for added protection. The platform was more adobe brick.

The floor was dirt. Narrow, backless wooden benches were the only seating. Its only identification as a church was a banner attached to the adobe behind the platform announcing, "*Iglesia de Paz*," "Church of Peace."

"So what kind of church is this?" Vicki asked as they ducked through the open rear of the structure.

Cesar looked puzzled. "Why, this is where we sing and praise God. We also read the Bible, which is God's Word. And pray to our heavenly Father and His Son, Jesus Christ, who is our Savior from sins."

"No, no, I mean what denomination? In my country there are many church groups. I was just wondering which one yours belongs to."

Cesar's face lit up with understanding. "Ah yes. We are Christian, of course."

Okay, so it didn't really matter. Either way, it was vastly different from the sedate community church Vicki had attended with the Andrewses or even the middle-class city church she'd visited in Mexico City.

Cesar and Vicki were not the only latecomers filing in, but the benches were already full, if not of the entire village, certainly a sizable portion. Late arrivals stood along the sides and in the back. Children squatted on the dirt floor or wandered between benches.

The congregation was on its feet, their singing shaking the rafters with enough force to sprinkle dust and twigs onto Vicki as she followed Cesar to an open spot near a support pillar. The intricate beat came not only from an assortment of hide-covered drums but the staccato of clapping. There was a guitar and reed flutes. The music itself was not cheerful to Vicki's American ears, the melody minor and plaintive, the lyrics in some Mayan dialect she couldn't understand. But from the enthusiasm of the singers around her, they didn't agree.

Then the song shifted to Spanish, the melody a familiar camp tune that had incredibly crossed continents and cultures to this highland Guatemalan village.

"He decidido seguir a Cristo." "I have decided to follow Jesus."

Heads turned as Cesar and Vicki settled under the thatch, but the singing didn't miss a beat. From the platform someone called out, "Cesar, up here!"

At his apologetic glance, Vicki waved him forward. A moment later he took his place behind a marimba. Vicki listened in delight to a ripple of chords from the padded mallets. Her WRC colleague was good!

The melody and song were again unfamiliar and wholly Mayan, but Vicki found herself caught up in the foot-tapping, hand-clapping rhythm until her hands were sore.

As more and more latecomers squeezed in, Vicki backed herself against a support pillar to keep from being jostled into the thatch. The light filtering in through the thatch and press of bodies was dim, so it wasn't until the instruments fell silent and those with seats rustled down onto the benches that Vicki was able to see across the interior—straight into a pair of green eyes.

How had she possibly missed Joe? But he too had backed against one of the support pillars, slouching against it in his usual, lounging posture, the dried fronds of the thatch blending in with his sun-bleached hair, which was currently neatly combed. He was even in jacket and pants, as Vicki had seen him wearing at the embassy.

If Vicki had been unaware of his presence, Joe had known of hers;

he gave her a civil nod as her eyes met his. When he straightened up and disappeared from the pillar, Vicki assumed he'd left.

But a few moments later, there was a rustle of thatch behind her. Then Joe murmured, "You might want to close your mouth before you catch a fly down your throat. You look so surprised to see me in church; I'm not sure I shouldn't be feeling insulted."

Vicki snapped her jaw shut. "I'm not surprised to see you in church," she defended herself feebly. "I just wasn't expecting you *here*."

"I could say the same."

And you wouldn't be here if you'd known, Vicki interpreted his sardonic expression.

Joe seemed to feel he had to explain himself, because as he leaned against the pillar where Vicki stood, he went on, "I may not have much chance to get to church when I'm on the road. But when I can, I like to come. If only to remind myself there really are decent, honest, caring human beings somewhere on this earth. This one—" Joe was close enough as he turned his head to survey the church interior that his jacket sleeve brushed Vicki's shoulder—"I like."

Vicki looked around. The women wore mostly the indigenous *huipil* and wraparound skirt, the men cheap pants and shirts like Cesar. The youngest children wore nothing at all. The singing had ceased, but it was hardly quiet, so Joe and Vicki's low English exchange was no distraction. A young Ladino preacher shouted enthusiastically above the whimper of babies, a babble of restless children and their mothers' shushing, a clucking of chickens, even the snuffle of a pig sprawled nearby under the thatched eaves.

This congregation held the poorest of the planet's poor, their wiry frames stunted and thin from a scant diet, the damp musk of inadequate hygiene so strong that Vicki was thankful for the open sides. It was for people like these that she had pledged herself to fight, raging against the injustice of their lives, battering her mental fists against heaven itself for answers to their plight. More incredibly, like Cesar and Maria and little Alicia and Gabriela, every one of this group had come to this place from tragedy greater than any Vicki had ever undergone.

So how was it they could sit here listening to whatever the Ladino pastor was reading from a huge Bible in their dialect with the contentment Vicki could see on bronze features all around her?

No, not contentment. Acceptance. Hope. Trust. Even joy.

Maybe the answer was in the final song that brought the congregation back to its feet, another of those oddly minor and joyous unfamiliar tunes. This time the words were in Spanish, so Vicki could translate the gist of the lyrics:

Así por el mundo yo voy caminando
So through this world I walk along
De pruebas rodeado y de tentación.
Surrounded by trials and temptations.
Pero a mi lado viene consolando
Yet at my side He walks, consoling me
Mi bendito Cristo en la turbación.
In all the chaos my blessed Christ.

The triumphal chorus soared to the rafters. *"Más allá del sol, yo tengo un hogar, hogar, bella hogar, más allá del sol."* "Far beyond the sun, I have a home, a home, a beautiful home, far beyond the sun."

Vicki found herself swallowing again and again. She stole a glance at Joe. He was listening with every indication of appreciation, his strong features as relaxed as she had ever seen them.

A similar thought must have come to Joe; he nodded toward the singers. "I guess it's like you were saying the other day on the plane. These people really *know* what we who possess so much more have a hard time believing—that there's something beyond all the dirt and poverty and problems that makes it all worth living. And that the God who created it all really does know what He's doing with the world."

Vicki shook her head, bemused. "That wasn't me on the plane. That was you."

His mouth curved slightly, but he said nothing more as the pastor, in fashion the world over, wound up the service with what were clearly announcements. The dim lighting allowed Vicki to study Joe's profile discreetly. He had to be the most contradictory person she'd ever met. It was as though he *chose* to be the unreliable drifter Bill had warned her against. But every once in a while, even against his will, another very decent human being slipped through the facade he had chosen to present the world.

"Why are you looking at me like that?" he asked.

This time Vicki didn't let her gaze drop as she answered with equal softness, "Because I'm starting to like you—the way you think. And I'm not sure I should."

Vicki considered him meditatively. Then a new thought came to her that in the dimness made sudden sense. "Joe, are you working for someone else besides Bill? Maybe some government agency?"

"Are you trying to rehabilitate me? I'm flattered, but the answer is no. I'm working for Bill Taylor—no one else."

Vicki swallowed disappointment. "But you aren't really who you appear to be either, are you?"

Joe didn't answer immediately. Vicki was sorry she'd asked, because the relaxed serenity that had transformed him was gone, his mouth thinning into what had to be an unpleasant thought. As though torn out of him, he admitted in a low voice, "No, I'm not. And I really shouldn't be here. If you'll excuse me."

CHAPTER TWENTY-THREE

CHAPTER TWENTY-THREE

Joe melted into the thatch and press of bodies. As the service broke up, Vicki didn't see him again.

Cesar introduced Vicki to the pastor and his wife. Then Vicki spotted the center cook working her way toward them through the crowd.

Maria invited them to stay for the hearty stew Vicki had seen simmering over the cook fire. Alicia and Gabriela emerged from the hammock for this. By the time she left, Vicki had even managed to coax a smile from them.

Vicki was glad she went, but the outing had spoiled the fragile tranquility she'd carved out for herself among the animals and flowers and tangled vegetation of this mountain sanctuary. Her beautiful surroundings were no longer enough.

Vicki didn't make the trek again to Bill's house. Running out of reading material, she leafed through the Bible she'd dug out after Evelyn's visit. Vicki reread the story Evelyn had told of Abraham and Sarah, then went on to others she remembered from Sunday school.

Joseph sold by his brothers into captivity in Egypt.

Moses wandering for forty years as a shepherd before being called to tend an even more recalcitrant flock.

Daniel and his three friends ripped away from their families for a lifetime of exile in Babylon.

The next Sunday Vicki returned to the village church, where she was now recognized and welcomed. This time Joe wasn't there. It had been days since he'd even shown up at the center.

Over the next week Vicki read of wandering prophets and missionary apostles. Of Jesus, the very Son of God, walking dusty streets of villages not unlike rural Guatemala, compassionately touching people just like those with whom Vicki had worked. None of the prophets and missionaries seemed to have had it easy. Nor had the people they'd come to serve always cared or cooperated. Vicki read of persecution and stoning and death. Yet they'd clearly found what they were doing worthwhile. Like that village congregation—and Joe—they'd seen something ahead that made their own troubles and the less-than-perfect world in which they lived eminently meaningful.

And Vicki?

Sitting cross-legged on the rock shelf overlooking *Pozo Azul* and Lake Izabal that had become her favorite thinking spot, Vicki closed the Bible. It was a rare clear afternoon. She took a deep breath, relishing the fragrance, the spray of the falls on her face, the waves dancing silver far below.

It's so beautiful! But beautiful though it was, the time had come to leave. Not just because of those e-mails from her employer demanding to know when she'd be back. There was simply no reason to stay.

Vicki had strong suspicions Rosario and Beatriz were siphoning animals into the exotic pet trade. And someone over at the army base was providing transportation. The two administrators handled the logs, and those didn't match Vicki's unofficial count of parrots, macaws, and monkeys. Though she'd drop a bug in Alison's ear, Vicki couldn't rouse herself to any serious outrage. Nor did she believe Rosario and Beatriz would kill over such a matter, however urgently Holly might have looked at such an affair. Such transactions were too much a part of life down here. Besides, they'd been at the center when Holly died.

The same could be said for the army base. If they were aware Holly had been wandering on her own through the biosphere, it was hardly a capital offense. Either way, if neither Vicki nor Michael with all Alpiro's help had turned up any further leads in what was now nearly a month, she had to accept it was unlikely to happen.

Maybe I was wrong all along. Holly really was in the wrong place at the wrong time. Maybe I really did lose the pendant when we moved her.

An Australian team was arriving tomorrow, and there were Spanish speakers among them. Vicki wouldn't be needed anymore. So what next? Maybe a longer-term assignment? Put down some roots?

She walked back up the path. *I'll have to let Michael know.* Would he be disappointed to see her go? Or relieved to have one problem laid to rest for the embassy?

Vicki had last seen Michael almost a week ago. But she'd seen UPN helicopters coming in this morning, so maybe he'd be by this afternoon. *Will he try to talk me out of going? Or is he just being . . . nice?*

The path led Vicki near the outdoor kitchen, and she heard murmuring before identifying the speakers. Cesar and Maria, heads close together, hands gesturing frenetically.

"Is everything all right?"

They whirled around. Vicki saw the urgency of their expressions before passivity dropped like a well-accustomed mask.

Cesar waved away her question. "Yes, everything is fine. Just a small difficulty that has arisen. Since all is in readiness for tomorrow, I have assured Maria no one will object if she departs before the dinner hour."

With a team arriving tomorrow, Maria had spent the morning sorting out a mule cart of market produce while Vicki worked with Beatriz to prepare the sleeping barracks. Joe had even flown in a cargo of canned and dry goods. Vicki had heard the DHC-2 drop in over the ridge not long after the UPN helicopters. A crunch of gravel she'd heard on her way out to *Pozo Azul* had turned out to be Bill's pickup delivering the supplies.

"You will tell Beatriz that Maria and I were called away? And perhaps, if it is not too much trouble, warm the food for yourself and the others?"

"It's no trouble. But what is the difficulty?" Vicki looked at Maria. She stood motionless with her eyes lowered, but the work-worn hands were twisting tightly in her apron. "Cesar, something's obviously wrong. Is there anything I can do to help?"

"It's nothing for which you need concern yourself. It is only . . . Alicia and Gabriela. They cannot be found."

"That isn't a small problem! Do you think they've just run off to play or that something's happened to them? How long have they been gone?"

"Since yesterday we have not been able to locate them."

Vicki managed to get out of Cesar that the girls had eaten their tortillas and beans the morning before but had been nowhere in sight when Maria left for the center. She had assumed they'd already headed to the village school. Since children their age wandered freely in these mountains, many even working for a living, Maria hadn't worried until the two girls hadn't shown up when she returned from work. A neighbor child had informed her that the girls never arrived at school. They'd searched the streets, calling, knocking on doors. But the girls had not turned up before it grew too dark to continue.

"Maria feels it is possible the children wandered too far playing to return before nightfall and found some place to sleep to wait for light. Or perhaps they were trying to frighten my cousin by staying away. Perhaps as punishment for a scolding. When Maria came to work this morning, others of the family agreed to search for them in the fields and woods. They were to let us know if the girls were found. But now it is afternoon, and Maria worries that they should be out so long without food. They are still quite small," Cesar finished.

"But of course you should go find out what's happening," Vicki said with exasperation. "I can't believe you came to work today. I'd like to help with the search. How are you getting into town?"

"I thought the bikes. Though Maria doesn't ride."

No, Maria walked. Close to an hour each way. Six days a week. Rain or shine. And no doubt considered this center employment a cushy lot in life.

"That'll take too long." Vicki glanced toward the sky. Now when she'd have welcomed the intrusion of a helicopter rotor, it was empty except for the gray of rain clouds beginning to spill down from the mountain heights. If only Michael had shown up, she could have asked his help. Vicki's gaze fell on the green pickup parked in the cul-de-sac. "Perhaps Señor Taylor would give us a ride into the village."

Vicki was never sure how much Maria understood of her Spanish, but Cesar spread his hands in acquiescence.

Vicki dashed over to the pickup. If Bill has time, maybe we could even ride around the plateau and try to spot the girls.

But it wasn't Bill who was walking out of the main building, looking down at a clipboard with an abstracted frown, a hand radio to his mouth.

Vicki stopped short. She hadn't spoken to Joe since that last strained encounter at the village church. Then she lengthened her stride. Alicia and Gabriela were of more urgency than any lingering awkwardness. "Joe, is Bill here? I need a favor."

The hand radio dropped. "No, he's occupied elsewhere. What is it?"

"I . . . well, I was hoping for a ride as far as the village." Vicki explained the situation. "And if the girls are still missing, maybe Bill or . . . or you might have time to drive us around to look for them."

Vicki saw Joe's surreptitious glance at his watch before she'd even finished. "Of course, if it's too much trouble . . ."

Joe didn't rise to the bait. "A couple of lost kids are never too much trouble. But I just got back from Guatemala City with these supplies. Taylor is expecting me to report in shortly. And this is his vehicle. Let me see what he has to say."

Stepping a few paces away, Joe raised the hand radio. "Yes, I got it. . . . They're on board. . . . I'm aware of the time crunch. . . . Not till dark. In the meantime, we've got a situation. . . . Maria's girls . . . Yes, I'm aware of our priorities." Clipping the radio to his belt, he walked back to Vicki. "Taylor says the truck's all yours. As am I."

Was that some obnoxious double entendre? And how could he smile so gently helping Maria into the cab while treating Vicki as though she had some contagious disease? No matter. At least they had the vehicle. With no cargo, Joe took the rutted track so fast that Vicki had to grab the seat to keep from being jolted off.

She'd hoped to arrive at Maria's and find the two girls safe. Or at least evidence of a well-organized search. There was neither, though swarms of people were milling around the dirt yard. Vicki recognized the Ladino pastor among them.

"Why aren't they out looking for the girls?" Vicki demanded of Cesar.

"It's getting late in the day. And now it's starting to rain. It's going to be freezing once night falls."

He shook his head. "It isn't easy. The plateau has already been searched. It is not so big an area. The girls are not here."

"You don't think maybe they've wandered up into the biosphere?" No wonder the villagers were still here. How could they even begin searching that vast, untamed wilderness? "Have you tried contacting the army base? If Michael is there, I'm sure he could get them to call out a search. Even if he isn't, maybe we could ask him to talk to his friends there. Or talk to Coronel Alpiro ourselves. If they could get their helicopters up into the mountains, maybe they could find the girls."

Cesar shook his head again.

Vicki studied his expression with sudden comprehension. "You know where the girls might be, don't you? At least you have some idea where they might be headed."

With a glance at the crowd of villagers milling around the yard, Cesar said in a low voice, "It is feared the girls have returned home to their village—the one that was destroyed. They have been determined to go home. That this is not possible, Alicia and Gabriela have refused to believe."

"But isn't that good news? If you know where the girls were headed, it should be simple enough to follow the trail and search for them. Look, if it's the distance, we can take the pickup. It's four-wheel drive, right?" Vicki shot a challenging look at Joe, standing silently a pace away, watching, listening but contributing nothing. "Or we can still contact the base. If a ground vehicle can't get in, maybe one of their helicopters can."

"No, that is not possible. Where the village was, where they may have gone—" Cesar motioned toward the mountain range, now shrouded with rain clouds, rising behind the plateau—"is up there where it is prohibited for anyone to enter. If it is even discovered that Alicia and Gabriela have returned to their home, *los militares* will be very angry." He hesitated before saying carefully, "Perhaps it is best to wait. To hope that the children will return of their own accord. When they are hungry enough, they will choose to come back."

Vicki saw with disbelief that he was serious. Saw the fear on the faces around her. The nods of assent on bystanders who were listening. What volumes this spoke of the past that these people could still be so frightened of their authorities. But this wasn't the past.

"And if they get lost or hurt? Or fall down the mountain? Or if they do find their home and freak out over what happened?" Vicki took a deep breath as she tried to keep her tone patient. "All these environmental regulations were meant to protect the biosphere from erosion and poaching. Not to keep people from looking for a couple of lost kids. Do you really think the UPN or the army is going to come after you for something like that? Cesar, you work for the Ministry of Environment. So do I, for that matter. Even Joe here, if not technically. We have as much right up there as these UPN soldiers. I mean, this is ridiculous! What are they going to do? Shoot us for going in there to look for the girls?"

She'd spoken in Spanish, and her challenging glance was now for the whole group of villagers who'd fallen silent around her. No one contradicted her assertion, but neither was there any response in the stubborn blankness of their faces.

"I'll prove you're worried for nothing. Cesar, is there a road up that way?"

"There was a track that market trucks and the army once used connected to what is now the nature trail," Cesar admitted. "There are men here who could show the way. If you truly believe *los militares* will permit it."

"We won't ask them. What's the saying—better to ask forgiveness than permission? If you don't think the army base will help, then Joe here can drive us there, and we can at least take a look."

Joe's expression was as neutral as the villagers', but he switched to English as he answered. "Vicki, I appreciate your motives for wanting to get involved. But my gut instinct tells me these guys are probably right. The military doesn't take kindly to having their orders ignored, no matter what reason. May I recommend your earlier suggestion? If these people are afraid to get the army involved—and I don't doubt they've had good enough reasons—then contact the base yourself. See if you can get Alpiro to mobilize some resources. Or if you can get through to Camden, have him put the pressure on. I'd be happy to drive you over there myself."

"And how long would that take?" Vicki cried out. "Nightfall? You know how slow everything moves around here. How about a compromise? Cesar?"

Vicki switched back to Spanish. She was undoubtedly being the stereotypical heavy-handed Ugly American. But she was feeling increasing urgency and exasperation. How long had those two precious little girls been without food, possibly even water? Vicki could almost feel the twisting of hunger in her own stomach. The chill of damp clothing. The fear and lostness. How could these people take such a serious affair so calmly? Especially since the sullen, dark clouds drifting down from the mountain heights had now settled low over the plateau, bringing with it the damp drizzle of the *chipi-chipi*. The heavy, cold tang of the breeze promised ground mists close behind. Once fog closed in, even without darkness, a search would be impossible.

"If you have some men who could guide the way, why don't we head over to the checkpoint where the nature trail starts? We can explain the situation to the UPN guards there. Have them contact their base to let them know we're heading up to look for the girls. If they send for more help, all the better. Either way, we don't lose more time, and everyone will be happy." Vicki gave Joe a hard look. "Bill did say we could use the truck and you until dark?"

An eager lightening of hope on dark faces told Vicki she'd won. As did Joe's shrug.

The plan's execution went as smoothly and quickly as she could have hoped. Four men—relatives of some sort, Vicki gathered—were chosen to accompany Cesar and the Americans. Hurrying indoors, Maria returned with a pile of handwoven blankets and a banana leaf wrapped around tortillas. "*Para las niñas.*" "For the girls." It was the first Spanish Vicki had heard her speak.

The Ladino pastor stepped up as the Guatemalans were climbing into the pickup bed. "May we pray for your success before you go?"

"Why don't you pray as we go?" Joe already had the engine running. "Vicki, far be it for me to push, but if we're going to do this, we're rather pressed for time."

"Yes, please pray for us." With a wave, Vicki hastily climbed in beside Joe. The pickup was spinning out of the yard before her door clicked shut.

Vicki's satisfaction lasted as far as the checkpoint. "What do you mean, you won't let us through? We're with the center. We have clearance. We were here a couple of weeks ago with a tour, remember? Just call your base. Let me speak to your commanding officer."

The sentries manning *la garita,* as the guard shack with its long pole across the road was called, numbered less than the pickup contingent. Just three in UPN uniforms. But each cradled an M16 automatic rifle, and Vicki saw no yielding in those stony expressions.

"That is not necessary," the guard leaning in Vicki's rolled-down window answered brusquely. "Our orders are clear. No one is to enter the biosphere without authorization and an escort."

"Then come with us! Please, you have to understand. There are two small children lost up there. We're only asking to follow the track. You're welcome to supervise that we don't touch the animals or flowers."

Vicki glanced in dismay past Joe to the metallic gray of a gun barrel thrust through his window. The third guard stood in front of the pole barring the road. They were not going to budge. It was raining in earnest now too, Cesar and his companions in the pickup bed hunkering down under woolen ponchos and Maria's blankets.

Vicki turned to Joe. "I guess we're going to have to go to the base after all. But by the time we get through to anyone, much less get things moving, it's going to be too dark to get a helicopter in the air. Or find them on the ground."

She caught Joe checking his watch, and her anger and despair blazed high. "Are you still worried about your schedule when those two little girls are out there freezing? Don't you get it? If they stay out in this all night, they could die! Or do you just not care?" She twisted cold fingers around each other. "Oh, if only Michael were here. Or Bill. There's got to be something we can do."

Joe turned his head, and Vicki was taken aback at the anger on his face. "You have no idea what you're saying. But fine. You want something done—here goes."

Ignoring the gun barrel in his face, Joe leaned out the window to say in polite Spanish, "Look, *sargento*—" an exaggeration as the sentry was at most a corporal—"we wouldn't wish to be uncooperative. If you will contact your commanding officer, Coronel Alpiro, or the rescue center liaison for the Ministry of Environment, Señor Guillermo Taylor, whom you know, they will assure you we have proper authorization to enter the biosphere. Please inform your superiors of our present mission and that we will be happy to accept any escort they would like to send. Now if you could step back so that I might move this vehicle."

Like I didn't already try that, Vicki refrained from saying aloud.

As the guards moved away from the pickup, Joe smoothly slid the gear selector into reverse. The wheels skidded in the mud as he backed away from the checkpoint. The sentries lowered their weapons and headed toward their guard shack.

The pickup had reversed a dozen yards when Joe hit the brakes. But instead of reversing farther to turn back into the main road, he shifted to drive.

Then, gunning the engine, Joe floored the accelerator.

CHAPTER TWENTY-FOUR

The sentries stood frozen in the trail, staring at the juggernaut of metal and rubber lumbering toward them. Vicki's voice rose to a squeak as she braced herself for the impact. But the guards weren't suicidal. They dived out of the way so that it was the pole that connected with the pickup's front grille. With a screech of torn aluminum, it landed to one side of the track.

"Bill's going to kill me for this," Joe gritted between clenched teeth.

The guards were already back on their feet, M16s coming up. The vehicle was in four-wheel drive, and with the muddy, rutted condition of the track, they were not going fast enough to possibly evade gunfire.

But it didn't come. Through the rear cab window, Vicki saw the guards lower their weapons, reaching instead for hand radios. Then the pickup slid around a corner, leaving them out of sight.

Vicki's hands were trembling in her lap. She couldn't imagine how the men in the back of the pickup must be shaking. "That wasn't what I was asking. You could have gotten us killed. You *should* have!"

"Not likely." Joe spun the pickup around another muddy curve.

Vicki glanced back again. Their Mayan companions were all still there, though they'd dropped flat into the bottom of the pickup bed.

"If you knew anything about guns, you'd know those M16s weren't loaded. And if you knew anything about law enforcement down here, you'd know they don't normally trust low-level sentry duty with ammo. An empty weapon is effective enough, since the locals are as ignorant as you are. Right now they'll be doing just what you wanted—calling their base for backup, which will be showing up sooner or later, so I'd suggest finding those kids before that happens. I'm counting on you talking your way out of this with Alpiro and Camden, because trouble with the local law I don't need."

"Don't worry. I'll take full responsibility," Vicki said stiffly, then added, "And thank you. If we can just find the girls, I'm sure we can clear it up with base later."

"Good. Then get one of those guys to tell me where I'm going." Joe took several more bends of the trail at a too-fast slide before he stopped.

Vicki walked back to the pickup bed.

Cesar conferred with his companions, then assured Vicki, "It is far by walking. But in this vehicle, perhaps an hour. Though it may not be possible to drive the full way. The village is not on this road but farther down the mountain."

That Vicki had already guessed since she'd seen nothing of the sort on her earlier excursion up here. A soft, steady drizzle fell on her as she looked around and above. Except for the brown ribbon of track, there was only a green tangle of trees and leaves and vines all around, so thick that even if they'd scrounged up that helicopter, it couldn't have done much good through the canopy.

"Are you sure the girls will be on this trail?" Vicki asked. "I mean, this all looks alike. Even if they were headed for their old home, they could have lost their way and be anywhere."

Cesar shook his head. "They have been this way often. And they are old enough to know their way."

Cesar detailed one of the four Mayan villagers to accompany Joe as guide in the cab. The rest stayed in the pickup bed to keep a watch for the two girls. Vicki insisted on joining them, one of Maria's blankets wrapped around her shoulders. Her lashes blinked away water as she strained her eyes and ears for two brightly woven *huipiles*—or the UPN escort that was bound to catch up with them.

Vicki didn't relish the inevitable explanation she was going to have to make to Colonel Alpiro. Surely he'd be reasonable, considering the circumstances. After all, he'd proved reasonable enough in the end on the airfield once Michael had shown up to explain. Still, a successful search would make it easier.

But whatever those angry guards were doing down on the plateau, no sight or sound reached them except the rumble of the pickup's engine and the long tunnel of the nature trail. Even the birds and monkeys huddled silent out of the weather. This was the trail Vicki had toured with the German team, and it would have been a delightful drive under other circumstances with occasional glimpses through the rain and mist of tumbling slopes, rearing peaks, a waterfall.

From one steep drop-off, Vicki spotted a circular pattern far below that looked like one of the clearings Joe had overflown on her arrival. Though any blooming of white and purple and scarlet was gone, leaving only one more weed patch hacked out of the cloud forest. Catching a flicker of movement down in the valley, Vicki leaned forward. A herd of highland deer feeding in the clearing, dappled hides blending into the greens and browns of the background?

But a fresh tangle of vegetation cut off her view as the pickup rumbled on, and Vicki caught no other glimpse of human encroachment. Or two little girls.

It was almost exactly the hour Cesar had promised when the pickup stopped. Vicki could see no difference between this stretch of track and that ahead or behind. But the men were already climbing out of the truck. As she joined them by the side of the road, she saw there was indeed a narrow, overgrown track snaking downward from the nature trail. The men were clustered around indentations in the mud. Even Vicki's inexpert eye could identify them as sandal prints. Small ones.

Joe bent down to touch one. "The girls have been here. And not long ago as the rain hasn't yet washed these away. They may not have even made the village yet, depending on how far that is. Which I hope it isn't, because this vehicle isn't going down that track."

It wasn't, the Mayan highlanders assured in chorus.

"Good." Joe looked up at a glimpse of gray between dripping leaves and vines and branches arched above the track. "If you can be back within the hour, we should make it down before dark. Barely."

A brief discussion concluded that the four village men who knew the area would follow the sandal tracks while the center personnel waited with the pickup. With no pursuit in evidence, the Mayan villagers had relaxed visibly. Taking with them blankets and the tortillas in their banana leaf wrapping, they disappeared at an easy lope into the brush of the overgrown trail. This time Vicki made no protest to go along. She couldn't begin to keep up with the speed and stamina with which these highlanders clambered around their mountain home.

Climbing instead into the cab, Vicki tucked the blanket tight against the chill. Joe joined Cesar outside. Through the rear window, Vicki could see them siphoning gas from a fuel drum into the pickup tank. The heavy weave of the blanket held in Vicki's body heat so that her damp clothing was steaming and she felt almost warm. No wonder the locals preferred their own handiwork to store-bought synthetics.

At least with all this rain, the girls wouldn't lack water. And those small sandal prints proved this mad expedition up here hadn't been so crazy. Surely even Colonel Alpiro with his cold gaze and unbending regulations would admit they'd been right to come before the children were caught in the rain and cold and dark of another night. *I'll happily pay for another pole and any dents in Bill's truck. Please, God, just let them find Alicia and Gabriela alive and well.*

Vicki must have dozed off, because she was confused and lost and frightened, and all around was the screaming of engines and angry shouts. She sat up with a start. It wasn't a dream. A *throp-throp* of helicopter rotors was directly overhead. The roar of a ground vehicle wasn't the one she sat in. Pushing aside the blanket, Vicki jumped out of the pickup and into the very confusion of which she'd been dreaming.

Men in uniforms ran toward her, automatic rifles unslung. Others were snaking down lines between leaves and branches of the forest canopy. As boots hit the ground, Vicki glimpsed the sleek, gray-green underbelly and runners of a Huey. More men were dropping down from a second helicopter to the rear. Then the ground vehicle she'd heard came into sight. Not from behind but around the next bend on the track ahead. It was an army Jeep, so splattered with mud that the camouflage fatigues of its occupants were the only real identification. If Colonel

Alpiro had dispatched it from the plateau, they certainly hadn't reached here by the track the pickup had followed.

Vicki looked frantically around for her companions. Joe stood in the middle of the track, hands in the air as he revolved slowly to show himself to the men racing toward him. "We're unarmed. We're unarmed," he shouted.

Vicki didn't need the ominous click of a slide along a machine-gun barrel to know these weapons were not missing ammunition.

Then a rifle butt slammed Joe against the pickup. Hands pushed Vicki to join him, patting her down. She caught sight of Cesar facedown on the ground, a boot in the middle of his back. *Not again!*

Restraining her impulse to strike away those groping hands, Vicki called out, "We're friends of Coronel Alpiro." A minor exaggeration. "And Michael Camden. We work for the Ministry of Environment. We have every right to be here."

The names had an immediate impact. Or the discovery that they were as unarmed as Joe had announced. Hands dropped, if weapons didn't. Joe straightened. From the corner of her eye, Vicki saw the boot removed, and Cesar staggered to his feet.

"We work for the Ministry of Environment. This is a rescue mission looking for two lost children. We have every authorization to be here." Vicki chose to repeat her announcement to the man who'd swung down from the army Jeep, the purposefulness of his march identifying him as the leader. At first, she actually mistook him for Colonel Alpiro, the UPN commander. But as he walked closer, Vicki realized it was only the Castro-style beard that created the illusion. This man was older and fleshier, gray streaking his beard and hair under an army cap, self-indulgence straining the buttons of his fatigue jacket.

"We're so glad you were able to catch up with us. We were hoping Coronel Alpiro received the distress notice we left to be communicated to him. This has been an emergency situation, and we had difficulty contacting your base. But Coronel Alpiro and Señor Michael Camden, from *la embajada americana,* can confirm who we are and that we have a right to be here." If Vicki could just repeat those two names long and loud enough.

The camouflage fatigues of the Jeep passengers offered no identification, but the troops who'd rappelled down from the helicopters wore UPN uniforms, and Vicki was sure some of them looked familiar.

Beside her, Joe said nothing, his expression stony. Well, he'd said any confrontation would be on Vicki's shoulders.

"We have two children who've been lost up here at least twenty-four hours. We've been very concerned to find them before nightfall. . . ." Vicki's bright babble faltered as Castro II reached her.

His cold expression offered no reaction to her explanation. And was that rum along with other unpleasant odors on his breath and fatigues?

"These children—where are they? And where are the others of your company?"

How had he known that? Of course. The guards they'd barreled through at the checkpoint. And the radio in the man's belt.

Vicki glanced involuntarily toward the overgrown trail where the four village men had disappeared. Yes, where were they? The hour Joe had allotted had come and gone, the glimpse of gray sky overhead darkening rapidly. Behind Castro II, the shadows at ground level were murky enough that the Jeep headlights suddenly sprang to life, the beam so bright in the gloom they'd have blinded Vicki had her head not been turned away.

Then she saw human shapes hurrying up the slope and the bright pattern of Mayan weave among the brush. One of Maria's blankets wrapped around a child-size bundle. Then they'd found at least one of the girls. No, there was a second bright blotch emerging from the brush. "Alicia! Gabriela!" Vicki started toward them gladly. She could see that both girls were conscious, black eyes open wide, arms tight around their rescuers' necks.

And they were alert enough to recognize a familiar face. "Vee-kee!"

Vicki was reaching for them when the roar of another ground vehicle drowned out their piping call. This time it came from behind the hurrying villagers. Vicki spun around incredulously as a dark box lumbered into sight up the track. Then headlights sprang on, pinning the villagers in their beam. An army transport truck. Vicki had time to wonder again where it could have come from. Then black shadows leaped down from the sides. The headlights transformed them into the brown and green of camouflage as they slammed the villagers to the ground, a thud of boots and gun butts audible even above the engine noise and angry shouts.

Vicki snatched at the girls as they began screaming, a horrible, thin, terrified sound, their arms strangling Vicki's neck. A blow across her shoulders knocked her to her knees. She heard the sharp order that left her kneeling free in the mud, the two little girls clutched so tightly that she could feel their frightened, racing heartbeats, the panicked rise and fall of their breathing.

Vicki didn't realize part of that terrible screaming was coming from her own throat until strong arms wrapped around her and the two children. A voice that was surprisingly soothing and gentle murmured over and over against her hair, "It's okay. You're safe now. It's okay."

"It will never be safe!" ripped involuntarily from Vicki.

But the screams had stopped, the two girls subsiding into the whimper of a hurt animal against Vicki's neck. For a grateful moment, Vicki let herself rest in the warmth of a steady heartbeat under her head, the unfamiliar security of a tight embrace.

Pulling herself away to accustomed independence, Vicki raised her head to whisper some polite thanks. Then the headlights caught the rugged features bent above her. The cold fury Vicki glimpsed there froze her gratitude on her tongue. Joe let her pull away without a protest. Rising with a fluid motion, he reached to lift the larger child into his arms. Alicia went with him willingly, allowing Vicki to straighten up with Gabriela.

The four village men had been yanked to their feet now. Vicki burned with helpless fury at the bowed despair of their posture, the filth that could have been blood or mud. Cesar had not hurried to his small cousins because two automatic rifles were thrust into his ribs. The girls were not even whimpering anymore. Vicki didn't like the wide, frozen stare of their eyes.

Then, as Vicki and Joe carried them into the truck, they saw their cousin and came alive again. "*Tío* Cesar! *Tío* Cesar!"

Vicki allowed her bundle to squirm loose. Running to Cesar, Gabriela buried her face against him. As Joe released his own charge, Vicki swung around to Castro II, who was surveying the scene indifferently, boots spread wide in the muddy track to balance his overhanging belly.

"You see? We were only here to look for these children. Now that we've found them, we will be on our way immediately. Please—I hope you will forgive any misunderstanding."

Castro II walked away and conferred briefly with one of the UPN men. Without a further word, he returned to the army Jeep, a snap of his fingers gathering his other passengers at his heels.

As the Jeep backed down the trail, disappearing around the bend, the UPN officer held out a hand to Joe. "The keys to your vehicle."

Digging them out, Joe dropped them into the outstretched palm. The man handed them to another of the helicopter contingent, who climbed into the pickup and started the engine. A rifle barrel gestured toward the back of the pickup.

As Joe and Cesar obediently lifted in the two girls, Vicki saw with dismay that the transport truck was also backing down the overgrown trail, the four village men still with them. "Hey, wait a minute!"

Joe looped his arm around her shoulder, ostensibly to help her climb into the pickup bed, but the strength of his grip was both warning and command.

The remaining UPN troops from the helicopters piled into the pickup, filling the cab before the less fortunate joined their captives in the back. Turning the pickup around, the new driver started back down the nature trail toward the plateau. No explanation was offered, and Vicki assumed they'd be driving all the way to the plateau. An unwelcome prospect as it was still raining, the temperature dropping sharply as night approached. Gabriela, curled up on Vicki's lap, and Alicia, hugging tightly to Cesar, still had the blankets in which they'd been wrapped, but the others were now soaked through. When Joe wrapped his arm around Vicki and Gabriela, Vicki didn't shrug it away, resting with relief against the warmth of his large frame.

In the end they remained in the pickup bed only until the track came to a gap where a landslide had ripped away the vegetation to one side of the track. Above a precarious slope of tumbled rock and earth hovered one of the UPN helicopters mere feet above the ground. Beyond it, higher above the valley, was the second helicopter.

The UPN leader emerged from the dryness of the pickup cab. Two of his patrol unslung weapons to accompany their civilian passengers down the slope. Nightfall was complete now, but the pickup headlights and the helicopters' own running lights made it possible to pick their way down over the precarious footing, Joe and Cesar carrying the girls. Waiting hands pulled them inside the hovering aircraft, and the door panel slid shut.

It was warmer inside but very dark and painfully noisy. The girls were crying softly again. Beside her, Vicki could hear Joe's voice soothing the one he held. Something in its gentleness made Vicki's throat ache. It had to be her own present helplessness and exhaustion that could leave Vicki almost envying a small lost child. *Why am I wasting my thoughts on him? He may be kind to little girls, but he's furious with me.*

Not that Vicki could blame him. She'd practically promised there'd be no repercussions when she'd commandeered his services. *He's the one who crashed through that pole. Yes, because I pushed him into it.* Was he afraid he'd lose his job? that Alpiro would throw him off the plateau? *So I'll reimburse him a season of surfing if I have to clean out my savings.* Though Joe gently soothing a sobbing child didn't seem someone who'd care only about his paycheck. *So he's a mass of contradictions.*

Vicki's unpleasant merry-go-round of thoughts seemed to go on forever. But it couldn't have been more than a quarter hour before they landed. Not on the airstrip. The door slid open to reveal the army base parade ground. A blue and white Guatemalan flag above the nearest building identified the base headquarters. Only the UPN leader accompanied them from the helicopter, a hopeful sign they were not actually prisoners.

The room into which they were ushered was a clone of every other administrative office Vicki had seen in this country. The mahogany desk. The gilt-framed paintings. The leather upholstery and plush rugs.

And the VIP behind the desk. This one was the original Castro lookalike of Vicki's arrival to this plateau. Colonel Ramon Alpiro, UPN commander. He was speaking on a radio phone that could have been the same one that connected the center to the outside world.

Vicki hardly glanced at the commander. "Michael!"

CHAPTER TWENTY-FIVE

Michael crossed the office quickly. Gripping Vicki's forearms, he searched her face, then pulled her into a tight hug. "Vicki, are you okay? I've been worried sick."

"Yes, I'm fine. We're all okay . . . sort of. Oh, Michael, I'm so glad to see you. I was hoping you were here when I heard helicopters this morning. It's been just . . . awful!"

Vicki caught her reflection in an ornate wall mirror. No wonder Michael had voiced concern. Her hair was plastered to her head, face and lips blue with cold. Behind her reflection, Vicki caught Joe's expressionless eyes on her. Beside him, Cesar's face was rigid with cold or fear. Vicki offered him a smile in the mirror that was meant to be reassuring but still looked wobbly. They'd been through an unpleasant experience, but it was over, and now they could relax. *Let the professionals take over*. That's what Michael had told her once, and this time she was more than willing to do so.

Stepping back from Michael's grip, she apologized with a shaky laugh, "I got you wet. I'm so sorry. I just can't tell you what it's been like."

Vicki liked that he didn't even brush at the damp splotches she'd left on his khaki shirt, and his easy smile banished the last of her anxiety.

"Well, that's exactly what you're going to need to tell me. This base has been on full scramble for the last hour or more. All I've been able to get straight was that a sizable party of intruders, including foreign citizens, had assaulted UPN enforcement and invaded the restricted territory. Possibly involving a stolen vehicle." Michael's gaze shifted to rest coolly on Joe, then Cesar. "All of which Taylor here has been insisting is impossible."

Only at his gesture did Vicki notice Bill standing in the doorway. She directed him a faint smile before she took in an icy glitter in the blue eyes and stony expression. Her heart sank. Somehow she'd expected him to understand.

Then she caught Bill staring at Joe. It was Joe he was so furious with. Vicki would have to make it clear that this was her fault and hers alone. She turned back to Michael. "It wasn't like that." She explained quickly.

Colonel Alpiro was still talking on the radio phone, a cold eye on his visitors, but otherwise ignoring them. He had very pointedly not invited them to sit.

Vicki wrapped up when Alpiro returned the receiver to its cradle. "Michael, I know these people are working with you. But you wouldn't believe the way they've treated us and the people who were with us. As though we were criminals. They've taken four of the search party somewhere. And those poor little girls. On top of everything else that's happened to them, I can't imagine how traumatized they've been by the way this was handled."

She searched Michael's face for agreement, but he looked grave. "I wish it were so easy. But I'll see what I can do."

Colonel Alpiro swiveled his desk chair around as Michael crossed over to engage in a low-voiced conversation. After a few moments, Michael beckoned to Bill Taylor. He joined them.

As they talked, Vicki drifted over to check on the girls. They had fallen asleep. A glance at her two companions showed Joe's gaze intent on the huddle behind the desk, but Cesar met her anxious smile with a slight relaxing of his tense stance.

Vicki was turning away when she noticed a collection of frames on the wall. Another clone of those other bureaucratic offices—the diplomas, military honors, VIP photos. She stiffened. It couldn't be! Not here too. This was beyond coincidence.

There was a movement beside her, and Vicki looked up to catch Joe's questioning gaze. Then he glanced at the photo, and she saw a flare of—recognition? He shifted his feet to settle the girl in his arms to a more comfortable position. The movement left his broad frame blocking the photo display.

"Vicki?" Michael's calm summons drew Vicki across the room. The three men had turned back around, Colonel Alpiro leaning forward in his chair, the other two standing on either side like a tribunal.

The questions that emerged from Vicki's mouth were not the ones she'd planned. "This office—does it belong to the army commander? Would it be possible to speak with him?"

Every eye in the place was on her as though she'd suddenly flipped her lid, Vicki thought with some hysteria.

Colonel Alpiro answered with cold indifference, "*Comandante* Pinzón is no longer at this base. He and his family are visiting your country for an indefinite period. Orlando, I believe. Dees-nee. This base has now been ceded to UPN command. My command. Anything you wish to inquire, you may address to me."

Michael had told Vicki that UPN was assuming command here. Then the photo was Alpiro's.

Without giving Vicki a chance to avail herself of his offer, Colonel Alpiro went on with icy authority. "It has been decided that despite your great transgression—" his eyes rested on Joe—"due to the mitigating circumstances of your distress, the valuable labor your facility provides our country, and indeed the very mission of la Unidad para la Protección de la Naturaleza that all charges will once more be dismissed. You are free to depart."

Michael cleared his throat softly.

Alpiro raised a hand. "And also, so that this unfortunate circumstance may not arise again, this facility will be organizing a task force to deal with such situations. Children do, after all, run into mischief on occasion. In the future, we are to be contacted as soon as such a situation arises. There will be no more need to take matters into your own hands. Nor mercy for those who choose to do so."

Perhaps his beaming smile toward the two sleeping girls was meant to be fatherly. To Vicki, it looked smug and self-satisfied. Nor had she forgotten—or forgiven—just what had happened up there on that cold, dark mountain.

Alpiro's settling back in his chair was a clear dismissal, but Vicki stepped forward. "What about the men from the village who actually found the children? Where are they? Have they been released too?"

The smug smile froze. "You are referring to *los delincuentes* detained this evening in the restricted zone. We will consider that you were not aware you were consorting with smugglers and poachers. But so my *teniente* informs me they have been identified. Perhaps this is the reason they were so easily able to assist you in your own search. They are currently being held for interrogation. Their future will be determined by the outcome of that interrogation."

"But that's absurd! They were just villagers helping us in the search. You can't—*we* can't leave here without them. If anything, we're the ones responsible because they just came along to help us. Please, Michael, if you could just explain!"

Vicki had turned to him with absolute confidence. Hadn't he resolved every other difficulty without blinking? It was with shock that she saw the shake of his head, felt the pinch of his fingers above her elbow. She looked to Bill for support, but he showed no expression at all.

"Vicki, Colonel Alpiro knows his job. He'll handle this," Michael said quietly. "Come on. Let's get these kids back to their home."

Vicki didn't so much as look at Alpiro again as Michael steered her out of the office, the others right behind. She waited until her feet touched the gravel of the parade ground to explode, her frustration only exacerbated by her efforts to keep her voice low.

"Michael, I can't believe what happened back there! Those men were not smugglers or poachers. They were just villagers, relatives of Alicia and Gabriela who were helping us look for them. And you know it. You can't let these guys get away with arresting them. This isn't twenty years ago when the army could grab people without cause."

"No, I don't know it! Nor do you. By your own account, you know nothing about those men." Michael ran a hand through his short hair. "No one's denying they went in there with you. But we've no reason either to doubt Alpiro's claim that these men are known smugglers who've been wanted by UPN for some time. If there's been a mistake, the interrogation will show it, and they'll undoubtedly be released. You said they knew their way around up there in a manner that must be considered suspicious."

An army Jeep sat under a nearby floodlight. Michael lifted a hand to catch the attention of the driver. The engine sprang to life.

"Sure, they knew their way. They lived there before the biosphere. Cesar can tell you about them, if I can't. Michael, I can't believe you're just taking Alpiro's word for this. We saw how they mistreated those men. So much for a new, reformed army. Or police! Surely Colonel Alpiro will listen if you put your foot down. Tell him you'll withhold funding if he doesn't release the villagers. Or . . . or *something*!"

"Frankly, I'm just relieved he didn't arrest you. As he had every legal right, by the way. Crashing a checkpoint? Vicki, what were you thinking? No, Ericsson, that was your bright idea, wasn't it?"

"We were thinking of saving Alicia and Gabriela's lives."

Michael swept inexorably over Vicki's protest. "Understand this: the only reason you're not in a detention cell with your village friends is because I pulled some strings. And because I could honestly assure Alpiro the three of you had never left the nature trail, which *is* cleared to Ministry of Environment personnel, if not in the way you went about it. Just take the break you've been given and be glad for it. Let Alpiro handle his own business. He knows this area—and its people—a lot better than any of us."

"Now you sound like Marion over at the embassy. Just be glad you didn't get arrested for something you never did anyway. Take the break and run. Meanwhile, forget about anyone else who's getting hurt and what's right and fair."

"This is not the place for this discussion." Michael's tone was harder than Vicki had ever heard it.

The Jeep had now pulled up beside them. Michael spoke briefly with the driver, then turned to the others as the UPN officer climbed out. "Taylor, I'm informed your vehicle is just coming down from the mountains. I'll drive you over to pick it up and drop off these kids. Then we'll continue on to the center, where perhaps we might finish this discussion in a little more privacy."

Michael opened the door for Vicki to climb into the front seat. With some reluctance, Vicki did so, then held out her arms to receive Gabriela from Joe. The others jumped into the back.

Vicki had assumed they were now completely free, but as Michael got into the driver's seat and pulled away, another Jeep fell in behind them. Beside the driver was the UPN unit leader who'd accompanied them from the biosphere. *Making sure we don't stray again.*

The journey to the village was a silent one except for a whimpering from Gabriela, who'd woken up with the bouncing of the bumpy road. If Vicki was now feeling the hunger and thirst and fatigue of the last hours, how much more these two children, despite those few tortillas? At least they seemed appreciative of their rescue, both girls sitting up with whispers of relief when the first lamplights of the village appeared.

Once in the village Cesar leaned forward to give Michael directions. But not to Maria's thatched hut. The church was bright with kerosene lanterns when Michael pulled into its earth courtyard. An audible prayer vigil going on inside broke up at the sound of engines.

Gabriela wriggled over the side into Maria's arms before Vicki could lift her out. Cesar got out with Alicia. The two girls didn't even look back at their rescuers as they were carried off to cries of delight and hugs and fussing. With any luck and the eager attention they were receiving, the nightmare of these last twenty-four hours would fade quickly and they would no longer feel the need to go searching for their old home. Vicki could only hope so. Up here there'd be no trauma counselors.

The pastor asked the question others were beginning to murmur. "But where are Ramon and Santiago and the others?"

Michael started the engine. "Let's get out of here. Your vet friend can do the explaining. He seems familiar enough with these people. Taylor, your vehicle should be waiting."

Cesar had indeed disappeared into a huddle with the pastor and other villagers. Vicki didn't protest Michael pulling away since Cesar was unlikely to leave his small cousins tonight anyway. She was saving her ammunition for bigger issues.

Vicki spotted the green pickup before they even reached the checkpoint. She winced to see the front grille visibly crumpled. But the metal pole, not looking worse for the wear, was back in place across the road.

As they climbed down from the Jeep, the UPN driver exited the pickup and held the keys out to Joe. At Bill's nod, he accepted the keys.

The troops who'd come down the mountain in the pickup were already squeezing into the second Jeep, perching on the tailgate and running boards to get everyone in. Their leader walked over for a brief exchange with Michael. Then they pulled away, leaving only the four Americans and two vehicles.

Joe slid into the driver's seat of the pickup. Bill leaned in the open window as the engine rumbled to life. His words were too low for Vicki to decipher, but from Joe's wooden expression, whatever he had to say wasn't pleasant.

"I can take someone with me." Michael glanced at Vicki as he started for the driver's seat of the Jeep.

Vicki didn't even look his way. Striding over to the pickup, she caught Bill saying, ". . . this stunt! Alpiro's talking about revoking all privileges. After being so careful for so long . . . I can't afford this; *you* can't afford this! . . . If you've messed things up—"

"You think I planned this?" Joe's low interruption was just as hard. "As for Alpiro—"

The two men stopped when Vicki leaned in the open passenger window. She was too full of her own furious thoughts to give any heed to their argument. "Mind if I ride in here?"

Joe reached over to open the passenger door. Bill stepped back from the driver's side, and as Vicki slid in, he called out, "I'll take you up on that offer, Camden. I've been curious for some time about your operations up here and the new UPN force. What did you say was your total capacity?"

CHAPTER TWENTY-SIX

Vicki sat rigidly beside Joe as he eased back onto the dirt track, not even looking out the windshield at their escort speeding away in front of them for fear she'd explode. The wind bit into her damp clothing, but she didn't ask Joe to roll the windows up.

They'd left the last yellow gleam of village lights well behind when Joe spoke up. "You'd better let out your breath at least. I'm not prepared to handle a stroke here."

His face turned to Vicki was only an indistinct outline, but his tone was mild enough that she might have imagined that earlier anger.

Her breath left her in a whoosh. "I just can't believe it. I feel like I've stepped twenty years back in time into some nightmare where the army's still steamrolling over anyone in sight, guilty or not."

"Not army. UPN. A duly constituted civilian authority, as Camden would say."

"What difference does that make? Do you think it matters to the villagers what uniform beats them up? As for Michael, I just can't believe . . . I mean, after all that's happened, how can our own people, our own embassy, be taking these guys' word for who's guilty and who isn't? And without checking if they're telling the truth. Even when they're talking about people's lives and freedom!" Vicki swallowed tears of disappointment and hurt, hoping Joe hadn't noticed.

She changed the subject. "That photo—you recognized it, didn't you?"

"Yes, I've seen it before. Though I wouldn't have recognized Alpiro in the lineup without someone pointing him out."

"Was it Holly who had the picture?"

Joe was silent for a minute. "Yes, that would have been where I saw it. Holly had a copy."

"Well, I've seen it at least three times now, not counting the archives where Holly got her copy." Vicki explained quickly. "Am I supposed to believe it's some kind of coincidence that the chief of police, minister of environment, zoo administrator, and now the head of this new environmental police unit *all* happened to be part of the same group trained by Americans way back when? Or that they've all ended up in related positions? There has to be some connection. And a reason why Holly was so interested in them. The environmental movement is certainly a strong connecting thread."

Again, Joe didn't answer immediately, giving time for the center's high barrier of vegetation to loom ahead. With the perverse variability of the mountain weather, the *chipi-chipi* had at last chosen to stop. Though mist was settling like gray snowdrifts across the coffee fields, the sky had cleared, and Vicki could make out an uneven black horizon that was the top of the cloud forest canopy.

"I know where you're going with this, Vicki, and I'm not sure I want to encourage it. I've no doubt you're right Holly had that photo because she'd seen it on these guys' walls too. But connection doesn't equate conspiracy. Guatemala isn't a big country, and the military leadership is—and was—a tight community. A group that's trained together at that level forms a lifetime bond. *Hermandad*, they call it here. A brotherhood. Say you and Holly are both right. These guys are one big, connected network. They're all involved in helping each other find cushy post–peace accord positions. High-paying jobs have to be tough to find these days for former military officers. That may be nepotism of sorts but not conspiracy. You've been in these kinds of places enough to know that."

He's right—again, Vicki admitted, deflated. Except for one stubborn reality. Holly was dead. And if this were just another straw, didn't enough straws add up to make bricks?

"So you're saying there's no connection between Holly's death and having that picture with—what is it . . . two, three, no, four of these guys in it?"

"Not at all. I've no intel one way or another. I'm just saying you don't have enough to run with it. You might want to talk to Camden and see what he's got on it. He seems to be tight enough with that bunch."

Vicki didn't respond immediately. The last person with whom she wanted to discuss Michael was her present companion, whose bias, whatever the reason, had been made abundantly clear.

But the words burst out of her. "That's what I don't get. I couldn't care less if the whole Guatemalan army is scratching each other's backs. What matters is that they—Alpiro—arrested four innocent men. They've got the village scared to death. They have *me* scared to death. This is supposed to be the new, peaceful Guatemala. But I'm seeing the same tactics that were around twenty years ago. And we know what happened then right under our noses. Two hundred thousand dead at the hands of forces we trained and supplied.

"So why is—?" Vicki couldn't say Michael's name. "Why is our embassy back to training and supplying them? Or believing whatever they say about who's an enemy and who's guilty without ever checking the facts? Or even insisting they use different tactics?"

"You're kidding, right?" Joe snorted. "Where do you think Alpiro and his like *got* the tactics they're using? The reason we were invited here to start with was because their military and aristocracy didn't have the muscle to stamp out a popular uprising. *We* gave them the muscle and the tactics right out of our own Special Forces handbook. Scorched earth campaigns so the locals have to turn to the army or starve. Strategic hamlets or model villages, if that sounds better, so the army can control the civilian population. Holding a village responsible for any enemy activity in the zone and wiping man, woman, and child out, so the next village will choose to cooperate. Organizing civil patrols and paid informants to divide the locals against each other. Targeted elimination—no, call it what it is: assassination—of opposition leaders.

"All taught to these goons by 'advisers' like the Green Berets in that picture who'd learned those lessons well over in Vietnam. And of course it wasn't just the Guatemalan army who got the benefit of our experience over there. Forget small matters like justice and human rights if we can make these third world militaries more efficient. We spread it around from the Shah's SAVAK Secret Police to the Nicaraguan contras, Colombian paramilitaries, Saddam Hussein himself when he was still our ally. Anywhere we felt our national interests or business profits might be threatened. Except there never was any outside enemy on the receiving end. Just local peasants and democratic opposition."

Vicki stared at the indistinct outline of his profile. "How do you know all this? You keep saying *we* like you've been out there. I thought you said you'd never been in the military."

"By *we*, I meant our American government policy. But I didn't say I'd never been in the military."

Still staring at him, Vicki took in what she'd never bothered to notice before. What even the night could not completely disguise. The relaxed tension of that muscled body she'd personally witnessed blurring into action. The narrowed watchfulness of green eyes, now a glint in the headlights as he turned his head. That peculiar catlike walk so like Michael's she should have registered the resemblance long ago.

"And just what were you? Special Forces?"

"For a while." The stars disappeared as the center's untrimmed canopy closed above the pickup. "Like I said, I didn't care for the spit and polish. Or the regulations. As you can see, I don't exactly fit into a box. And that's what the army requires. Nice, neat box shapes that can be easily stacked in a warehouse and shuffled around the world. Don't get me wrong. I'm not knocking those who do. I've got nothing but respect for our military, who are for the most part just doing their part to keep America safe. Following orders and all that."

Joe's glance shifted past Vicki. "Right, Camden?"

The center generator hadn't been turned on, so it was only when Joe eased the pickup to a halt that Vicki realized the taillights ahead had blinked out and caught the crunch of gravel outside her window.

Michael yanked Vicki's door open. "What do you know about following orders, Ericsson? Let's go, Vicki. Now that we're out of earshot of half the country, I've got something to say to you. *All* of you."

His grip was not gentle as he helped Vicki from the cab, but his glare was directed toward Joe. "Vicki, far be it from me to criticize your choice of associates. I'm doing my best to use language appropriate to a lady, so let's just say tonight was not the wisest course of action. Alpiro had every legal right to lock all of you up and throw away the key. If Ericsson wanted to take a joyride through a restricted zone, he could at least have had the decency not to get you involved."

Joe's only response was to switch off the ignition.

"But it wasn't Joe—"

Michael interrupted Vicki's protest. "It's not that I don't understand your motives. As usual, you were only trying to help. But this could have been handled another way. If you'd approached Alpiro instead of going it on your own, all this could have been avoided, including these arrests that have you so upset. Not to mention, you'd have had Alpiro's resources at your back instead of against you."

"But—" Vicki stopped. The worst was that she herself had suggested exactly what Michael was saying. And from the swift response she'd witnessed, maybe there really had been time to get official help before dark. But could they—should they—have counted on it? How could she explain the fear and distrust and desperation that had impelled their decision? They'd done the best they could at the time. Didn't that count for something?

"I'm not blaming you, Vicki. You couldn't have known." Michael's tone turned acid as a shadow loomed in front of them. "But if you haven't been here long enough to understand the local situation, Ericsson certainly has."

The darkness was so complete that Vicki wasn't sure where the buildings lay around them until a blue-white flame sprang to light. Its glimmer reflected off wood and thatch, then revealed weathered features and gnarled hands as Bill Taylor lifted a Coleman lantern onto a hook just up the steps of the community shelter.

It was a signal Michael had been waiting for because he immediately steered Vicki in that direction. "I don't know what kind of twisted nonsense Ericsson has been filling you with—"

"Actually—" the crunch of Joe's boots fell into step beside Vicki, and he sounded not at all chastised as he cut into Michael's icy speech—"I was just explaining to Vicki where your guys inherited the tactics we saw them use tonight. Tell me, Camden, are you all still using that Vietnam-era training manual? Sure looked like it."

"So you're beating that dead horse," Michael said. "Maybe you have no respect for law and order, judging by tonight's stunt. But don't you be pointing your finger at better men than you for doing a job they were trained and ordered to do."

"Oh, I wouldn't think of it," Joe agreed. "Like you said, they were just following orders. I'm sure they had no control over what was done with the excellent training they handed out. You'll excuse me if I'm a little less generous to those who actually formulated the policies of who received our military aid. Or those high enough to know good and well to what use it was being put. Oh yes—that would be your department over at the embassy, wouldn't it, Camden? Your predecessors, of course. Not you personally."

They'd reached the community shelter now, the glow from the lantern morphing their shadows into human form. Vicki didn't need light to feel the fury vibrating through Michael's hand on her elbow as he led her up the steps.

The shelter with its scattered tables stretched empty and dark beyond that single yellow pool of light. Bill was nowhere in sight, though a flashlight flickered from the far side of the shelter. The somnolent tranquility from the animal cages indicated Rosario and Beatriz had stooped to perform the usual night rounds. But if a meal had been prepared, it was long since put away. Vicki glanced toward where the kitchen shelter would be in the dark. *I can't stand another argument on an empty stomach.*

As Vicki tugged her arm free of Michael's grip, Bill approached. The tray in his hands held white local cheese, rolls, butter, guava paste, and chunks of pineapple and papaya. He set it on a table directly below the lantern, his features more resigned than angry.

Vicki spoke up as she reached for the cheese. "Bill, I just wanted to let you know this was my fault, not Joe's. I talked him into looking for the girls. He—"

"No one talks Ericsson into anything. He makes his own decisions. But what's done is done. The kids were recovered; end of discussion."

Vicki wasn't satisfied, but Bill's closed expression was as dismissive as his wave. Then she bit into the cheese, and the salty, chewy texture in her mouth drove away any other thought. Dropping into a chair, she followed the cheese with the sweetness of pineapple, then a roll slathered with butter, the bliss of food in her stomach taking precedence over the continued discussion going on around her.

"You seem to be forgetting the most important element here. We were at war. We did what was necessary."

"Necessary for who?" Joe dropped into a chair across the table, hooking a second one to prop up his legs. Crossing his boots at the ankles, he reached for a chunk of pineapple. "Certainly not for me. And I doubt those Mayan villagers wiped out by your local allies would concur it was necessary. Or the union leaders or journalists or human rights activists."

"No one is denying there were occasional excesses. But a lot of those activities were suspicious in context."

Michael hadn't reached for a chair or food, the sharp authority of his tone easily dominating the scene.

Joe, in contrast, was as disheveled as Vicki herself must look, his hair matted with rain and dirt, mud-splattered clothing clinging damply to his lounging frame, his unmoved drawl countering the tightness of Michael's voice. Did he really care about what he was arguing, or was he deliberately prodding the embassy staffer to anger?

"You mean, like organizing to get a decent living wage? marching for freedom to work or speak or associate where they wanted? Yeah, really suspicious! Isn't it time we let go of the myth that Mayan peasants were fighting for some ideal of Soviet global domination and recognize they were fighting for a lot of the same things Americans took up arms to win? And that arming dictators around the planet to whip their own people into line hasn't exactly proved a prize-winning strategy for spreading peace and democracy."

"What do you know about winning a war, Ericsson? Because the proof is that we did win! Communism is a dead game around the world, thanks to the stand we made. And if that requires forming alliances with less than savory characters, so be it. You don't win a war by refusing to enter the battlefield until all your allies have passed some human-rights litmus test. You focus on winning the battle first. Then you can use the clout of victory to pressure for any reforms you want."

Michael's tone was tight now with scorn. "As you might be capable of understanding if you'd ever stepped off that surfboard long enough to serve your country."

Vicki braced herself for Joe's rejoinder. But he simply reached for a roll. "And you don't think that just maybe, if we'd made a stand on what we claimed to believe was right, the Soviet Union would still have fallen? Maybe even a little faster if people like the Mayans had seen us support human rights and democracy and the people trying to bring them about instead of weighing in on the side of their oppressors?"

"That's wishful thinking. The world doesn't work that way."

"Well, I guess we'll never know."

Vicki had had enough. "What difference does it make?" she cried, slamming down a half-eaten roll. "That's all in the past. Why are you two wasting time arguing about it? What matters is *now*. And four men who aren't with their families tonight. Not because of people our government armed and trained once upon a time but because of people we're arming and training right now. Our own embassy. Michael, you can't stand there now that Alpiro isn't looking over your shoulder and tell me you bought that lie about those poor villagers being criminals and smugglers. Okay, so like you said, the war is over. The peace accords have been signed. Well, then, you can use that pressure for reform you were talking about. What are you going to do to make sure these men get their civil rights and a fair hearing? That isn't theoretical. It's here and now."

It was like a blow when Vicki saw Michael's expression close over. Joe didn't move a muscle, but he narrowed his eyes at Michael.

"It's not that simple," Michael said. "The Cold War may be over, but the Guatemalan military is still our most vital strategic ally in this region. Guatemala has become a key transfer point for drugs and human trafficking across our southern border. And we know terrorists have cells down here. We need the military's cooperation. Not to mention their continued support against a new swell of left-leaning regimes like Venezuela and Bolivia and Brazil."

"So in other words, you won't lean on Alpiro." Vicki was on her feet now, moving toward Michael. "You're just going to let this go."

"I'm saying that our embassy has to carefully consider where best to spend its influence in the interests of our own national security. I will do what I can, but interfering in a local arrest is not likely to be a high priority."

"You see, Vicki, there's your problem," Joe said. "There's always another war. If not the Cold War, it's counternarcotics or the war on terror. And once again, if we have to lay aside minor issues like human rights or religious freedom for the peoples of those nations, what does it matter as long as our own interests are served? National or personal."

"Not 'our'! Not 'we'! Stop saying that!" Bill had slid into a chair, but he was suddenly on his feet, white head shaking vehemently. "There *is* no royal *we*. Only an *I*. That's been the problem all along. Everyone says 'we,' as though countries and people groups make these kinds of decisions. It's a whole lot easier to blame the Americans. Or the Guatemalans. Or the military. Or the CIA. For one, it gives a nice target to keep hating. *And* keeps the real perpetrators from being called to account. But it's not a *we* who chooses to do these things. It's always an *I* who gives the order. Or a lot of *I*s! Individuals who choose to do—or allow—things they'd never ordinarily condone, out of self-interest or fear or maybe even out of good intentions. Either way, it's all personal. It's all *I* because as long as I can make it *we*, I don't have to make my own decision *at* the time *on* the spot as to the right thing to do. I can just sit back and blame it on some nebulous *we*. A superior. The group."

Bill was breathing heavily as he finished. Vicki had to wonder what he was seeing in that faraway gaze. Again, she was reminded of how little she really knew of William Taylor.

"'Do what is right and do not give way to fear.'" Vicki hadn't even realized she'd spoken aloud until all three men stared at her.

"What did you say?" Bill said sharply.

Vicki faced him. "It's just something Evelyn McKie, the missionary who runs Casa de Esperanza, likes to say."

Under three unblinking pairs of eyes, Vicki felt compelled to expound. "It's out of the Bible from the story of Abraham and Sarah—what Evelyn calls being Sarah's daughter. What do you do when you're faced with a mess and you've got a hard decision to make? 'You are her daughters if you do what is right and do not give way to fear.' Anyway, it seems like pretty good advice. . . ." Vicki trailed off in discomfiture, a sudden hysterical giggle welling up at the blank expressions from all three men who'd just been arguing so furiously.

"'Do what is right and do not give way to fear,'" Bill repeated heavily. "A nice philosophy. And when it's too late?" He pushed past Vicki and Michael, blundering into a chair when he left the circle of lamplight. The thud of his boots was slow, aged, as he descended the steps. He called back, "Joe, are you parking yourself for the night, or have you forgotten you've got work undone?"

Michael turned to Vicki. The tightness of his mouth had relaxed to humor. "So that's why you came here? Some proverb from a missionary who should have retired decades ago? All this foolishness tonight was about proving you're this 'Sarah's daughter'? Well, you've proved your point. I appreciate and respect your intention, including tonight's shenanigans, however misguided. So let's just leave it alone. None of this is what I came here to talk to you about."

His hard glance went pointedly from Joe to the direction Bill had disappeared; then he went on. "Now please believe me that we—I—am also doing what I believe is right. Right to protect my country. Right to win this war. I hope we can all agree the world is better off with a strong America than without it. And right to protect you, Vicki. We've wasted enough time. Let me say what I came here to say. I want you out of here. It's nothing to do with tonight. That may have precipitated things but only by a day or so. The plug has been pulled on your sister's investigation. I hope you'll agree it's time. A lot of man hours and effort have brought us right back to where we started. Whatever very valid concerns Holly might have been dealing with, there's simply no evidence her death was more than being in the wrong place at the wrong time.

"I'm flying out tomorrow afternoon, and I'm not planning on a return in the near future. I'd like you to come with me." Michael held a hand out to Vicki. "There's nothing more you—or anyone—can do here."

Which was exactly what Vicki had already decided herself that morning.

Michael stood relaxed and confident, the curve of his smile already sure of her answer.

Looking down at his long, strong fingers, Vicki wanted suddenly, desperately, to reach out and lay her hand in his. To flee to the relief and expectation with which she'd greeted him in Alpiro's office earlier that night. So why was she hesitating? "And the villagers? Are you going to let them go?"

"The villagers?" An impatient note slipped into Michael's tone. "You mean, the men arrested tonight? You do realize these locals you're so worried about are only too likely part of the smuggling enterprise your sister was trying to ferret out. But I'll certainly pursue the matter with Alpiro. Though understand it isn't up to me. Now—are you coming?"

Vicki surprised herself by taking a step back. "No, I'm sorry, Michael. But I can't just walk away from those people. You said you—the embassy—could use your influence if you decided it was a priority. If you want me to come, then I'm asking you to use it. Maybe it's not national security, but these are people's lives. To their families that's certainly as important. Once I know they're free—and I want to see for myself that they're back with their families because I don't trust Alpiro—then I'll go with you. And . . . and I'll stop investigating Holly's death. I won't ask anything further *ever* of the embassy. If not, then I'll have to do what I can myself. When I'm ready to leave, I'll make my own arrangements."

Michael dropped his hand. "I can't accept that, Vicki. For your own protection, I'm asking—no, I'm *insisting*—that you trust me to make the right decision—"

"The lady said no."

Michael and Vicki whirled around.

Michael glared at Joe. "Stay out of this. Haven't you caused enough damage for one night? If I had you under my command—"

"Well, fortunately, I'm a civilian and not under your orders. As is Vicki. So it isn't up to you. Let her make her own decision."

Michael's hands relaxed. "Fine, you've made your decision, Vicki. But if you change your mind, the invitation still stands." Spinning around on his boot heel as sharply as though on a parade ground, he left the thatched shelter.

Vicki had to admire his self-control. She walked over to Joe. "Was that necessary? I'm perfectly capable of fighting my own battles."

"I know, but it sure felt good. By-the-book stuffed shirts like that are one reason I got out of the army." His eyes glinted emerald as he looked up at her. "'Do what is right and do not give way to fear.' I like that. Yes,

I can see you as Sarah's daughter. Don't let Camden put you down. I'll take someone following what they think is right, even into hot water, over a coward watching out for their own back any day."

"I appreciate the advice." Vicki hesitated as she looked at Joe. From this close vantage she could see bits of twigs and leaves in his tangled mane. His body heat was drying the Hawaiian shirt to wrinkles, but it was still damp enough to cling like a second skin over the powerful muscles of chest and shoulders. Vicki could suddenly feel the warmth of that broad chest under her head again. The calming, steady beat of his heart. The gentleness of touch and voice when he'd soothed her and Gabriela and Alicia. The safe feeling she'd felt even in the terror of darkness as long as his arms had been around her.

"Joe, I never really thanked you for what you did tonight. I am *really* sorry for all the trouble I dragged you into. I . . . I didn't expect any of this, especially for you to get blamed for it. I'll pay for any damages to Bill's truck. But . . . well, thank you for doing it."

Behind Vicki, headlights stabbed at the dark. An engine gunned as the army Jeep accelerated out of the cul-de-sac. A long horn beep was followed by Bill's impatient command. "Ericsson, now!"

Swinging his boots to the floor, Joe got to his feet. "Don't thank me. Bill was right and so was Camden. It was the stupidest thing I've done in a long time."

He might as well have slapped Vicki. "How can you say that? Are you saying you could have left Alicia and Gabriela out there? that you wouldn't have done it if . . . if you'd known all this would happen?"

"No!" Joe tossed over his shoulder. "That's what makes me so stupid." Two swift strides, and the night swallowed him up.

CHAPTER TWENTY-SEVEN

Vicki was alone at last.

Not only in the physical isolation of this room, the Coleman lantern on the converted crate keeping shadows and thoughts at bay.

She'd waited until the sound of the two vehicles faded before bestirring herself to clean away their impromptu meal. Then she'd lifted down the lantern and checked the sleeping animals before climbing the back stairs to her room. Rosario and Beatriz had indeed retired for the night because Vicki could hear a faint snoring through the dividing wall. She should be following their example.

But Vicki didn't turn off the lantern when she went to bed, staring instead at the printed images on the bunk overhead. The camouflage fatigues. The hard, satisfied faces. Those tiny American flags on lapels.

Something in the relaxed, even bored, self-confidence of one American adviser evoked Michael Camden. Vicki hastily turned her head to happier images of animals and landscape, the wavery glimmer of the lamp flame making colors and shapes shift and sway as though alive. She had spent so much time poring over that group portrait that she hadn't looked closely at the landscape shots. They weren't as random as she'd assumed.

Lake Izabal as seen from the lookout rock of *Pozo Azul*.

Another from that rock outcropping of the ridge rising up from the waterfall where Vicki had run into Joe's interference.

Vicki wouldn't have differentiated the next scene had she not seen it that very afternoon. The valley with its overgrown clearings that lay beyond the dividing ridge from the plateau. This one had been taken from much the same vantage point as Vicki had seen it today. But here were no tall weeds or indistinct shapes of feeding animals. Holly's photo showed the thick, lush carpet of white and pink and lilac and red blooms over which Joe had circled that first day.

And from which the DHC-2 had drawn ground fire that so nearly knocked them from the sky.

Vicki stared at the photos till her eyes burned. It was easier—*safer*—than closing her eyes, allowing her own thoughts to sweep her away. She didn't mind her physical aloneness. These close walls were a welcome sanctuary. It was the inward aloneness that sat like a hot, hard lump in her chest, stung at her eyes. The recognition that even if she abandoned the solitude of this small room, there was no longer a single person in all these highlands to whom she could confidently turn. She wouldn't even think of Michael. Nor would she go again easily to Joe or Bill.

Not even for transportation.

Because Vicki was still leaving. There was no more reason now than this morning for her to stay. Michael had been right about that. Even for the four villagers, Vicki could do nothing further here. Back in Guatemala City, she could at least register a protest with the embassy and chief of police.

As for the bubble of enchantment that had held her here, it had burst beyond repair under angry shouts and guns and running boots and frightened faces and crying children. There was no more retreat or sanctuary from human cruelty and greed and pain in these beautiful mountains than in the burning stench of Guatemala City's garbage dumps.

So Vicki would leave.

And as she'd told Michael, she would make her own arrangements. If air flight was inaccessible, there was always the evening "chicken bus," a refurbished school bus redolent of gas fumes and cigarettes and crowded with locals hauling market goods, even livestock, into the city. If not a comfortable way to spend the night, it would get Vicki to the capital by morning. If the bus didn't go over a cliff as white crosses marked so many along the way. Or a *mara* didn't stake out Vicki and her duffel bag as an easy target.

"Do what is right and do not give way to fear."

Vicki had thrown that challenge at Bill and Joe and Michael. She'd followed it blindly, hopefully, to this place. But if it had made any difference—if *she'd* made any difference—she couldn't see it. Except that single piece of luggage, she was leaving these mountains empty-handed, with no more idea than when she'd come of who had killed her sister. And more importantly, why.

Yet . . . was she really leaving so empty-handed? Or even alone?

A breeze rattling the screen above the door gusted the scent of a cloud forest night into the room. Green, wild, moist with a taste of flowers, and underlying it all, the chill, metallic tang of the mists. A curl of quietude, even peace, stole through Vicki at its familiar, clean sweetness.

I came up to these mountains to uncover a murderer. You led me instead to a sanctuary. I came here to understand Holly's death. But it's her life I've come to understand. And . . . and her faith.

"This is my Father's world."

But so was that world outside the center where people hurt and fought and cried. Yes, and loved too. With all its beauty—and all its pain.

And it was to that world which Vicki, unlike Holly, had been called to make a difference.

Father God, I still don't understand why You let the world be such a terrible place. Why You can't make it all better now. But if I can't see my way forward from this place and time, if I've no idea what You're doing with me, at least I can believe You do. That You see the end, and that it's worth it. That You're down there in the world I'm going back to as much as up here in these cloud forests. I always believed the world had to be right—that I had to make it right—for You to be there with me. But if these villagers who've lost home and family and been hurt so much more than I can sing with such peace and faith of You and the future You have for them, then surely I can believe You're there for me, too.

If Vicki took nothing else of Holly from this place, that would be enough.

Which left only one task before boarding that bus tomorrow evening. Rolling over onto her stomach, Vicki hauled out the small cardboard box that had sat untouched under the bunk all these weeks.

Holly, tomorrow it's you and me.

Vicki knew just where she'd say good-bye. The memory trail that must have been a favorite of Holly's because she'd left it laid out for her sister. Vicki tugged the crate and lantern over to the bunk. Holly's photos were vivid and crisp, another inheritance from a father she'd never known. The *Pozo Azul* lookout. The thin line of a path running parallel to the waterfall up the ridge. The carpet of wildflowers clear enough under the brighter lighting for Vicki to make out individual blooms.

Vicki sat up so suddenly her skull made painful contact with the planking. Lifting the lantern high in one hand, she leaned closer.

No, there was one other task she had to do before leaving these mountains.

As Vicki blew out the lamp, plunging the room into darkness, a new flame of excitement and uncertainty burned away the last of her resignation.

Tonight the villagers were not singing.

At first there'd been screaming and running and frightened tears. Children, mostly, young and forgetful. The adults knew only too well why they were being rousted from hammocks and floor pallets. A few men had braved automatic rifles and bayonets to rush forward when lighted torches began raining down on thatch. Several women scuttled after children who'd slipped away.

The latter had been resolved by snatching up small runaways and tossing them into the throng. Lacerations and groaning bodies in the dirt showed how the others had been dealt with. Now they stood passively, he noted with satisfaction, huddled into a single mass, women clutching children close, men shielding their families.

Standing back in the shadows of the vehicles, he tilted his hat against the betrayal of leaping flames, bandanna covering mouth and nose against gasoline fumes and smoke. The only sounds were a crackle of fire, the whimper of some child too small to be terrified into silence, shouted orders, and a coarse jest from the man beside him. Only when the timbers holding up the roof crashed down did a young Ladino step forward with a cry.

He winched as a baton crashed down, slamming the man to the ground. But he didn't interfere. After all, they were alive.

And for that, they could thank him.

His hands clenched on the night-vision goggles with enough force to crack them had they been of civilian make. He lowered the NVGs as flames blazed white in his scope. The running figures, metallic containers splashing a liquid that was definitely not water, the vehicles and distinctive shape of weapons were now identifiable in the mounting inferno, if not the individual faces above them.

Fury burned acid in his stomach, tightened his jaw under green and black paint to stone. But he didn't interfere either. There was nothing one man could do after all.

And how many times have people like me used that same excuse? he questioned bitterly as he lowered himself silently, invisibly, from the canopy height of his perch. *And in these same mountains?*

Too many.

And too many had died because of that.

Well, this time something would be done. He had them now at last. This time they wouldn't get away with it. He wouldn't let them get away with it.

Twenty-four hours.

It was a vow.

CHAPTER TWENTY-EIGHT

Vicki was up before sunrise the next morning. It took only minutes to restore her few belongings to her duffel bag. All but palm-size binoculars and the cardboard box, which she settled carefully into a knapsack she'd come across in the women's barracks when she cleaned it. She stripped the bedding from her bunk, then detached Holly's photo lineup, sliding it into the knapsack, before running dust cloth and broom over the room. It was now ready for whichever WRC staffer was bringing up the team that should be arriving in time for supper and the evening animal rounds, which Vicki would no longer be available to carry out.

Leaving her bag on the stripped bunk, Vicki took the knapsack with her. Cesar hadn't yet returned when she began preparing the animals' breakfast, and it was Rosario who did the morning rounds with Vicki and Beatriz who prepared breakfast in the kitchen shelter. Her expression as she slapped a mug in front of Vicki shouted, *This is beneath me.*

Well, it couldn't be pleasant to have a nonstop parade of foreigners through one's home. Though Rosario and Beatriz had been unfriendly and possibly dishonest, Vicki hoped they would soon move back to the capital. For the center as much as their own sakes.

Cleaning up breakfast, Vicki added a canteen, rolls, oranges, and the small, tough-skinned "finger" bananas to the knapsack. As she wheeled the mountain bike from the shed, an excited animal babble turned her head. Cesar was threading toward her through the animal cages. Vicki caught a whiff of wood smoke as he came near. Maria's cook fire? It was unlike Cesar to linger over morning coffee and tortillas when he had duties waiting, but after last night it was certainly understandable.

Vicki looked past him. "Is Maria here yet? How are Alicia and—?"

"Where are you going?" Cesar cut in sharply. "Are you not still departing today?"

Vicki sighed. She'd have preferred to slip away without anyone knowing she was taking this excursion. On the other hand, it might be prudent to leave notice as to which direction she was heading. *It's what I'd insist on if it were Holly.* Vicki tugged Holly's photos from the knapsack. "I *am* leaving today. But first I'm going to take a memorial ride along this trail Holly shows here."

Cesar shook his head.

How could she make him understand? Or at least not interfere? Opening the knapsack again, she lifted out the cardboard box with its mortuary logo. "My sister loved these mountains. From these pictures, this trail was a special favorite of hers. So I want to follow it today on a pilgrimage to say good-bye to Holly. And . . . lay her to rest.

"The animals are all fed. The rooms are ready for the team. So there's no reason I can't take off for a few hours. I know exactly where I'm going, and with the bike it's not so far. I'll be back in plenty of time to leave tonight as I told you."

"No, it is too dangerous. You cannot go into the mountains alone." Cesar stepped in front of the mountain bike. "Not even Ho-lee followed that trail alone."

"How is it dangerous? We went that way yesterday and didn't see an animal bigger than a monkey. If it's the soldiers you're worried about, don't forget the biosphere is supposed to be off-limits to them, too, except for their war games, and I happen to know those have finished." Vicki repacked the knapsack as she argued. "Besides, this time I've no intentions of announcing myself or being seen. And if I do run into some lingering patrol, so what? So they throw me out again. I'm leaving these mountains tonight anyway, and I'll have already finished what I came to do." *All of it, I hope.*

Then what he'd just said registered. "Wait—alone? You said Holly hadn't followed that trail *alone*." Vicki let knapsack and bike drop to the path. "So she *did* go up there. With who? With you? Can you show me exactly where she went? If you don't want me to go alone, come with me."

The reek of smoke and burning grew stronger as Vicki moved closer to Cesar. Only when she tilted her chin up challengingly did she realize that it was all wrong for Maria's cook fire. Taking in a smudge of soot against bronze skin, a dusty sifting across shirt and pants she could now see to be ash and cinders, Vicki demanded, "What is it, Cesar? What's wrong?"

Cesar glanced down to brush at his shirtfront, leaving an even bigger smudge. He shrugged. "It is nothing to concern you. The church burned down in the night."

"What happened?" Vicki gasped. "Was it an accident?"

His expression closed, and Vicki knew with dismay that the tenuous connection she'd worked so hard to develop was gone. Cesar had retreated behind that defensive wall of stolidity and silence where he'd barricaded himself since she'd arrived.

Laying a hand on one sooty sleeve, Vicki looked at him pleadingly. "Please, Cesar, you were a friend to Holly, and I thought you were my friend too. Can you at least tell me if Alicia and Gabriela and Maria are safe?"

His eyes flickered at the mention of the girls. He turned his gaze to the distance, weighing, Vicki guessed, her status as an outsider, a foreigner, one of his people's light-skinned conquerors, with the help she'd provided last night. She didn't push him, tamping down her impatience until she was hardly breathing. Then he looked back at her. "Maria and the girls are unhurt. They will be arriving soon to work. And, no, it was not an accident. It was a warning. A punishment."

"A warning? You mean, because of yesterday? It was the soldiers? The UPN?"

"It is not possible to say. They wore camouflage but no identification. They said nothing when they came out of the night. We thought they would kill us like that other village. But they only came into our homes with their guns and sticks. They took us to the church. Then they made us watch as it was burned. They did not need to say that if they come again, it will be our homes and our lives."

"This is terrible! Did you report it to Coronel Alpiro? No, I can see that wouldn't be the best idea if maybe some of his men were involved. But if you could get word to Guatemala City. Get the police or someone up here to investigate."

"Investigate? Like your sister's death?" Cesar dropped clenched hands to his sides. "And what are we to say? The church burned. There is only our word as to how. And if they believe our witness, the army will say it was *la guerrilla.* Or just common *bandidos* who do not want outsiders in their territory. And who is to say it was not? Since no one died and our homes were spared, the villagers will be grateful for this and keep quiet. And they will not again easily disobey and enter the forbidden *zona.* So all will be well."

"But they destroyed your church. Surely you don't think they should be allowed to get away with that."

The slightest of smiles lightened his face. "No, you are mistaken. They did not destroy our church. A church is people, not the thatch and wood under which they gather. You cannot destroy a church by burning. As to the meeting place, it will be built again. Perhaps with tile or tin that does not burn. But we will also be careful to provoke no more difficulties. So you see why it is best you do not go back into the sierra. And why it is best that you leave as you have planned."

Why was it everyone knew what was best for her? *I just wish I knew so clearly.* She put all the conviction she could into her tone. "Yes, I certainly do see why you can't come. I'm sorry I asked, and I'm really sorry about your church. But this is something I have to do. If there's any trouble, I promise I'll make sure it falls on me and no one else."

Cesar made no move to get out of Vicki's path. "No, I can't do that."

"Please, Cesar!" Vicki bent down to pick up the mountain bike and the knapsack. "I'm not asking that you understand or help me. But if you were Holly's friend, I'm asking that you not interfere. Or tell anyone where I'm going. At least not unless something happens, and I don't come back."

"No, what I mean is that I cannot let you go alone. Not if you truly must go." Cesar turned to look up into the foothills as he said slowly,

"You are right. Ho-lee was my friend. She encouraged me to dream. To believe I could make a difference for my people here. That the future did not need to be like the past. And you are right that it was I who took her into the sierras. Like you, she believed it was her right to enter the biosphere when she chose. And her duty to ensure all was well there. Many times we explored trails with no difficulties until . . ."

"Until what?" Vicki prompted when he stopped.

Cesar nodded toward the knapsack. "The last time we went, she took those pictures you showed me. It was a trail we had followed once before. But this time we went farther than we had ever been. I did not want to go so far. But she insisted. She had a camera with a telephoto lens."

The shards of Holly's digital camera had been among the personal belongings smashed by Sergeant Torres and his pals back at Casa de Esperanza.

"Yes, she spent much time looking through it. I don't know what she saw, and she would not show me the pictures. But that she was troubled, I could see. The next day she went to the capital, and she never spoke of this again."

"How long ago was this?"

"I do not know the precise day, but perhaps you do, because when she returned, she informed me her sister had come to Guatemala."

So those pictures had been taken just before Holly's worried confidences at the airport. Were they connected to that cry for help or just pretty pictures of spectacular scenery?

"Do you have any idea what she might have seen there that could have worried her? Maybe something that's not in the pictures? Is it possible she saw someone poaching? Maybe even someone she knew?"

"Anything is possible. But she would not speak to me about it, though she was my friend. So I did not think it was about the animals we both care for but perhaps some worry from beyond the sierra."

Or someone Holly hadn't wanted to worry Cesar about. Was it possible that Michael and Colonel Alpiro were right about those men, family members of Cesar's, who'd volunteered so quickly to accompany them in the search?

"There is one other thing. I think she may have gone back without me. After she went to the city, she brought back maps. I saw her looking at them. The kind that can be printed from the computer that show the mountains from above."

"Satellite maps, you mean, with latitude and longitude."

"Yes. She left one day before morning chores. I thought she'd gone to the city with Señor Taylor. But when he came that afternoon, he assured me the plane had not gone that day. She returned before dark, so it was not necessary to announce she was missing. But she did not say where she had been. The next day she went to the city . . . and she did not come back."

Vicki swallowed as Cesar glanced at the box showing against the canvas of the knapsack. "So, if you don't think it was poachers, what else could it be? You must have some idea."

"I know nothing of which I haven't told you. Only that it is an evil and dark *zona* of the sierras, and I did not wish to go there. Nor do I wish to go back. But I will take you, if only because I do not wish you to be lost or hurt, and you are her sister and, like her, will go whether I say yes or no. But you must in turn swear to me that you will leave tonight as you have said."

Cesar looked so unhappy that Vicki would have backed down if the urgency of her mission were not so strongly upon her.

"I promise," she said gravely.

CHAPTER TWENTY-NINE

CHAPTER TWENTY-NINE

Vicki curbed impatience as Cesar wheeled out his bike and tucked a water bottle and food into a handwoven bag looped across his chest. But the sun was barely clearing the far shore of Lake Izabal when they finally started up the trail rising from the waterfall to parallel the stream that supplied the center with its water. At first the path was so steep, the underbrush so thick and tangled, that they had to walk the bikes.

But the vegetation thinned as they climbed higher. Pausing to look back, Vicki was amazed again to see how quickly the canopy had swallowed up the center buildings. Her calf muscles were protesting when the slope flattened toward the top of the first ridge, the path becoming a meandering zigzag that still led upward but not steeply. When Vicki saw Cesar mount his bike, she swung a leg over hers as well, finding the shift of muscle use a relief.

Until now they'd been paralleling the rush of water, but as they reached the top of the ridge, the path made an abrupt left to wind its way along the summit. The undergrowth was less dense here, the trail clear enough to ride. But the cloud forest canopy was still well above Vicki's head, closing in on both sides, so she had time to catch her breath before a curve of the trail and a gap in the vegetation gave her the first clear glimpse of what lay beyond the ridge.

She lost her breath. Straight ahead the mountainside tumbled down for hundreds—perhaps thousands—of feet into a long valley. To either side, fold after emerald fold rose up from that valley to merge at last into a gray-blue that could be even higher mountain peaks, cloud banks, or the distant horizon of the sky.

Here was the wilderness Vicki had flown over with Joe, but this was far more intimate than a plane's cabin. The chatter and caw and twittering of the fauna. The pungency of leaf and moss and earth. The taste of sweat trickling down her face and the coolness of a breeze fanning her cheeks dry.

The gash in that curtain of green had been ripped when lightning had struck down a hardwood of a species Vicki didn't recognize. Dismounting, she propped her bike against the exposed roots of the fallen hardwood and climbed onto a moss-covered trunk. From here she could see a brown ribbon of water winding through the valley. A flowering tree thrust out yellow blossoms from the steep slope a few meters away. Far in the distance, the silver thread of a waterfall sprang out over a rock face.

But there was no sign from this angle of the overgrown clearings in Holly's photos, and when Vicki heard Cesar's impatient whistle, she remounted and rode on up the trail.

The path did not again become too steep to ride, though they had to lift the bikes across occasional fallen trees or streams. Greenery closed back in around Vicki, and she caught only intermittent vistas of sky and mountains and valley below. From those glimpses she knew they'd left the first ridge behind the center and were now following the left flank of that mountain valley. Somewhere in this same flank was the biosphere service road. But of this Vicki saw no sign, though other trails crisscrossed their path. She soon realized she'd have been hopelessly lost without the metallic glint of Cesar's bike as her focus point.

Most of the trails were wide enough only to give passage to their bike wheels and might have been worn by either human or animal feet. Or both since two- and four-legged wanderers alike tended to trace the same paths of least resistance. But two paths they intersected were wide enough for a cart with ruts still distinguishable through a riot of foliage. A reminder that these mountains had once been home to any number of human habitants.

As Vicki had assured Cesar, they saw no sign of human life, neither armed patrols nor the Mayan highlanders who'd lived scattered throughout these ridges and valleys. Of animal life, by contrast, there was ample evidence. Without the noises of engines and too many humans to spook them, the forest residents made no effort to evade these two odd but quiet intruders. A herd of brocket deer had to be shooed from the trail. A peccary burst across Vicki's path so that she almost lost control of her bike. A troop of howler monkeys chose to follow the bikes, their leaping figures and excited chatter keeping pace in the branches overhead.

When across the trail dipped a flash of color that might have been a macaw or even a quetzal bird, Vicki found herself letting out a sigh of pleasure. Tonight she'd be leaving these mountains, and the hours ahead promised any amount of unpleasantness. But for this moment, she'd been offered a gift she'd been longing for since her arrival—to see these mountains, the cloud forest habitat, as they'd been created before humankind had touched them.

Up ahead, Cesar showed no hesitation as to where he was going. So for this brief reprieve, Vicki let slide away the purpose for this journey and gave herself up to the delight of sights and sounds and smells, the adrenaline of pushing herself and the bike over the curves and bumps of the trail so fast she couldn't have spared time for thought had she chosen.

It was almost a shock when Vicki had to brake to keep from running into Cesar's back wheel. He'd stopped at a massive rock slide that had ripped open the view to the valley below. Perhaps even the same they'd scrambled down to reach the helicopter. She immediately recognized the source of Holly's photograph as she joined Cesar at the edge of the rock fall. The same vista she'd glimpsed yesterday from the service road not long before the pickup stopped.

There was the valley floor with its winding riverbed. Beyond, the Sierra de las Minas range rose like cresting green waves. The silver ribbon of the waterfall was much nearer now and bright in the midmorning sun. Down on the valley floor and scattered along the nearest flank were the overgrown clearings that in Holly's photo had been white, pink, lilac, and red.

Vicki glanced at her watch. Not much over an hour. The trek hadn't taken as long as she'd anticipated. But then the mountain bikes had probably made as good time as the pickup over that rutted service road. Beside her, Cesar was studying the valley as intently as Vicki.

They hadn't exchanged a word since leaving the center, and Vicki's voice echoed louder than she'd anticipated as she asked, "How far are we from the service road?"

If the sound of her own voice startled Vicki, Cesar started as though he'd been stung. He was shivering, his rapid breathing not from the hard ride they'd just completed.

"It's okay," Vicki whispered. "There's no one here. We haven't been seen. We're not going to be seen."

His shivering abated, but he shook his head. "This is not a good place. We should not stay here."

She looked around, puzzled. Except for the vista the landslide had allowed, she saw nothing different from any other piece of the trail over which they'd ridden. The horror in Cesar's eyes would seem no more rational than the panic that had struck Vicki so vividly and painfully those first minutes on the plateau.

And perhaps just as real. Which made it all the more remarkable that he'd brought her all this way, exactly where she'd asked him to, without protesting or turning back.

"We won't stay long. I promise," Vicki assured gently. "Just a few minutes, okay?"

Vicki unslung her knapsack. She didn't reach for the binoculars she'd placed there. Not yet. If what she expected to see was there, she'd know at last—or thought she would—why Holly had died, if not at whose hand. But for just a short while longer, she'd hold on to the contentment of this pilgrimage. Long enough to say good-bye.

She took time for a drink of water, then lifted out the cardboard box. As she did so, Cesar pushed the bikes off the trail deep into a tangle of ferns and elephant ears. An unnecessary precaution, surely, but maybe it would make him feel easier.

Vicki focused completely on the box she cradled. Scrambling across the broken rock to a shallow ledge that had survived the landslide, she sank cross-legged at an angle that didn't show the overgrown clearings.

Settling the box on her lap, she opened it. But she didn't immediately reach for its contents.

Near her boot, a fern curved upward to form a feathery arch through which Vicki could see the vast panorama of the Sierra de las Minas range. Above her head a tangle of wide fronds and vines had woven her own private shelter. A rush of water couldn't be the falls across the valley but some closer cascade out of sight. A monkey screeched from a branch overhead. The smell of rich loam where her boots had broken through moss caught at the back of her nostrils.

Only a few weeks ago, these same sights and sounds and smells had provoked in her as much panic as Cesar had just displayed. Now they were familiar and vastly comforting. So familiar that when Vicki shut her eyes, she could almost imagine herself the small child who somewhere in her elusive memory had played in these mountains.

Yes, we were digging in the dirt. We were building a house. Holly was humming. There was a monkey. And a boy too. A Mayan boy.

The tranquility of her reminiscence must have reached Cesar, for Vicki felt a quiver of moss under her boots as he joined her. With a quiet sigh that no longer held fear, he sank under the green roofing of their shelter.

Vicki didn't open her eyes. Was it only Evelyn's photos and stories that were bringing images to her mind? Or did she really remember a tall, blond giant with laughing eyes and strong arms lifting her high? Long dark hair spilling across a gentle face and a soft, sweet voice singing lullabies? And a love that was suddenly as warm and real around her as a soft comforter?

I was loved! The thought actually stunned Vicki with its force.

All my life I've thought of myself as somehow alone and abandoned, fighting for my place against a world that was so full of injustice and cruelty and grief. And yet I was loved. Not by just one set of parents but two, because Mom and Dad Andrews loved me too. And Holly. And Evelyn, though I never knew it.

And You, Father God, who made me and created all this. Even when I couldn't see You, didn't want to believe You were still there, You loved me. You sent me people to love me. How could I have been so blind?

Yes, Vicki had been more fortunate in her life than she'd ever been willing to recognize.

It had been Joe who'd first pointed that out. And how angry she'd been with him for it. Just as it was Joe who'd quietly prodded Vicki toward Holly's unquestioning faith that there really was a purpose and design and loving hand behind the mess humanity had made of this world.

Only now was Vicki realizing just how many times Joe had been there in these last weeks, for all that he'd seemed to avoid her. Shielding her from prying eyes and tongues at Holly's funeral. And from Alpiro's cold fury at the airstrip. Singing beside her in the little thatched church. Smashing through that roadblock. Gentling a hysterical child. Backing Vicki up, calm but unyielding, against Michael's icy demands.

In fact, Joe had stepped forward—reluctantly, caustically, but there—every time Vicki had called on him, and often enough when she hadn't. So why had she turned so automatically to Michael when she'd needed help?

Because Michael had offered, to be sure. Because he was confident and handsome and in authority. *And because I snap-judged Joe by his appearance. And his employment.*

No, it hadn't just been that. *Because he's deliberately pushed me—pushed everyone—away. There's something he's hiding. Which is too bad because if he'd just let me, I could really like him.* It was the same unwilling conclusion Vicki had come to on the plane ride.

No, I do like him.

How much Vicki had never really realized till now. Whatever Joe was, whatever it was he felt he couldn't share of his past, she had come to trust *who* he was. The kindness and strength—yes, and faith—that crisis brought out of him, however he tried to mask it behind that brusque, remote facade he insisted on presenting to the world.

When this was all over, maybe she'd get a chance to thank him again. For being a friend. For opening her eyes to all she had and not what she'd lost.

"This is my Father's world."

I am not alone.

I am loved.

Vicki reached into the box. Its contents were as soft and powdery as talcum powder. Tossing a handful outward, she watched gray flecks drift over the valley below. Some orchid, some flowering tree would bloom just a little greener and stronger this spring. She tossed another handful. *Until I see you again, Holly. Oh, and say hi to our parents for me. All of them. Tell them I love them and . . . and I think I remember them.*

Her glance fell on Cesar watching silently beside her. Some of her own serenity reflected in his expression as he looked back at her. Holly's friend. Peacefully, she held out the box. As peacefully, Cesar made his own toss. When the box was empty, Vicki shook it out into the breeze.

Then, because this moment would not quite be complete without it and the mountains and valley lay with such complete stillness around them and her instinct for stealth seemed suddenly unnecessary silliness, Vicki began to sing. Softly. Rustily. Words she hadn't uttered aloud in twenty years. "'This is my Father's world, and to my listening ears, all nature sings, and round me rings the music of the spheres. . . .'"

Her eyes were shut tight again. It was twenty years ago, and her world was still whole. A soft, cool breeze was stirring the shelter overhead and wafting sweet fragrance to her nostrils. *I do remember!* A blonde toddler was scooping mud into the hands of their small Mayan companion, her contented hum adding to Vicki's song.

"'This is my Father's world: He shines in all that's fair; in the rustling grass I hear Him pass, He speaks to me everywhere.'"

When an off-key whistle rose to join the chorus, Vicki thought it too was a memory. Then she stopped singing and registered with heart-jolting adrenaline that the whistle was still carrying the tune.

"It was you!" Vicki pushed herself to her knees, turning around under the broad fronds. The bronze features, the black eyes staring at her with shock, were a lifetime older but suddenly so familiar she couldn't believe she hadn't known them before now. "You were the boy!"

CHAPTER THIRTY

“You were the boy who used to play with Holly and me,” Vicki said. “You used to whistle just like that when we sang. You do remember, don’t you?”

The caution that had Vicki hunkered down under this patch of elephant ears seemed suddenly far less important than what lay behind Cesar’s stunned look.

Only an explosion of monkeys leaping and screaming overhead startled Vicki into dropping her voice again. “We were playing in the woods just like this. You showed us where to go so we wouldn’t get lost.” It was all so clear now. “We were building a house out of bamboo and palm leaves. Holly and I were singing, and you were whistling. Then it started to get late. Holly was crying that she was hungry. And when no one came to look for us, we started back.”

She was almost through the curtain veiling the “before” of her past. In the small space, she clutched at Cesar’s arm. “Tell me you remember too. Tell me I’m not crazy.”

Cesar’s expression went from stunned recognition to incredulous joy. “Yes, of course I remember. You were—” The phrase he used was unintelligible. “And Ho-lee, she was—” Another unfamiliar phrase. “I cannot believe it! All these years I have wondered what happened to you.”

"Then you *were* the Mayan boy who played with us? Or at least—that wasn't my name you just said or Holly's."

"It was your Q'eqchi' name. The dialect of my village. I did not speak Spanish then. Nor did my village except for a few of the elders. Your sister's name in Spanish would be 'moonbeam,' because her hair was the color of the moon at night. And your name—it means 'little monkey.'"

"Little monkey!" Vicki's indignant repetition was enough to provoke the real simians overhead to a fresh burst of chatter. An apprehensive glance showed a panorama as serene and empty as it had been, but she scooted back under the broad leaves, tugging Cesar with her, until the tangle of greenery closed around them. "Why a monkey? Moonbeam is a whole lot prettier."

"Well—" Cesar pushed a fern away from his face—"your hair was the soft color of a baby monkey, and you laughed and chattered around the village as happy as a small monkey at play."

Happy. Yes, so Evelyn's photos had shown a small Vicki. "I wish I could remember more clearly."

"And I would know how it is that Ho-lee never told me she once lived here. She told me she knew nothing of Guatemala or the sierra. That song you sang—she sang it too, and though I do not know the English words, I whistled for her as I had heard it when we were children. But she said nothing. And her name, Ho-lee An-droos—it was not familiar. Though if I ever knew your father's gringo name, I do not remember."

"No, Holly wouldn't remember. She was so little when we left here. I didn't remember either until you started whistling." Vicki didn't even try to explain the dark veil of her past, the foster homes, her adopted parents. "Please, just tell me what you remember. Was it your village, then, that we lived in—my parents and Holly and me?"

"I remember everything," Cesar said simply. "I remember when you arrived in the village. Now many foreigners come to the center and for the aid projects. But then we had never seen hair that was not black. Nor eyes the color of sky when the mists are gone. Nor skin as pale as a moonbeam. My mother gave you your Q'eqchi' names. She worked for your mother. It was my task to watch for you and your sister to keep you from being lost in our sierras."

"You mean, you were our *babysitter*? But you couldn't have been any older than I was. I remember—" Vicki broke off. The small boy she remembered had been no taller than a five-year-old Vicki. But since then Vicki had dealt with malnourished children who looked years younger than their American counterparts. Even now Cesar was no taller and little heavier than Vicki.

"I was old enough your mother was teaching me to speak and read in Spanish. In the refugee camp, they estimated I was eight years."

"Do you know what my parents were doing in your village? Why they came? Were the people happy to have them there?" *Or did someone murder them for intruding into your world?*

"Everyone knew why they came. To tell the world of what was happening in our sierras. The evil. The injustice. That was the name we called your father. 'Truth-teller' in Q'eqchi'."

"And my mother?"

He smiled slightly. "She was called only 'Truth-teller's woman.' Times were different then, and we did not speak her language nor she much of ours.

"Yes, the people were happy your family came. At first because it had been a bad season on the plantations, and your father offered payment for the building of his house and for his pictures and for telling the stories of our people into his recording machine. My mother, who had lost her man to the fever on the plantations, was happy for corn and even meat to feed herself and her son.

"But then it was because Truth-teller and his woman were kind and did not treat us like animals as the Ladinos and the plantation owners did but as people of dignity like themselves. When children became ill, your mother cared for them so they did not die. Your father spoke for our people when soldiers came and the guerrillas, too. I did not know then what a camera was, but he let me help in the making of his pictures." Cesar paused. "Señorita Vee-kee, why are you crying?"

Vicki didn't realize tears were streaming down her face until Cesar gently traced a finger through the moisture. With a shuddering breath, she wiped the back of her hand across her eyes and face. "It's just . . . I never knew my parents—who they were, what they were like. I feel as though you've given them back to me. I . . . I think I even remember them, a little anyway. But, if your people loved them, then how did they die? Who killed them?"

The softening of memory was wiped instantly from Cesar's face. "They died as the rest of the village did. As my mother did. You do not remember? You were there."

"*Where?* Where was I? And your village. I thought you told me it was destroyed by the army. . . ." Vicki's voice trailed away as she recognized with horror what she'd just said. "Wait. My parents were in your village when it was destroyed? Holly and I were there? But the embassy said it was a robbery."

Blackness was pressing in again. In that blackness was the pounding of boots and unintelligible shouts, the smell of smoke. Vicki's heart was racing so fast she couldn't breathe until the force of her will pushed the darkness away. "Where?" she got out through stiff lips. "Where was this village?"

A gesture indicated somewhere beyond Vicki's shoulder.

Swiveling around instinctively, Vicki took in nothing but vegetation. "You mean, *here*? Close by?"

"I told you this was an evil place."

Vicki hardly heard him. Before her resolve could falter, she leaped to her feet, pushing fronds and leaves out of her face. "Then I was right. I *have* been in these mountains before. Can you take me there?" A step landed in a tangle of lianas, and she grabbed at a palm frond. "That is, if you can find it again."

"You think I do not know my own birthplace? I have not returned to this place since . . . *then*, even when others did. But I know these mountains as I know the animals in my care."

Vicki was taken aback by his harshness. Loosening her foot from the liana, she turned around. Cesar too had risen, and she moved backward to keep from bumping into him. "I didn't mean anything. It's just, all my life I've had this hole where my past was, wondering about my birth parents, how Holly and I ended up alone. And now I think I'm starting to remember, and I have to see it through. To know what really happened."

Then Vicki saw the horror and fear back in his eyes, the quickness of his breathing, and realized just what she was asking. Unlike Vicki, Cesar remembered the past only too well.

"Oh, Cesar, I'm so sorry! No wonder you didn't want to come here. I didn't think of how hard this would be for you. I shouldn't have asked you. If you give me directions, I'll go by myself."

Closing his eyes, Cesar breathed in and out deeply, then shook his head. "No, I have already told you I will not let you go alone. It is a strange thing. Long ago I asked your father why he took his pictures. He said it was because truth set people free. I didn't understand then what he meant; I thought it was because he did not speak our language well. But when I learned to speak and read in Spanish, I found what he said in God's Word."

"'You will know the truth, and the truth will set you free,'" Vicki murmured that long ago Sunday school lesson in English. She waved a hand for him to continue.

"I came then to understand what he meant. When the Truth Commission revealed to the world what happened in our mountains, we began to feel freedom. To know that if the past could not be erased, our suffering and pain was no longer hidden. That we were no longer invisible and could lift our heads in dignity. You are Truth-teller's daughter. It is your right to see the truth. And perhaps for me too, it is time to go back."

Squaring his shoulders as though he were summoning his resolve, Cesar lifted the broad fronds aside to step into the open. He was no longer trembling, his features set in determination. Now it was Vicki who hesitated as he held the fronds out of her way.

"Don't be afraid," he urged, whether to Vicki or to himself. "God will be with us. And it is not far."

They returned to their bikes, and Cesar turned onto a path that was even more overgrown than those they'd negotiated to this point, but its surface was packed firm. After a time, though the path had not changed, Cesar dismounted his bike. As Vicki followed suit, she watched him scan the forest around and above and behind him. His apprehension was contagious, and she found herself straining for every shadow and sound.

But the forest was silent, even unusually so, the monkeys that had traveled with them now gone. Vicki's steps were automatic as she pushed the bike along, the grip of memory growing stronger. Surely she'd walked this very trail before. Picked the orchids curling down into her face.

Then Cesar wheeled his bike around a tiny cascade bubbling over mossy rocks into a small pool. The pool was cloaked with vegetation, but abandoned among the undergrowth, Vicki spotted a rusting five-gallon can and knew where she was. Villagers had climbed this path for the pure, clean drinking water of the spring. *She* had climbed here.

Cesar's raised hand stopped them, but not even the caw of a parrot suggested alarm, so they went on. The next time Cesar paused, Vicki saw sunlight dancing through the leaves and vines and tree trunks from open ground ahead. As though sleepwalking, she leaned her bike against a tree trunk. Somehow, she found her hand clutched tightly in Cesar's, his palm as damp as her own. As the two slipped forward through the brush, Vicki was again the five-year-old returning home, hand-in-hand with her Mayan guide and playmate. A blonde toddler might have been clutching her other hand as they emerged into the open.

It was exactly as she'd imagined it. Or remembered.

Still being cautious, Cesar tugged Vicki to a halt short of a sparkle of sunlight. A grove of orange trees spread their limbs, the rotting fruit underfoot signaling that this season's crop had not been harvested. The low-hanging branches didn't screen what lay beyond. The hamlet held perhaps twenty to thirty houses. These were just four bamboo walls roofed with thatch, clustered around an open area, once worn bare but now a tangle of grasses, vines, and brush. The village commons, soccer field, gathering place.

Around each hut, weed-choked patches of corn and bananas and fruit trees made a yard of sorts. To the left across the open ground was the hamlet's only solid construction: a cinder block rectangle with a corrugated tin roof. At the far side of the commons, Vicki could see the ruts where vehicles had made their way into the village.

Like a battered red Jeep.

I remember! I remember Papa driving.

Everywhere she looked was familiar. How had she forgotten so completely what had once been her whole world?

Except that in Vicki's memory there was no empty silence, but women stirring food pots under the thatched cooking shelters. Children kicking a soccer ball. Men swinging in hammocks under the fruit trees. And beyond the dirt track on a wide veranda edged with flowering pots, a dark-haired woman with Vicki's face fussing over the bandage on a child's leg. A tall blond giant raising a 35-millimeter camera. A toddler with hair like the moon at night peeping through an open door.

Vicki turned. The wood and brick home with multiple rooms that her father had created for his family had been a novelty to the villagers. But where it should have been between two thatched huts was instead an irregular mound overgrown with vines and brush that might have been charcoaled debris. The sight of it was a blade ripping through twenty years of rejected memory.

No! No!

The light filtering through branch and leaf was no longer sunshine but flames leaping high against a black night. In front of those flames, men in uniform argued over possessions she recognized. Someone lifted a camera and laughed. Then tall shapes separated from the others, voices frightening in their sharp anger. *"No witnesses . . . Those kids aren't local. . . . Get away from those cameras!"*

Now Vicki reached frantically to retrieve that veil, not wanting to remember. But she could no longer push memory away. The bodies piled in a careless heap, bloodied and still, dead eyes wide and staring. Faces of children who had been her playmates. Adults to whom she'd run for an indulgent smile and pat.

Papa! Mama!

Vicki didn't know the retching sound was hers until Cesar shook her hard. "Vee-kee! Señorita Vee-kee!"

She came back to dappled sunshine, the scent of overripe oranges crushed under knees and hands, Cesar's drawn face above hers. Only the emptiness of her stomach had kept her from making a total fool of herself.

Yanking an orange from a branch, Cesar sliced it open with a pocketknife. "Here. This will help."

Vicki sucked at the fruit gratefully, its sweet acidity settling her stomach enough to push herself back to her feet.

"Come! It is enough. We should go." Cesar looked around apprehensively. How loud had she been?

But Vicki shook her head adamantly. "No, I'm all right now. Please, I remember . . . everything! I just want you to tell me—why? Why this village? Why my parents? Surely even then killing American citizens was hardly standard practice. And why was it reported as a robbery? How could they cover up what happened all these years?"

Despite herself, Vicki's voice began to rise. "You knew the truth of what happened here. How come in all these years you never told it?"

"The truth!" Cesar's tone lost some of his own restraint. "I still do not know all the truth of what happened. As to why our village, why not? There were many villages destroyed in those days by the army. Then I believed it was because of the guerrillas. They came the day before the army, demanding food for their troops, bringing us into the schoolhouse."

He gestured toward the cinder-block rectangle. "They did not hurt us; they wanted only to speak about our rights to a better life. The elders could not say no, because the guerrillas had guns. But we were afraid the army would find *la guerrilla* had come. Then your father came and asked the guerrillas to go. And because he was known to be a good man and to help our people, they went, taking only some bags of corn to feed themselves. But there must have been a *soplón* because the very next day the army came."

The term *soplón*, literally a "blower of air," had come to mean the countless informants who for fear or greed or even revenge carried tales to the eager ears of police or military.

"They demanded the guerrillas be turned over to them. Again your father spoke for the village. Oh, but he became angry. He told them there were no guerrillas here. He told them he was a *periodista* and would tell the world of their abuse if they did not leave us alone. And they went. But that night they came back. I thought then it was because of the *soplón*, that this traitor had informed the army that *la guerrilla* had been welcomed into our village. But now . . ."

As Cesar hesitated, Vicki urged impatiently, "Yes? But now what?"

Cesar looked away from Vicki as he said slowly, "When I became a student and came to know more of *la situación* and all that happened beyond our village too, I came to wonder if it was not because of the pictures."

"What pictures?"

"Your father's pictures. *Los militares* do not like to have their actions questioned or their violence publicized. And your father took pictures of the soldiers rounding up the people, striking women and children. More, the soldiers had with them three bodies they said were guerrillas. They demanded to know their names. Everyone knew who they were—men from the next village. But no one spoke for fear *los militares* would turn next on their families. Your father took pictures of the bodies and the soldiers with them. I saw the pictures myself when he printed them. He made the soldiers leave without completing their mission. Their *comandante* would have been very angry. He would not wish those pictures to find their way into the media. Not when the authorities had been lying to the Americans that *los militares* had changed their ways so that American aid would begin to come again into their pockets."

Vicki's stomach was roiling again. Was it really possible her family's presence in the village had brought death and not the other way around?

"As to why I did not tell of what happened that day, it is simple. I was never asked. It was a common enough tale after all, and I spoke only the little Spanish your mother had taught me then. I did not know after that day what had become of you nor what had been reported to your family. I knew only that you were gone, and I was alone in the refugee camp with people who did not speak my language and despised my people. And later, when I had learned from their schools and *Tía* Maria had found me . . . You are not the only one who chose to forget the past. Besides, only the foolish protested against the army. I remained silent and took what was offered and became the first of my village to go to university. Do you think that was a betrayal?"

The harshness of his demand was a sharp reminder that Vicki had not been the only injured party. Who was she to judge? She'd at least had the foster care system. And the Andrewses. Would she have done as well in his place?

"Of course not. It's just the embassy wrote it up as a robbery. Not even as an unknown cause. It's in the death report. They had to know it wasn't true, that an army massacre had killed American citizens."

"Perhaps they did not. Perhaps they knew only what *los militares* chose to tell them—that their citizens had been robbed and killed in the sierras."

"No!" Now the harshness was in her own tone. If Cesar had spoken no Spanish twenty years before, neither had Vicki. Other words came to her mind. *"Don't cry, sweetheart. Everything's going to be all right. You're safe now."*

"No, the embassy knew all right. At least someone did. Because there were Americans with the army that night. Americans who not only knew but were involved with how—and why—my parents died."

CHAPTER THIRTY-ONE

"But of course it was the gringo who took us away that day." Cesar looked uncomprehending at Vicki's vehemence. "I didn't know their words to say they were *americanos*, only foreign. But who besides *los americanos* would be in the mountains alongside our *militares*?"

Yes, who?

"Why should you think they would hurt your parents? Was the gringo not the one who took us away and did not allow the soldiers to touch us? I remember well. Though I never saw him again, I have always believed it was the gringo who left instructions at the camp for my schooling. *Los militares* would not think of such a kindness. Do you not think it is possible the gringos came only to find your parents dead? I have always heard *los americanos* do not kill without reason like *los militares*."

"That isn't the point. You don't understand our government. If Americans working down here with the military even *knew* they'd butchered American citizens, if they were involved even in the cover-up . . ."

Vicki shook her head. Something she'd just said struck a chord. But the thought receded when she groped for it. And now that the first shock of memory was easing, there were other incongruities she was taking in. It had been twenty years since she'd stood under these same fruit trees looking out at the aftermath of a nightmare.

Yes, a terrible thing happened here, but it was a lifetime ago. I'm not a five-year-old anymore but a twenty-five–year-old PhD who's managed just fine all these years without cracking up. So get a grip!

But if it had been twenty years, why was this place so completely familiar? Why was the whitewash only slightly faded on bamboo walls? In the yard closest to her, why was a hammock still hanging limp between two citrus trees, a wooden hoe not yet rotted?

For that matter, why were the huts themselves not destroyed in the damp and mold of twenty rainy seasons? And if the village commons needed mowing, it certainly didn't hold two decades of growth.

"Where are you going?" Cesar hissed as Vicki stepped forward. "You said we could leave now."

Vicki eluded his restraining grab. "I have to see."

One more step, and she was in the sunlight. The sun was almost directly overhead, its radiance welcome after the damp chill of the cloud forest. Vicki walked over to an aluminum pot lying on its side under the cooking shelter just beyond that hanging hammock. She rolled it over with her foot. Ants were scouring its interior, and there was still crusted food on the bottom. Charred firewood around it still held its shape.

Pushing open a bamboo door, Vicki stepped into the hut. The interior had been ransacked, any furniture now pieces of broken wood scattered around the dirt floor. But in a corner, a piece of ragged clothing had not been worth taking. She looked down as something touched her sneaker. It was a cheap, pink Barbie doll knockoff, bought by some Mayan parent for her daughter as a treasure from the outside world. Its sprawled limbs and staring eyes twisted at Vicki's chest, and she stepped out quickly.

Walking swiftly across the commons to the ruins of her childhood home, she braced herself for emotion. But here at least was nothing familiar, and she felt only a somber absorption in tracing the outline of crumbling brick and concrete foundation still discernable under its cloak of vegetation and moss. Only four rooms but a mansion to the Mayan villagers. A common living/dining area and two bedrooms forming a square.

Holly's and mine was on this side overlooking the cooking shelter. There was . . . yes, a wooden bed we shared and a chest for our clothes.

The Mayan cook—it must have been Cesar's mother—used to let us help shuck the corn and pound it with a big, wooden pestle.

The cooking shelter was just a thick growth of brush, as she'd have expected the other huts to be, but behind the second bedroom was the tumbled-down ruin of a fourth room. Vicki conjured up a hazy recollection of a windowless place full of strange objects sternly forbidden to small girls' questing fingers. Jeff Craig's darkroom.

But only the outline was familiar, so Vicki walked on to where the village's single road curved away from the commons to disappear into the cloud forest. Here too was incongruity, because ruts pressed deep into dried mud had not yet melted under the *chipi-chipi.* And not just the ruts of a mule cart. The wide treads of a motorized vehicle.

A new dread was building up in Vicki's stomach. She could almost smell the reek of death. Pressing the orange peel still in her hand against her nostrils, she breathed deeply to keep from retching again. How tense she was, she didn't realize until a clap of sound spun her around. She was scrambling for a banana grove when the sound came again, not so violently. This time Vicki witnessed its origin and relaxed. A gust of wind was catching at the schoolhouse door, slapping it inward to bang against its hinges.

Another slam jolted Vicki's nerves, and she rushed toward the schoolhouse. Cesar rose from where he had thrown himself flat under an orange tree. Reaching the concrete structure, Vicki climbed the steps. All she had in mind was to pull the door shut. But as she stepped over the threshold, she stiffened in shock.

This place also brought back sharp memory. Sitting on the narrow wooden benches with other small, squirming bodies. Shrill voices reciting lessons she didn't understand. Chalk letters on the blackboard. Holly had been too little, but a five-year-old Vicki had insisted on joining the village children for their lessons.

But these stains puddled everywhere, on the concrete floor, splashed across the walls were not in Vicki's memory. Stains of a rusty brown she had encountered too often in too many places not to recognize. Stains that should have long faded.

Vicki's limbs seemed turned to stone, her mind fitting together ugly facts and images into an equation she should have already reached. The tragedy that had happened here was not of the far-distant past but only too current. And that smell of death was no imagination. Somewhere close by was a fresh mass grave.

Cesar coaxed Vicki out of the schoolhouse and down the steps. He tugged the door closed, a broken branch through its latch to hold it shut. Vicki made no protest as he drew her back across the commons to the orange grove.

She breathed deeply of its cleansing acidity before she rounded on him. "That didn't happen twenty years ago. The massacre two months back—Alicia and Gabriela's family—it was here, wasn't it? It's happened all over again." She ran a shaking hand across her face. No wonder it was so quiet in here. The animals could smell the death.

"I didn't know what we would find here, but I was afraid it might be so," Cesar admitted. "I had heard it whispered that there were those who wished to leave Verapaz and go back to the sierra. Those whose *familiares* once lived in these mountains who knew there was good land and were tired of living under the fist of *los militares*. That it was forbidden meant little. Have not *los españoles* always taken our land and given it to others?

"But I was away then at the university finishing my studies. When I came to the center, *Tía* Maria whispered to me that my cousin—Alicia and Gabriela's father—was among those who'd chosen to go. I wondered if they had returned to the old village. It is easier to clean up old fields than to clear fresh jungle. And the schoolhouse at least would still be standing. I was not happy that they went. Not only because it could bring more grief to our people but because I had learned of the importance of this biosphere to our country. But I am no *soplón*. And it was only one village.

"Then word came of the massacre. What could be said when to even admit of their presence in forbidden territory could bring trouble with *los militares*? So once again nothing was said, and our *familiares* were mourned in silence. It wasn't until I saw where Alicia and Gabriela's path led yesterday that I knew it must be our old village. That road—" he gestured toward the dirt track leading out of the village—"goes to another which in turn joins with the biosphere trail. When we were children, it was the only road to the army *cuartel* and markets down the mountain."

"Then the girls were trying to get back here. The men must have caught up before they arrived, because I didn't see any fresh sandal prints coming into the village. Or tire tracks. So where did that army transport come from last night?"

Cesar shrugged. "There are many tracks in these mountains."

Yes, Vicki had seen any number yesterday as well as on the bike ride, remnants of other hamlets these mountains had sheltered. "But who would do this? Alpiro might be hard-nosed enough to arrest those men for being in the wrong place looking for lost kids. But I can't see him ordering a full-scale massacre over a little trespassing. Not when it would be easy enough just to bulldoze the place and deport them back out of the biosphere. And roving bandits—they go after tourists with money and cameras. These people could have nothing they'd want. It doesn't make sense."

It had been Vicki's cry for weeks—since Holly's death. Had she been wrong, after all, in the revelation that had come to her last night? Was it the massacre that had troubled Holly that day at the airport? That she had been investigating in those last days?

No, wait—Holly hadn't even known about that before Lynn brought it up. Nor had it seemed to trouble her particularly. Far less in Holly's single-minded environmentalism than her lost jaguarundi. Unless . . .

A thread of thought was again tugging at Vicki. Unless it was all connected. The past. The present. The massacre. The photos. Holly's last words. Her death.

Vicki hadn't realized the massacre had happened so close to the plateau. She had thought little about it beyond a detached indignation until she'd met Alicia and Gabriela. Now she remembered something Joe had said. The overgrown clearings they'd circled in the valley, the same that showed in such a wealth of colors in Holly's pictures, had been abandoned by the massacred villagers. The shock of gunfire following had driven that comment from Vicki's mind until now.

Vicki's knapsack had remained over her shoulder in all her striding around. Lowering it, she dug out the photo printouts, as she'd meant to do up on the ridge before her recognition of Cesar had driven every thought from the present into the past. She shuffled to the shot of the flower-cloaked clearings. "Do you know what kind of flowers these are?"

"No; they do not look native to the sierra." Cesar's tone questioned why it mattered. "But I am a veterinarian, not a botanist."

No, he wouldn't know them. The flowers were no more indigenous to Guatemala than to the sierras.

"Is there a lookout nearby where we could see these fields clearly as we could from the mountainside?"

Cesar looked baffled. "On the far side of the village."

For their hamlet, the villagers had cleared a fairly level shelf of land partway up the mountain flank. From the orange grove where Cesar and Vicki had dropped their bikes, the mountain rose steeply to the spring and on up to the ridge they'd followed.

Cesar led Vicki the opposite direction across the village commons onto the dirt road. He turned almost immediately onto a trail leading past the ruins of Vicki's childhood home. Like the path to the spring, its firmness indicated a well-used walking path, though by its overgrown state, it had been months since anyone passed through. Vicki followed Cesar through leaves and vines for only a few minutes before the mountainside dropped away to offer a panorama of the valley below. The waterfall was now directly opposite them, the valley floor no more than a hundred meters below.

The path wound downward, but Vicki had found what she wanted. An outcropping of rock a few meters off the path. Tapping Cesar on the arm, she scrambled into the brush. The rock surface was flat enough for Vicki to worm in on her stomach, scooting up to where she could see the whole valley with its abandoned clearings. There were more than she'd seen before, more than Joe had had time to scout out before that blast of gunfire, not only on the valley floor but climbing the slope below them. How many hectares in all? Dozens at least.

Cesar scooted in beside her as Vicki dug the binoculars out of her pack. Though small enough to fit into her palm, the magnification was excellent with the zoom capacity of a good camera, and the distance no longer great. It was what Vicki had braced herself to see. Without the multicolored petals, the flower stalks in the closest clearing were identical enough to be seen now as a crop. They were at least a meter tall, each ending in several bulbs like green pomegranates. Vicki increased the magnification to its maximum. Though fuzzy, she could make out scores sliced down the side of the bulbs, streaks that might have been brown gum.

Vicki let out the quietest of sighs. This had to be why Holly had died, what she had come across in her unsanctioned wanderings through the biosphere. Unlike Cesar, Holly had known what she saw and had in the end asked too many questions. The sheer extent of those poppy fields represented more processed heroin than Vicki could contemplate. They would have had to be seeded here months ago, neatly camouflaged among wild corn and weeds, left to spread their beauty until the bulbs were ripe and the falling of petals signaled the harvest.

Was that what had once again doomed the village? Had its new residents moved back in, built fresh homes on the rotted remains of the old, then set out to plant their crops, thinking nothing of the strange flowers that had invaded the abandoned clearings? It must have been a shock for the caretakers watching over their prospective fortune.

But just who was responsible? Alpiro for sure had to be in it up to his teeth. Who else could ensure the opium growers were left undisturbed? Or that certain parts of the biosphere weren't included in any "training operations"?

And who else? That obsequious and unhelpful minister of environment, under whose province the biosphere fell?

"You were right," Holly had managed to get out as she died. And what exactly had Vicki warned her about? Only the possible corruption of Holly's high-living local colleagues.

No, it all fit. Vicki's tumultuous thoughts jumped to the U.S. drug czar who'd been dining at the airport on her arrival. How had this big an undertaking been kept from Alpiro's American advisers and outfitters? She considered the pride with which Michael had recounted his counternarcotics victories. However angry his support of Alpiro had made her, Vicki couldn't have mistaken the sincerity with which the embassy staffer had spoken of his duty and commitment to country and mission. And he'd been decorated for wiping out countless drug trafficking operations just like this. So how had they kept him in the dark about this one?

The same way they'd done it for decades. By lying and deceit and ensuring that foreigners like Michael got just enough small "victories" to report back to DC that their dirty double-dealing in other areas wouldn't even raise a red flag. *At least now maybe Michael will listen to me about Alpiro.*

There had to be others involved, because Vicki had learned in Myanmar how much labor the opium trade entailed, supplying work to far too many Burmese peasants. Once the petals fell off, each bulb had to be scored as night fell, the opium gum oozing out scraped off at dawn, not once but several times, the dried sap molded into brown blocks of raw opium. If the poppies were finishing their bloom when Vicki arrived at the center—*then these last couple of weeks someone's been harvesting the opium.*

No wonder Alpiro had forbidden overflights of the biosphere. And she could bet the gunmen who'd shot at the DHC-2 had been caretakers of the crop. Though from the lack of life Vicki was seeing below, the harvest looked to be finished. What exactly had Holly stumbled onto out here? And who had been responsible for her death?

Though it didn't even really matter. If Vicki could bring this to authorities who could actually *do* something about it, then she could strike the blow for the biosphere and against this illicit drug empire that Holly must have been after. Even if she never found out who'd actually pulled the trigger, these last weeks would not have been fruitless.

"Do what is right and do not give way to fear."

Is this why I'm here, Father God?

At a tap on her arm, Vicki turned to meet Cesar's anxious glance. "We'll go in just a minute," she whispered.

She got to her feet, looping the binocular strap around her neck for safekeeping as she balanced at the rock edge. Standing, she could see considerably farther, including another handful of clearings down the valley the undergrowth around her had masked. Vicki's survey had reached the far left of the valley floor, and she'd actually begun to drop the binoculars when movement registered in her field of vision. Though she'd relayed Michael's assurance that Alpiro's men had abandoned their biosphere operation, it had still been with caution and stealth that Vicki and Cesar started out on this expedition. But the passing of hours without any other human life, the silence and emptiness of the landscape below, had lulled her into the careless assumption that their caution had been needless.

So it was with a jolt of adrenaline that Vicki snatched the binoculars back to her eyes. She adjusted the magnification. No, it had been too much to hope that she was mistaken. Nor were the shapes in that field some feeding herd of deer. They were human. Vicki counted four in the mottled green and olive of camouflage fatigues, automatic rifles in their hands. The rest wore the cheap clothing of peasant laborers. Scythes in their hands mowed the tall poppy stalks as though it were grass. Vicki's thoughts flashed to the "deer herd" she'd glimpsed yesterday. Another clean-up crew?

Because that's what it had to be. The harvest must be over, and now the evidence was being eradicated. Those peasants under the gun barrels were the grunt labor Vicki had expected.

Grabbing a nearby liana to steady herself, Vicki stood on tiptoe to focus the binoculars on one of the uniforms. It was not UPN but the unmarked camouflage last night's ground patrol had worn. Was she wrong again? Was there yet another group operating in this rain forest? Some rogue military unit or even guerrilla band that had staked out its own kingdom in the biosphere?

Either way Alpiro has to know about it. Just look at how his men showed up last night.

Just then a worker stepped into the binoculars' field of vision in front of the uniform, a scythe in his hand. After an hour together in the back of a pickup, Vicki recognized the dark, Mayan features instantly. So this was where yesterday's seized volunteers had ended up.

Then as Vicki shifted her focus, the binoculars caught another uniformed man leaving the clearing. She panicked as he started climbing the slope in her direction. But when she dropped the binoculars, Vicki realized he was so far away she wouldn't have even spotted the green and olive of his fatigues if she hadn't known he was there. Without field glasses, he couldn't possibly make out the beige shirt and cargo pants Vicki had chosen for this expedition.

Finding him again in the binoculars, Vicki turned perilously on tiptoe to follow his progress. Twice she had to readjust the focus closer, and she was considering a prudent drop to cover when he vanished. Vicki twisted farther to scan the mountain slope to her left. All that appeared was a mass of greenery. Where had he gone?

Vicki adjusted the focus even closer—and almost lost her hold on the liana. She'd missed the encampment because it wasn't down in the valley but up the slope only slightly below her and not more than fifty meters to her left. Camouflage nets explained how they'd escaped notice when Joe had circled in overhead. Why hadn't they just used the old village site? Then Vicki recalled that pervasive odor of death. Besides, from here they could keep watch over their treasure without bestirring themselves.

A number of army tents were tucked among trees. Vicki had a clear line of vision into the largest. Inside she could make out a table and radio equipment. She stiffened as her binoculars moved across a canvas lawn chair, its occupant lounging with a bottle of gold liquid as though enjoying a day at the beach. It was yesterday's ground patrol leader who'd loomed out of the night. Castro II.

Releasing the liana, Vicki used that hand to scrabble in the top of her knapsack. She tugged loose the group photo that had trailed her across Guatemala. Yes, Castro II at least had changed little over the years. There he was right next to Alpiro, without the peppering of gray but curls and beard just as luxuriant, his florid face as smug. *He looks so much like Alpiro; they've got to be blood relatives.*

Which would explain the involvement of a high-ranking law enforcement officer like Alpiro. And how he could keep something this big from leaking out. He wouldn't need more manpower than Castro II and his band of merry men with their conscripted peasant labor. Alpiro's own UPN troops need know only their legitimate mission of protecting the biosphere. They might even have been told some kind of training mission was going on in here. That would explain the cooperation Vicki had witnessed last night.

Vicki's plans of immediate departure evaporated instantly. Instead she shifted her focus to study the camp. At the nearest perimeter under its own netting, she noticed the Jeep Castro II had been driving last night and beside it the army transport. Just beyond was a rutted track. That would be how they'd emerged to intercept the pickup. And that radio in the tent would be how they'd known Vicki and the others were coming.

The camp held a number of the unidentified camouflage fatigues. Two ambled around with unslung weapons. If they'd looked up the slope, they might have spotted Vicki, but they seemed more interested in the other activities than their sentry duties. Under a square canvas pavilion, its side walls rolled up, two more men in fatigues scraped a brown rubbery substance from a metal basin into fist-size balls. The congealed opium gum scraped from the poppy bulbs. Two others were working with a press that turned out brick-size blocks. Another was wrapping the bricks in brown paper.

Vicki's arms ached with the effort of holding both binoculars and liana. She let the glasses drop on their strap to adjust her balance.

As she did so, Cesar took the binoculars from her hand and turned the glasses to where he'd seen her attention focused. Almost immediately, he dropped them with a furious hiss. "Señorita Vee-kee, that man—the one in the chair—he was the one who directed the burning of our church. Who are these men? What are they doing?"

Why am I not surprised? At least that cleared Michael's UPN troops, if their *comandante* was undoubtedly involved.

"*¡Narcotraficantes!*" Vicki answered as she took back the binoculars. It was all the explanation necessary. If heroin was a new industry for Guatemala, drug trafficking was an ancient problem.

Vicki heard Cesar gasp. Then he tugged at her arm in fresh urgency for them to leave.

Vicki nodded. Cesar was right. It was time to get out of here—and without being seen.

With those scythes, it looked like Castro II and his gang were winding down their operation. Had the harvest actually finished, or had yesterday's intrusion into their territory spooked them? It would be easy enough to move on and start over. The biosphere was vast, and there were other abandoned settlements, if not so easily accessible. If they cleared out before Vicki could get some authority out here . . . No, she couldn't let that happen. Not after all this.

If I had Holly's digital camera for proof. It'll just have to be my word. I hope that's enough. I need to get to Guatemala City, get through to the right people at the embassy, make them believe.

Time was the greatest urgency. Michael had offered transport, but she'd have to go through Alpiro to reach him. Her best option was the DHC-2. And Joe had seen those earlier plantings. He could vouch for her story. He might even have a camera, if he'd be willing to risk flying over this for some shots.

Vicki was now as anxious as Cesar to leave. But she still didn't move. A new sentry, M16 slung over a shoulder, had just emerged from behind the command tent and was sauntering through the camp. He faced Vicki and was less sloppy than the other guards, head raised under a floppy brim, scanning his surroundings. Vicki froze lest any movement pull his eyes up the slope.

The sentry disappeared between the Jeep and army transport, lingering long enough that Vicki had made up her mind to move when the binoculars caught him striding out the near side. To Vicki's dismay, he was heading up the slope. She swung the binoculars to follow his movements—and swung too far. Frantically, she scouted to recover her target. She was panicking again when a slight movement against the greenery allowed her to home in on a recognizable pattern of mottled olive and green. Was the sentry coming in her direction?

He rested against a tree, the features too shadowed to make out but turned away from Vicki.

She relaxed. But only until she focused in on the motionless figure. This wasn't the same sentry after all. He had no M16 slung over his shoulder, and the shadows obscuring his face proved to be a pair of binoculars that looked far more powerful than Vicki's. He'd been looking toward the encampment, but now he turned to survey his surroundings, and the relaxed ease of his stance held none of the carelessness of the men below.

Vicki's first wild fancy was that her own earlier thoughts had conjured up the resemblance. There had to be others with such a tall, broad frame and muscular grace of movement. Then something caught the sentry's attention, and the glasses came down. Vicki caught a strong profile she'd know anywhere even under the green and black of camouflage paint.

Joe Ericsson.

There has to be a mistake. Maybe . . . maybe I was right before, and he's undercover, watching them like I am.

Then Vicki spotted what had drawn Joe's attention. Another man in camouflage fatigues was walking into her field of vision. The sentry who'd emerged from the camp. And he was expected. Joe stepped immediately forward to speak with him. It was only a brief exchange. Then the other sentry walked off, not back toward the camp but angling up the slope. The disappointment and betrayal was as sharp as a physical pain. *No! I won't let it be true!*

But now at last the thought that had been nagging Vicki all day burst to the surface. Holly's last words. All of them. *"You were right. . . . No, I was right."* Vicki had been so focused on the first part, so sure one of Holly's Guatemalan colleagues had to be involved, as Vicki had sardonically suggested. But what had Holly retorted? *"Why not one of the American volunteers—Roger, or Joe, or even me?"*

Joe.

This then was what Vicki had sensed the handyman was hiding even when she'd been drawn to him. Why she'd found him on the mountain in hunter's gear and weapon. A man her sister had trusted and admired. Maybe even been half in love with. Of whom she wouldn't have wanted to believe any ill. And so would have held back from reporting him to any authority.

The thought of Holly was enough to burn away betrayal and disbelief in a flood of fury. Vicki's grip tightened around the binoculars. *You won't get away with this. Not if I have to find a way out of here and off this mountain and drag the proper authorities to arrest you all by myself.*

But Vicki's movement had also tightened the liana she'd wrapped around her arm to balance herself. The snapping of it resounded in the quiet like the cracking of a whip. Frozen in horror, the binoculars still to her eyes, Vicki saw Joe spin around, his glasses coming up. For one instant, the two sets of field glasses locked on each other.

Then Joe's binoculars fell, and from the cold ferocity of his expression, Vicki knew he'd seen her.

CHAPTER THIRTY-TWO

Joe wasn't the only one to take notice. The snap of the vine was followed immediately by a shout from the encampment.

Vicki dropped into the cover of the underbrush. "Let's go!" she mouthed.

She followed Cesar down from the outcropping.

Had they seen her? *Not that it matters,* she answered herself bitterly. Joe would let them know fast enough.

They were off the outcropping now, but to reach the path, they had to step into the open, and this time a chorus of shouts left no doubt they'd been seen. Men in fatigues fanned out across the slope to their left. Stealth was no longer an advantage, only speed. Vicki and Cesar reached the overgrown trail, twigs and vines grabbing at them as they waded through. A branch slapped Vicki in the face as she struggled to stay on Cesar's heels. At least they had the path while the pursuit below was battering its way through untamed brush.

Then Vicki heard an engine roaring to life. Cesar tossed over his shoulder even as he pushed on faster, "They will know we must have come there from the village."

He didn't need to amplify. They had to reach their bikes before that racing engine cut them off. How far would the pursuit have to detour? Not far enough from the swiftness with which that transport had sped up the track after those villagers yesterday. Adrenaline redoubled Vicki's speed.

The pursuit was still a distant rumble when Vicki stumbled after Cesar onto the track at the edge of the hamlet. Ahead was the open stretch of the village commons. And that orange grove on the far side was their hope. If they could lose themselves on the mountain bikes up in that maze of trails . . .

The jouncing of her knapsack and the knee-deep brush that had overtaken the commons were a distracting annoyance as Vicki ran. She resisted the impulse to look over her shoulder.

When the citrus trees were no more than ten meters ahead, she heard the engine roar into the open. A babble of shouts told Vicki their progress across the field had been spotted. She risked a glance back. The Jeep held at least a half dozen men. Joe wasn't among them, she took time to catalog bitterly. The Jeep accelerated onto the field, the four-wheel drive making nothing of the brush. But they were too late. Two more strides would bring Cesar and Vicki to the cover of the orange trees. And their bikes.

Vicki had just ducked under a low-hanging branch when a crack of sound split the air and a ping nicked a piece of bark from the nearest tree trunk. The pursuit wasn't waiting to overtake them. The single shot became a *rat-tat-tat* of automatic gunfire. The erratic jolting of the Jeep saved the two fugitives, deflecting the gunfire over their heads, a whistle of bullets tearing through leaves and smacking into wood. Then Cesar yanked Vicki beyond the first line of trees. The Jeep engine went dead as he scrabbled to lift their bikes. Thudding boots and hoarse calls replaced the indiscriminate gunfire. Cesar shoved Vicki ahead onto the trail as they mounted the bikes. Only when a fresh spray of gunfire broke out did Vicki register the selflessness of that gesture.

But the trail made an immediate bend so that the gunfire was wasted on oak and cypress. Pedaling furiously, she glanced over her shoulder to see Cesar close behind her and unhurt. Thrashing and shouts came from the undergrowth behind them but no more gunfire.

By the time Vicki reached the drinking spring, the sounds of pursuit were distant enough that she dared slow to ease her aching calf muscles and laboring lungs. They were safe—at least for the moment.

Vicki didn't wait for Cesar to take the lead when she reached the first intersecting path but took the right fork unhesitatingly. Broken vegetation and tire marks were as clear a guide as a signpost. They would also be an open map to the pursuit, but she refused to linger on that. The men knew now that Vicki and Cesar were mounted. They'd have to be foolhardy to continue the chase on foot. But even when the last echo of pursuit was long gone, Vicki didn't slow, pushing herself faster and harder than she ever had in her life, unerringly taking each turn of path over which they'd come, slowing only occasionally to check that Cesar was still with her. The burning anger in her chest gave her strength even after the first rush of adrenaline had ebbed.

Once a helicopter flew low overhead, but Vicki didn't even break rhythm. Under this thick canopy, they were invisible from the air. Twice she fell when she was going too fast to see an obstruction. By the time she reached the steep zigzag where they'd first mounted the bikes, Vicki was dripping with sweat and itchy with dirt, face and arms stinging where leaves and vines and branches had lashed across them.

Here at the top of the ridge was less cover, and when Vicki heard the drone of a helicopter returning, she dismounted. Shoving the bike into the undergrowth, she dropped beside it, wrapping her arms around her knees as she tried to think. She'd tried to plan her next step while racing along, but there'd been room in her mind only for the next curve in the path. Now as she looked down over the plateau, she could no longer put it off.

Plan A—the night bus down the mountain—was out of the question. The Verapaz bus stop in the town plaza would be an automatic target of any search order.

Plan B—the DHC-2—was out too. Which was something else that didn't make sense. The gunfire directed at the small plane on Vicki's arrival had been real. Unhappiness lifted slightly until Vicki remembered what Joe had shouted at the soldiers. *The new plane and flight plan never got passed on to the right people. No wonder he was so furious. He must have been circling around to calculate their crop when they shot at us.*

No, Vicki didn't even want to think of Joe. The possibility of Michael's involvement in this had been little more than a distasteful thought while

Joe's betrayal still stabbed like a physical pain; that distinction was something else she wouldn't let herself probe.

Going back to the center was out as well. Rosario and Beatriz were no friends.

And Michael? Vicki's earlier anger over the missing villagers no longer seemed such a priority, and he had given her until afternoon to change her plans. But his transportation was a UPN helicopter, and whatever Alpiro's involvement in this biosphere narco-scam, she'd bet he had his own forces on high alert by now. She'd be walking into the lion's den to try to reach Michael.

Despair was growing in her when Vicki's eye fell on a red tiled roof raised on a knoll in the middle of the coffee fields. A green pickup sat in the driveway, and at the sight of it, Vicki straightened with what was perilously close to a sob of relief.

Of course! Bill had told Vicki to come to him if she ever needed anything. This wasn't what he'd have had in mind, but if she could trust him with her parents' identity, she could trust him with this. Better yet, Bill had embassy contacts. And his own radio setup. He'd know what to do.

Besides, Vicki reminded herself with a fresh stab of betrayal, she had an obligation to let him know just what the employee he'd treated so generously had been up to. Had Bill some inkling of what kind of man Joe really was? Was that why he'd warned Vicki to stay away from him?

Vicki pushed down that renewed unhappiness as hard breathing alerted her that Cesar had overtaken her. He flung himself from his bike and hunkered down beside her.

Vicki raised her head to meet his gaze. Cesar had every right to blame her. He hadn't wanted to come and had warned her from the start. Now who knew what kind of trouble she'd landed him in. But she saw no hint of condemnation in his eyes, only urgency.

"Come! We must get to the village before *los militares*."

Vicki looked at him blankly. "The village? They can't help us. We need to reach Señor Taylor. He has a radio and contacts with *la embajada*."

"No! There is no time for that," Cesar answered. "Do you not see, *los narcotraficantes* will not know who we are, only that we have invaded their territory. They'll think we are from the village, that we came to spy out their *narcotráfico*."

Joe at least knew exactly who'd been on that rock outcropping. But Cesar hadn't seen him, and Vicki didn't waste time raising the point. "Then the village is the last place we should go. They'll be looking for us there."

Cesar shook his head as he said harshly, "They will not care which villager it is—only that we have disobeyed their command. No, *los narcotraficantes* will come back to carry out their threat. The villagers must be given warning to escape to the hills. And do not think the authorities will stop them. Were not *los militares* with *los narcotraficantes* when we found Alicia and Gabriela? Do you think this has happened in *la reserva* without their knowledge?"

By what arrogance had Vicki somehow assumed Cesar couldn't add two and two as easily as she had? or that she was the natural leader here? In fact, his life had faced far more of such situations than hers.

"Then go," Vicki said. "Go do what you have to—and don't come back to the center until it's safe. I'll get to Señor Taylor. Maybe he can help. I'll be fine now by myself. Your family, your people need you."

Cesar seemed to weigh whether she meant what she said. Then he took off down the mountainside, bike slung over his back.

Vicki didn't immediately follow. Her binoculars had remained around her neck on that mad trek back, and she lifted them to study the slope between her and Bill's coffee plantation below. The path Cesar had followed was out since it dead-ended at the center, and she didn't know Cesar's detours. But up here at least the undergrowth was scant, and if she worked her way through it, she could angle down to come out directly behind the plantation house.

Avoiding guards and laborers was more complicated. There were no coffee plantings within a fifty meter radius of the knoll, only smooth, trimmed lawn. The closest laborers Vicki spotted through the field glasses were on the far side of the road. But the usual sentry was in the guard shack at the front gate, and the binoculars zoomed in on a man in a sombrero on Bill's front veranda. The guard Joe had chewed out after Vicki's last unsolicited visit? And any of those laborers out there could be a *soplón* for Alpiro.

With no path, there was no advantage in the mountain bike, so Vicki left it in the brush. It took longer than she'd hoped to work her way to

Bill's fields, though she stayed high on the ridge until she was directly behind the plantation house. By the time she slid through the brush to where Bill's back veranda was directly across from her, she'd added rips to her shirt and cargo pants.

To Vicki's disappointment, the veranda guard had drifted around to the back, where he was smoking a cigarette. Crouching in the underbrush, she didn't dare even reach for her canteen for fear the movement might be spotted. She considered throwing herself on the guard's mercy to call his employer when he flicked the cigarette to the veranda floor, ground it out under his boot, and walked around the side of the house.

Vicki covered the open lawn in less than ten seconds. Slipping across the veranda, she froze as her foot accidentally dislodged an open beer bottle. The guard's afternoon refreshment by the liquid trail still dribbling from it.

But the sound had been negligible, and an instant later Vicki was at the back door. Noiselessly, she slid the latch downward. The door didn't budge, and she panicked when she heard footsteps on the side veranda. Then she pushed the latch upward. The door swung open. The latch snicked quietly behind her just as footsteps rounded the corner of the veranda.

She was inside.

CHAPTER THIRTY-THREE

After the early afternoon sunshine, the interior was dim. Vicki paused to orient herself. She was in the kitchen. Part of the dimness came from a white blind pulled down over the window. Bill Taylor clearly didn't care for prying eyes.

Vicki stepped farther into the kitchen. A door stood open into a pantry. "Bill?"

No answer.

She walked into the living room. It was empty. The two bedroom doors stood ajar, so Vicki didn't have to step inside to see they were unoccupied. Poking her head into the office, she called softly again, "Bill?"

No one was there, but a mug of coffee sat on the desk, recently poured from the wisp of vapor.

Vicki returned to the living room and peeked around another blind. Since the green pickup was still here, Bill hadn't gone far. Maybe he'd stepped out to deal with some plantation business. She'd just have to wait and hope that Bill would be right back.

Meantime, Vicki slipped into the bathroom between the two bedrooms. She wiped dirt and sweat from her face and arms. Pulling her ponytail loose, she raked debris from her hair before twisting the hair tie back into place. As she peeled a banana and assuaged thirst from her canteen, she felt almost human again but increasingly edgy. Where was Bill? Pressing in on Vicki was the urgency that they were running out of time. Had Cesar reached the village yet? What would happen even if he could get the villagers into the hills? They couldn't stay there forever.

I've got to get help to put an end to this. If we can make it public enough, the authorities will have to do something or be embarrassed before the whole world. That's the only way the villagers and Cesar can go back to their lives.

Was this how Vicki's birth father had felt? Why he'd been so passionate about taking his pictures? "Truth-teller," the Mayans had called him. *Jeff Craig—no, Papa!—maybe I don't really know what I'm remembering and what I'm imagining, but I'm so proud to be your daughter. And Mama's. Let me be like you. Let me tell the truth to the world like you were trying to do here—and Holly.*

Restless, Vicki wandered back to the office. Maybe something in here would indicate what had taken Bill away and how long he'd be. But the desk held only a neat blotter and a stack of what looked like junk mail and magazines, the computer monitor showing a blank screen. Vicki glanced longingly at the radio equipment. It looked high-tech, a far cry from the center's UHF radio, but she didn't know how to work it. And if she did, whom would she call?

Vicki was turning to leave when she noticed the pottery shelf standing slightly away from the wall, as it had been when she'd seen Joe working in here, and if it hadn't been for a soft whistle of wind, she would have walked away. She stared at it for a moment. Then she reached for one of the pottery figurines. Or tried to, because as she tugged, Vicki discovered it was glued in place. She pulled instead at the shelf. Noiselessly, as though on oiled wheels, the entire bookcase swung another two feet into the room. Vicki stepped around it.

The fireplace gave the illusion an entire room didn't exist. Not that it was a big room—the width of the fireplace and half the depth of the office.

The whistling came from an air vent high in the back of the fireplace, cleverly positioned to allow for a flow of air through the chimney, even if the pottery shelf was shut. The room itself was warm and dry. Touching the back of the fireplace, Vicki found it pleasantly hot. A built-in dehumidifier. The room was also surprisingly well lit, considering it had no windows. She tilted her head back. There was no ceiling except for the roof tiles. Right alongside the ridgepole, a square meter or so of these had been replaced with what looked like a solar panel. Through the skylight Vicki could see the satellite dish that had masked the solar panel from above. The height of the ridgepole and smallness of the room gave the impression of standing at the bottom of a well.

A safe room. A wise precaution for a lone foreigner living in this lawless region. Did Bill know Joe had found it? Because Vicki had no doubt what Joe had been doing that day she'd seen him in here.

At first glance, the safe room's contents hardly seemed worth the concealment this hiding place entailed. A small, wooden table disordered with papers and files, a pair of night-vision goggles tossed on top. A single chair. File cabinets. Vicki tugged at the nearest. Locked. An open laptop seemed superfluous with the desktop version in the other room until she saw wires snaking up the wall and a modem. The satellite dish above her was not only for cable. And from a still-damp coffee ring, it appeared Bill had been here when he responded to whatever interruption had come.

Then Vicki saw a satellite phone. Black and sleek in its bulky base, it was the kind of setup Holly had dreamed of for the center. Vicki could understand Bill keeping it locked away. It had to be worth what a coffee picker earned in a decade.

Vicki didn't consider she was snooping as she walked over to the table. The papers scattered on top looked to be some sort of aerial maps. Pen markings and some sort of scribbled diagrams in the margins looked rather like notes a football coach might use to outline a game plan.

Vicki pushed aside a stack of folders to reach for the phone. *I could call someone. No, I have no numbers, not even Evelyn's. But 0 is for the operator even down here. If I could get through to the embassy, talk to Marion Whitfield . . .*

But she didn't lift the phone from its cradle. Her hand trembled slightly as she reached for the PDA that had been exposed when she moved the folders. If it wasn't Holly's, it was an identical model. Whether her passionate hope was that she were right or wrong, Vicki wasn't sure. Any doubt evaporated as the liquid crystal screen came to life.

The screen saver was one of Holly's photos: the landscape shot of fields of flowers. Vicki's fingers felt as cold as the stone in her chest as she began running the unit back through its most recent usage. If Holly had intended that screen saver as the clarion announcement it was, surely she'd left some message here for her sister. But Vicki found no personal communication at all, only file after file Holly must have downloaded from the Internet.

What they did show was that Holly had been researching along the same lines as Vicki's own deductions. Several documents addressed the rising heroin traffic in Central and South America. A dozen of them dealt with the Guatemalan regime's decades-long war. Vicki soon spotted the common denominator. The files Holly had chosen to save dealt less with military wrongdoing than the United States' own involvement in Guatemala over the past half century. Vicki scanned through each file until the group photo Holly had posted for bedtime viewing scrolled across the screen. The document was a Human Rights Watch testimony from more than two years back. A number of photos were buried in the text. Vicki was interested only in the group photo. The caption was the same as that Guatemalan newspaper account from which it must have been scanned, but here a question mark had been satirically added: "America and Guatemala: Allies Against Communism?"

The report mentioned the scathing coincidence of how many CIA informants in the region just happened to be graduates from the special counterinsurgency training programs. No explicit connection was made between photo and the text, but the implication was clear.

Vicki eyed the tiny turned head of the American in civilian clothing and floppy hat. *I figured you as CIA. Were you recruiting while they were training?*

That was the last text file. Interesting material under more leisurely circumstances, but was there any relevance? So these men had been trained by the US, maybe even recruited as an intelligence asset by the CIA. Vicki had no real argument with the recruiting practices of her nation's intelligence service. Sometimes you had to deal with scumbags to get information. She'd done so herself. And once again, this was all far in the past. *What are you trying to tell me, Holly?*

Nor was it relevant to the more urgent question. What was Holly's

PDA doing in Bill's safe room? *Joe must have had it after all—one more lie.* But why not simply return it to Vicki? There was nothing particularly incriminating in this hodgepodge of downloaded research files. *Except then he'd have to explain where and how he got it.* Had Bill come across it? Or had Joe mislaid it here when he was snooping around?

The pain was hot again in her chest as Vicki turned next to the photo album her sister kept on her PDA. Most of the photos were variations on the ones Holly had posted on her bunk. A number were different angles of the poppy fields, though none showed the ripened bulbs. Though of course they wouldn't, since Holly was dead by the time the petals had fallen.

Vicki flicked almost impatiently past a larger version of the small image in that last text file. Speed-reader though she was, it must have been close to fifteen minutes since Vicki had slipped into the house, over an hour since she and Cesar had fled from the encampment. Joe and his rogue military allies would not be sitting still. *Please hurry up, Bill!*

That mental plea gave way to cold dismay as the next JPEG flashed onto the screen. It had been cropped and blown up from the prior group photo.

"Why not one of the American volunteers—Roger, or Joe . . ."

Or William Taylor, WRC's most generous and long-serving volunteer.

Vicki would never have recognized that turned-away profile under the tilted brim if it hadn't been cropped and blown up. But then she hadn't worked as closely nor admired so deeply the center's elderly benefactor as Holly had. He hadn't been young even when the photo was taken, the hair longer than his present crew cut, the aquiline profile sagging only a little twenty years later. When Vicki flicked back to the last JPEG, that straight-backed, ageless posture screamed for recognition.

Vicki turned off the PDA, snatching up the knapsack she'd allowed to rest on the table. She glanced at the sat phone. *I have to call for help. It's my only hope.*

The sat phone was cordless. She'd have to hope it had range outside the house. But in her haste to snatch the receiver, Vicki hadn't watched for the knapsack on her shoulder. As she swung around, it slammed into the sat phone and folders, sending them scattering to the floor. Diving to her knees, Vicki caught the bulky weight of the phone's base before it crashed against the hard tile floor. But the receiver had tumbled out amid a welter of folder covers and what looked like dozens of full-page snapshots. Not paper copies such as Holly had posted. The colorful gloss of professional prints.

Pushing the phone base back onto the table, Vicki grabbed the receiver. She scrabbled instinctively to shove the photos into a pile as she checked anxiously for a dial tone. The phone was still functioning. Recognizing the absurdity of her frantic gathering, Vicki let the photos in her hand fall. But she didn't rise from her knees. The bright rectangle from the skylight overhead fell directly on the scattered prints. Despite her urgency, Vicki's first reaction was of wonder. The photographs were so beautiful, a work of such love and vision that she was left confused.

There was a young Mayan father swinging in a hammock, playing his guitar for two small, naked children. An elderly woman patting out tortillas to bake on a hot stone. Laborers, stooped and worn beyond their years, lifting huge sacks of coffee on bent backs. A young couple dancing together. Children sitting on narrow, wooden benches, wearing neat, white pinafores over their ragged clothing. *If Bill took these . . . !*

It was the last photo that held Vicki to her knees. *I know this place. This is the village schoolhouse.* Then she noticed the words in the photo's lower right-hand corner: *Jeff Craig Productions.* These were no work of Bill Taylor. They could only be the compilation of Mayan village life her birth father been working on when he died.

No, was murdered.

Vicki spread the photos out. Yes, there were the photos Cesar had mentioned. Army trucks swirling up a dust cloud on the village commons. Soldiers jumping free with weapons unslung. An officer on a cab roof with a megaphone. Women and children running and screaming. A baton slamming brutally down on an elderly Mayan woman. A soldier's boot crashing into a prone body's ribs. A crying child cringing from a rifle barrel. Three dead bodies in the dust. All bore the stamp of Jeff Craig Productions. Her birth father must have shot the roll before the soldiers had spotted a foreign observer in the village. No wonder they hadn't wanted to see these hit the international media.

There were a handful of guerrilla shots too. A line of them, ragged and underfed with their leader alone in uniform so that only their weapons distinguished them from a crowd of villagers passively listening to the leader's arm-waving exhortations.

Vicki shook loose the last folder. These pictures alone bore no stamp of her father's trademark. Dim, fuzzy, no longer shot by an expert eye, they were the images of her nightmares. Flames shooting high against a mountain twilight. A mound of bodies. She could almost make out a paler gleam in the tangle of limbs and hair, and with sickness rising to her throat, she thrust the print away. Soldiers laughing and holding up plunder. An officer in command beret talking into a hand radio. Vicki no longer had any surprise left in her as she recognized the officer. Castro II.

Then nightmare resolved into memory as Vicki brushed prints from the last two photos. Three tall figures striding away from the camera, and beyond them, emerging from the tree line at the very edge of the flash, three small, ghostly blurs.

The last print had caught the three larger figures whirling around, and even in the twilight gloom, the features were identifiable. Two under army caps, annoyed, furious. The third under a floppy hat, impassive, watchful. All unmistakably foreigners.

Vicki's head swam as the words echoed in her mind. *"No witnesses. Hey, get away from those cameras! No records. Do I have to spell it out?"*

I have to get out of here! Her hands were shaking so badly she was losing valuable seconds as she scooped the prints into a stack and shoved them into a single folder. Her father's legacy was coming with her. Stuffing the folder into her pack, Vicki snatched up the sat-phone receiver and fumbled on the tabletop for the PDA. *Please, let the guard be away from the back veranda.*

Footsteps and the scraping of the pottery shelf whirled Vicki around. Then a large hand, gnarled but with a grip of steel, closed on her wrist. "I'll take that, if you don't mind."

CHAPTER THIRTY-FOUR

The weathered features looming over Vicki were no longer of a kindly old man but bleak and harsh, the blue eyes chips of ice.

Still, it wasn't her terror that burst out in Vicki's first accusing words, rather the hurt and bewilderment of the small child she'd been. "You're CIA, aren't you? You were one of the Americans in that photo in Alpiro's office. And in the village that night when my parents were killed. You were the one who told us not to be afraid. Did . . . did you have to kill them?"

Bill released Vicki's wrist, letting out a tired sigh as he stepped back from her. "No, we were not around when your parents were killed, or things would have been very different. The last thing we were after was killing American citizens, even a busybody journalist like Jeff Craig. Unfortunately, we got there too late."

"But you covered it up. You lied to the American people, not just us. And the State Department, the embassy—they told the world it was a robbery, while all that time they *knew* their war buddies or allies or whatever you called them had murdered American citizens."

"The embassy knew what we told them," Bill answered. "And for your information, we don't take the murder of our citizens lightly. Unfortunately, in this case we had no choice. We'd just trained a network that was not only the best qualified in the Guatemalan military but the best connected for future intel, related not just to half the top political families in the country but, thanks to some serious inbreeding among the local aristocracy, to each other. They had a stake in each other's lives, and we made sure they had a stake in us."

"As CIA informants, you mean," Vicki said.

"Intelligence assets," Bill corrected. "And letting it get out that one of our expensive protégés had a notion of battlefield censorship that slaughtered a couple of Americans instead of ripping up a few rolls of film—that would have been an intelligence and PR disaster. Do you think we approved? That we didn't do our best to rein these guys in? But once it was done, there was no point in derailing our entire regional policy by having one unfortunate excess splashed all over the evening news. Besides, you don't think those pictures you're about to give back to me were the only copies made that day."

Vicki didn't try to resist as Bill took her knapsack and removed the folder from it. Twisting a combination lock on one of the file cabinets, he slid open the top drawer and tossed the folder inside.

"Those were turned over just to keep us well reminded of what they had on us. Clear, recognizable shots of high-ranking American personnel in the middle of a civilian massacre. Who would believe we'd walked in on the aftermath? Every media source and enemy of the administration would have given their eyeteeth to parade that in front of the American people and the world. The scandal could have ruined our entire strategy against global Communism. Let's not forget it wasn't much later that the Berlin Wall came down and with it the entire Soviet empire. How many potential American lives did that alone save?"

And how many others—maybe not Americans but humans and surely deserving of life and dignity—had died because the CIA adviser's "protégés" had never been called to account? How many other mass graves had followed, including the latest that held Alicia and Gabriela's family?

Bill looked more weary now than angry as he shook his head. "I regret deeply you had to find out this way—or at all. My purpose then and now was to protect you. I made sure you and your sister and that Mayan kid were taken care of. You had no extended family. Your mother was raised in foster care, and your father's parents were dead. And you were so traumatized you couldn't even talk. The best thing for all of you was to forget and start a new life. Once you went into the system, you were out of our hands, but they told me you'd been adopted by a good family. Believe me, it was as big a shock to me as you to find out you and Holly were Jeff Craig's kids.

"You think I wouldn't give anything to roll back the clock that day? I might even have made a different decision, if it had been up to me. I'd been screaming for months it was past time to lower the boom on some of our, let's say, more enthusiastic allies. But it wasn't up to me or my colleagues in training that particular unit. My superiors made the decision that seemed most expedient at the time."

"Expedient, not right. How can you even make that excuse? You said yourself every decision's personal. That it's all *I*, not *we*. You and those other Americans could have made the right decision. But it was your own backs you were watching, weren't you? You talk about fighting Communism, but it was your careers that were at stake if those photos went public. So you let them blackmail you and get away with it. And what about now? Are they still holding those pictures over you? Or is your CIA pension just not enough for all this?" Vicki's gesture encompassed the sat phone, the dish overhead. "Is that why you're still cooperating with them?"

"Cooperating?"

"Yes, I saw what you're doing out there in the biosphere. It was the same man in the photos. Your protégé. You said yourself he ordered the village and my parents killed. I know he murdered that other village. And burned the church. Was all that worth the money you made? Or your CIA intel?"

"You saw Hernandez in the biosphere?" The old man's demand was sharp.

"Yes. And Joe, too. He's working for you, isn't he?"

Bill looked blank for a moment, then grasped that Vicki wasn't referring to the center. "Yes."

The unperturbed deliberation of his answers, the mildness of his expression was lessening Vicki's terror. Bill was taller and heavier than Vicki, but he was still over seventy years old and unarmed. She edged toward the table. Bill had stepped far enough into the safe room that she was now as close to the opening as he. If she could fight her way past him, make a dash before he could call the guard . . .

Vicki sidled another step as she faced him defiantly. "It doesn't matter. I just want to go home. You can't keep me. I'm an American citizen, and this isn't twenty years ago. People will come looking for me. Just . . . let me go!"

"To Michael? I'm afraid we can't let that happen."

Vicki whirled around right into a tall, broad frame filling the entrance.

Joe held her, steadied her.

Vicki yanked herself away, retreating with despair into the safe room. "How did you get here?" She looked past the pottery shelf, half expecting to see Hernandez or Alpiro with a unit of soldiers. But the outer office was empty.

"You aren't the only one with a mountain bike. You made better time than I'd expected, but it was an even bet I'd find you here." As Joe stepped inside the safe room, the shelf wall closed behind him with a click.

Though Vicki hadn't heard a sound from the rest of the house, he had somehow found time to change from the camouflage fatigues and wash the paint off his face. Perhaps on the trail. Combat attire would certainly have drawn unwanted attention from the laborers and guards outside. But he looked no less big and dangerous in a khaki work shirt and civilian hunter's pants, and though his tone was level, even conversational, his strong features were taut with anger.

"The question is, what were you doing out there? No, I can guess that. Snooping again. I told you once you were treading on dangerous ground."

"She says she recognized Hernandez," Bill broke in. "But it's done? We're ready to go?"

"Yes, mission accomplished; at least until she showed up and tossed a smoke bomb into the hornet's nest. The whole plateau's boiling over now." Joe's eyes hadn't left Vicki's face. He closed the gap between them. She could feel the furious energy of his taut body, see a quick pulse at the base of his neck. "So where's your partner? Who was he—Camden? No, I can't see him on a bike. That vet you work with at the center? Do you have even the slightest idea of what you've just put yourself in the middle of?"

Vicki fanned anger to keep her terror at bay. "I know everything. I know Bill's CIA. I know you're working for him. I know about your drug dealers out there. Just tell me this: Why Holly? What happened? Did she see you out there? Did you stay in town after you were supposed to have flown back that day and follow her on her way to see me? Or was it both of you together?"

Vicki was talking to both men, but she was looking at Joe, her hands clenched to keep from pounding her fists against his chest. "You didn't need to. You could have made up some lie. She'd have swallowed it, believe me. She thought the world of you. She trusted you. *I* trusted you."

"You're accusing me of killing Holly?" If Joe wasn't a consummate liar, drug dealer, and only too certainly a murderer, Vicki might almost have imagined a flicker of shock, even hurt, before his gaze hardened to stone.

"I found *this*!" Vicki snatched the PDA from the table. "You had it, didn't you?"

Any doubt—hope?—was removed by silence, the abrupt emptying of Joe's expression. All the pain and grief that had been building up since Vicki had discovered him chatting with a drug-dealing sentry on the mountain burst through in such a torrent of rage she forgot to be afraid. "You *lied* to me! About the PDA. About being Holly's friend and protecting the environment and . . . and your faith. And you were so good at it; I bought every word."

If she'd hoped to provoke a response, it didn't work. Joe simply stepped back, leaning against the shelf wall, his face wiped blank, arms folded across his chest. "Who—*what* do you think I am?"

"Like Holly, I was stupid enough to believe there was something special about you, no matter how you chose to live your life. That . . . that you were more than a beach bum or handyman. Now I know you're just an ex-military who's found an easier way to support your life on the beach than odd jobs for an NGO. So are you on Bill's CIA payroll too? Or are you just in it for a big enough cut of the drug profits to finance every surfing season for the rest of your life? Well, I'm not afraid of you." The quiver in Vicki's voice gave lie to her defiance. "I hope you drown before you catch a single wave with dirty money."

Bill stepped forward. "Vicki!"

Joe's hand went up so fast Vicki flinched until she realized that it was raised at Bill. "No, let her get it out of her system."

But Vicki was done. Mutinously, she lifted her chin and tightened her jaw.

Joe straightened from the wall. "Taylor, we've got no time for this. We've got to assume we're blown. We'll have to push up the timetable. If we don't get that plane off the ground now, we may not get another chance."

The plane in which Vicki had only an hour ago hoped to make her own escape. Was it even now being loaded with opium? Was that—not the center's needs—why Bill had invested in a larger plane?

"And the girl?"

So quickly she was not a person they'd known but an anonymous object. An obstruction. Vicki might have been invisible for all that either man looked her direction.

"We can't take her. She'd draw too many eyes. And we can't let her go. She'll run straight to Camden."

"So leave her here with Garcia?"

"No, we'll need him." Joe glanced around. "But this'll do unless she's a monkey." He scattered the contents of Vicki's pack on the table, shook the half-empty canteen, and glanced at the food she'd brought. "She's got supplies to hold her until we can deal with her. Do you need to use a restroom?"

Vicki didn't realize he was addressing her until she caught the arched eyebrow. She shook her head.

"Better take the sat phone and computer though. You can bet she'd figure out how to make use of them." Disconnecting wires, Joe scooped up the laptop and sat-phone setup, even lifting the modem off the wall, leaving only the dangling wires. He touched something on the shelf wall, then pushed it open. "Bring the maps. And we need to move. We've lost too much time." Without a backward glance, he was through the opening.

Bill grabbed the aerial maps. He lingered briefly in the entrance, and Vicki saw what might have been regret, even compassion, in his eyes as he turned to her. "I'm sorry about this. I wish you hadn't gotten involved. It'll be okay. I prom—"

"Taylor! We're on a countdown!"

The wall panel clicked shut behind the old man.

And Vicki was alone.

CHAPTER THIRTY-FIVE

Despite Joe's confidence, Vicki spent her first minutes determined to find a way out. She quickly found the button Joe had used to open the pottery shelf wall. Her own repeated jabs produced no response. Though that would have been too easy.

There must be an override lock in the outer office, or the two men would have never left her in here. The wall itself had looked like ordinary shelves bracketed onto a plastered wall just like the other shelves around the office. But on touching it, Vicki could feel solid metal under the paint, and where her fingers traced the edge, it fit smoothly into a steel jamb. She broke a nail prying on it before she gave up and turned to the rest of the safe room.

The other three walls rose sheer to the ridgepole, easily three times Vicki's height, the plastered concrete offering not a single handhold. Vicki climbed onto the table, feeling it sway precariously under her weight. But this closed less than half the distance. Next she turned her attention to the file cabinets. They were all locked and too heavy to even budge. She broke another fingernail on the drawer into which Bill had dumped her birth father's photos before giving up on its lock. With phone, computer, and map gone, the room's remaining contents were Vicki's food and water supplies, the empty folders still scattered on the floor, a few wires hanging from the rafters, and the night vision goggles still sitting on the table. Maybe MacGyver could engineer an escape plan out of them, but Vicki was no prime-time adventuring genius.

All that remained was what any self-respecting heroine in captivity did next.

Scream.

"*¡Socorro!* Help! *¡Socorro!*" Vicki's throat was sore, her body trembling, when she finally gave up. It wasn't just the thickness of concrete and brick, soundproof enough that Vicki hadn't heard the pickup leaving, though the men must be long gone by now. A clear image came to her of the empty fields she'd seen from the ridge around the hacienda. Even if Joe had pulled the veranda guard, there was still the guard at the gate and a workforce drilled to maintain a respectful distance from Bill's living space. Something Joe had certainly taken into account.

Sinking into the single chair, Vicki dropped her face into her hands. But only for a moment. Banishing weakness with a deep breath, she straightened and reached for the canteen. She was unscrewing the lid when her gaze chanced on one other object left on the table among strewn finger bananas, oranges, and rolls.

Holly's PDA.

It made little difference now except to hold her thoughts at bay, but Vicki turned it on and started perusing its contents again, this time reading line by line through the Human Rights Watch report and other documents. In the context of her birth father's photos and Bill's own admissions, paragraphs leaped out at her with new relevance.

Most striking was just how extensive the CIA's involvement had been in Guatemala, at least according to footnotes from numerous declassified documents, including some Holly had managed to download in their entirety. Lynn had been right that day at the WRC hostel. With a free hand offered them by a grateful aristocracy, the CIA had made the Central American isthmus their experimental laboratory for decades. Not just in the distant past but more recently, even during the decades when the country's blatant human rights abuses had evoked a congressional moratorium on US military and government aid.

Worse, if these declassified documents were accurate, any number of informants on CIA payrolls were not only trained by US military aid programs but were among the more well-documented human rights abusers.

A connection to Holly's drug-dealing downloads became clear toward the end, where a DEA whistle-blower complained of the CIA sabotaging their counternarcotics operations to protect intelligence assets who were known traffickers. The Iran-Contra scandal rated a mention as a primary case in point.

Vicki took particular notice of the indictment by a US judge of a Guatemalan colonel and CIA informant for the murder of an American expat innkeeper, a certain Michael Devine, in a remote tourist destination, presumably for having stumbled over the colonel's drug operation. Had that killer also been Castro II?

But, no, Bill had given Castro II a name. Hernandez.

If Vicki had the newspaper printout currently in her duffel bag, she could dig up Hernandez's full name among that list of training program graduates, but it definitely wasn't the one in this report. Not that the American innkeeper's killer had been called to account either, despite that indictment. In fact, the report concluded with the denunciation that no Guatemalan military or government personnel had been held to account for any atrocities committed in the last fifty years. Nor had the US government ever ceased to laud Guatemala as their staunchest regional ally.

That's right. Didn't they just try to nominate Guatemala to the Security Council? Things still haven't changed.

The final recommendation: an immediate cutting of all military aid and strict accountability measures for any further State Department involvement in Guatemala. Since the report was two years old, it had clearly been ignored.

In the PDA's picture album Vicki found more JPEGs beyond the close-up of a younger Bill Taylor. Holly had cropped and enlarged the other two American advisers as well. Vicki recognized neither, but both had the tight-jawed determination and narrowed, watchful gaze Vicki had seen in Michael and Joe. The look of an elite soldier.

The individual graduates had been enlarged as well. Vicki ticked off those she'd come to know. Hernandez. UPN Commander Ramon Alpiro. Chief of Police Gualberto Alvarez. The minister of environment, Francisco Soliz. And one would be the zoo administrator, Samuel Justiniano, though Vicki didn't know which face belonged to him. These at least had moved into the well-connected positions Bill had anticipated when the CIA chose and recruited them twenty years earlier.

The battery died in mid-JPEG, and Vicki set the unit back onto the table. What impressed her most was just how much Holly had pieced together even without Vicki's discovery of their birth parents.

Now with nothing else to occupy hands or mind, thoughts Vicki had been trying to stave off came crashing down. Had Cesar managed to alert the village? What would happen to them if Vicki failed to rouse official help? Were the poppy fields being scythed, the camouflage netting and tents coming down, the opium bricks being loaded into the DHC-2, so even if someone did come to look, no sign would be left that the Sierra de las Minas Biosphere had ever held a sizable narcotrafficking operation? And how long did she have before Bill and Joe came back?

What would happen when they did?

Vicki didn't see how they could let her go. Not with what she now knew. Yet whatever murderous rage Joe had so quickly veiled with indifference, she hadn't forgotten the look of regret, even compassion, Bill had given her as he'd stepped out of this prison cell. The kindness he had shown a number of times over these last weeks. Even all those years ago when he'd snatched two small girls and a Mayan village boy from that massacre and made at least some personal effort to give them a new life. Whatever the former CIA agent had been or done all those decades he'd flown in and out of Guatemala, he clearly had his own code of ethics, and wantonly killing civilians was not part of it.

So Vicki was back at the question she'd thrown at the two men. Why Holly?

If a lifetime of practice in lies and deceit wasn't enough to deflect Holly from her bulldog course, why not just kidnap her? Once the biosphere was scoured clean of evidence, Vicki had seen nothing in Holly's possession that would hold up in any court of law. And both the CIA and Guatemalan authorities had ample experience in screaming injured innocence against far more substantial allegations than Holly would be able to bring.

As for the photos in Bill's possession, not only had Holly known nothing about them, but despite what Vicki had thrown at him, she didn't see what leverage they could still hold on him after two decades. Those were sins of the past, not the present, the Americans involved and their superiors long retired, the happenings themselves no longer state secrets but documented in the hundreds by the UN Truth Commission. And as the report she'd just read had made clear, none of the perpetrators had paid any penalty. Other than survivors like Vicki herself, who would really care? Not enough to be worth Holly's life.

Or had the Americans once again simply walked in too late?

Vicki folded her arms on the table and dropped her face wearily into them. *I still haven't made sense out of all this. I just know I've messed things up so badly.*

"Do what is right and do not give way to fear." I really thought I was doing that when I came here. That I could make a difference. But what good have I done? If I hadn't run to Bill, there'd still be a chance. And if I hadn't come here at all, at least the villagers would be safe. Now they're going to get away with it. I'm trapped in here like Sarah in her harem.

And Bill and Joe—I still don't know how I could have been so wrong. Everything they said—everything Joe said . . . I let myself like him, maybe even start to care about him, even when I knew he was hiding something, because what he said had so much truth and beauty. What he said about You. He helped me see You again. See the beauty and not just the pain in the world You created.

And what he said was true. I won't let him take that away just because he proved false. I believe that this is Your world, and no matter what's happening out there, You're still in control. And I believe You can rescue me just like You rescued Sarah. You can send someone, or even intervene directly like you did to Pharaoh for her. Because it wasn't Abraham who got her out of there; it was You.

But even if You don't, even if what happened to Holly happens to me, I know You're with me, and I know You were with Holly when she must have been as scared as I am right now. And . . . and I choose to believe what Joe said—that You have something waiting beyond all the wars and the pain and wicked people getting away with murder that's going to make all this worth going through. Something so beautiful I can't imagine it.

Then, because she wouldn't let herself give way again to tears and if she didn't rouse herself soon from this slumped position, she'd be too stiff to move at all, Vicki pushed herself back to her feet and began to call out again, *"¡Socorro!"*

The only answer was a faint echo of her voice against the roof tiles, and after a few minutes Vicki's voice gave out. She picked up the night vision goggles and slammed them against the pottery shelf wall. The collision of goggles on painted metal made a gratifying noise, so she repeated it again and again. *I'll keep it up till Bill and Joe come back, or someone comes by to let me out.*

It wasn't her strength but the NVGs that let Vicki down. First the casing cracked. Then the pieces began to fall apart in her hands until in frustration she threw the remnants into a corner and raised her voice instead, alternating shouts with pounding her fists and kicking her boots against the steel.

At first she thought it was only that faint echo of her own voice. But she fell silent, bruised fists dropping to her sides. No, there it was. Just a whisper of wind that had sounded almost human through the air vent above her.

She'd raised her boot to renew her assault when it came again. Still soft, this time it was as clear as though broadcast from an intercom.

"Señorita Vee-kee?"

CHAPTER THIRTY-SIX

CHAPTER THIRTY-SIX

"Cesar!" Vicki threw herself across the safe room, pounding her fists against the back of the fireplace, but the pain of her bruises forced her to stop.

Cesar's voice came again, cautious but louder. "Señorita Vee-kee, are you in the chimney?"

Vicki almost smiled at the image. She understood how she'd heard him. He'd been close enough to the fireplace that his voice had carried up the chimney and through the air vent. Now he must be kneeling on the hearth itself.

"No, I'm in a room behind the fireplace," Vicki called up to the vent. "I'm locked in. Come into the office. The door—the wall—is behind a shelf of pottery. On this side there's a push button to open it, so look for any kind of button or lock on the pottery shelf."

Vicki could appreciate the soundproof quality of these walls because though she knew Cesar must have gone to the office, she heard no sound until a thump clanged against the pottery-shelf wall. She thumped back and called, but Cesar's voice was too muffled to understand. Then there was silence. Vicki waited impatiently, sore hands twisting around each other.

When Cesar spoke, it was through the air vent again. "I found the mechanism of which you speak, but the button does not work. There are numbers like a calculator so I think some kind of combination is required."

Vicki sat wearily against the edge of the table. If she'd spotted that earlier, she'd have known Joe couldn't have been in here without Bill's cooperation. Now what?

"I will be back!"

That brought Vicki to her feet. "No, Cesar, don't leave me here!" She bit her lip at the selfish childishness of that cry. There was no answer. He'd gone then.

Vicki sank into the chair. At least Cesar would be safe, and he must have been successful in his original mission. Perhaps he'd be successful too where Vicki had failed and find some means of communicating their plight—and the village's—with the outside world. A moment later Cesar's voice floated through the air vent. "Stand away from the wall. I'm going to break it in."

Vicki heard crashing sounds from the office side. Cesar must be breaking every piece of pottery on the shelf. Then the wall began to shake.

Oh, please, please! Vicki prayed, eyes glued to the doorjamb. Surely even an ax couldn't cut through solid metal.

It didn't have to. Chips of plaster and paint showered Vicki as the wall popped outward. Cesar stepped around it, crowbar in hand.

Relieved tears would be a distraction right now, so Vicki fought them back as she said shakily, "Cesar, I can't believe you're here! God really did send someone!"

At his mystified look, Vicki leaned forward impulsively to kiss him on the cheek. "Never mind. I'll explain it later. Let's just get out of here."

A kiss on the cheek was a common greeting among the Spanish upper classes but not the Mayans, who had an indigenous reticence about casual touching between sexes, Cesar included. Something Vicki, also reticent about her personal space, had appreciated and been careful to respect. But her gesture drew a rare smile from him, and he nodded. "*Sí,* I think you are right that it was God who sent me. Come!"

Vicki threw her canteen, food, and Holly's PDA into her knapsack and followed Cesar out of the safe room. The outer office was in shambles as she'd envisioned, and she could see behind shards of pottery a control panel with number pad and button, now smashed in.

Before they left the living room, Cesar stopped. "You can't go out like that. You will be noticed. One moment." He added to his demolition job by snatching some of Bill's *típica* collection from the walls and sofa.

Grasping what he had in mind, Vicki tugged an embroidered *huipil* over her head. It was big enough to fit loosely over her shirt. Cesar added a length of red weave around her waist. This was too short for a proper skirt, revealing Vicki's cargo pants from calf to ankle, but that only allowed more freedom to walk, and Cesar bound it in place with a few wraps of a long sash.

A wall shelf held one of the halolike knottings of homespun and tassels Mayan women wore as a headdress, but Vicki knew better than to try to balance that on her head. Instead, she tied a smaller red cloth over her hair like a bandanna while Cesar tied her knapsack into a striped carrying cloth. Pulling the ends of this over one shoulder and under the opposite armpit, Vicki knotted it in front the way a peasant woman carried a bundle or a baby.

The whole thing had taken only a minute, and at least from a distance they'd appear as any humble peasant couple. Vicki felt not the slightest compunction at raiding Bill's collection. The way she felt right now, if it weren't for the flame-retardant construction of brick and tile, she'd look for a box of matches and torch the place like that thatched church last night.

"How did you find me here? What's happened to the village?"

"Wait!" Cesar cautioned Vicki to silence as he inched open the back door. If there'd still been a house guard, they couldn't have made the fifty meters to the coffee bushes, since a Mayan couple emerging from the patron's house would rouse as much suspicion as a fugitive American. But as Joe had told Bill, the veranda guard was gone.

Vicki waited until they'd reached the cover of the coffee rows before demanding again, "So tell me—what made you come back? Did you make it to the village? What is happening with your people?"

Cesar didn't slow his rapid stride as he answered over his shoulder. "I reached the village, but it is filled with soldiers. They are looking for you—for us. *Tía* Maria had already gone to work, but the pastor and elders were at the church removing the burnt wood. They will wait for the search to end before leading the people out. I do not think *los narcotraficantes* will come before dark because of the market bus that comes every day. They will not wish for outside witnesses. Or so we must hope.

"I started then to the center to find *Tía* Maria. That is when I saw *el vehículo* of Señor Taylor go by with his gringo *ayudante* and other men. You weren't with them, so I thought perhaps you had returned to the center. But I found only *Tía* Maria there with Alicia and Gabriela. Rosario and Beatriz had already left to meet the bus with the new volunteers. *Tía* Maria had not seen you. I told her to take the girls into the sierra.

"Then I came here because I was concerned that something had befallen you. I came around back through the coffee *finca* because of the guard. But he was not there, and though the back door was locked, it was not difficult to break."

Proving Bill's wisdom in building that safe room!

"The house appeared empty, but when I heard your pounding, I knew you must be there though I could not see you. Now perhaps you will tell me why Señor Taylor left you so."

"Because he's in league with *los narcotraficantes*," Vicki answered bitterly.

Cesar stopped so suddenly Vicki stepped on his heels. He swung around in the middle of the coffee bushes with as much incredulous dismay on his face as Vicki had felt. "But Señor Taylor has been a good man and a good patron to Verapaz for many years."

"He was *el americano* who took us from the village when my parents and your mother were killed."

Cesar shook his head as Vicki gave a synopsis of Bill's admissions.

"What shall we do now? Search out your other American friend? But he is a *colega* of Coronel Alpiro."

"I know. We can't go near the base. I've been thinking. I left my bike on the ridge, but if I could stop at the center to get another one, if I can just get to Alison without anyone seeing me, make her understand what's happened, then maybe she can get through to her embassy, and I could get down the mountain on the charter bus. If we can get help today before they clear all the evidence away, get the embassies and media involved, there's got to be some honest police and army who could be called in; then the villagers wouldn't even have to leave."

The heavy homespun flapped against Vicki's cargo pants as she started walking again. "But we'd better hurry before the soldiers decide to search the center, too."

"It is too late for that. One of the army trucks was already coming down the road as I left. That is why I told *Tía* Maria to leave with the girls."

"Oh no!" Vicki stopped. "It would take forever to reach the bus on foot, especially without being seen. We'd never make it before the team leaves there—or that charter bus."

"I have already thought of that." Beckoning Vicki to follow, Cesar started walking.

A few minutes later, they reached the center boundary of tall trees and vegetation. Through it Vicki could hear a diesel engine and raised voices.

Before her anxiety level could rise, Cesar picked up a mountain bike from against an oak tree. "You will have to ride with me. There is a path that will take us to the village unseen."

The mountain bike was not designed for double occupancy, but Vicki had seen poorer Guatemalans balance an entire family on a bike, and neither she nor Cesar were large adults. Hiking up her skirt to slide onto the seat behind Cesar, she wrapped her arms around his waist.

He took the trail with reasonable caution until it intersected with the long, winding gravel driveway connecting Bill's plantation with the center. Vicki caught no glimpse of buildings or soldiers as Cesar pedaled across, though she could still hear the latter. Then they were back in the underbrush, and Cesar picked up speed. Vicki burrowed her head against his back, realizing with chagrin just how much faster he could have gone without her that morning.

At first the trek was at least reasonably level. Then a zigzag distinctly downhill forced Vicki's eyes open. All of Lake Izabal was spread out before her, while to her left the steep slope dropped away for hundreds of meters. At least Cesar had slowed to negotiate the treacherous descent. Clutching him tighter, Vicki spoke into his ear, "Where are we going? Verapaz is the other way."

"There are too many people, too much cleared land up there. This is better," Cesar called back.

Shutting her eyes again, Vicki held on tight and prayed. Any moment a swerve or rock in the path was bound to send them over that terrible drop-off.

But it wasn't long before Vicki felt the g-force of a zigzag ascent. When she felt level ground again, she raised her head and opened her eyes to see fruit trees, banana palms, and corn patches.

Glancing back, Cesar jerked his head to the left. "The coffee *fincas* of *los militares* are beyond there. Verapaz is not far ahead. We will leave the bike before the checkpoint and pass around it on foot. Then it is only a short distance to the bus stop."

True to his claim, Cesar braked a short time later under the fronds of a banana plant. They slid with silent caution from the bike, then slipped forward through the banana stalks.

Cesar's circuitous route had clearly taken them across the undeveloped cloud forest the center occupied at the end of the plateau, down around the rim to avoid populated areas, then back through a belt of crops and fruit trees, because directly ahead was the dirt track that divided the plateau lengthwise. Just ten meters to their left was the military checkpoint marking the outskirts of Verapaz, where the nature trail departed to climb up the ridge into the biosphere. Vicki shrank back into the banana stalks as an army Jeep pulled up to *la garita*, wishing her Mayan attire wasn't so brightly colored.

But the Jeep carried only a driver, and as two guards emerged from the guard shack, he didn't signal them to raise the barrier but stepped down. Now Vicki could see that what she'd thought was a uniform had been an illusion of khaki clothing.

As the driver took off a floppy brimmed hat to run a hand through his hair, Vicki clutched Cesar's arm, all thoughts of reaching the bus stop leaving her. "It's Michael," she whispered in his ear. "Señor Camden."

CHAPTER THIRTY-SEVEN

This was a break Vicki hadn't even dared envision. "If I can speak to him, tell him what's happened in the biosphere, he can call *los antinarcóticos*, even the American DEA. Oh, Cesar, this is an answer to all my prayers!"

Cesar didn't seem to share her delight. "Are you sure he can be trusted?"

"Of course," Vicki hissed indignantly. "He's been decorated by the American *antinarcóticos*. He's a colleague of their drug czar."

"So is Coronel Alpiro."

Vicki waved that aside. "I have to speak to him alone. If I could just get his attention, or if there were some way to draw off the guards—"

"That I can do." Cesar started to move.

Vicki grabbed at him. "Wait; what if they shoot at you? After yesterday, they're bound to have ammunition now."

"That is a risk that must be assumed."

Another sharp reminder that Vicki was not the only one with much at stake. In a rush of affection and gratitude for this man who'd once been her playmate and had shown himself more of a friend than she deserved, she squeezed his hand. "Thank you, *mi amigo. Que Dios te acompañe.*" "May God go with you."

A smile glimmered in Cesar's eyes. Then he loped through the banana palms along the edge of the road. The two guards were talking to Michael, and only Vicki saw Cesar slip across the road, using the Jeep as cover. But she wasn't the only one to hear a loud rustle from the underbrush behind the guard shack. Then Cesar scuttled onto the nature track a dozen meters beyond the metal barrier.

"¡Alto!" The two guards immediately opened fire and gave chase.

Cesar dived into the brush on the opposite side of the track.

Please, God, don't let him be hurt, Vicki prayed as she moved out onto the road. Michael had turned to watch the chase. Picking up a pebble, Vicki tossed it so it landed against his pant leg. He glanced at Vicki hurrying toward the checkpoint. Then, as Vicki came abreast with the Jeep, he went still, his eyes widening with disbelief and recognition. Michael's reflexes were superb. In two steps, he had Vicki by the arm and was drawing her into the guard shack and out of sight.

"Please don't let the guards see me," Vicki whispered urgently as he tugged the door shut.

Michael snatched a hand radio from his belt and barked, "Have you found the fugitive?"

Vicki couldn't follow the spatter of static, but Michael responded curtly, "Continue in pursuit. I will remain at *la garita* until you return."

Then Cesar had made his escape. Vicki let out her breath in relief.

Sliding the hand radio onto his belt, Michael stepped back to take in Vicki's costume. "Now, what are you doing here and dressed like that? I've been hoping you'd change your mind from last night. But are you aware Alpiro's got the entire garrison searching for you?"

Vicki didn't dispel his assumption. Instead, she demanded, "What did he give as the reason?"

"Well, the official story is that the gringa from the center is lost in the sierras, maybe even hurt. And since *el cuartel* announced themselves last night to be good neighbors, Alpiro is spearheading a search so the locals won't have to worry about it—or butt in where they aren't wanted. I'm assuming you have a different version?"

Michael's last question was dry but unperturbed, and Vicki found herself shaking with relief to see him. His confident figure and unruffled tone represented law and order, sanctuary, the juggernaut power of Vicki's own government behind her.

"You won't believe the real story," she said unsteadily. "Or at least I hope you will because I'm counting on you to call in the cavalry. Alpiro and some guy named Hernandez have been running an opium-trafficking operation in the biosphere all the time Alpiro's been pretending to cooperate with your UPN training program. This Hernandez has a whole gang out there in the mountains."

"Raul Hernandez?" Michael's expression was no longer so unperturbed.

"I don't know his full name. You know him?"

"Alpiro has a cousin named Raul Hernandez who was an army commander in these parts during the war. But I haven't heard of him being involved in anything illegal. Where did you hear this?"

"I saw it myself in the biosphere today. I saw the poppy fields and their encampment and the opium they were getting ready to ship. And I saw this Hernandez. He's an old military buddy of Alpiro's, and he even looks like him, so he's probably this cousin. Not only that, but I'm pretty sure he massacred that village a couple of months ago and burned the church last night. He's definitely the one who killed my parents and wiped out the village they were living in—in fact, the same village that was massacred in the biosphere. I saw pictures of it with Hernandez in them. Worse, there were Americans involved in the massacre. All the time the embassy wrote my parents' death off as a random robbery, but they'd been deliberately murdered—just like Holly!"

This time Michael's handsome features did lose their composure, the gray eyes going blank with shock before he demanded sharply, "Are you telling me you're Jeff and Victoria Craig's daughter? And Andrews would be . . . ?"

"That was our adopted name. Then you've heard of my parents?"

"I'm with the embassy. It's my business to know of Americans who've been killed here. Especially unsolved murders. There aren't that many on the books, whatever you may think." Michael's eyes never left Vicki's face. "So why didn't you tell me? I thought we were in this together."

In all that had happened, Vicki had actually forgotten that Michael alone still had not heard this earth-shattering fact. "I didn't know it myself until I came to Guatemala. And when I found out . . . well, it didn't seem relevant to Holly's investigation."

"Relevant? That wasn't something for you to decide in an investigation like this. Now tell me everything and quickly before we're interrupted. For one, where have you been? It's been a good two hours since Alpiro called out the troops." Michael's hands were now hard on Vicki's upper arms, his eyes blazing with impatience, as though restraining himself from shaking her.

"Ouch!" Vicki protested, and he relaxed his grip but didn't release her.

"Bill Taylor and Joe Ericsson are both in on this too. Bill was in that village with Hernandez twenty years ago. He was one of the Americans. He was CIA, and Hernandez was one of his informants. He must still be working with Hernandez in the drug trade. And Joe—you were right in suspecting him. He's working for Bill. Not just at the center but whatever they're doing out there. I think they're planning to use Bill's plane to fly out the opium shipment, because I saw people mowing down the poppy fields and packing up the opium. I . . . I still can't believe it. I thought Bill and Joe were my friends. Bill seemed like such a nice old man." Vicki was appalled to discover that tears were sliding down her face.

She couldn't even wipe at them because of Michael's grip, which had tightened again painfully. "What is it? Did they hurt you?" He released her and produced a handkerchief.

Vicki used it gratefully. "No, no, I'm not hurt. They just locked me up—at Bill's house; that's where I saw the pictures. I only got away because Cesar, the vet from the center, found me and let me out. He's the one who distracted the guards right now so I could talk to you. I just hope their crazy shooting didn't hit him."

"I'm sure it didn't, or we'd have heard by now. Did Joe or Bill mention me in any of this?" As Vicki gave him a blank look, he added flatly, "They know what I do. They weren't worried I'd stop them?"

"Yes! That's why they locked me up. They said they couldn't let me get to you before they finished what they were doing. Which I guess meant that last shipment of opium. If they can get away from here with it, I suppose there'll be no way to prove what they've done."

"We'll see about that." At Michael's tone, Vicki looked at him. For a moment his expression was as cold and hard and dangerous as Joe's had been earlier.

"What is it about you, Vicki, that you manage to keep stumbling over intel an entire investigation team couldn't dig up?" He smiled briefly, a hand going out to brush back a wisp of Vicki's hair coming loose from the bandanna. "Are you okay now?"

When Vicki nodded, Michael took his hat off and ran a hand through his hair, then straightened. "Okay, here's the game plan: I've got a chopper on standby at the base. No—" he raised a hand as Vicki opened her mouth to protest—"they're not Alpiro's men; they're under my direct command, and I'd trust them with my life. They can be in the air in ten minutes. The road out there's wide enough for them to land."

Michael slid the radio from his belt as he explained. He'd just finished issuing orders when Vicki, still keeping a lookout through the window, spotted the two guards returning. At her apprehensive start, Michael laid a calming hand on her shoulder. "It's okay."

Opening the door, he called, "Did you find any sign of the fugitive? . . . No matter, I've already alerted the patrols in the biosphere to keep watch for him."

Following the guards' glance, Michael added with a nod toward Vicki, "As you can see, the señorita from the center has been found unharmed. You may return to your normal duties. I've called off the search and requested a helicopter. When it arrives, I will escort her to the capital for a medical checkup. I'll send someone to return the vehicle to *el cuartel*."

It had taken considerably less than ten minutes to get that helicopter in the air, because he'd just finished speaking when Vicki heard the *throp-throp* of rotors heading their direction from the army base. Moments later it hovered over the widest area available, created by the junction of the plateau road and biosphere service road. The wind of its settling stirred up a dust storm that rattled *la garita* and sent its guards scuttling for cover.

The helicopter looked so similar to the one that had accosted the DHC-2 that Vicki shrank back. Especially as the side panel slid open, and she glimpsed not only a crouched olive uniform but the ugly, gray shape of a bolted-down stationary machine gun.

Michael gave Vicki an encouraging smile and took her by the hand. Hunched over against the continued wind blast of the rotors, they ran together toward the helicopter. She caught a helmeted face watching them through the windshield. Then helping hands pulled her aboard. The helicopter was already lifting as the side panel slammed shut.

For the first time that day, Vicki felt her tension ease. Michael steered her to a jump seat at the back of the cabin. She shrugged off her peasant disguise before allowing him to pull a shoulder harness down and fasten her in. She closed her eyes briefly to let out a quiet sigh of relief, then opened them to look around.

The only other seat in the cabin area was another jump seat beside hers, though the cockpit held both pilot and copilot. The two soldiers who'd pulled them aboard squatted on the floor, automatic rifles across their knees. Michael headed toward them.

It was the burlap sacks that first reawakened Vicki's disquiet. They filled every available space of the cabin. Stacks of them carefully tied down against a sudden banking of the helicopter under heavy canvas netting. And their contents weren't loose like sugar or grain but pressed against the sacking in rectangular lines like so many small postal packages.

A terrible dread was building in Vicki. Easing herself upright, she opened her mouth to call Michael's name.

But just then the copilot turned to speak to the approaching attaché, his voice raised above the noise of engine and rotors. "This is the last shipment. But we will need to move quickly because my sources tell me *los antinarcóticos* have been alerted."

With the side door closed, the Huey's cabin offered little lighting, but a late afternoon sunbeam was angling through the windshield so that the copilot's florid features, unkempt curls, and too-full beard were outlined in vivid technicolor.

It was Hernandez.

CHAPTER THIRTY-EIGHT

There had to be some mistake.

Vicki called sharply in English, "Michael, that's the man I saw in the jungle. The one who killed my parents—who's dealing drugs!"

Michael shot her the indifferent glance of a stranger, then addressed the copilot in Spanish. "Yes, I know it was *la americana* here who alerted them."

"*¡La americana!* I told you she would be as much trouble as her sister. But you would be merciful. Have I not told you before that you *americanos* are too sentimental, too soft? You do not understand the hard decisions."

"Yes, Raul, and you were right, unfortunately. But we're clear now, and we're about to find out how much damage she's done."

So this *was* Raul Hernandez, Alpiro's cousin. The Guatemalan was looking at Vicki as he must have looked twenty years ago at Jeff and Victoria Craig. And at Holly. Not angry but with the indifferent brutality with which he might have considered swatting a persistent insect.

But Michael? Vicki's bewilderment was no longer *what*—that had just become appallingly clear—but *why*. She unsnapped her harness and rose, though what she hoped to accomplish hundreds of feet in the air in a helicopter full of hostile men, she hadn't even formulated.

This time in Spanish, she cried out, "Michael, what are you saying? This isn't some war game. This . . . this *animal* killed my parents! And that village!"

The soldier in front of her didn't even shift expression as he slammed the butt of his weapon into her stomach. A boot thrust her back into the seat. From the front of the cabin, Vicki heard the distinct click of a pistol being cocked and saw the metallic length of the barrel leveled at her over the back of the copilot's seat.

"So—*la americana* speaks Spanish." The brutality on Raul Hernandez's face was no longer indifferent, the gun barrel actually shaking with eagerness.

Michael slapped the gun down. "Are you *loco*? You want to blow a hole in this?" He took out another much smaller gun from the small of his back, elbowed aside the soldier who'd struck Vicki, and knelt in front of her. His eyes were warm with a smile she had come to know well, and she knew then that she'd never really known what lay behind them. Vicki put up no fight as Michael snapped her back into her harness.

"Let's not have any more problems, okay?" he announced in loud Spanish. "This Glock won't make such a mess of the cabin as a .38."

"Give it to her! Get it out of her, okay, hombre?" Hernandez called.

Michael switched to English, looking even regretful as he shook his head. "I really am sorry about this, Vicki. I like you. And I did my best to keep you out of this. To save your life, though you may not appreciate that right now."

Vicki looked at the gun in his hand, then turned toward the copilot. "You said a .38. Wasn't the gun that killed Holly a .38 police revolver?"

As Michael went still, she said, "Why are you of all people helping a bunch of drug dealers and murderers? Everything you are, everything you do at the embassy—why would you risk it for this? It can't just be the money. And you believe in your country, believe in serving it. Whatever else, I know I wasn't wrong about that."

Then it hit her, and Vicki stared at him, stunned, before she breathed out, "Joe was right. You're CIA too, aren't you? Your DAO position—that's just your cover. And Raul Hernandez—he's *your* informant, not Bill's. You're his handler."

"Embassy attaché is an overused device," Michael agreed conversationally. "But useful and a lot more convenient for dealing with my kind of sources than the usual foreign businessman."

"Like Bill Taylor. Then . . . then who is he?" Vicki demanded. "I thought he was working with this Raul guy and Alpiro. That he was CIA. No, I know he was; he admitted it. And Joe—who's he?"

"Actually, I was hoping you could tell me." The jump seat was low enough that, even hunkered down, Michael loomed over Vicki, forearms propped on his thighs, the Glock balanced loosely in his right hand. It was only the short distance between them that allowed Vicki to catch Michael's words above the noise in the cabin, and she was reading his lips as much as hearing them. "DEA, maybe? They're always meddling in our ops. Though I'd know if any official DEA postings were intruding in my territory. And I've got counternarcotics—US and local—nicely sewn up with one of my UPN units hitting Raul's Colombian competition up in the Petén rain forest. No, I checked out Ericsson myself. He's just a drifter with a petty rap sheet Taylor must have hired for muscle. But Taylor—he's been around these parts a long time, and he's got a thing for that nature reserve. If he's chosen to stick his nose in there . . ." Michael's tone hardened abruptly. "So what exactly did Taylor and Ericsson tell you?"

Then her instincts had been as right about Joe as they'd been about a stranger lurking behind Michael's handsome face and charming smile. *I should have trusted my heart, not my eyes.* With death staring at her through a sleek, metallic barrel, Vicki should have been terrified, but her mind and heart had room right now only for elation. *Whatever Joe is, he isn't a drug dealer. He isn't a murderer.*

Then why hadn't he even tried to stop her hysterics, to explain? *Because I wasn't listening. Because I said such terrible things.* Joe had simply tuned Vicki out and gone off to do what he could to stop this thing—because Vicki had no doubt now, though it still didn't make sense, that this was the reason for Joe's presence in the woods. He'd left Vicki stashed safely away where she wouldn't be hurt and couldn't interfere. Except that once again, Vicki had messed things up so badly. *If only I could say I was sorry.*

Meanwhile, what damage had her interference done? Michael certainly seemed confident he had nothing to worry about. And there were still those photos and Bill's own confession.

Michael stared at her, and Vicki realized he was still waiting for her answer. Well, there was nothing she could say that she hadn't already given away.

"I already told you. They locked me up and said they couldn't let me warn you. And something about getting to the plane before they could be stopped." Vicki glanced at the burlap stacks around her. "I assumed they meant to get the opium out."

Michael spat out a stream of unpleasant phrases she'd never expected to hear from him. "If Taylor had Ericsson snooping around out there for him, we've got to assume they've made me and Alpiro and probably have a whole video production of the camp. If they reached the right ear for home movie night, that place is going to be swarming with law enforcement. I hate cleanup! It always means someone's messed up bad."

He called up to the front of the helicopter, "Raul, are you sure you've got the sierra emptied out?"

Vicki couldn't hear the response over the noise of the rotors.

"They're bringing the trucks down now? . . . No, *los campesinos* don't matter anymore. But you won't be able to take this load into Guatemala City for processing. They may have *antinarcóticos* alerted at the airport. Head for the coast instead. You have ships on call. See who can meet us in the Gulf."

This time Raul's turned head allowed Vicki to make out his words. "As you wish. And do not worry about *los antinarcóticos*. My cousin is second in command there. He will delay any mobilization until it is too late."

More *hermandad*—blood or otherwise.

Michael faced Vicki. "At least you've got your wish to save your *campesinos* buddies. We sentimental Americans."

It was again a dichotomy that made no sense. "I don't get it," Vicki burst out. "How can you deal with a killer like Raul Hernandez, then turn around and intercede for a bunch of *campesinos*?"

"Because Americans don't take out civilians," Michael responded curtly. "Not when it can be avoided."

"No, you just work with psychopaths who do," Vicki said. "Just tell me why. That Hernandez creep can't be holding those pictures over you like he did with Bill Taylor and those other Americans. And that's another thing. Bill Taylor practically admitted he was CIA and involved in recruiting Raul and the others in his unit. So how come you didn't know who he was? And why didn't Alpiro recognize him?"

"Good question." Michael seemed willing enough to keep talking, maybe because it was the easiest way to keep a prisoner quiescent.

For Vicki it was preferable to letting her own terror engulf her. *If I die, at least let me finally make sense out of this.* The thought was such a stereotypical last wish of a die-hard investigative journalist, she could almost smile.

"For one, it shows he's higher placed than I could have hoped. Somewhere no doubt there's a sealed file I don't currently have access to. But I know exactly who Taylor is—or was—if he's one of the Americans in Raul's blackmail archive. Though that wasn't the name he used back then. See, you're mistaken about one thing. Taylor wasn't Raul or Alpiro's recruiter. There were two others who headed up the training of that particular unit. One was the Special Forces training liaison—a Green Beret with Vietnam under his belt. The other was . . . well, let's just say he was an embassy attaché with additional responsibilities."

"CIA, you mean."

"Fine—CIA." Except for the roar of the helicopter and three weapons angled her direction, Michael might have been simply entertaining Vicki with stories of his work as he'd done so often back at the center.

"This guy's mission was to bond with the trainees, recruit them if he could, build a country network for the future. Taylor was *his* handler. His Langley supervisor, to be precise, in Guatemala for the graduation and to evaluate the new intel assets. He must have been fuming when *el generalísimo* in charge of the ceremonies pulled him into a photo shoot. Like any well-trained operative, he at least managed to keep his face out of the papers. The only other time Alpiro would have seen Taylor was in the aftermath of a battlefield, and I doubt he was cataloging features."

"The massacre, you mean," Vicki accused.

"Whatever." Michael shrugged. "In any case, twenty years later when a UPN unit showed up at Taylor's retirement pad, there's no reason Alpiro would know the difference. I'm guessing Taylor did recognize him, since Raul Hernandez, area commander on the day in question, made sure Taylor and the other two Americans had a full set of the photos his officers managed to take before their American advisers could stop them."

"With my father's cameras," Vicki said. "But how can you possibly know all this? You were just a kid at the time. Or is this all in your CIA files even while you people are telling the American public that things like this never happened?"

"Oh no. Liars are too easy to trip up. And nosy journalists are as good at that as any CIA interrogator. You can be sure the overwhelming percent of agency drones are as innocent and pure and idealistic as the American people want to believe—and have never had to deal with tough reality in the field. As to how I know . . ."

Michael shifted position on his heels. "It can't matter now, and considering who you've turned out to be, you'll find it an interesting piece of family history. You see, I've kind of followed in the family business. My father originally recruited Raul and the rest of that network."

"*Your* father?" Vicki exclaimed. "Then how come Bill didn't know you—or at least your name?"

"I go by my mother's name. They divorced when I was young, and since my father didn't care to mix agency and personal life, I never did carry his name. I was barely in middle school and living in the States during that whole time period, so I didn't know anything about what happened or those photos. Not until shortly before my father died when he passed the file on to me with the rest of my inheritance.

"By that time I'd followed him into the agency and had hit my first Central American post, so he told me the whole story—wanted me to understand what he'd done and why. Unlike him, I burned the photos first thing. But he was never sorry about the field decision he'd made that day. The Cold War was at a critical juncture at the time, and my father saw Raul and the other recruits as the future of US HUMINT—human intelligence assets—in this region.

"He wasn't even sorry for Jeff Craig's death—though he'd have never lifted a finger to bring it about—and certainly not the wife. But he hated left-wing journalists. He was one tough old man, willing to do whatever it took to protect his country and the American way of life. Now as Raul says, my generation is a little more sentimental about collateral damage and a little more tolerant of diverse points of view."

"Then why are you still supporting Raul?" Vicki asked. "I get Bill Taylor and your father. I mean, I don't believe for a minute they were thinking of their country before their own careers, but I can see what it would have meant to have those pictures all over the news back then. But those are all sins of the past. They couldn't have been held over your head. Wouldn't it have been a lot bigger PR coup to turn Raul Hernandez in when you found out he was dealing drugs, especially in an endangered habitat? to be able to show the world you were serious about cleaning house in this country—even if you're not? Unless . . ."

Suddenly, finally, it all made sense. "Unless it's *not* sins of the past. Raul is still on your CIA payroll, isn't he? Still doing your dirty work Americans are too good to do. That's why you have to let him have his drug operation and keep the DEA away, just like the Human Rights Watch report accused. That's why you had to get rid of Holly. Because she was going to expose that *you* were still working hand in hand with drug dealers and war criminals instead of turning them over to justice. And the American people would never put up with those kinds of methods to protect their freedoms."

"Don't kid yourself." Michael sneered. "What the American people want are results. They know better than to ask for details, and we know better than to give them. Raul Hernandez has been one of our most valuable intel assets in this region for twenty years. When Guatemala got too hot for him—not even his own military colleagues had the stomach for the enthusiasm with which he performed his duties during the war—he was one of our most capable contra commanders in Nicaragua and Honduras.

"Unfortunately he's smart. Twenty years ago may have been the first time he protected himself with a visual record, however inadvertently. But it wasn't the last. Nor were all my predecessors as careful as I. Suffice it to say Hernandez has made it clear that if he goes down, he sings like a canary. Everything he's ever done for the CIA. So Hernandez gets one small drug op to fund his personal pleasures with Cousin Alpiro running interference on the local end—"

"Who I'll bet *you* ensured would end up commander of UPN."

Michael ignored the interruption. "Meanwhile, the DEA gets to clean up the competition, courtesy of Hernandez's outstanding, if somewhat unorthodox, intelligence network. Taking out, I may add, a lot more drug ops than they ever would on their own. And the American people continue to profit from the best intel network in the region. It's win-win for everyone."

"Except Holly."

Michael's expression hardened. "Holly was a foolish young woman who figured she didn't have to obey the rules. That's the irony. If she'd simply minded her own business and stayed out of the biosphere, she'd be alive today, and her precious cloud forest would soon be returning to normal, minus a bunch of invading peasants."

"Then *you* were the American she found out about, not Bill or Joe."

"Possibly. Somewhere in Holly's unauthorized wanderings, she stumbled across the poppy fields and decided to do some further investigation. I just happened to be out there at the time checking the crop with Raul and Alpiro. I'd never have known Holly'd spotted us if she hadn't come barreling up to the base as I was boarding the chopper back to the capital. When she told me she had embassy business to discuss dealing with the biosphere, I knew she had to have seen me. I brushed her off—told her to contact me in town. When I ran into her the next day at the airport—"

"When she introduced us. Then that's why she was so funny talking to you. I thought—"

"That she had a crush on me?" Michael's eyebrows went up. "Oh, I'm afraid she did—thankfully. She wasn't sure I might not be conducting some counternarcotics op in the area and didn't want to go to the authorities without giving me a chance to explain. Except when she couldn't get ahold of me right away, she didn't quit digging. My mistake. Unfortunately for me—and her—she chose to go back out there just as Raul's men were setting up camp for harvest and their *campesinos* laborers were thinning out the poppy stalks.

"Holly took some interesting pictures—which once again could have ruined everything, except that she was considerate enough to call me to make sure she wasn't throwing a monkey wrench into some counternarcotics bust. She told her friends she was going to see you, but when I checked my messages—oh yes, I did get back that night—I hightailed it over. Holly was out on the curb with her radio taxi running late. She was only too happy to get a lift and tell me all about it. Except we ended up at Hernandez's processing plant over in Zone 4. If I'd thought for a minute she'd buy a line about national security and classified intel, I'd have used it. But even with a crush—"

"You knew Holly wouldn't turn a blind eye! Not after the stink she was willing to raise for a few missing animals. You knew she'd go right to the press. With those pictures, they'd believe her about you too. So you took her out over the dump in one of your helicopters—maybe even this one—shot her and then threw her out. Only she landed too far out to be a simple mugging. You never expected her to live long enough to speak to me, and you forgot to take this off." Vicki's hands were shaking with fury as she pulled the jaguar pendant free from her khaki shirt.

"Yes, I did miss that. But I managed to rectify that little mistake while my homicide unit was prowling around the dump. I dumped it where I knew it would never turn up again. I swear, if I were superstitious, I'd think something—or someone—has been working against me since the beginning on this mission."

"You keep calling this a mission like you were saving the world. Don't kid yourself—or me—that this was about national security, any more than it was with your father. This was your own back and career at stake, and you know it." Vicki wanted to strike out at him, verbally if not physically, to force a reaction.

But he only shook his head. "I'm just doing my job as any good soldier would—or my father. You think I wanted any of this? I tried to keep you out of it, to get you out of the country, and when you insisted on staying, to keep Raul from deciding you were too dangerous. My guys got rid of Holly's camera and computer in your room and looked for that PDA just in case Holly had uploaded those last pictures onto it. Not just for myself but for you. To ensure this mission had no further unfortunate collateral damage. But like your sister, you couldn't stop poking, and now you've taken away any choice. And if I had one, I'd take it."

At the flat conviction of Michael's tone, Vicki actually believed him.

"You have no idea how tenuous the world situation is right now. The war on terror is at as critical a juncture as the Cold War ever was. Support is failing. The American people are just too soft for a protracted fight, even for their own freedom. We—people like me who understand—are the ones who have to hold the line until reality sinks in that our very existence may be at stake here. It's not just frontline soldiers who sometimes have to make sacrifices—even the ultimate sacrifice. Aren't two lives—or a few hundred villagers'—better than our entire civilization going up in smoke?"

"Funny, that's just the kind of thing the terrorists say," Vicki answered scornfully. "The bottom line is, after all these years, you and your buddies are still claiming to stand for democracy and justice and human rights even while you've been using these people and plenty of others like them to get work done that's too dirty for your own hands. Because like Joe said, there's always one more war, one more excuse for you to play God. This time it's the war on terrorism, but it's all the same underneath. And if your methods here came out in the open, some ugly comparisons might be drawn. So you—or your bosses—decided damage control was more important than the life of an American citizen."

Vicki stared at Michael with conviction to match his own. "But you'll never get away with it, no matter what happens here today. 'Do what is right and do not give way to fear'—that's not just for people; it's for countries, too. Every time you guys forget that, it always winds up going sour on you. In the end it's the American people you say you're trying to protect who suffer the most for it."

Michael's expression was so furious that Vicki braced herself for him to strike. But she wouldn't let his rage, the hostile twitching of the two crouched soldiers, Raul's self-satisfied smirk from the copilot's seat, daunt her. Lifting her chin unflinchingly, she demanded, "So what now? I presume you're going to kill me, too."

Michael slid his Glock into the small of his back. "Not at all, no more than I killed your sister. Remember—we Americans don't get our own hands dirty. I'm just going to hop a flight back to the embassy once our cargo's off-loaded, just in time to celebrate the latest US-Guatemalan counternarcotics success. I'll have an airtight alibi when a distraught tourist takes her own life on the site of her sister's murder."

He lifted the jaguar pendant so that the emerald eyes glowed in a shaft of light. "This clutched in your hand will make a nice touch. You can be sure I'll attend your funeral and be genuinely regretful."

Michael went forward to look out the windshield. His question shouted above the roar of the helicopter was in Spanish. "You have enough fuel to get to Belize?"

Raul Hernandez turned his head. "Yes, but it will not need to be so far. We'll drop the load for my cousin when we are close enough. For a commission, he'll hold it until it can be discreetly recovered. Then we'll be able to fly to the capital freely for anyone to search."

"Drop me off at Río Dulce. I'd like to be in plenty of company for the next twenty-four hours. I should be back in the capital by morning."

"And the girl?"

"She's in your hands. You know what to do."

Vicki paid little attention to the shouted conversation. There was a certain peace in total resignation. She turned away as Michael headed back in her direction.

"What the—?"

A scream of engine drowned out Michael's swearing, shaking the Huey as though in a whirlwind. The helicopter banked with such force that Vicki was thrown sideways in her seat harness. But not before she caught sight of the plane that had been coming straight toward them as though to run kamikaze through the windshield.

The DHC-2.

CHAPTER THIRTY-NINE

The Huey dropped groundward at a sideways angle, the blue of Lake Izabal rushing up at them. Then the helicopter straightened out and rose slightly.

Picking themselves off the floor, Michael and the two soldiers kicked away burlap stacks that had tilted onto them. English and Spanish curses and accusations flew around the cabin.

Vicki kept absolutely still, not allowing exultation to show on her face. How had Bill and Joe found her? What they could be planning, one small civilian aircraft against an armed military helicopter, she couldn't even imagine. It didn't matter. She only had to be ready for whatever came. She found herself on the edge of her seat, straining against the harness.

A yell came from the pilot. In the copilot's seat, Raul Hernandez gestured frantically toward Michael and waved out the left cockpit window.

From her jump seat in the rear, Vicki had little vision out the window panes in the side doors, but to her left she caught a glimpse of a propeller, a wingtip. Then the helicopter slowed abruptly enough to slam her against her harness and send the smaller and faster single-engine plane shooting ahead.

Vicki immediately recognized the purpose for their slowing, because as the helicopter reduced speed to little more than a hover, one of the soldiers wrestled the left side door open. She was grateful for the seat harness as wind surged into the cabin. Blinking against the airstream, Vicki scanned the sky for the plane. She couldn't see it.

But a moment later it screamed overhead from the right, so close as the DHC-2 cleared the left side that Vicki couldn't believe its landing wheels had missed the rotors. Again, the helicopter banked sideways and dropped. Through the open side door, she could now see the lazy curl and crashing of waves less than a hundred feet below.

Michael grabbed at an overhead strap to keep from sliding across the cabin. "Ignore the plane," he shouted at the pilot. "Can't you see they're trying to force us down? Just head for the coast. Once we're in international waters, they can't touch you."

That must be what Bill and Joe had in mind. If they could keep the helicopter forced down below where it couldn't clear the tall jungle canopy and buildings of Río Dulce ahead, it wouldn't be able to escape the lake. But how long could the smaller plane possibly keep that up? Already, the Huey had leveled off and was *throp-thropping* toward the distant green of Lake Izabal's eastern shore.

Above the noise, Raul yelled at Michael, "What about my shipment? My cousin is waiting."

"Are you *loco*? Forget the shipment! If you have to lose the drugs, then do it!"

The expression on the rogue commander's face made it clear that would be a last choice.

The DHC-2 had circled around again and was keeping pace with the helicopter not more than two wingspans away. The cargo door that was directly under the wing was slid back. Only when Vicki spotted Joe in the doorway did she realize the floppy hat she'd glimpsed in the pilot's seat must belong to Bill. So he was a pilot too. A minor surprise after all the other revelations this day had held.

Joe was crouched in the open door, and though his face was shadowed by the wing above him, Vicki knew the instant his gaze zeroed in on her face. She saw him take in her position, the jump seat harness. Did he know that she was not a willing passenger but a prisoner? Could he forgive the horrible things she'd said?

Joe leaned out to grab one of the struts supporting the wing overhead, and something in the purposefulness of his expression chilled her heart with fear. Surely he wouldn't try anything reckless. Glancing down at the dancing blue waves below, she noticed a pleasure yacht heading in their direction. Raul's cousin waiting for their cargo? By the perspective of the boat, the waves were larger and rougher than they looked, but if she could jump into their cushioning . . .

Before she could lose her nerve, Vicki released the harness. A few steps, and she'd be out the door. But even as she tensed her muscles to move, a flash of shock and actual fear on Joe's face told Vicki he'd read her intentions and didn't approve. In the same instant, the second soldier swung the barrel of the bolted-down machine gun.

Joe's glance flickered from Vicki's face to the gun, his shout of warning drowned out by the rapid *chunk-chunk-chunk* of machine-gun rounds.

The DHC-2 fell away just in time for the stream of gunfire to clear the plane's nose.

Michael was across the cabin before the machine gun stopped firing. His backhand across her face lifted Vicki off her feet and back into the jump seat. In one swift movement he had the harness back in place. He pulled out a pair of plastic cuffs and tightened them around her wrists. "Are you trying to save us the trouble by killing yourself? You move again, and I'll shoot you myself."

Then as the pilot turned toward them, Michael shouted, "Higher and faster, *estúpido*! Don't let them distract you. They won't come close enough to crash their plane."

Vicki slumped down in despair. All the Huey had to do was keep flying until it reached the ocean. Once they made it to international waters, the helicopter was untouchable, especially if Raul Hernandez had shipping contacts. They could even afford to ditch the Huey. At least Raul and Michael wouldn't be able to arrange Vicki's "suicide."

No, just dump me into the ocean with the opium. If I disappear, they'll have a dozen lies for anything Bill and Joe can say.

Vicki saw the DHC-2 dropping again from above, the square-tipped wings shuddering in the wash of the rotors but maneuvering too high and quickly for the gunner to angle up at them. She raised her bound wrists to the crouched figure in the doorway. At her action Michael slapped her again. Through her tears, Vicki caught an expression on Joe's face as dangerous as the one that had earlier sent her on a panicked race through the woods.

Then as the gunner swiveled the machine gun in the plane's general direction and as the deafening *chunk-chunk-chunk* of its firing filled the cabin, the DHC-2 dropped out of sight. It didn't reappear as the helicopter droned on. Coming up too quickly was the eastern shore of Lake Izabal. Straight ahead was Río Dulce, and beyond that only a small lake and river separated the Huey from international waters.

Fifty kilometers, no more. Thirty miles. At their speed, less than fifteen minutes.

A new thunder of engines and rotors screamed from behind. This time Michael offered no criticism when the Huey dropped toward the lake. There was astonishment on his face as he spun around.

From the cockpit Raul Hernandez yelled, "*Antinarcóticos*. How can they be here? You said they were far away in the Petén!"

The cavalry had arrived at last. Two of them—one racing forward in front of them, the other banking around to take up position on the Huey's left, where the DHC-2 had been. Nor were these Vietnam-era Hueys. Inexpert though she was, Vicki knew the multi-bladed rotor and sleek, gray-green bulk of a UH-60 Black Hawk helicopter, at least half again the size of the Huey.

Unlike Bill's old bush plane, these carried weapons. The Huey's gunner dropped his hands from his machine gun as he saw the powerful cannon-style mini-gun facing him through the side door of the Black Hawk, the well-armed soldiers outnumbering the Huey's contingent two to one.

Then high up and beyond the Black Hawk, Vicki noticed the DHC-2. So that was their plan. Bill and Joe had been thwarting the Huey's escape until their backup could arrive.

From the door of the Black Hawk, a man in uniform made hand signals as the longer helicopter pulled forward to where the pilot could see him. The Huey dropped farther, settling at a hover above the water, the gunner's hands spread wide in the air. Above the noise of multiple rotors and engines, Vicki heard loud, furious cursing.

Had the other soldier misunderstood and actually thought his M16 could make some impact on that huge, hovering aircraft beside them? Or had he made the desperate choice of a blaze of glory over dishonor? Vicki saw only an automatic rifle coming up, peppering the Black Hawk's fuselage with a spray of bullets, and heard a scream as someone inside was hit, Michael's furious swearing beside her. Then the Black Hawk reacted, the *brrrrrr* of its min-gun deafening.

A shout of fury came over the radio. "Don't shoot! You'll hurt the hostage!"

It was too late.

The crack of sound came directly behind Vicki. The tail of the Huey was gone, daylight streaming through. But just for a moment. Overhead the rotor turbine died. The broken tail went up, the nose down, and the Huey dropped like a stone.

Anguished screams rang in Vicki's ears, but she was too busy fighting her seat harness to add to them. The plastic cuffs bit deeply into her wrists as she tugged at the buckle. She was still yanking at it when they hit the water. From any higher up, the Huey would have broken to pieces. As it was, the windshield smashed on impact, sending a tidal flood through the cabin.

The water was cold, striking Vicki with a shock that drove the air from her lungs. Water rushed through the open door as well, the weight of the cargo packed behind the machine gun tilting the helicopter to its right as it flooded. The buckle had finally come loose, and her cuffed hands pushed the harness over her head.

The cabin was now filled with water, the open side door of the Huey above Vicki's head. She kicked desperately upward as the helicopter sank around her. Something—a hand, a rope, a harness?—grabbed at her ankle, and she struck out in panic before she felt it give. Her hands were on the sill of the door, then her feet.

And she was out.

Vicki managed a single gasp of air before the downward suction of the sinking aircraft pulled her back under the waves. She kicked upward, rolling over onto her back so her bound hands were less of an impediment. Her nostrils were full of water, her mouth opening to inhale as her head broke the surface. She was free.

But her situation wasn't less desperate. One of the Black Hawks dropped to hover above the waves. The DHC-2 banked in low. But around Vicki the waves were high, tossing crests. A roller, green and gray, curled lazily above her head to crash down finally in a churning of foamy white, slapping Vicki in the face as she kicked on her back to stay afloat. Choking, she sank beneath the water. Only frantic thrashing propelled her to the surface again.

The chill of the water bit into Vicki, and she could no longer feel the throbbing sting of cuffs cutting into her wrists, the slowing movement of her lower limbs. She sank underwater until the waves could no longer reach her. The late afternoon sunshine danced an opal light spectrum through the foam and churning and turmoil, but she no longer had the strength or will to move toward that light.

I'm drowning. Surely there should be emotion in the thought. But no feeling was left in Vicki at all but deep, biting cold. Then as consciousness drifted away, she was no longer cold but almost warm. *Into Your hands I commit my spirit.* From what long-ago Sunday school lesson had that come? *Holly? Mama? Papa?*

When a sharp pain at the roots of her hair yanked her back to consciousness, she could almost feel resentment. An iron grip tugged at her clothing, a steel arm tight around her waist. Vaguely, Vicki felt an upward thrust of long limbs against her. Then a final powerful surge tossed her head and shoulders out of the water before she splashed down limp against wet cloth that was rock-solid and supporting. Warmth covered her cold lips, breathed life into her lungs.

Coughing and sputtering up lake water, Vicki opened her eyes. "Joe!" She didn't know whether the wetness in her eyes was from the lake or tears. "Oh, Joe!"

"It's okay. I've got you."

Turning her head against his shoulder, Vicki saw the DHC-2 circling above, the open cargo door under the wing from which he'd dived into the water. A life ring landed close by with a splash. Beyond it, a Black Hawk hovered only a scant few meters above the water.

Joe grabbed the life ring and balanced Vicki's head and shoulder against it while a knife appeared in his other hand. Painful life returned to her wrists as he sawed at the plastic cuffs. As they fell free, Vicki threw her arms around Joe's neck with a fierce relief that swept them both underwater before Joe's strong kick brought them back to the surface.

Embarrassed, Vicki pulled away, but Joe didn't loosen his tight grip. Two of the Black Hawk's crew were now in the water, pulling in the line of the life ring. Taking a firmer grip on the ring, Joe let the rescue team haul them in, his arm still around Vicki. The beat of his heart, quickened from exertion, was strong beneath her ear, his drawl as gentle as to a hurt child. "It's okay, sweetheart. Everything's going to be all right. You're safe now."

This time Vicki believed it.

CHAPTER FORTY

It had been five days since Joe lifted Vicki from the waters of Lake Izabal into the safety of the Black Hawk. Five days of chaos and conferences and camera flashes and more media attention than Vicki hoped to have again for the rest of her life.

The Huey had been recovered with Raul Hernandez and the pilot still strapped in their seats. One of the soldiers had made it out of the sinking helicopter; the other had drowned. The opium strapped in its cargo netting was hauled up and placed into evidence.

Michael hadn't been found. Lake Izabal was vast and deep with strong currents, so he had been presumed drowned.

Meanwhile, counternarcotics troops were swarming around the biosphere. How Bill and Joe had managed to summon the cavalry just in the nick of time was still a little hazy to Vicki, though it would seem only her rescue was spur-of-the-moment. The Black Hawks had been heading in to raid the encampment when Bill and Joe's frantic SOS detoured two of them.

The remaining force, another Black Hawk and three Hueys, had reached the plateau in time to catch Hernandez's transport truck and Jeep coming down the nature trail. Their contents were suggestive with the camp and harvest paraphernalia, but as Raul had assured Michael, hardly incriminating without that air-lifted opium. Vicki still didn't have those details either, since the minute they'd all landed back in Guatemala City, Bill and Joe had disappeared into a madhouse of American DEA and local counternarcotics meetings, which had been to the accompaniment of a media barrage. Unfortunately the air show over Lake Izabal had not gone unnoticed.

Vicki had again made multiple statements in English and Spanish. Early in the proceedings Evelyn showed up, bringing with her a change of clothing. Vicki's knapsack and Holly's PDA were somewhere at the bottom of Lake Izabal. Except for the occasional summons to embassy or police station, Vicki had stayed at Casa de Esperanza until yesterday, when a DEA fact-gathering team heading to the biosphere allowed her to hop their Black Hawk to pick up her belongings.

Vicki had found the center noisy with the Australians. Their own arrival in the middle of that counternarcotics raid had proved rather anticlimactic with their hosts in hysterics over the Black Hawks and Hueys and an AWOL camp cook. But Maria had returned by that evening, and within two days, Rosario and Beatriz were gone.

Alpiro, shrewdly sequestering himself in his office during the counternarcotics raid, had gotten off with a slap on the wrist and a demotion, swearing that he'd simply done a relative the small favor of ignoring his presence in the biosphere. But a treasury police raid of home and bank accounts had confirmed Vicki's suspicions that he was also using his UPN position to funnel black market wildlife from the biosphere through Rosario and Beatriz.

Vicki had little doubt the couple's own superior, the minister of environment, along with the zoo administrator, had been Rosario and Beatriz's Guatemala City receivers. But those two, more cautious in their accounting, managed to escape with only slightly dusty hands, while the media was satisfied with the scapegoats offered. At least there'd be a stronger scrutiny now on the two men's activities.

Of greater interest to Vicki was the news that Cesar would be taking Rosario and Beatriz's place. The refuge would finally have a director more interested in its future than city lights and comforts. Vicki had arrived in time for Alison's announcement at dinner last night and was the first to congratulate the Mayan vet with a hug and kiss.

Vicki knew Cesar too well to think of offering him aid, but she'd pressed into his hand a thick stack of quetzales she'd changed in Guatemala City. "To rebuild the church, my friend. After all, it was my doing that it burned."

"No, it was your doing that saved Alicia and Gabriela. It was the doing of *los malvados*—the evil ones—that burned it." But Cesar had accepted the gift. "For God and the people of Verapaz. *Que Dios te bendiga.* And you will come again to visit us?"

"You can count on it," Vicki promised.

It was after supper when Alison brought Vicki the message that the DHC-2 would be able to give her a lift back to Guatemala City the next morning. Vicki's ticket was already booked on an afternoon flight back to Washington DC.

Vicki had set her alarm to go off before sunrise. She didn't want a crowd around when she made her good-byes to the center and plateau and the Sierra de las Minas. Mist swirled across the gravel path as Vicki made her way through the animal cages, the sky above the oak branches just paling to gray. The *chipi-chipi* brushed her face with a cool mist, a fern laying beads of dew across one arm.

But when Vicki emerged on the rock outcropping above *Pozo Azul*, the last stars were fading from a cloudless sky over Lake Izabal, a shiver of pale jade and pink above the jungle canopy across the lake promising a perfect sunrise for her farewell.

From this distance the lake water looked flat and calm, its gray already tingeing to blue. The night orchestra of frogs and cicadas was giving way to dawn's symphony of bird songs, parrot caws, and the chatter of monkeys rousing from slumber, all to the glorious bass thunder of the falls. Settling herself on the damp stone so she could wrap her arms around her knees, Vicki watched the sky lighten over the lake, listened to the morning song around her in speechless delight. Below her, mist pooled white and thick above the hot spring, the spray of the cascade as it churned down into it catching the early light to create the faintest soap-bubble glimmer of a rainbow.

It was as though the mountains and cloud forests and very animal life around her had gathered to offer Vicki a magnificent farewell. Their joyous serenity stole into her mind and heart, infused peace through the very muscles of her body. She didn't even turn her head when she heard firm footsteps on the rock behind her. They were part of this perfect morning, and she knew them immediately.

Vicki waited as Joe settled himself down beside her, stretching out his legs. Though Bill or Joe had been there at every interrogation and press conference, she hadn't seen either privately since those terrible moments in the safe room. In his hands he held a small knapsack, and this he set carefully down on the rock at his side before leaning back to rest on his hands. Together they watched the jade and pink of the horizon brighten to oranges and reds.

Only after a comfortable silence did Vicki turn her head to ask the question that had been burning in her for days. "So who are you really? DEA?"

Even as she spoke, Vicki was blinking in sudden unfamiliarity. Then she took in what made her companion look so different. Joe had cut his hair. Not short like Bill's but shaped and trimmed well above his shoulders. Instead of his wild Hawaiian look, he wore a thin polo sweater and jeans. With a fresh-shaven jawline, he looked almost . . . respectable.

The irony on Joe's face told Vicki that he knew exactly what she was thinking. "Well, in a manner of speaking, yes. How did you guess?"

"It seemed logical with everything that's happened, especially the DEA showing up so conveniently. Then you *were* working for some government agency when I asked you that day?" *You were lying to me?* Her disappointment hung unspoken in the air.

Joe held Vicki's gaze, irony darkening to intensity. "I may not have told you everything I wanted to, but I have never lied to you. Not about my job, my faith, anything."

Clearing his throat, Joe looked out across the treetops. "I've been with the DEA since I got out of the army five years ago. But these last months with Taylor wasn't for them. That was private. A crusade, you might say."

"How in the world did *you* get involved in all this?"

He looked at Vicki again. "It's a bit of a long story."

Vicki wrinkled her nose at him. "We've got until my plane leaves. So long as the pilot has no objection."

Joe grinned. "So be it. But first, I want you to understand about Bill.

You know what happened that night twenty years ago. But afterward . . . well, Bill never quite forgave himself, firm believer though he was in what they were doing down here. Especially when it became evident over the next years what a monster they'd let walk that night in Raul Hernandez. Within five years of your parents' death, he was out of the CIA. Before he left, he warned the agency that Hernandez was out of control and too dangerous to keep using.

"When things calmed down a bit, Bill bought his land and did what he could to help the people create jobs, establish the center. If he couldn't make up for that past miscarriage of justice, at least he could make a difference for the future. But then things started getting uneasy again. Alpiro was moving in with that UPN handover coming up. His units had already taken over biosphere security. When the massacre happened, Bill didn't know what was going on. Certainly not that Raul Hernandez was back in town. He just knew it was all beginning again.

"Unfortunately, the biosphere was under Alpiro's jurisdiction, and Alpiro had a lot of clout. Bill had no proof, and he was in no condition to mount any serious investigation. So he called an old friend."

"You?" Vicki asked.

"No, my father."

"Then your father's still alive?" Why had Vicki assumed Joe was as alone as she? Because of the drifter persona he projected?

"Alive and kicking, though long retired from the military. I hope you can meet him sometime. You'd like him. He's a lot more respectable than his son." A ghost of a smile.

Joe was silent for a moment before going on slowly. "You see, he was the third American in those pictures. For him it was different. As a Special Forces instructor, he'd come down, train these guys, and leave. He was horrified to walk in on what his latest graduate had done. Funny thing is, the only reason my father and the others were there was because Raul Hernandez, the highest ranking of their new recruits, wanted to show off to his American buddies—and maybe show them how much they were indebted to him.

"If it had been up to my father, Hernandez would have been hung out to dry from the first. But CIA trumps armed forces, and they were screaming national security. I never knew why we left Guatemala so quickly. Oh yes, I was here then. That was actually my father's first overseas position. We were living with my mother's family. She was Guatemalan."

As Vicki's look of astonishment took in his lanky frame, the sun-streaked hair, Joe smiled slightly. "One of the German coffee families—and with strong military ties. My grandfather was a high-placed general, my uncles all up to their teeth in local politics. That was why my father put in for this particular post. We'd come down at least once a year to visit my relatives. So it was natural to put in for long-term deployment here.

"Only my father hadn't been here long when he saw the other side of military rule here. After your parents were killed, he immediately put in for transfer and asked my mother to go with him. She ended up choosing her family over my father. And me. A year or so later she married another coffee baron, some childhood playmate. A few months later, both of them were killed when he was drunk and crashed his Ferrari."

Joe gave Vicki a rueful grin. "Of course, all I saw as a little kid was my grandfather's estate. I was pretty ticked when my father carried me off, as much for the loss of a luxury lifestyle as losing my mother, to be honest. I knew my nanny better than I did her. Still, she was my mother, and when she didn't even bother calling after the first couple of months . . . Like I said, I blamed myself for a long time. But I'm glad now she let my father take me, or my life might be right where Alpiro or any of these guys ended up.

"Anyway, Taylor knew my father had a son who was now DEA. He had this idea I could get something moving, even if he couldn't. That's when I learned about all this. Of course, they were wrong that I could do anything or get the DEA on board—for the same reason as Bill. No concrete evidence. But I took a leave of absence, not totally approved by my supervisor, and came here."

Vicki listened with growing absorption as Joe quietly, even matter-of-factly, told his own side of the last three months.

"I chose one of the personas I'd used undercover floating back and forth between California and Mexico—the drifting expat surfer." His hand rose briefly to where his long hair had been. "Since I can't quite blend in as a Ladino, even if I do speak the language."

"So are you really Joe Ericsson?" His hesitation back at that airport party when Vicki had made a joke about his name sounding like an alias now made sense, as did so many other small happenings over these last weeks.

Joe grinned. "In a manner of speaking. My father's name is Eric Thompson, so . . . Ericsson. Or 'son of Eric.' A background check would come up with Joe Ericsson, international drifter, a few minor possession priors in Mexico and California. That must be what Camden turned up. But WRC was so desperate for help that no one even asked any questions when Bill hired me.

"Once I had their radio frequency and heard enough to confirm Bill's suspicions that *something* was going on, I made myself discreetly known to the DEA country attachè over at the embassy, just to let him know I was unofficially in his territory. He was willing to talk a serious op if I could come up with some hard data. What I was specifically after were aerial maps of the biosphere that would detail the valleys and ridges—and any recent clearings and plantings there. DEA had just done a joint op with the locals mapping likely drug-producing areas with SOUTHCOM surveillance planes. The Sierra de las Minas should have been a given, but somehow that entire area of the biosphere had been left off the list. I know now that was Alpiro's doing.

"So, I talked the DEA into seeing what they could do to schedule me some discreet satellite maps while still keeping my presence covert. Funny thing is, I saw Camden at the embassy that day. The attaché had been telling me about this new UPN unit. I even thought of roping him in, but he was working closely with Alpiro, who was at the top of Bill Taylor's list of likely suspects, so it seemed prudent to keep those in the know to a minimum. Fortunately, as it turned out."

"I think I saw you at the embassy," Vicki put in. "I'd gone there for my parents' death report."

"That's right; you were jumping into a taxi. In any case, there wasn't much the DEA could do, especially over Alpiro's head, without concrete proof. But if I could get a visual record and GPS position, he'd bring in the local counternarcotics troops and their US equipment. Problem was, there are so many valleys and ridges out there, and except when the poppies are in bloom, there isn't much to see. Plus, any serious air search would have roused all kinds of questions, since everyone in these mountains knows Taylor's Cessna. So we were kind of stuck waiting for those satellite maps.

"Meanwhile, I'd take a swing out over the mountains when flying to and from the city, working my way gradually across the biosphere. In fact, that particular valley was one of the first we'd checked and seen nothing but a few overgrown clearings; the poppies weren't up yet. But Bill was sure it all had to be related to that massacred village, so he asked me to fly back over those abandoned fields with the de Havilland. With a new plane, Taylor figured it wouldn't raise any questions—our mistake. I'm just thankful I didn't get us both killed.

"At least once I spotted these poppy fields from the air, I knew we had them. Except Alpiro put the brakes on air traffic over the biosphere. We still needed visual proof, which meant tracking back to that valley on foot—not so easy when the biosphere was swarming with Camden's UPN op. I'd talked the DEA into loaning me a couple of their local counter-narcotics team, Guatemalans who've been trained, polygraphed, and are paid well enough by us to minimize odds of corruption."

"Your guards," Vicki identified.

"Yes, that was their cover."

"So that's what you were doing in the biosphere when I saw you that day and earlier on the mountain," Vicki said sadly. "No wonder you were so furious about me coming here. I messed up your entire investigation."

"No, don't think that way," Joe countered swiftly. "I'll admit I wasn't too happy about you poking around—if nothing else, for your own safety. But in the end that little side trip after Alicia and Gabriela was what nailed Hernandez's position for us and broke the whole thing wide open.

"When I was in town that morning picking up supplies, I'd also finally picked up those aerial maps, along with a GPS tracker, night vision goggles, and a couple of mountain bikes. You actually gave me that last idea. The maps confirmed the coordinates of the poppy fields, but of course they didn't give us the opium lab or those running it, which is what we really wanted. Our plan was to wait till dark, when the UPN op would be out of the biosphere, and use the bikes and NVGs to track down those coordinates and hopefully come up with something more concrete than just a few poppy fields.

"Then came that search for the girls. Bill was furious at my getting involved—especially when Alpiro told him he'd just arrested his gringo employee—until I told him about that Jeep and transport truck appearing out of nowhere and who was driving the Jeep. I immediately recognized Raul Hernandez from his photos. We knew then who was responsible for the opium—and that massacre.

"After I left you that night, Ramirez, one of our counternarcotics loaners, and I were getting ready to follow that track back into the biosphere when we saw Hernandez show up with his guys to burn the church. It was the hardest thing I've done in a long time not to interfere. But there was nothing I could do except follow them back when they returned to base. That saved us any search time by leading us right to the encampment. We hid out till morning to get some visual proof. My binoculars have some special high-tech options, including digital video.

"A call to the DEA country attachè scheduled a strike for that afternoon, the same forces Michael believed were safely in the Petén. I stayed in the woods to guide them to target . . . until your arrival threw the op into chaos.

"When you saw us, Ramirez had just managed to filter through camp as one of their own sentries and slap a GPS tracker on that Jeep for the strike team to follow in. I had just finished filming the loading of the dope when I heard you, then saw you."

It was an explanation, not an apology. Vicki didn't need to explain her own role. Joe had been there for both her English and Spanish statements.

Joe didn't pause or look at her as he went on. With the biosphere and plateau boiling over with armed search parties and Raul's men scrambling to dismantle their camp, Joe and Ramirez had been forced to retreat. With the element of surprise gone, they had to get the DHC-2 off the ground and call in the Black Hawks immediately. Joe might not have cared for Michael's politics, but he still had no reason to suspect his involvement.

But even if Michael was just a little too bonded with Alpiro to be objective, Joe and Bill couldn't trust Michael not to blow the operation to his local colleagues, especially after his ardent support of Alpiro the night before and his only too patent antipathy toward Joe himself. So they couldn't afford to let him get wind of what was going down until it was all over. Only when their rescrambled strategy had been set in motion and the DHC-2 was in the air had Bill radioed for Garcia, the veranda "guard" and another counternarcotics loaner, to head back in the pickup and check on Vicki. The small plane was monitoring from a safe height that last liftoff of opium from the encampment, Joe impatiently calling for counternarcotics to move in before it was gone, when Garcia reported Vicki's breakout. The guard was driving the pickup toward Verapaz to search for her when he'd seen the UPN helicopter land at the biosphere *garita*. When he informed Bill and Joe the UPN gringo adviser had taken Vicki aboard, they'd known just what Michael had to be.

Joe glanced sideways again at Vicki. "And you know the rest."

Yes, Vicki knew the rest. "Joe, all those terrible things I said—"

He cut her off. "Don't! Yes, I do remember what you said: that you believed I was special, more than a beach bum or drifter. The rest . . . Well, I'd have made the same intel assumption on the data you had. Besides, I could have handled things differently myself. I could've at least tried to say something to dispel your misconceptions, maybe even spared you a terrible ordeal. I admit I was ticked off that you could believe I'd hurt Holly. I guess I thought—hoped—you knew me better than that."

"Well, you had Holly's PDA, something only the killer was supposed to have. I'd known for some time you were hiding something, even when I wanted to believe in you. And all those things Bill said about you. When I saw you out in that camp talking to one of their guards—I . . . I really did hope I was wrong until I saw the PDA."

"I'm sorry about that. I didn't know where the PDA was when you asked me about it, but the instant it didn't turn up in her stuff at the children's home, I guessed where she'd have stashed it. Bill had this small hidden compartment in the Cessna for valuables. While I was cleaning out the Cessna to turn it over to the new owners, I found it right where I'd expected.

"When I saw her pictures and downloads, I knew you were right—Holly's death was no random mugging but connected to our investigation. Holly must have recognized Alpiro and Raul as the men she'd seen in the poppy fields. She'd recognized Bill in that photo too, which explains why she didn't come to him for help, though neither Holly nor Bill and I at that point had any idea you two sisters were connected to that past massacre. Either way, I couldn't exactly explain that PDA to you without blowing my cover. The best option was to convince you to go home and get in touch when this was all over and we had Holly's killer in hand. Only you don't convince too easily."

When Vicki prudently refrained from responding, Joe finished catching her up on the last few days of the investigation. "Michael's comment you passed on to us about Zone 4 led counternarcotics straight to the heroin processing lab, a warehouse owned by Hernandez. They got most of it. But with Hernandez dead and Camden missing, there's no real proof of any current CIA involvement. Officially, Camden's been written off as an embassy 'bad apple' using his connections to run narcotics—hardly the first and probably not the last. With him out of the picture, both the Guatemalan and American powers that be have decided to let the pictures of that massacre twenty years ago come out and take credit for bringing a war criminal and murderer to justice, even posthumously.

"Bill and my father have agreed to make statements as to what they walked in on that night and their orders to remain silent. As for the CIA, admitting that long-retired personnel made one bad call has actually made them look pretty good—the new transparency and all that. At least your parents and those villagers will at last have justice."

"Justice." Vicki snorted. "That's something I still don't get. Why didn't they just do the right thing from the beginning? Not just Michael or Bill Taylor and the others. All the way back to when they were deciding it was easier to make a few extra dollars by accepting forced labor instead of pushing a minimum wage law down here—at least for American companies—or that it was ever okay to play God with other people's governments and countries."

Joe's broad shoulders rose and fell as he said reflectively, "I guess it's like you said that night at the center—about doing what's right and not giving way to fear. Problem is, we humans always have had a tendency to do it the other way around, making our decisions by fear, not what's right. With the plantation owners and big businesses, it was fear that if they made reforms, they'd lose economic dominance and wealth.

Even for the ordinary Spanish and Ladinos, there was always the fear that the Mayan majority would rise up and sweep into power if not kept repressed. And among the Mayans, there was plenty of fear for their own skins that led to denouncing their neighbors, taking revenge."

"I suppose for Michael and others like him, it was fear that if people found out what they were doing, they'd actually have to start being accountable for their activities. Though in the end, it looks like Michael got his wish. No real scandal for the US or CIA." Vicki looked out across Lake Izabal, now warming to the same blue-gray as the sky above, the eastern horizon a glorious splash of oranges and reds. "So do you think he's really in that lake somewhere?"

"I don't know. Without a body, we'll never know. Though being who he is, Camden's capable of being back in some Black Ops unit at Langley by now." Joe gave Vicki a keen look. "Which is it you're hoping?"

Vicki shrugged. "I don't know. It's hard to wish someone you've known dead, even though he'd have killed me in a heartbeat and was ultimately responsible for my sister's death, whether or not he actually pulled the trigger."

"Does it worry you he might still be out there? That he might still come after you?"

"Not really. Michael's a professional, and he has his own code. I don't think he'd hurt me except for a greater good or even hold a grudge. That much I've learned about him." Vicki shook her head. "He was so sincere, so sure of what he believed, so committed to his country and his duty. That's why it didn't even enter my mind to suspect him. I didn't agree with everything he said, but I trusted him implicitly."

"People who truly believe what they say and act on it are the most dangerous. Especially if they believe their cause sets them above the rule of law."

"Dangerous." She turned her reflective scrutiny on her companion. "That's the other thing that confused me so much, that . . . that made me believe what I saw, even when I didn't want to. Bill said you weren't a safe person to know. And you agreed. Up there on the mountains and even on the search . . . well, you looked so angry; you really did scare me."

"I was more than angry," Joe answered. "I was furious, not to mention scared stiff. I'd discovered that the person running this drug op wasn't just some crooked UPN commander but a mass murderer likely responsible for your sister's murder as well. And here you were, once again poking your nose into a hornet's nest without a thought for the danger you were in. When I saw you in those woods and in that helicopter . . ."

Once again, he hadn't even mentioned the jeopardy in which she'd placed his own mission, but Vicki felt her cheeks burn. "I know. I'm so sorry. It was stupid. I could have ruined everything."

"No, you weren't stupid. As far as you knew, you were the only person taking Holly's death seriously. It was just one of those things that can mess up the best-planned op. In any case, it's ended and ended well.

"As far as Bill's crack about being 'safe'—again it was the truth, though maybe not the way you took it. I had a persona to maintain, and it wasn't safe for you to start seeing me as a different person. That warning of Taylor's was meant as much for me as you. He could see I was letting you get under my skin and maybe not maintaining the impersonal distance needed for the mission at hand."

"Because you felt sorry for me about Holly and about my family."

Joe's eyes were suddenly intense and very close. "No, because you were one of the most incredible people I'd run into in . . . well, too long. I've spent so much of these last years undercover, and most of the people I deal with are scumbags on their way to prison if I've anything to say about it. Then along came you—strong, caring, determined to do good and save the world even when you didn't think it would matter."

Joe cleared his throat before he went on. "Anyway, I guess I just wanted to shake it through your head that the world really isn't a lost cause. That it's still a pretty awesome creation in the hands of someone big enough to take care of it—and us."

Vicki found herself speechless under the intensity of his gaze. She swallowed before she managed to get out, "Yes, I . . . I've kind of learned that myself these past weeks."

"I'm glad. At least that much good has come out of your coming back here." Joe's voice grew somber as he said, "I didn't know then you had your own connection to this place beyond Holly. After Bill's crack that day, he told me the other reason I had no business getting close to you—that you happened to be Jeff Craig's daughter and had no idea that I—or rather my father—was closely involved in your parents' deaths."

Vicki put a hand on his arm and felt it tense under her fingers. "Joe, you can't think I'd blame you for anything your father did or didn't do. I—I don't even really blame *him* anymore now that I understand better how it all happened. And you're the one who helped bring Raul Hernandez to justice after all these years—and your father and Bill. That's what I choose to remember, not what happened twenty years ago."

The muscles under her hand relaxed fractionally. "I'm glad you can be so forgiving. Because my father really is a pretty special old man. As yours was, from everything I've seen. I saw his photos Bill had. He really had an extraordinary gift. And a passion for this country and its people. Like his daughters."

At his slight smile, Vicki seized gratefully on the change of subject. "Yes, I have those pictures now. Bill brought them over to Casa de Esperanza. Said they really belonged to me. He'd rescued them that night before Alpiro and Raul could burn them. All they wanted were their blackmail shots." Bill had also begged Vicki's forgiveness. Touched and disconcerted by actual tears in the man's eyes, Vicki had hugged him fiercely. "Evelyn gave me the ones she had of his as well. I'm going to have the collection printed as a book, as my father had in mind. I can't say how much it means to me to finally have a legacy of my birth parents."

"Not the only legacy." Only when Joe lifted the knapsack beside him did Vicki take notice of the bundle he'd brought. He unwrapped it to reveal an urn, weathered and encrusted with dirt.

"Something else Bill wanted you to have. You know your parents were cremated, courtesy of the embassy. There was no family to collect their ashes. Bill kept up a burial niche for them in Guatemala City." Joe didn't need to explain. Vicki was well aware that except for the wealthier family crypts, burial space was usually rented. When rent ran out, unclaimed remains were tossed into a common grave. "He asked me to deliver this to you."

Vicki lifted the urn. It was heavier than her sister's funeral box but still so light to represent two human beings. *Because it doesn't. What my parents were—what they are—is not in here.* For a long moment, she cradled the urn in her hands. *I* will *see you again, Mama . . . Papa. Until then . . .* Then she looked down at the swirl of mist and foam and spray below and in one swift motion emptied the contents of the urn out over the rock outcropping. "There! Now they're with Holly. At least . . . You know what I mean. Thank you. I can't imagine a more beautiful place to remember them."

Setting the urn back on the rock beside her, Vicki shook her head. "You know, it really does seem an incredible coincidence that we should all end up here together like this now. Holly. Me. You. Michael. Bill. Raul and Alpiro. All these people from twenty years ago coming back at the same time."

Joe tucked the urn back inside the knapsack. "Not as much a coincidence as one might think. Bill was here because of his past connections, and it was those same past connections that brought Michael to take over for his father as handler for Raul and his network and caused Hernandez and Alpiro to choose these mountains. And I was only called in because those past connections had reared their ugly heads.

"The real coincidence is Holly choosing this place as her environmental crusade without even knowing who she was or that she'd once lived here. Even you chose a project in Guatemala because she was here. Though maybe even that wasn't all coincidence. Holly may have been too young to remember these mountains consciously. But there must have been some subconscious memories—sights and sounds and smells—that drew her here out of all the places on this planet."

Vicki remembered her own first reactions to this place. "Yes, I know what you mean."

"But truth is, I don't really believe in coincidences. I think God had a plan that entailed bringing you back to your past. And not just you. All of us had unfinished business here."

"I don't believe in coincidences." How long ago had Evelyn McKie said the same to her?

Vicki looked at Joe sharply. "A plan? For Holly to come back here to die? For another village to be massacred? For me to almost mess everything up?"

"Don't go there." Now it was Joe's hand that was on Vicki's arm, his fingers warm as he lifted her cold hand and folded it in his own, his voice gentle. "Whatever happened here—of good or evil—is still in God's control and His plan. As Holly is His child. She lived on this earth until she'd finished God's plan for her life. Then she went home. Don't forget: this life isn't our real destination or our real home. In fact, it's just the start. More like, well, our boot camp, you might say, from the point of view of eternity."

"Now you do sound like a soldier." Vicki managed a smile. "No, I know you're right. I've been thinking too of what the villagers were always singing—that our real home is a long way beyond this world. Still, after all this, it doesn't really seem like we accomplished much. It's not like we saved the world. Alpiro and the others are still getting away with an awful lot. There're plenty of other drug dealers out there. And all those . . . those fires of corruption and violence and hate that seem to be just under the surface as much as the fires down at the dump. Do you think Holly's death—any of this—has really changed anything?"

"Who knows? But one mass murderer is dead and can't hurt anyone again. The media coverage has focused a lot more attention on the plight of the cloud forests as well as its Mayan residents. Holly would find that alone worth all of this. We've stopped one explosive situation and one narcotics network—put out one small fire, you might say. For me that's enough. After all, we were never called to save the whole world, just our part. You're the one who told me what we're called to do, the difference one person can make."

"'Do what is right and do not give way to fear,'" Vicki repeated slowly.

"Exactly. Like Taylor says, it's all personal in the long run—*I*, not *we*. One person's decisions really can change history. Abraham and Sarah's single mistake with Hagar changed world politics forever. A decision twenty years ago changed many lives. All because people chose to act in fear. But on the flip side, what might one child you've saved in your work grow up to be? Who knows what Alicia and Gabriela might contribute to their people someday?"

One situation.

One child.

One fire.

Vicki conjured up the image of a young couple holding a small Vicki and Holly in that faded old photo of Evelyn's. Jeff and Victoria Craig hadn't been much older than Vicki was now when they'd given their lives in these mountains. Her thoughts moved to Mom and Dad Andrews, who'd lovingly accepted two small, hurting girls into their home. To Evelyn McKie with her enormous family of heart, if not of blood. Bill Taylor, sacrificing his own anonymity to make amends for the past. Joe, patiently watching and waiting for months in these mountains.

Just one person here. Another there. But they added up; oh, how they added up!

The green tangle of cloud forest was now emerging from the mist below the rock outcropping, the eastern sky brightening from pink to blue above the lake. At any moment the sun would spring up over the distant jungle canopy.

God, I can't run Your universe or fix it all. Forgive me for being arrogant enough to even think it's my job. All You call me to do is my part. To be Sarah's daughter. "Do what is right and do not give way to fear."

"You're right. It's all we can do. It's enough." Vicki glanced at Joe. He was staring at the lake. They'd now finished all the pertinent topics, and Vicki was suddenly feeling inordinately conscious of his closeness, the faint masculine musk of his body warmth.

"So, what's next for you?"

The query came out in unison. Joe waved a hand for Vicki to go first.

"I'm flying back tonight to Children at Risk headquarters. I plan to concentrate on pursuing contracts with other faith-based organizations now that we've seen the success of Casa de Esperanza as a prospect. I'll be staying put for a while except for short-term trips. And you?"

"Well, I've been thinking about getting out of undercover work. I'm tired of having to pretend to be something I'm not, of spending my time with the world's scum. I'm slated next for a resident agent posting since the DEA decided not to can me for my leave of absence. That would be a more supervisory position running a field office. But for now I've decided to take up an offer I had pending before this side trip—an instructor stint at the DEA training academy in Quantico, Virginia. Undercover tactics."

"Really?" Vicki toned down the delight of her exclamation. "I don't know if you're aware, but Children at Risk is based in Washington DC. Not too far from Quantico."

"Yes, I'm aware of that," Joe said coolly, but there was nothing cool about the disturbing smile in his eyes, and Vicki's heart began to race.

"I wanted to say—"

"By the way—"

Again they spoke together. This time Vicki laughed and waved. "Okay, you first."

"I just wanted to say I've been doing some reading on Abraham. I remember the story from Sunday school, but somehow they always left out those harem parts."

"Yes, well, that's what I wanted to say." Vicki felt flushed. "I never said thank you for coming after me, and . . . and I want to before we're out of here. I know God saved me when I really thought I was going to die, but you were the one He sent. And Cesar too. Unlike Abraham in that harem, you chose to risk your life to come after me."

"Abraham turned out to be a pretty incredible guy in the end. I guess he learned from his mistakes. But I have a hard time understanding him letting a woman like Sarah go without fighting to keep her. I read that part about being Sarah's daughter—and the description it gives of her. She wasn't just a woman beautiful enough to tempt a pharaoh; she was beautiful on the inside, too. The kind of woman you could count on wandering through a wilderness in a strange land. The kind of woman you'd want at your side whether times were good or when they got rough. The kind of woman you are, Vicki. No, don't turn your head away."

Somehow now, both her hands were in his, the green eyes close enough to see yellow flecks, his mouth curved to tenderness. "All these weeks I did what Bill asked. I held back and focused on the mission, because that's why I was here and what it took. But the mission is over, and I don't want to let you just walk out of my life. Is there any chance I can come see you in Washington?"

The amber light of her eyes, the warm delight of her smile gave Vicki's answer.

Joe's hands crushed Vicki's too tight, and she heard in his voice a diffidence she'd never heard before. "I've got to tell you, I can't offer much. Like Abraham, I've been a bit of a wanderer all my life. And Bill's right—my job isn't so safe, and I never know where it'll take me next—"

Vicki covered his mouth. Softly, she said, "Shut up and kiss me."

He did.

Over Lake Izabal the sun was finally shooting its bright radiance above the jungle canopy. If the two on the rock outcropping didn't notice its arrival, around them birdsong was rising in noisy chorus to greet the morning. Overhead the troop of monkeys chattered its own celebration.

And down below on the plateau, standing hand in hand, two small girls in *huipiles* and black braids, a glimmer of healing smile in their black eyes, tilted wondering faces to its glory.

This is my Father's world.

The man behind the desk looked up as he walked in but didn't stop turning pages of the file he was reading. "So you made it back. Took you long enough."

He hooked a straight-backed chair with his foot. "Yes, well, I had to take a roundabout route."

A page turned. "So I gathered. The old man isn't too happy about what he's been seeing on the news."

He shrugged as he sat down. "Sometimes an op goes down without a hitch; sometimes it hits the fan. You know that. Looks like you've handled damage control well enough."

"No thanks to you. You do realize you're dead. You'll never be able to work with an open cover again."

Another shrug. "I did what I had to do. I'd do it again. I *will* do it if it proves necessary."

Several more pages turned. "Yes, well, I'm told you need a new passport, a new name, a new assignment." It was a statement, not a query.

Stretching out long legs, he waited.

After a moment the file closed. The man behind the desk folded his hands on top of the folder. "So . . . how's your Persian?"

ABOUT THE AUTHOR

As the child of missionary parents, award-winning author Jeanette Windle grew up in the rural villages, jungles, and mountains of Colombia, now guerrilla hot zones. Currentlyw living in Lancaster, Pennsylvania, Jeanette spent sixteen years as a missionary in Bolivia and travels as a missions journalist and mentor to Christian writers in a dozen countries. Her detailed research and writing is so realistic that it has prompted government agencies to question her to determine if she has received classified information. She has fourteen books in print, including the best seller *CrossFire* and the Parker Twins series.